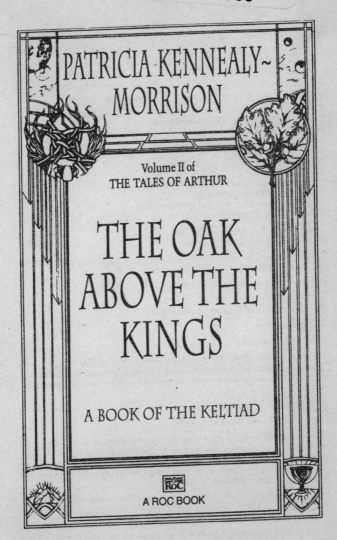

PATRICIA KENNEALY~MORRISON

Volume II of
THE TALES OF ARTHUR

THE OAK ABOVE THE KINGS

A BOOK OF THE KELTIAD

ROC

A ROC BOOK

ROC
Published by the Penguin Group
Penguin Books USA Inc., 375 Hudson Street,
New York, New York 10014, U.S.A.
Penguin Books Ltd, 27 Wrights Lane,
London W8 5TZ, England
Penguin Books Australia Ltd, Ringwood,
Victoria, Australia
Penguin Books Canada Ltd, 10 Alcorn Avenue,
Toronto, Ontario, Canada M4V 3B2
Penguin Books (N.Z.) Ltd, 182–190 Wairau Road,
Auckland 10, New Zealand

Penguin Books Ltd, Registered Offices:
Harmondsworth, Middlesex, England

Published by Roc, an imprint of Dutton Signet, a division of Penguin Books USA
Inc. Previously published in a Roc hardcover edition.

First Mass Market Printing, June, 1995
10 9 8 7 6 5 4 3 2 1

"A GRAY-HULLED BOAT WITH A SILVER MAST ...

moving toward me over wild waters; five riders upon the breast of a green hill; a ship falling like a shot swan into the red throat of a firemount; a wounded king with three veiled queens round about his bier ... At that sight I started forward uncontrollably with a cry, for the king bore the face of Uthyr; but as soon as I stirred, the pale pain-filled face shimmered, like a pond's surface ruffled by the wind, and when the shimmering had stilled again, the face of the king was the face of Arthur, and he was not wounded but dead ..."

So Taliesin, Chief Bard of Keltia, tells the tale as only a true bard could tell it.

THE OAK ABOVE THE KINGS

ACKNOWLEDGMENTS

Thanks are due this time to the usual suspects: the Keltic kitchen cabinet, for assorted and sundry plot thickeners— James Fox-Davis, Susan Harwood Kaczmarczik, Regina Kennely; the Kelts board on GEnie, for real as well as virtual aid and comfort; and Mary Herczog for wise counsel and general 'tude.

Thanks long overdue to Tom Canty (Thomas the Limner!), by whose incredibly beautiful covers I am so very proud my books are judged.

And thanks beyond thanking to all you loyal, loving and *patient* lieges of the Copper Crown and the Lizard Throne, whose support, belief and faith have meant so very much to me and to my beloved lord.

For my brother Timothy Joseph

KELTICHRONICON

In the Earth year 453 by the Common Reckoning, a small fleet of ships left Ireland, carrying emigrants seeking a new home in a new land. But the ships were not the leather-hulled boats of later legend, and though the great exodus was indeed led by a man called Brendan, he was not the Christian navigator-monk who later chroniclers would claim had discovered a New World across the western ocean.

These ships were starships; their passengers the Danaans, descendants of—and heirs to the secrets of—Atlantis, that they themselves called Atland. The new world they sought was a distant double-ringed planet, itself unknown and more than half a legend; and he who led them in that seeking would come to be known as Saint Brendan the Astrogator.

Fleeing persecutions and a world that was no longer home to their ancient magics, the Danaans, who long ages since had come to Earth in flight from a dying sun's agonies, now went back to those far stars, and after two years' desperate wandering they found their promised haven. They named their new homeland Keltia, and Brendan, though he refused to call himself its king, ruled there long and well.

In all the centuries that followed, Keltia grew and prospered. The kings and queens who were Brendan's heirs, whatever else they did, kept unbroken his great command: that until the time was right, Keltia should not for peril of its very existence reveal itself to the Earth that its folk had fled; nor forget, for like peril, those other children of Atland who had followed them into the stars—the Telchines, close kin and mortal foes, who became the Coranians, as the Danaans had become the Kelts.

Brendan had been twelve centuries in his grave when a time fell upon Keltia at which the Kelts still weep: a reign of blood and sorcerous terror, civil war and the assassin-murder of the reigning king and the toppling of the Throne of Scone itself, all at the hand of Edeyrn the Archdruid, known ever after as Marbh-draoi, 'Death-druid'—and rightly so.

Edeyrn fastened round Keltia's throat the iron collar of the Druid Theocracy and Interregnum; and, with the help of traitor Druids, collaborating Kelts and the terrible enforcers called Ravens, kept it locked there for two hundred fearful years. The royal House of Dôn—such of it as did survive the Marbh-draoi's methodical slaughter—was forced into hiding, while a great resistance movement, known as the Counterinsurgency, was raised to fight against the Theocracy's forces.

Yet even iron collars may be broken by a single sword-stroke, so that the sword be sharp enough, the blow well enough placed; and if the arm that wields the sword be strong enough—and so fated. . .

In the year 1946 of the Common Reckoning were born in Keltia three children: a girl and two boys. As has been already told in *The Hawk's Gray Feather*, Gweniver Pendreic, Arthur Penarvon and Taliesin Glyndour—princess, prince and bard—grow up in the Marbh-draoi's despite. Hunted by Ravens every hour of their young lives, nevertheless they survive and thrive, to lead the Counterinsurgency in what are to be its most fated hours.

Arthur and Gweniver are royal cousins, scions of the all-but-perished House of Dôn, though Arthur is kept in ignorance of his true parentage for many years, until it is revealed at last by his mother, Lady Ygrawn, and his teacher, the mighty sorcerer Merlynn Llwyd. More than that, they are co-heirs, equal lawful inheritors to the

Throne of Scone, the rulership of Keltia; and it is thought from their early days that when their years allow, they shall wed and win back their birthright together. Arthur and Gweniver agree on this, but on nothing else: Indeed, they loathe each other, and each takes another partner for lover and for mate.

Taliesin, who will become the greatest bard of Keltia since the order's founding, himself falls in love with Morgan, Arthur's half-sister, and she with him. He and Arthur were reared by Ygrawn, as foster-brothers, from early childhood; and when they come to their years as men, they work together with their trusted Companions, men and women alike, to win back Keltia for the House of Dôn.

So well have they wrought that now, for the first time in two hundred years, by Arthur's arm and mind and the valor of his Company, a victory of arms has been won against Edeyrn, at Cadarachta on the planet Gwynedd; and the rightful High King of Keltia, Uthyr Pendreic, has been proclaimed with Ygrawn his Queen.

But victory, as ever, comes at great and terrible cost . . .

Twelve musics we learn in the Star of Bards, and these the twelve:

Geantraí, the joy-song,
whose color is gold and whose shout creation;
whose number is one, and one is the number of birth.

Gráightraí, the heart-lilt,
whose color is green and whose descant rapture;
whose number is two, and two is the number of love.

Bethtraí, the fate-rann,
whose color is white and whose charge endurance;
whose number is three, and three is the number of life.

Goltraí, the grief-keen,
whose color is red and whose cadence sorrow;
whose number is four, and four is the number of death.

Galtraí, the sword-dance,
whose color is black and whose blazon challenge;
whose number is five, and five is the number of war.

Suantraí, the sleep-strain,
whose color is gray and whose murmur calmness;
whose number is six, and six is the number of peace.

Saoíchtraí, the mage-word,
whose color is blue and whose guerdon wisdom;
whose number is seven, and seven is the number of lore.

Créachtraí, the wound-weird,
whose color is brown and whose burden anguish;
whose number is eight, and eight is the number of pain.

Fíortraí, the honor-hymn,
whose color is purple and whose banner justice;
whose number is nine, and nine is the number of truth.

Neartraí, the triumph-march,
whose color is crimson and whose anthem valor;
whose number is ten, and ten is the number of strength.

Dóchtraí, the faith-chaunt,
whose color is silver and whose crown transcendence;
whose number is eleven, and eleven is the number of
hope.

Diachtraí, the soul-rune, sum of all before it,
whose color is all colors and whose end perfection;
whose number is twelve, and twelve is the number of
God.

—Taliesin ap Gwyddno

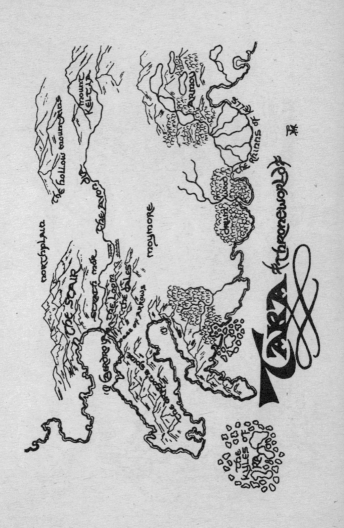

"As the oak stands above all other trees, so shall you stand above all other rulers—to be the oak above the kings."

—Merlynn Llwyd

FORETALE

Say of the dawning: or rather, that moment just past, when the sun that has been rolling up from shadow stands balanced on the edge of the world, its white fire like a flung spear between your eyes, dazzling you, dizzying you, so that you lift a hand to it as much in self-defense as in salute.

The night this new sun dispelled had been a long hard night for Keltia—two hundred years and more of black despairing—but for us who stood that day on the field of Cadarachta, true morning had come at last; and he who had led us to that field was the sun himself.

Hard it is now to cast back my mind upon it, across so many sunsplashed years of peace and freedom: Light has been so long with us now as to drive away even the memory of shadow; or much, at the least, of its darkest shade. Still, I have heard the healers say that the body retains no real memory of pain; not the pinprick, not the deepest wound. We can recall the fact that there was a hurting, even the remembrance that terrible pain had been; but the Mother in Her wisdom has decreed that more shall not stay with us, lest we in fear of hurt should fear to live—for to live is to hurt, and so it must be. But though the body can militate so against pain's recollection, it is far otherwise with the pain of the soul . . .

Here in Caerdroia, city of Brendan and Raighne and

Athyn and Arthur, and others greater still perhaps to
come, how often easier it is to not *forget,* just so, the
past's pain, but rather to look upon it with a kind of
*dis*memory, as one who has survived an all but mortal
wound—aye, or even a well-placed pinprick—will hold
in mind the fact if not the feeling of that wounding. One
remembers; but one does not *remember.*

Even, it would seem, a bard of the order can be subject
to such a failing: For so I am, I Taliesin, son of Gwyddno,
of the House of Glyndour, called by some Pen-bardd. Yet
it is all my task, and all my joy likewise, that I should and
must remember; not for myself alone but for all you who
hear the words of this my tale, not for Keltia alone but for
other worlds beside: to remember forever how it was for
us then—how it was for *him,* for Arthur . . .

And Seren Beirdd, Star of the Bards, is the kingplace
of remembering that ever there was or will be. Our home
from of old at Caerdroia, it is home for all and any with
the bent for bardery: a college and a library and a
songhall all together. I dwell here by choice as much as
chance, for I am alone now; those I loved best and hated
most have all gone before me, and even had they not still
would I sooner be here than any other place. I teach a little, still, and still I learn—aye, and shall until I can no
longer lift harp to shoulder—but most of all I strive to set
down these histories, for I sense that I have need of haste.

Yet in that very haste I see that I have outpaced my
own story: a bad thing in any teller of tales, but fault un-
pardonable in a bard. To begin aright, then, come back
with me two hundred years and more: back to Edeyrn.

Passing strange, is it not, that so complete a lord of
darkness should be called by so bright a name. And yet
not sò, perhaps, for it has been many times seen that a
fair morning can oft as not turn to full storm before high
twelve has struck.

That dark of Edeyrn's making had a name as black as
it merited: We who lived of force beneath its evil pinion
called it the Theocracy. As for Edeyrn himself, he who
had been the mightiest of sorcerers in a realm whose soul
is sorcery—Archdruid, Ro-sai of the Pheryllt, friend and
confidant and trusted minister to his master, the High

King Alawn Pendreic—*him* did we call Marbh-draoi, 'Death-druid,' and never was name more truly earned.

For Edeyrn betrayed Alawn, betrayed him and over-threw him and murdered him; killed his Queen, Breila, and his heir the Tanista Athonwy, and her brothers the princes Brahan and Cador, and her two half-grown chil-dren and their father with them. Indeed, more died than those alone for Edeyrn's will, for it was his plain purpose to put an end forever to the House of Dôn, that had reigned in Keltia for half a thousand years, and all those loyal to that House and its members.

Therefore were slain alike Alawn's brothers and sisters, another infant grandchild, uncles and great-uncles, aunts and grandaunts and cousins to the fourth and fifth degree. Not his widowed father, Rhain the King-dowager (Rígh-duar, as we call such a one), nor his grandmother Queen Kentiarn, ancient lady though she was and no danger to any, nor any child of his body or even of his fostering was spared; save one only—the Princess Seirith, Alawn's youngest daughter.

Though 'spared' be perhaps the wrong word ... By dán, then, and the grace of the gods, Seirith narrowly es-caped the slaughter of her kindred and those who had served them. She who had never thought to be High Queen herself—who had wished it still less—took with her into exile her lord, Rhys, and such companions as were loyal enough and loving enough—and brave enough, and alive enough—to follow her. Her second and last child, the boy Elgan, was born in that exile, and Rhys his father perished in it; but through that young prince, only last survivor of all his House, would pass the entire descent of the Dôniaid.

In my own youth the latest inheritor of this outlawed dominion was a lass of my own age: the Princess Gweniver. She in her turn had felt the sword's steel kiss as near as any of her line, for her father, the Ard-rígh Leowyn, was himself slain by Edeyrn's order. He fell by chance one evil night into the claws of Ravens, those butchers sworn to the Marbh-draoi's service, by whose arms (as by his bent Druids' magics) he kept Keltia so fast against us.

But as I have recounted elsewhere and earlier, when secrets long held close and careful were declared openly at last, Gweniver's right to the Copper Crown of Keltia's sovereigns came to be shared by another, one with as lawful a claim as hers to that crown, a claim of blood and, well, blood; and he my friend and fostern: Arthur of Arvon.

It is said by the metaphysicists that every force has by dint of its very existence not only its own opposite but also a twinned opposite, one outwardly to face and one contained within itself that must also be faced; and for all his long dark mastery, Ederyn himself could not in the end escape that law and judgment.

His outward enemy had been born in the very moment of his great treason; no single dam or sire but many parents did it have—all whom in that moment he betrayed. We who this day had fought at Cadarachta were but its latest offspring: Branded 'rebels' against the Marbh-draoi's rule, we rejoiced in the name of Counterinsurgency, and had called ourselves so from that first moment forward. (As for Edeyrn's 'inward' enemy, well, let me save somewhat for the tale yet to come—but that enemy too came to be in that fateful instant, and outlived it in stranger ways than any of us could have imagined . . .)

No need to recount yet again the Counterinsurgency's many advances and reversals down the years: Those have been most scrupulously chronicled otherwhere by better historians than I. Not that those other tellers are of necessity any better than I at the actual telling, mark: They have words as I have words—other words, different words. If they deal with facts, I deal with truth; and if perhaps you have heard from other voices what I shall speak in these pages to come, have heard the tale cast in other mold, heard it told otherwise and diversely, know that what you have heard from them is no less true for all that, and that what you shall be hearing from me no more false. For the truth wears many cloaks; and bards are trained to weave, on a different loom, a weft that is built to last.

Let me say only—lest this foretale should itself become a saga—that although the Counterinsurgency had endured two centuries against the Marbh-draoi, had preserved five monarchs and uncounted millions for an unguessed and oft despaired-of future, had even turned Edeyrn's own dark tide against him times not a few, not until the coming of Arthur did that striving light-tide become the mounting swell that would rise in its own time to a flood of change.

We had been together, Arthur and I, from our early childhood; had seen both our fathers fall to Edeyrn as so many others, men and women alike, had fallen before them, and would fall before the end. Arthur's own city was destroyed before his eyes, and my whole province before mine; and all this before we were scarce more than lads.

Gwynedd, third world of Keltia to be founded and first of the Kymric system, was our world then—indeed, we had never known any other—and there it was that we grew to manhood, studying for Druids together under the iron tutelage of Merlynn Llwyd himself, before Arthur went to the Fians and I to the bards, each to pursue his own particular calling and do honor to his Gift.

After those early learning days were done, together we had worked side by side with friends and kin and strangers, all of us part of the same dream and daring: to win Keltia back, one province at a time if so we must, from the grip of Edeyrn; and from the many puppet lordlings who ruled those provinces, or even worlds, in Edeyrn's name, who served as willing fingers upon that bloody hand.

We had worked, and we had won; so that now above the field of our first triumph—Cadarachta, below the horns of Agned—flew the Gál-greine, the sunburst banner of the Counterinsurgency, the white-and-gold vexillum that had floated in defiance and defeat over too many stricken fields.

And beside it flamed the sign and seal of that triumph: the Gwynedd stag, gold-antlered, white on blue, the Royal Standard of the House of Dôn that had not been flown beneath any heaven for two hundred years. It flew today for the first High King since Alawn openly to be proclaimed so: Uthyr Pendreic, uncle of Gweniver and Arthur both. And it flew also for his Queen who shared the day with him: Ygrawn Tregaron, my own foster-mother; mother by her first lord, Uthyr's brother Amris, to Arthur.

And it flew against Owein Rheged, our first real adversary, who until this day had ruled the planet Gwynedd as Edeyrn's adopted heir; who this day had gone down before us, we whom Arthur wielded as his arm did wield his sword; and deliverance was what that wielding had won us.

For us at Cadarachta, then, it seemed that at last our sun had risen. Yet even in the hour of its rising would it be plunged into bloody eclipse . . .

BOOK I

Créachtraí

CHAPTER
1

I raced through the sleeping camp as if the Far Darrig, the Red Man himself, and the Cwn Annwn that are Lord Arawn's hounds, and all the barguests ever whelped were close upon my track, crying out to any who might hear me that by all gods they should hasten sword in hand to the King's tent, for all our lives; but either they were leadfoot that night or I was wingèd, for I came there before them all.

And all the while as I ran I cursed myself and everyone else I could think of for fools and boneheads and fatal idiots, that we had not seen and did not guess. No matter, that the thing had been so cleverly contrived—who among us, even the sorcerers, even Merlynn or Morgan, would have dreamed in darkest nightmare or most furious of fancy that Owein Rheged, whom all had thought to have slunk off after losing of the fight, had instead used sorcery for his vengeful riposte? Had cloaked him with the outward semblance of his hated adversary: had cast a fith-fath upon him, to steal the face and form and seeming of Arthur himself.

All this I saw in an eyeblink, as I threw wide the doorflap of the King's tent and skidded to a stunned halt: I saw Uthyr the King fallen to the floor in a welter of blood, two Arthurs blade to blade above him. A moment of frozen chaos: no sound, no movement—not even the swords sang or shifted—no thought, but only a kind of blank mazed horror.

I know that I cannot have stood there for more than a few seconds at the most; but to me then, and, aye, even now, it seemed I stood so for ages. Then the scene came roaring back to life around me, as the help I had so desperately shouted for came bursting in at my back (only seconds behind me, for all my panicked fret); as I myself moved forward, hand outflung, a mad thought of somehow stopping the fight—and I utterly unarmed, and no Fian to go barehand against six to one together—the only thought in my mind, if thought it could in truth be named.

Words take more time than deeds: All in that same blazing moment, the Fians burst in and I moved forward and the two Arthurs broke their sword's-edge balance, to strike one another down beside the King on the red floor of the tent. Ygrawn, the Queen, I could not see at all.

There was blood everywhere: Uthyr lay as he had fallen, and though I saw that he yet lived, I saw in that same frantic glance that there was little other hope for him. Yet as I looked so, and saw so, through my tears of grief and frustration and fury, even then I was already looking past him, to the two others who lay as unmoving as did he, a little way away upon that ghastly floor.

Under the stress of murder and wounding and combat, the deceit of the lying fith-fath he had set upon himself had passed off Owein Rheged; so that he wore once again his own face and form, not the cheating image of Arthur that, together with the slaughter of the tent-guards, had earned him unchallenged admittance to the King's tent. He was not dead, for our eyes met then; and I turned away, as much to direct the help I had called for as to no longer have to look upon his face.

That help was already to hand: not only the Fians who had followed on my heels but others who had heard— with deeper senses than hearing—my despairing summons. Tarian Douglas was now here, and Grehan Aoibhell, and Keils Rathen—warlords all three; a few others of our—Arthur's—Companions; and ahead of them every one, my beloved, Morguenna, known to all as Morgan, sister and daughter to the two who yet lay so very fearfully still.

Heedless of the ruin she was making of her gúna, with-

out so much as a glance even at me, still less at anyone
else, Morgan went to her knees in the midst of that terrible red lake, and put her hand upon her brother's shoulder, to pull him back from its farther shore.

"Arthur, hear me."

To everyone's unspeakable relief, he heard; and, leaning
heavily on both Morgan and myself, managed to pull himself to a sitting position. *Not so badly hurt as he had looked
and I had feared; thank gods for* that, *at least . . .*

He caught my unsaid thought, as he so often did when
I had a thought I would have sooner kept from him.

"Indeed, braud, scarce hurt at all," he said, though all
of us there could see that that was a proud lying word:
Owein's last thrust had laid open his side. But though it
was surely a painful hurt, just as surely it was not a grave
one, and I allowed myself to breathe again.

"My mother?" asked Arthur then, with a dart of swift
fear in his eyes. Of Uthyr he did not ask; but had cast one
hooded look at the limp form that careful hands were now
conveying to a field-couch by the tent wall.

Morgan took his hands in hers. "She is well, Arthur,
look—" She nodded to where Tarian and Keils were supporting Ygrawn between them; though Ygrawn, as usual,
looked as if the support of others was the last thing in the
seven hells that she required. Uthyr's queen and Arthur's
mother, and Morgan's mother also, Ygrawn had been
knocked to the floor by Owein when he forced his way
into the tent. Yet even so she had not failed to try to protect her lord: The slashes across her palms gave witness
to how, unarmed, she had tried to thwart the striking
blade. But she had been stunned by Owein's buffet, and
had fallen dazed to the floor behind a chest, and had seen
nothing past her son drawing his own sword and leaping
all in one move to the defense of his uncle and his King.

With an unreadable glance at me, Morgan left Arthur in
my hands—literally—and went to her mother's side;
while I, for my part, was passionately relieved to pass Arthur along in my turn to the Fian healers who now came
crowding up to attend to them all.

That done, I took myself out of everyone's way, to
stand by the tent wall where I could shake quietly with
none to see me do so. The mood in the tent now was one
of black despair and white-hot anger: That Uthyr should

be struck down in the very moment of his reclaiming the throne was almost beyond bearing; that Owein, having failed to defeat us in fair fight, should be the sorcerous cause of Uthyr's fall was not to be borne. Even as I stood there I could sense the grim news sweeping outward from the tent, as the dark windstorm we Kelts call cam-anfa will grow in an eyeblink from a small tight funnel to a whirling wall of destruction.

After a while Morgan came back to me. She had been healing her mother's hurts, and overseeing the Fians who attended to her brother, and watching a while by her father's bedside; and now, with all three of her wounded kindred made comfortable, or as much so as was possible for the moment, she came to me for comforting of her own, walking without a word spoken straight into my arms.

We stood for some time unmoving, our arms round each other, her head bent to mine; there were no tears. After a while I felt her stir and gather herself, but I could not look down just yet to meet her gaze, for a great and shameful reason.

My guilt was by now past pretending, my soul howling in a wordless passion of what-ifs and if-onlys and how-nots. Why had I not been swifter to sense that it had not been Arthur passing by me in the camp-way below the tent but Owein in his counterfeited likeness? Why could I not have been quicker in alerting the Fians and our Companions? How came it that I alone was unarmed on entering the tent? Had I been so, I could have stopped the fight sooner, if only I had come there sooner to start with ... And so I tortured myself; but if my guilt was so ungovernable, how much more so Arthur's, who *had* been in the tent, sword in hand too, and who even so could not keep his uncle and his mother from harm ...

"Nay, cariad, do not ..." That was Morgan's low rippling voice, so like her mother's, pitched now for my ear alone; and I forced myself to meet her eyes, desperate as I was for consolation, feared as I was to see in those eyes either hate or blame.

And knew as I looked at last what folly it had been to fear so; there was a shadow in the hazel depths, but it was pain alone had put it there. "How, then?" I muttered savagely.

"They were giving one another goodnight, Arthur and my parents, when Owein entered. As you saw, he had cast my brother's likeness upon him; a fith-fath, and a good one too"—that assessment given with a sorceress's professional judgment—"if not quite good enough to keep *you* from pointing the difference." She laid an open palm flat upon my chest. "No blame, Talyn. Had you not seen what you did when you did, who shall say what Owein may not have managed to encompass?"

It was a generous forgiveness; all the more so since she clearly considered there was naught to forgive, but knew also that I needed her absolving for what I held to be my fault. This she saw too; but said no more of it, only went on with her careful, controlled account of the night's events.

"It was only by means of that mask that Owein passed by the Fians who stood guard in the faha below the tent."

"But if Artos was already here—"

"Aye so, but the lower faha guards knew not that he had returned to bid the King and Queen goodnight. The Fians by the tent door did know, and so moved to stop Owein—how could one seek entrance who was already within? But he drew on them first, and cut them down, and came inside. My mother tried to stop the sword, but—Then Arthur—"

I kissed the top of her head, where the dark-gold hair was piled and pinned soft and deep and clean-smelling, and after a moment she continued.

"Owein had not seen Arthur just at first, and went straight for the King; and then Arthur came against him with Llacharn."

Llacharn ... I remembered well, as I knew Morgan herself remembered, the winning of that magical sword: how she and I and Arthur had worked together to gain it, how Arthur had drawn it from the stone, in a secret place of earth, deep below the Forest in the Sea. And yet in the end, not even Llacharn's temper or Morgan's magic or Arthur's arm had been enough to hold off disaster ...

I threw a glance at the author of that disaster. The Fians, wild with grief and rage, had dragged Owein up at last from the floor, where all this time he had lain under the close points of a dozen swords. Like Arthur, he was drenched in blood: Uthyr's, Ygrawn's, Arthur's, his own.

Again like Arthur, his wounds were not so grave as they had at first seemed, though sore enough; and yet not one hundredth, one thousandth part so grave or so sore as the whole of our army would have had them to be.

I was no more immune to that vengeful sentiment than anyone else: I had not troubled myself to think of Owein until I knew that my dear ones—or at least the two I could reasonably hope for—were reasonably unhurt. Now, as I brought my gaze unwillingly to meet Owein's again, I found myself consumed by the burning desire to rip out his throat with my bare hands.

Never had I felt so about another living being, not even Edeyrn, who had wrought so unspeakably with me and mine. As Druids we are taught unceasingly that all life has value and reason and purpose, even if we in our limited vision can discern none of these; and not even in the hottest, bitterest battles I had fought by Arthur's side— not at Cadarachta, not at Glenanaar—had I been possessed of such a longing for another's blood.

It seemed that Owein sensed my mood—certainly he felt the weight of my glance, it must have fallen upon him like a sword across his shoulders—for as they began to half-lead, half-drag him out past me he halted, and looked full into my face.

"Mabon Dialedd, I think?" he said, with a small stiff bow and stiffer smile; the best of each that he might make, under bond and point of sword and pain of wound. "I should have known you long since, Glyndour, if only from that name alone. For five years in Caer Dathyl I had Gwyddno's son beneath my hand, and knew it not."

But the memory of my service as bard in Owein's hall was not one I wished to recall just then ... "No more than I knew *you,* not straightway, when we could not find you after the fight." I spoke carefully, for I did not trust my voice to keep from word-whip—and Druids can kill with a word—any more than I did trust my hands to keep off from his throat. "We thought you had simply skulked away, like the carrion-dog when the lion has shaken his mane."

Owein flexed his shoulders against the ropes that bit deep, fixed so by grim Fians, to take what ease they could in petty vengeance in the face of the greater anguish.

"The skill was not my own that hid me, as your

lady"—he bowed here to Morgan, who was regarding him steadily and serenely, with no expression whatever visible upon her face—"knows well. I was dodging her and that thrice-damned Merlynn all day; you'd have thought they had somehow scented me out."

"Treachery has no time a sweet fragrance, and Edeyrn's sorceries never aught but stench." I nodded to the guards. "Take him to the clochan of the Fianna command; and, Keils"—this to Uthyr's warlord—"do you yourself mount watch. We will deal with him when this here is settled." In the presence of Ygrawn, Arthur and Morgan—queen, prince and princess—I had no business whatsoever giving orders to the King's guards in the King's tent, and still less commanding Keils Rathen. But I was obeyed instantly; and after Owein had been led out, Keils following grimly after, I felt as if a great vile uncleanness had been suddenly washed away.

It seems ages in the telling, but in truth no more than fifteen minutes had passed since that first terrible moment; the tent was full of folk now, word of the calamity having run through the campment like the Solas Sidhe. And now for the first time I allowed myself to look full at Uthyr, and to hope in the midst of despair. Might it be that the King could yet be saved? He lay still and silent on the low bed, Ygrawn beside him with his hand in both of hers and her eyes fixed on his face. *Maybe magic . . .*

All at once the enormity of what had happened here caught up with me, or I with it, and I reeled on my feet as giddiness took me. I was seized and steadied by Tarian, who stood by, and the friendly hands of others as well. But a torch had gone up in my brain: *Gweniver.* Uthyr's niece, Arthur's cousin, who had been formally named heir—well, co-heir—to the Copper Crown only a little time past: Surely she had been told of her uncle's wounding?

But even as I thought it, and turned to speak of it to Tarian, the doorflap blew in as on a gale, and Gweniver herself was the wind that flung it wide.

CHAPTER
2

She had obviously heard of the events in the King's
lodging; but though her face was a little paler than
usual, her mouth a little more tightly set, her expression,
like Morgan's, gave otherwise no clue to her feelings. She
swept one blazing glance round the tent to see how things
did stand, and why, and with whom: noting those who
were present, those not, how they seemed, what they did
or did not do or say, what was or was not betrayed by
their voices or gestures or eyes; then went straight to her
uncle, kneeling by his couch on the other side of Ygrawn.

Friends though we were from our youth—and one time
more even than friends, though that one time only—still
I rated no more from Gweniver just then than a curt nod,
the which, even so, clearly conveyed 'Aye, I see you,'
and 'Aye, glad that you are unhurt,' and 'Aye, you did
well'; while Arthur—co-heir with her to Keltia, after all,
by Uthyr's own decree; not to mention being her pledged
lord of three hours' standing, also by Uthyr's decree—
rated not even so much as that, though she had seen
straightway how it was with him.

All at once I could not bear one moment more; and
turning on my heel, not looking to see what anyone
thought of it or did about it, in any case not caring, I
grabbed up my cloak and went out into the cold unquiet
night. I have little memory of where I went, only that I

walked fast and with purpose; or so at least did I try to do, for at every step people caught at my arm or my cloak like imploring children, full of fears and tears and questions, and at every step the rumors grew wilder and the askings ever needier and my responses terser and, aye, even impatient and unkind. That last I could not help: For I was frightened too.

At last I found myself once again on the little hillock where I had already stood twice that day with Arthur, and so often before that alone in my dreams. I was seeking some answers and assurances of my own, and until I found some, from whatever source supplied, I could have no comfort for anyone else.

In my desperate need I stared out into the darkness that rose up before me like a wall in the west. To the south stood the enemy camp, or what was left of it after our forces had broken through; and our own lines to the north, where quartz-hearths sparked and torches stood before almost every tent.

But all at once I was not seeing any of it: I was seeing a hall I had never yet seen in life, that great chamber far away on Tara where my father had died; and yet I was standing on a cliff above what had once been Gwaelod, that was now only the blue skin of the sea over the bones of a drowned land; and also I was standing on a hillside across from a small bright city in the Arvon hills, a chestnut-haired boy of my own age watching hawk-eyed from a little way away; and again that same hillside, only now it was night, and the little city was bright with laser-fire from attacking ships that swooped and darted in air, lights like corpse-candles that flared and flickered and went out.

I trembled in the grip of the vision, but it had me fast now, unrolling before my othersight like a tapestry of years: everything I had ever seen or would ever come to see—a gray-hulled boat with a silver mast moving toward me over wild waters; five riders upon the breast of a green hill; a ship falling like a shot swan into the red throat of a firemount; a wounded king with three veiled queens round about his bier.

At that sight I started forward uncontrollably with a cry, for the king bore the face of Uthyr; but as soon as I stirred, the pale pain-filled face shimmered, like a pond's

surface ruffled by the wind, and when the shimmering
had stilled again, the face of the king was the face of Arthur, and he was not wounded but dead. And all around
was a bare and blackened land, sere trees, blood on snow,
ruined crops, choked rivers, parched earth, dead seas and
dying skies.

When I came to myself I was whimpering like Cabal in
a thunderstorm, and Morgan's arms were round me. I
clutched at her as if she were my last hope in a dying
land; she drew my head down into her lap, twisting her
fingers in my hair, summoning calmness into me as
steady and warm as a candleflame.

After a while I felt sufficiently recovered to sit up,
though I took care to keep myself well-coddled in Morgan's arms, my head against her breast. I began to speak,
trying to frame in words some of what I had seen, but she
was there before me.

"I know it all, cariad," came her voice in the air above
my head; and though that voice was soft as ever with love
and solace, something in it rang faintly ominous, like the
far-off chime of a sword being drawn from its scabbard.
"I have Seen, too."

I twisted in her arms to stare up into her face. "Say you
so? Then perhaps it is *you* can tell *me:* What of Uthyr?
That was no ashling I saw just now, lady. That was an-da-
shalla, if ever I knew it!"

The hazel eyes veiled themselves for a moment: Morgan might be versed as none before her in the sorceries of
the Sidhe, but she was still her father's loving daughter,
and in any case it is never easy to watch those you love
in pain.

"No ashling," she said slowly. "But a true Seeing—
Let us go back now to the others, and I will tell all of you
what must be."

The news that awaited us in the King's tent was better
than I had dared to hope; and yet, and yet—

Ygrawn met us with outstretched hands. Somewhere
she had found a few moments to shed her stained garb
and wash away the blood; but I saw the fine red lines that
still scored her skin: the now-healed marks of Owein's
sword that would fade from her palms in a day or two—if
never from her heart.

"He sleeps, careddau," she said, embracing us both. "And Arthur's hurts are healed—" But to a bard's ear her voice held something else.

"Methryn?" I asked then, carefully, when Morgan did not speak.

"My lord—his wounds are healed, save for one. And this one wound will not—aye, they say *cannot*—close: the wound in his thigh." Ygrawn turned in sudden fear renewed, a quick glance over her shoulder; but Uthyr was quiet, and the healers sitting vigil beside him gave her grave smiles of assurance and support.

"But he *will* live!" The protest burst from me before I thought.

Ygrawn nodded. "Aye. He will; at least a while yet, but—"

The word hung in the air between us: 'maimed.' According to Keltic law, a crippled king was no king at all; and unless he was swiftly—and rightfully—deposed in favor of his named heir or another, elected, successor, his land was doomed to barrenness and death.

So if Artos and Gweniver do not take the throne now ... I laughed grimly to myself: The throne was still effectively to be won from Edeyrn; premature by far to trouble about the name of its lawful occupier. Suddenly I saw again the face of the wounded king in my vision, and began to shake anew. Was this what my Seeing had meant? That the wasted land and Uthyr's wounding were all one? Or was the ruined land Edeyrn's doing, and the dead king not Uthyr but Leowyn, or even Amris, who should have been King and never came to it? And what of the three veiled queens, who were they?

I came out of my reverie to find Morgan peering up at me with concern, and with an effort called up the echo of her question.

"Aye, I will come now; only let me first bid the King goodnight."

She withdrew to the adjoining pavilion with her mother, summoning selected friends and counselors with them, while I went to stand by Uthyr's bed.

He was deep asleep, and seemed comfortable enough; but I could see where the ugly, angry wound in his right thigh had been vainly tended, and at last bound up as best it could be. An open gash with ragged edges, it still bled through its packings, though little, and slowly; and as I looked on the King's face I thought on the royal sacrifice, the ruler's life that must so often be given for the life of the land.

We in Keltia have never had a true tradition of sacrifice, what barbarousness some say we had once on Earth along with so many other races; indeed, as so many other nations have even now. But we have ever had among us the tradition of the given death, the unstinting gift freely offered so that others might live and thrive—a gift unthought of, unprepared for, unplanned and undevised, but in the instant of its offering intentioned well and completely, without reserve, felt to the soul's roots, given and accepted.

And this it was I saw in Uthyr's face, and tried to drive from my mind the thought that some time to come I might see it likewise in Arthur's . . .

When I stepped through the curtained doorway into the pavilion that adjoined the royal tent's sleeping quarters, I saw that I had been waited for by those already assembled. The pavilion had been furnished for the King's conferences with his commanders—a long table, campchairs, field-desks—and to this particular conference the King's daughter had summoned not only his commanding officers but family and friends and close advisors: Tarian, Keils, Grehan, Marigh the Taoiseach, Merlynn, Ygrawn's nephew Tryffin, who was heir of Kernow; most of those, in fact, who had been present at that night's earlier assembling, when Uthyr had named Arthur and Gweniver to an unprecedented joint sovereignty of Keltia.

Something, someone, though, was missing; and as I made my way to the seat left for me between Ygrawn and Morgan, I puzzled on it. Who, or what, could it be? Not Arthur whose absence was in question: The healers had by now dealt with him, and he was grinning up at me from a pillowed longchair a few feet from my own place, Cabal's huge head resting on his knee—since his master's wounding, the great wolfhound had not let Arthur out of his sight, nor taken his eyes from his face.

I knew well how the beast felt . . . "I thought Elen would have long since packed you off to bed," I remarked. Elen Llydaw was the healer for our inner circle of Companions; not to mention one of the best generals we had, and heir to half the planet Arvor.

"Not I!" boasted Arthur. "It takes more than Elenna to put *me* out when I would stay awake to talk. Though she it was who insisted on this softling's couch—one might think I had been something like injured . . ."

"Bonehead!" I told him fiercely. "Will you never learn, Artos? Very well then, stay and speak; only, if I see you tiring at any instant I will order you carried—aye, carried—straight to your tent; so mind how you tax yourself."

Arthur only grinned again and rolled his eyes; but I sensed him schooling himself to relax. Well, insofar as any of us *could* relax . . .

For Morgan now had risen in her place beside me, and lifted her hands, gathering the room together with one compelling glance. Before she could speak, however, Gweniver turned her whole attention on her cousin, her eyes as gray as winter, with a kind of focused ferocity that actually made me flinch—as even the day's battle horrors had not done.

"Well?" she snapped, all of her fears to be heard in that one word. "What has been done for the King?"

Morgan took the fears into her own calm. "What the King will have to be done for him; nothing more nor less."

That gave Gweniver pause a moment; but before she could rally with another question Grehan Aoibhell spoke up from the far side of the table, with all his usual bluntness.

"Will the King die?"

All eyes went not to Morgan, but to Ygrawn as Morgan answered.

"It might be better for him not least did he so," she said quietly. "But that is not his dán, nor yet ours. Nay, the King does not die, not this night nor any time soon, not until—"

"Until?" That was Gweniver again.

"Until the time comes for it, as it shall. But the King will live to see Edeyrn cast down, and Arthur nearly the same"—even in my shock to hear her say so I smiled; for almost never did Morgan call her brother as did all the rest of Keltia, by the shortname 'Artos.' *Not since her*

*childhood at Coldgates; surely not since her time in
Collimare* ... Nay, it was ever 'Arthur' to Morgan,
though she was often as not 'Guenna' to him ...

But the room was in a tumult, and I wondered briefly
if I were not losing my mind under the stress of it all.
Even Tarian, our usually unflappable war-leader, had
been so far shaken as to stare at Morgan as if the Princess
had unaccountably lost her wits. And as to her speaking
of defeat, even near-defeat, in connection with *Arthur*—

"It may well take months, Guenna—years, even, if dán
holds against us—before ever we get to Tara," said Tarian
protesting. "Let alone throw down the Marbh-draoi—and
as for Uthyr ..."

Merlynn stirred, and the room stilled. "The King will
live until then all the same: live weak and wounded, live
in pain and in patience, live bound and bleeding, but live.
And as the King lives, so shall the land live with him; until in the end both land and King find healing."

Such was the power and sureness that had grown in his
voice as he spoke that the room was struck into silence;
even Gweniver, it seemed, was disposed to accept the
Archdruid's words. Looking up then, I met Merlynn's
eyes, and saw him smile; and turning my head, I found
Arthur's eyes on me in my turn, and in my turn I smiled.

But that pronouncement of Merlynn's had hit them
hard, with all the force of law or prophecy. Suddenly the
tenor of the moment had changed, and now all the talk
was of how to make things as easy for Uthyr as we might,
when we should begin the advance on Caer Dathyl, when
that on Tara itself ... But I was still caught up in that
nagging thought I had earlier entertained: that somewhat
was lacking here, that something had not been said,
someone had not been summoned ...

Then I had it, and icy dismay swamped me as the answer came storming to my mind; even as its living expo-
nent came storming into the tent.

CHAPTER
3

It was never like Marguessan to make a gentle entrance
where a wildly dramatic one could be made instead;
and, despite her father lying sore wounded in the outer
chamber, her mother and brother themselves not un-
scathed by the events of the night, Marguessan did not so
now.

During the fighting that day at Cadarachta, the Princess
Marguessan, elder of the twin daughters of Uthyr and
Ygrawn, had been safely kept out of it, far behind the
lines at our hidden shieling of Llwynarth. The reasoning
had been that as she was no warrior nor yet sorceress, and
could be of little count in the battle, and also as she was
near her time with a babe who, did we lose the day, might
well be the last heir of the House of Dôn for many years
to come, for her to have joined us on the field would have
been purest folly.

Those were the noble reasons, somewhat too eagerly
and too loudly subscribed to by all consulted to be quite
real. The truth was nearer this: that not one of us Companions was fond enough of Marguessan to wish to die in
her company; and so we kept her away.

But now she was here, standing like dán itself in the
door of the tent, her sense of slighted self furiously apparent in every line and lineament. In my cowardice I re-

sorted at once to thought-speech, and besought Morgan in desperation: *Who in all hells was it sent to Marguessan?*

Her answer came back swift and tart: *Not I! Nor any here, I think; but my sister has never needed any bidding but her own, to come where she has not been asked.*

I looked over to where Ygrawn was standing talking in a low calming voice to her daughter, and I was a little abashed for my lack of delight. However much I might detest her—and by all gods I did so, and my loathing went long time back, and had good cause—still was Marguessan Arthur's sister as well as Morgan's; and daughter to Ygrawn who was my foster-mother, which bond among Kelts is as strong as, ofttimes stronger than, the bonds of birth.

Also Marguessan was as I have said near to term with a royal grandchild—fathered by her lord, Irian Locryn, heir of an old loyalist family—and would, in time not far off now, be my sister-in-law, when Morgan and I should come to wed. A little charity on my part might well be called for, no matter what I knew of her from of old ... Then Marguessan's voice came cutting through the low hum of talk, and charity was all at once the last thing I felt disposed to offer her.

"Nay, mother, your pardon but I *will* see the King, and I will see him now! He is my father, and like to die, and before he does so I would have his blessing on his grandchild."

The undercurrent of talk redoubled: folk in their embarrassment desperately feigning to ignore the Princess's outburst. Ygrawn looked for one tense moment as if she would box her daughter's ears in public; then gave a small tight nod and went back into the outer tent with Marguessan smirking alongside her.

Seeing that Arthur was taking my earlier warning to heart, and was now talking quietly with Grehan and Tryffin, I judged it safe enough to leave him unwatched for a moment or two; any road, I was mightily curious about what would be Marguessan's reaction when she saw her wounded father.

So I sloped off as unobtrusively as I could manage, though I did not escape Arthur's mocking raised eyebrow as I did so; nor Morgan coming casually after me.

In the outer tent all was as before, or at least it was so

until Marguessan altered things to suit herself: Making as much stour and difficulty as was in any way possible, she crossed the chamber and knelt, her heavily pregnant condition making her less graceful than she might have liked, by her father's couch.

I leaned against the tent-pole and watched with interest, the most charitable thought I could summon up—in keeping with my new resolve—being that were *I* the one who lay so wounded, Marguessan Pendreic would be the last person in this world or any other that I should choose to have hovering over me. I did not realize I had been sending in thought-speech until I felt Morgan give my ribs a sharp dig with her nearest elbow.

It seemed that Marguessan had heard my thought as well; or perhaps it was just that she was no fonder of me than she had ever been—which was to say not at all—for the glance with which she favored me just then would have soured milk in a cow's bag. But then she turned all her attention to her father; and for no reason I could put name to, not then, I tensed as if to ward off some unseen blow or harm, and beside me I felt Morgan draw in breath to do the same.

But now Marguessan had lumbered down to her knees, weeping showily—pure piast-tears, no more—and kissing her father's hand, and in general making the kind of spectacle that Ygrawn and Morgan and Gweniver themselves had thought scorn to make. But Marguessan was ever cut from lesser cloth.

For all her noisy lamentations, though, it took some time for Uthyr to take note of her presence. He had fallen into that deepest sleep which is more akin to trance than to slumber, that to awaken from which is to awaken not to alertness but to disorientation and daze; and as I watched Marguessan's selfish importunings I was half-moved to put a stop to it, and order her removed. But again I felt my lady's elbow—and none had an arm more to the point than Morgan—and again I held my peace.

It seemed that Marguessan's efforts were not in vain at the last, for Uthyr stirred a little, frowning; then his hazel eyes came slowly open. He looked up straight at Ygrawn, as if he had seen her even with his eyes closed—as perhaps he had—and smiled a real, if tired, smile. But when his gaze moved past her to Marguessan, such a look of appallment came over his countenance that even I, clear across the tent, shrank back a little.

Marguessan plainly felt no such compunction, but began at once to babble on about herself, not Uthyr: how *she* had felt, how *she* had suffered. Still, soon or late even such an insensitive self-absorbed trimmer as Marguessan must see such rage and recoil as Uthyr's; and as it began to sink in, bringing with it an uncomprehending terror, Marguessan began to babble more wildly still. And when Uthyr struggled to rise up off his pillows, to point a trembling finger at her where she knelt now cowering by the bed, even I felt impelled to pity her.

"Father? Nay, father, it is I, Marguessan—do not look so hard upon me—will you not bless your grandchild which is here within me—"

"To *bless*?" Uthyr's voice, if harsher with pain, had lost but little of its strength, and indeed was growing stronger with every dán-echoed word. "A better blessing for Keltia if that child you carry died of its bearing and you with it; sooner that a thousand times over, than have him raised to treachery and treason, to lift his hand against his King . . ."

He was shaking now, and fell back speechless and breathless alike upon the pillows; Morgan dashed across to try to calm him, while Ygrawn and I hastily helped Marguessan from the chamber, the Princess so wild with injured self-pity that she was well pleased to be removed.

"Not in with the others again, Talyn," murmured Ygrawn. "They will mean well, perhaps, but they will only upset her the more. Help me get her to my own chambers, and leave her with me."

By the time we had gotten Marguessan, who was still weeping copiously and overloudly, settled in bed in her mother's quarters, an hour or more had gone by. I looked in briefly on Uthyr—*peacefully asleep,* said Morgan's voice in my mind—then went back to the pavilion to see what had become of those we had so abruptly left there.

Most of them had by now drifted away, returning to their own duties, and at this hour only Tarian and Keils remained. They greeted me cheerfully, and invited me to join them for their refighting of the day's battle. But it had been a long and strainful day, crammed with incidents any one of which would normally overtax even the strongest soul, and all at once I was unspeakably weary. Still, there was one thing more I needed to do before I could allow myself my rest ...

He was ensconced in his own tent by now, having taken my words of warning very much to heart; but he *was* working, and he looked up guiltily as I entered. Cabal lashed his tail furiously, but did not stir from his usual bed on an old cloak of his master's: the great hound seemed cheerful enough now, but I remembered well— and I daresay so did much of the campment—his anguished howling at Arthur's injured state; and the silent imploring vigil he had kept by his master's side until the hurts were healed and he had been reassured by Arthur himself.

"Where in all the hells have *you* been?" demanded Arthur crossly, and I knew by that very crossness that he was hoping to forestall a scolding. "Never mind, come and sit by me and tell me what you think of this; we must move on Caer Dathyl before the week is out, and you having spent so much of your time there—"

"*You* are moving nowhere just now, save to that bed over there in the corner." I pulled the order diptych from his hands and made great show of closing it up and stuffing it out of sight. "In the morning, we will see. But just now, bed you, and not another word on it."

He made some token grumbling protest, but obediently stripped off tunic and trews and boots and flung himself down amid the soft blankets.

"A long and bloody day, Talyn," he said, already all but asleep. "But a wonder?"

Indeed ... But *my* only wonder was how he had managed to stay so long awake, with all the demands on body and soul, all the weight of battle and victory and wounding and worry that had been on him. After all, in the space of barely twice ten hours he had led his army in their first great battle, and had won; had fought epically himself; had seen his uncle and his mother struck down before his eyes and had been himself both wounded and wounder ... Had I been in his boots, by now I had been crawling on the ground, cloak over my head, wailing piteously to myself and to any who would hear of the manifold unfeeling ways of dán. But that was ever the difference between Arthur and me ...

Still, in spite of my own weariness I watched over him awhile as he slept, and my mind was a whirling blur of all the times I had watched thus; or those times I never knew of, when our places had been reversed and he the one who kept watch over me. Four decades and more had there been of such vigils: more than forty years of perfect loving trust. We had seen much together, Arthur and I, had known much and lost much; and now, gods willing, were in a fair way to win much, much more—and not for us alone—or else to lose all, forever.

I must have dozed off then, for all at once I jerked sharply awake. The air was colder, and the camp more silent; I had been asleep for some time, then. Arthur, who had been so reluctant to yield to unconsciousness, now slept the sleep of the utterly exhausted and the deeply happy. Even Cabal did not stir as I went quietly from the tent and along to my own a few yards down the line, where Morgan half-woke and sleepily made space for me in the warmth beside her before sinking back once more into her dreamlessness.

But for all my weary woe, it was yet some time before I managed to join her there.

The next morning was clear and cool and bright: blue skies, white puffs of cloud racing their shadows over the ground. I took a small breakfast with Morgan, speaking idly of what each of us must labor at that day; then with one last touch of mind on mind, I went outdoors, my steps turning, as if some outside force did rule them, to take me to the Fianna clochan across the faha, where Owein Rheged was being held close under the most vigilant of guards.

It was a large, many-chambered structure, sturdier than the field tents most of the army employed. I nodded to the guards at the officers' entry, and was saluted and passed unchallenged. Within, Fians and Companions together turned to greet me, with small nods and quiet words and grins of relief and delight, and I saw friends I had not seen since battle's prelude the preceding day. Then a curtain parted in an inside wall, and Tarian put her head around it, to bid me come within.

I stepped through to join her and some others in the inner chamber, and stiffened at once like Cabal when quarry comes in sight.

Owein Rheged met my glance with a settled countenance and no sign of surprise. He looked rather the worse this morning, for Keils and Tari and Grehan had been less than gently patient in their questioning, and beyond the clochan walls the army was howling for his head on a pike without further delay. Not that that would have troubled him: Owein, whatever else he might have been, was no coward. Behind the weariness of defeat and the bitter gall of abandonment (for Edeyrn his master and adopted father had sent neither word nor help), the old malicious glint I knew so well was still alive and sparking, though I was less inclined than of old to respond to it.

He noticed that, too; he had ever been quick as a palug-cat. "Ah. Then it is not my onetime bard, latterly known to us in Caer Dathyl as Mabon Dialedd, who comes to call this morning, but the Lord Taliesin Glyndour ap Gwyddno."

"Even he." I disengaged Tarian's cautioning hand from my shoulder and crossed the room.

Owein stretched his aching arms, where they were pinned by a tight-set restraint field to the back of the oak settle. "I did not know you rabble had such technological toys in your play-chest," he said with a rueful smile as he did so. "But this is a great advancement for you, not so—up from bardery to bed with a king's daughter?"

I had been expecting some remark of the sort, and had resolved beforetimes not to let it sting me. So now I merely returned the smile and said nothing; but Keils Rathen was not so restrained.

"The Princess Morguenna's name has no place upon your lips, maggot of Rheged!"

Owein raised his brows, and I rolled up my eyes, knowing what was coming.

"Nay? Then perhaps you, Rathen, would prefer I spoke of the Princess Gweniver, and what lord she spends *her* nights with . . ."

He got no farther than that, which was quite far enough: All three of us moved as one, but it was Tarian got there first. The sound of her hand meeting his scored face with force cracked through the tent, as the blow broke his cheekbone.

"Filth," she said pleasantly. "Speak so again and I rip your tongue out by the root." Ever the lady even in excess, Tarian fastidiously wiped Owein's blood from her fingers with his cloak and turned her back on him.

Silence awhile; presently Owein looked up at me. "I know not what you delay in hopes of," he said quietly, "and care less. But I tell you plain that my life will buy you naught from the Lord Edeyrn; and will serve only to harden his resolve to crush all you under heel like casual adders. Where is that Fian honor I hear so much of, to kill quick and clean?"

"When it comes to that," I heard myself saying, and meaning, too, "my word on it that you will merit the same end as any other enemy. But when it *shall* come to it, any road—that will be for the Ard-rígh and Ard-rían of Keltia to determine, not for me."

As I had intended, the use of the double title surprised him out of his composure.

" 'Ard-rígh *and* Ard-rían'? But who—"

The curtain parted again, with the timing of a perfect cue; and at once all in the room, save only Owein, rose in silence to their feet.

Arthur stood there, and just in front of him was Gweniver: both of them were in field armor, and neither of them looked overjoyed.

"Who?" repeated Arthur, smiling. "Why, Rheged, who think you it might be else?"

CHAPTER
4

It seemed to be a spate of timely entrances: first me, in the King's tent the night past; then Gweniver; Marguessan to follow; now Arthur and Gweniver together—folk popping in and out like foxes from their holes.

But these were the first words that Arthur and Owein had spoken, to anyone's knowledge, since those two grudging sentences before the battle had been joined; and plainly they were no more pleasing to Owein than those other, earlier words had been.

He tried to put an optimistic face upon it all the same. "Does this unprecedented titling then mean the upstart Uthyr is no more? If so, I congratulate you both; but Edeyrn Archdruid may have other words, and more than words, the better suited to your new dignity."

Gweniver smiled and took the chair I offered her. "To your distaste, the Ard-rígh Uthyr lives and thrives, and will for many months yet, gods willing. But in his wisdom and farsight he has so ordered it, that when the time comes he shall be succeeded by a double sovereignty: my cousin, Arthur Pendreic, Prince of the Name"—she used name and title deliberately, and Owein as well as I noted Arthur's faint fleeting flinch—"and I myself, Gweniver ferch Leowyn, as Ard-rígh and Ard-rían together; to bring twice over the blood of Dôn against the Marbh-draoi."

"That will count for little in the end," said Owein in a

voice of honest warning. "Edeyrn has defenses would make your blood turn to sand did you but know them; as doubtless you shall. As for your ragged claims to succession, know that on my death—which I have a tiny thought may be soon—my son and heir Malgan will be raised up in my place, to stand as Edeyrn's heir to Keltia."

Was it my imagination—and bards never seem to lack of *that*—or mere guilty knowledge, that made me think Owein as he spoke this bent a glance of mocking malice on Arthur? Did he know then, I wondered, about Gwenwynbar—Arthur's first wife, before she left him and ran off to win Owein to her bed; or worse still, did he suspect that Gwenwynbar's son, the boy Malgan of whom he spoke so proudly, was perhaps no son of his after all but rather Arthur's firstborn? Or, suspecting, even knowing, did he care? Or was he but pleased to have any heir at all, for his own purposes, and so cared not who might have sired the lad, himself or Arthur or any man else?

If Owein cared not, then Arthur surely did: He had flushed near as dark-red as his own hair in sunlight, though he met Owein's gaze full on. All at once he seemed to come to some decision, one he plainly knew would cause him grief in time to come, and in which he would stand alone, then as well as now. It seemed also to be a decision he had taken all on his own: Gweniver did not share it with him, nor Ygrawn, nor any other of those on whom he ordinarily could count to give him aid— none save, as I later learned, Merlynn himself. But that was later, as I say, and Ailithir, our old teacher, the true Archdruid of Keltia, had as ever his own reasons . . . Just then I could think only of my dizzying fury, all the blood in my body rushing to my brain until I thought I would explode head first, as I heard Arthur my fostern pronouncing Owein's doom.

"I have no other messenger to send," Arthur was saying in a cool everyday voice, as if he did naught of more consequence than order a new cloak or a change of supper plan. "Therefore I must make shift with what I have to hand: Go then, in freedom, and tell your master what has befallen here at Cadarachta. Tell him fairly and freely, what you have seen, and heard, and fought; what strength we have, and what spirit. I charge you deliver all this to Edeyrn, as I have spoken it and you have seen it."

Owein had been listening to Arthur closely, his expression growing gradually more and more astonished, though he struggled mightily to keep it otherwise; and when Arthur ceased to speak, before any of the rest of us could protest or forbid or deny, he spoke in his wonder.

"I wish to make no mistake here, Prince"—the first time he had ever given Arthur his rightful royal title, and there was respect in the word as he spoke it—"yet I cannot but think that I have heard in error, and would that no mistake be made by the others who serve your rule. Do you set me free?"

Arthur nodded, twice and tightly. "Utterly against my own heart, and utterly against advice, but solely for that I know you may be trusted in this if in naught else: to deliver my message to the Marbh-draoi."

"How shall this be done?" Owein's eyes were veiled, but I and the rest could sense his mind all but visibly running through possible shifts and dodges.

"You will be taken to Caer Dathyl with us—we advance on the city within the next day or so, and I doubt not but that we shall find it already ours—and there you will be given a ship in which you must find your own way to your master on Tara. No more than that will you be given, and thus far only, no farther, can I undertake to guarantee your safety. For you see I do all this in the face of my army's resolve that things should be very much otherwise."

"The *army's* resolve?" cried Gweniver, who seemed at last to have rediscovered her powers of speech. "Nay, my lord, that resolve begins here, now, with me! And with your commanders"—her hand swept round to include the rest of us, Tarian and Grehan and myself and the others there present—"and with your—*our*—kindred above all others! What think you your mother will say, when she hears you have let free the one who thought to slay her lord the King?"

Arthur did not reply to her just then, only repeated his orders to the Fian commanders who clustered round outside the chamber door, and left the tent, nodding to me to follow. With one backward glance at Gweniver, so I did.

He vouchsafed me no word as we walked through the

campment, his ostensible purpose being to inspect our
readiness to march next day, or perhaps the day following, and I knew him well enough to know that inquiry
would not be welcomed. But I knew just as well that he
would speak when he was ready, and that restraint ever
gained more from him by way of response than all the
questioning in the worlds.

And so it proved . . . "Well, Talyn?" he murmured after
some ten minutes had passed. "Do you too think I do ill
to let him go?"

"Artos, it is not mine to say aye or nay," I replied with
careful calm; not for aught would I allow blame to creep
into my voice, and yet—I could not help it—blame was
no small part of what I *did* think. "I daresay you are right
when you say you could have no messenger who would
be the more believed by Edeyrn; that *is* it, is it not?"

"Mostly," he said. "There is more to it than that,
though."

"With you, anama-chara," I muttered, "there ever is."

He laughed unwillingly. "That may be. Well, he *will*
give good account of us to the Marbh-draoi, and that of
course is my chiefest reason. As to the rest of it—I
thought thereby to earn some stature, trust, maybe, even,
in Gwenar's eyes."

For one bewildering instant I thought he had spoken
his sister's name, and turned to face him with a puzzled
frown. Then it dawned on me.

"*Gwenwynbar*?! What—whyfor—" So many words
came crowding to my tongue that I could get not one of
them out unmangled; but in truth I was dumb with astonishment. Arthur had not spoken his onetime wife's name,
so far as I knew, in all the years since she had fled his bed
and his cause together, and gone to Caer Dathyl to become Owein Rheged's mate; that he should speak so now,
I thought, could mean no good.

And as he had not spoken the name of his wife, how
much the more had he not spoken the name of the one
who might be his son: Malgan—called ap Owein, but
who knew the truth of it? Save only Gwenwynbar, and
she not telling . . .

For a bard, an ollave yet, there were times I could be
duller than a slug; still, it did not need a house to fall on
me . . .

"Malgan," I said with perfect certainty, and Arthur looked away. "Nay, come, none of *that* ... You would know after all these many years if he is in truth your son, yours and Gwenwynbar's, and not hers and Owein's as all the worlds have thought."

"He would be near, what, twelve years by now?" He made a question of it, but he knew very well the correct number of years on the boy, and knew just as well I knew he knew it. "And if—I say 'if' only, Talyn—he is indeed mine, he may well be the only heir of the body I shall ever have; and at the least he will be blood of the line of the Dôniaid."

And as such, therefore, of the rígh-domhna, eligible for the Ard-tiarnas, the rulership of Keltia ... I pondered on it awhile as we walked. Though Uthyr had last night commanded what all of us closest to him had known for long must be—that Arthur his nephew and Gweniver his niece must wed (and in Keltia it is neither sin nor shame for first cousins to do so, though admittedly it is not often done)—not even Uthyr himself thought the union would prove to be aught but one of sheerest duty. For my part I could not by any reach of fancy see Gweniver so far bending to duty's dictates as to bear an heir of Arthur's siring; and yet the producing of such heir would be the chiefest point and foremost purpose of their union ...

So then. If no child came of that, then it would be indeed as Arthur had said, and Malgan Pendreic ap Arthur would be heir of line to the Throne of Scone; and perhaps the certain knowledge of his parentage could only be surely purchased by sparing of Owein's life, and that was why Arthur did so.

All at once I was racked by pity and pain, for my fostern and his fears and quandaries, and the straits to which I saw him being forced. And though I still most violently did not agree with the liberation of Owein, at the least I could see Arthur's reasons plain at last, the great gamble he had made of it, and the greater hopes—and greatest good—he had of it.

But whether anyone else would see as much, *that* I could not see.

In the end all fell out as Arthur had willed; as it most always had done over the past two decades since our fight

had begun in earnest. Though there was protest aplenty,
even Gweniver came round to hold with him by the time
he had done talking—and Arthur was one of the most
persuasive folk that ever I have given ear to, so that privately to twit him I named him 'Honeymouth,' after a
far-famed bard of old.

As for Ygrawn and Uthyr, they never needed any 'sua-
sion from the first: Whatever Arthur thought his right
course to be, that was the course they held to; for all the
worlds as if he were Ard-rígh already. And indeed, on the
eve of our departure for Caer Dathyl, Uthyr named him
Rex Bellorum, before all the army and the folk alike,
royal war-leader, to have supreme authority over the entire fabric of the fight; and now even Gweniver must bow
to his word in war.

For war it now was, openly and no mistaking: Three
mornings after that dawn over Cadarachta, we broke our
camp and began the long march to Caer Dathyl in the far
southeast, seat of the Princes of Gwynedd since Keltia's
founding, and stronghold of Owein Rheged since first he
rose to power.

Our way there was made considerably easier by the
captured transports and other bits and bobs of hitherto un-
obtainable technology that Owein had reserved for his
own use; though I take pride to say that our scientists of
the Counterinsurgency had wrought surpassing well for
us over the years, and indeed had in some inventings surpassed even Edeyrn's drones.

Though most of the heavy troops and enginery had
been sent on ahead, there yet remained a formidable force
of horse and foot; and these did Arthur choose to lead
himself, riding to Caer Dathyl as he had done once so
long since, though that time with but three companions
only, and all of them set as iron against his riding. Now
thousands rode at his back, and thousands more flocked
to his standard as he rode: But we his Companions caught
one another's eye and nodded, no words needed—Arthur,
for all his satisfaction at how the fight had gone, held still
just that last littlest cantlet of longing sorrow for the days
that had been. Oh, he would never have traded this day of
triumph for those of too-frequent defeat, he was desperately glad and proud of what we had won, and full 'ware
of what we had all paid to win it. Still, he missed those

times of sharing and caring; and though we would all do both unabated until the end of our days, we too knew it was never to be the same again, and we missed those times also.

Purest sentiment to dwell on that, though: We were taking our war to Tara now. It had long been determined that once we had won back Gwynedd from Owein—as it appeared we had now done, and with scarce a sword drawn save at Cadarachta and Ravens' Rift alone; villages, towns, whole lordships even, were sending their submissions to Arthur faster than Marigh Aberdaron could keep count of them—we would then use the planet as a base from which to launch our campaigns against the other worlds of Keltia.

But Tara was the Throneworld, and we had ever known that that must be our prime objective. Not only was the chiefest part of the Marbh-draoi's forces centered there but Edeyrn himself, in his tower of Ratherne, or in Turusachan even; and so there must the strongest blow be struck. Once we had Tara behind our shield, we had won three parts of our fight, so powerful a symbol was that planet, and so mighty a control did she wield over the hearts of Kelts.

For all that, though, we did not come to Tara for near a sixmonth . . . But let me tell the tale in right order.

It took us near a fortnight to reach Caer Dathyl—well, it was a progress, not a forcemarch—and the thing most to our wonderment was that we saw so little fighting along the way. This was all due to Keils Rathen's generalship: His plan had been that once we had won at Cadarachta and the Rift—and he never did tell us what his plan had been if we had lost those fights—our auxiliars, the irregular troops Arthur had been training up for years all across the planet, should move from every shieling on Gwynedd, to take strategic towns and hold them for us, until what time we came ourselves.

Keils's plan worked beyond all right expectation, as we now saw wherever we rode: people streaming out from liberated towns and townlands and walled cities—even Talgarth, of unnerving memory!—to kiss Arthur's hand, and Morgan's, and Gweniver's, and even mine; any hand they could reach, any forearm they could clasp, anyone

they could get near enough to embrace in their delirium
of joy.

I made many songs on that march, songs that are sung
even now, not perhaps for any artistic merit but for that
they were composed when they were, and where, and for
what reason; there is joy in them, and lamenting too, for
Uthyr the wounded King was no better, and we were beginning to accept that word of Morgan's—though we
liked it as little as when she had first pronounced it.

But in spite of our triumph over Owein, and the efforts
of our auxiliars, we had still to smoke out nests of Ravens
in odd corners of Gwynedd; and after that there were the
other Kymric worlds of Dyved and Powys to be won.
Though we as yet could not mount a real campaign for
any world other than Tara, Gweniver even so sent Grehan
to win Erinna—as the Prince of Thomond's heir, he could
command such Erinnach loyalties to fight together as
would not in other time be seen passing water on one another; and Tarian Douglas's brother Aluinn was sent to
wrest back Caledon. They had little with which to work
in the way of arms and ships and troops; but there had
ever been especially virulent enmity against the Marbh-
draoi on both those worlds, and neither was notably
gloomy about the prospects.

It was about this time that the problem of hostages
arose. Until now we had not been successful enough for
the Marbh-draoi to take much note of us, save as annoying cleggans that buzzed and bit and did but little more.
But now, as we grew a force to make a real threat, we
found to our horror that parents, sibs, wives, husbands,
friends, children even, were all being seized indiscrimi-
nately by Edeyrn to use as counters against our advances.
It broke our hearts, and near bowed our spirits, to see
those we loved taken so and treated so: but Gweniver and
Arthur, with the full approval of Uthyr and Ygrawn, proclaimed early on in this siege of shamefulness that no
matter the loss, we would never deal with demands that
turned on the safety of hostage Kelts. We ourselves refused to do likewise, to take hostages of our own; but if
we had, Edeyrn would not have been swayed. Nor would
he have been moved: But we loved, and love was the
whip he thought to hold above our heads.

Yet however we loved those who had been taken—and

many there were we loved most dear—sooner would we give them up to death at Edeyrn's hands than treat with shame for their release. And, when their messages could be contrived to reach us, not a one of them but urged us to stand firm in our resolve; with one voice, so brave a voice, they said to let them perish rather than cut cloaks to Edeyrn's pattern. And, with grief and pride, we did as they did bid us. But, Mighty Mother, it was hard.

"I had forgot it was so fair a place," whispered Morgan, gazing up wide-eyed as we rode under the landgate of Caer Dathyl and turned into the main castle approach.

I looked sidewise at her. She was so fair herself, clad that day in the blue and silver of her House, her hair burning gilt above the indigo tunic.

"When were you here to see it?" I murmured casually, and she fell right into it.

"Oh, one time, with Birogue, we rode down from—" She sighed, then laughed. "I never learn to look out for those little bardic deadfalls of yours, you do them so well they sound as proper questions."

"Aye, that is how they teach us in Tinnavardan," I said equably. "But I would hear more of this jaunt of yours. I knew not Birogue ever left her island."

"Well, she has done, and doubtless will again . . . But we had a fine time here," she added, eyes sparkling with the memory. "We stayed in that inn right over there, and bought cloth and leather and even some unset stones that were offered in trade."

"Oh aye? And did you pay for them in faery-gold, that turned to leaves in the merchants' mailins after you had gone?"

"Certainly not!" she said, indignant. "We paid honorably, in silver, like anyone else: I had pouch-money from my parents every quarter-day, and when she had need, even Birogue seemed to have no lack of coin."

I grinned and stared straight ahead, and our banter carried us up into the castle precincts before either of us could give in to the feeling that had gripped us, a feeling even I, a bard, could put no name upon. It seemed to be a sadness that drifted over us like woodsmoke, like seamist, like cloud in the hollow of an autumn valley.

"Aye," said Arthur later, when I had gone to his chambers after settling into my own rooms. "I felt it myself as we rode up here."

"And? And?"

"And nothing. It was a feeling like any other, and now it is gone." He was unpacking his gear as he spoke—not overmuch, Arthur ever travelled light—and pacing between chest and press as he did so. He had commandeered for himself chambers not far from mine, and had ordered that Uthyr and Ygrawn be housed in Owein's splendid suite of rooms. The former occupant was himself securely held in a tower strongroom, until such time as Arthur should choose to keep his word and set him free.

"Did you see how they cheered the King and Queen, when we entered the city?" he added, himself looking more cheerful as he said so. "I knew the folk would turn their hearts openly to us, when once we might openly solicit them. Oh, *what*?" This last to me, when he turned to look at me at last. "You look as sour as a thistle."

I shook my head and shrugged. "As Gwennach did say that night in the King's tent—the other boot has yet to fall, and I mislike waiting to hear the thud."

He sat down, looking suddenly deflated, and I regretted my words at once. "What think you, then?" he asked, in quite a different voice. "Some disaster apparent to your bardish instincts, that none of us grosser folk perceive just yet?"

"You know very well it is not so at all," I said roundly. "But since you speak of disasters, what of your sister?"

He stared at me as if I had taken leave of what few wits he deemed me still to possess. "My *sister*? Oh—Marguessan."

A good question: Since that night in Uthyr's tent, when the wounded King had prophesied treachery in his own daughter's heart—and in the babe she carried beneath it—few save her mother and ladies had even seen the Princess Marguessan. She had come with us to Caer Dathyl, riding in state in a horse-litter, the best conveyance we could contrive for the rougher parts of the way; then when better roads were reached she had taken to a carriage, one of the few we had—more a great enclosed chariot than a proper carriage, which was rare in a realm of riders.

Arthur's face had taken on a look I knew from of old: a kind of weighing look, as if he were judging just how much truth his listener could stand to hear, and how it might be taken.

"Do you know, Talyn," he said at length, "the King does not recall that prophecy he made concerning Marguessan. Recalls not one word of it ... when my mother spoke of it to him, it was as if she told him a story of someone else entirely, and he was most—distressed."

"I will wager on it," I said grimly. "Before the battle, back at Llwynarth, he spoke privily to me of his misgivings concerning Marguessan and Irian, that he feared some mischief to you from them in time to come. I promised I would keep 'ware of them both, and he seemed content." I moved forward a little in my seat, for now I must ask the thing I had been dreading and fearing most to put to him. "But Artos—what of Gwenwynbar?"

Plainly he was prepared for me to ask, had been expecting it; for he looked straight at me and smiled.

"She is not here."

"Are you sure of it?"

He nodded. "Oh aye. The castle has been searched by our Companions—I had not allowed Uthyr brought into it else—and she was not found. Some of the servitors say she has fled, though I doubt she would have gone to her own place of Saltcoats, or any other place obvious to pursuit."

"And taken the boy with her?"

"Aye."

I could not determine from such brevity the true nature of his feelings—which was of course just as he did wish it. Even Druids need a little more to work on than five operative words—the rest were mere masking—and Arthur had ever been above the common run at concealing his state of mind or heart when he did wish to keep hidden either one. He but tried to put me off the trail, and hoped I would not press him.

Well, it takes more than that, *braud* ... "What does Owein say?" I asked for a moment, all casual inquiry, then looked up sidewise and swiftly, just quick enough to see his face change before he could control it. *Ah, that's a touch, now!* ...

"You and Guenna have no child as yet," he said then in

apparent thus-not. "And it may be that I myself have
none as yet, nor ever shall—but think how *you* must feel,
Talyn, were it your son kept from you as maybe Malgan
has been kept from me."

And all at once I felt sad and sorry, and shamed indeed
that I had pricked him so, and I thought of Malgan as I
had known him in Caer Dathyl, what time I had been
bard to Owein and spy for Arthur all at once . . . True it
was I had no way just yet of knowing what Arthur must
feel—and, unnatural father that I must be, even when I
did come to have a son of my own I never came to feel
as Arthur seemed to be feeling now; yet I daresay I loved
Geraint ap Taliesin as well as any father loves any son . . .
But Arthur was made differently, and as I saw his grief
for one who might or might not even be his child at all
I repented me of my ploy.

"My sorrow, Artos," I said formally, and he heard the
true-feeling in the words and nodded.

"Aye, and mine . . . But just now there is more for us
to do than fret." And he turned his mind—gods, how I
envied that ease of his; though it was not in the slightest
easy but the exercise of a disciplined will—from what
could not be helped to what could no longer be halted:
the disposition of Owein Rheged and the beginning of the
campaign for Keltia. And never doubted for the smallest
instant that the rest of us would turn as well.

CHAPTER
5

If I have seemed to scant our triumph, know that it is not for lack of material; I could 'broider on the theme from now till Nevermas, were it not that there is so large a tapestry yet to unroll. Too, I think we were all somewhat boggled, even Arthur, at the *completeness*—or at least what then seemed to be so—of our victory at Cadarachta. It was like a fidchell match: With one hand—Tarian's—we had played out a daring game of risk, while with the other—Keils's—we had dealt distraction, and so won twice over. Heady stuff, for poor rebels who had known naught but the pinprick triumphs of reivings and small skirmishes for so many years gone by.

But now all was changed, utterly and forever altered. No more the rash chief of a ragtag resistance, Arthur was now Rex Bellorum, supreme and uncontested commander: In the eyes of the army and the people, if perhaps not just yet in Edeyrn's reckoning, he was the sword that Uthyr wielded to win back Keltia for the folk; and as for Edeyrn's measuring, well, that too would change ... But Arthur took over Caer Dathyl as if he had been heir to it from birth as a prince of Gwynedd; from that strong place he sent out his forces across the planet, like the narrow burning rivers that course down from the volcano's heart, and he himself that great blazing center.

By Lughnasa we had won the entire planet for our

own; by Fionnasa we were ready to move, for the first time in two hundred years and more, off-planet: We were ready to take our war through the stars, to Tara.

But before we could begin to move so we began to hear that which we had long been dreading to hear: Edeyrn the Marbh-draoi had at last deigned to take note of us, and his noting took a most evil form indeed, from which all Keltia will be a thousand years and more in the mending . . .

"Galláin!" echoed Gweniver, staring at Arthur as if she deemed him to have lost what judgment she had reluctantly conceded him to possess.

She was not the only one who thought so; but all the rest of us, every scrap as surprised as she, did keep it a thought only. Still, we were all heard even so . . .

"Fomori and Fir Bolg," said Arthur evenly, and my glance met Daronwy's, as I remembered our converse by the bath-tent the night of Cadarachta. She raised her fine dark brows and nodded once, then we returned our attention to Arthur.

But my mind was running on our foes . . . Fomori and Fir Bolg, we had called them, back in the days of Brendan; these enemies were not strangers. We had named them after our old Earth enemies; indeed, we had called them thus so long and so insistently that they came in time to call themselves as we did, their old names forgotten even among themselves, save for the loremasters. Human in form, both races; good fighters too, with even a smattering of honor.

All and all, though, they were mercenaries, bought and brought by Edeyrn, to help him defeat this son of Dôn that had come out of nowhere to destroy his reign.

"He must be fearing indeed," remarked Kei, "does he bring in galláin to splint his arm."

Arthur shook his head. "Nay, I see how he does plan it: Throw the galláin against us first, as expendable levies, straw for our swords to bite on; while all that time keeping his seasoned troops as far intact as he might, hoping to exhaust us before he must commit his own armies to battle."

"As loathsome a plan as we might have expected from him," said Morgan. "But, Arthur, no warrior of Keltia has had to face galláin for a thousand years and more; not since the very early years, and even then—"

"And even then it was just these same Fomorians and Fir Bolg," said Arthur cheerfully. "Let us be thankful indeed that it is not the Coranians that have so taken the Marbh-draoi's coin."

At that a shiver ran round the room that none of us could hide; I, who shuddered with the rest, thought even as I did so that no man who faced what Arthur now was facing had any right to jest as he jested now. For where the Fomorians have only been *named* after ancient Earth enemies, the Coranians *are* ancient Earth enemies: sprung from the Atlandean race of the Telchine folk, as the Kelts were come from the Danaans.

They are a fierce, cruel and hateful people, and were chiefly the cause of the Danaans leaving Atland, our first homeplace on Earth, to find refuge in other, happier lands; and in the end, of course, they were our near-destruction ... But this is not the time for the history of the Atlandic Wars; perhaps I shall yet be spared to write them—In any case, the Coranians were not in this present coil of Edeyrn's—at least not that we knew of—and for that we were ever grateful.

Daronwy, never a one to avoid the obvious, asked the question we had all framed in our minds.

"But, Artos, what will this mean for us?"

And strangely, it was not from Arthur that the answer came ... From his place against the wall, flanked by Tarian and Betwyr, Owein Rheged spoke to answer Ronwyn's query.

"Naught, you may be sure, of good."

Arthur turned a thoughtful gaze his way, but his face was otherwise bare of expression and he said nothing in response.

Not so Kei ... "This needs no dog of the Marbh-draoi, Artos, to tell us so ... Have you nothing to say of more merit, Rheged, or is that the sum of your wisdom?"

Owein smiled; he was thinner than when I had known him at Caer Dathyl, and looked rather more haggard than he had a few months since at Cadarachta. Still, he was used in those days of captivity to wear a face more appropriate to a victor than one who had lost a planet—and who would soon be giving an accounting of that loss to an angry master.

"What would you have me say? That you will come to Tara on sails of silver and take the Throneworld with feathers, not swords? Your master has the right of it: Edeyrn will be saving his best troops to meet you do you gain the planet; he will be spending his hired swords to see that you do not. Any idiot can see as much."

"Well, this idiot sees a lai or two more," said Arthur pleasantly. "I think, Rheged, the time has come for you to complete your purpose—or the purpose we have devised for you—and depart for Tara, to serve a herald's calling."

In spite of his best efforts to conceal it, Owein's face lighted with sudden doubting hope. "Then you will free me as you promised?"

"Did I not just now say so?" said Arthur with a rare snap of exasperation to his tone. "Aye, go, and go now. I ordered a ship to stand ready this morning; it will convey you to a place in the Throneworld system from which you may with reasonable care come to safety. How you come to it is your own concern, and how you deliver my charge to Edeyrn is your concern still more."

Owein rose while Arthur was still speaking, and Betwyr and Tarian with him; at Arthur's glance I myself quietly moved round to join the escort party.

"Then I take leave of you all," said Owein formally, "and in especial of you, Penarvon; though I know well the leave is not the last."

"Indeed not," agreed Arthur, and at the other end of the table Gweniver stirred and glanced at him with puzzled sharpness.

Owein was more than usually quiet as we passed through the corridors of Caer Dathyl, corridors that he knew well from all his years here residing. Stealing a sidewise look at him, I wondered if he thought now of that time: those five years I had been bard to him; those we had known. Wondered if he thought of Gwenwynbar, and the boy Malgan; if he knew to what hidden sanctuary they had fled ...

It seemed he had read my thought ... "Nay, Glyndour," he said suddenly, "I know not where she might be. She did not deem it any concern of mine, it seems; though I am *quite* sure"—here his voice was dry and cool—"that the lady has arranged matters to her advantage."

"And the boy?" I asked after a moment.

He was not quick enough this time in his control, and his mouth twisted before he could help it.

"I do not know that either ... But one thing I will tell you: It is possible—possible only, Glyndour—that the boy is whose your leader thinks him."

I saw in his face, heard in his voice, what this admission had cost him to make—insofar as it *was* admission. *So, Gwenwynbar has not dealt in honesty with you either, Rheged* ... And that Owein should say even so much as that was by way of repayment to Arthur, a return on the debt of freedom that lay now between them. *Yet not paid in full for all that* ...

"He is gone then?"

I answered Arthur's question but looked at Gweniver as I did so.

"Aye, gone; Betwyr and Tari are following as escort until he clears the system."

I flung myself into a chair and shaded my eyes with my hand. Not for worlds would I have let them know how I was feeling about this: I had such a presentiment of oncoming disaster as made me queasy as a pregnant woman or a seer in the throes of trance. And not that alone to make me loathsick: For several appalling hours I had been off-planet in one of the escort craft that had been dispatched to see Owein beyond the gravity well of Gwynedd; other ships would be accompanying his craft on from there.

It was the first time I had been truly in space; though we barely ventured past atmosphere and clouds had hidden the lands beneath, still the sky above was black and thick with stars, thicker than I had ever seen, even on all those cold winter nights of wandering. It was a short first trip, and the crew of the little craft obviously well versed in its handling; even so, I had been seized by panic as never before. To fight Edeyrn, and the galláin forces he had brought to face us, we would be travelling through space a good deal farther than this; would we be up to it, and still able to fight when we came to our journey's end? Travelling to Tara would mean flight through hyper-

space, and that was a chilling prospect, not only to
Taliesin the space faintheart but perhaps to many of the
others as well.

"Well, you know, Talyn," said Gweniver kindly when I
broached the subject later, "we have been training for just
such an invasion for some years now. Aye, even in hyperspace! It is not so fearful a place as you would make it
to be; many of us Companions have sailed it—you remember even Tryffin went in secret to Kernow when we
were preparing the ship attack down Glora, and I can tell
you that he did not sail there straight! You will do as
well, I promise. Or ask Merlynn for a rann if you do not."

I looked keenly at her as we spoke: Since the events at
Cadarachta Gweniver and I had had little time together;
she was usually occupied with one task or another concerning the imminent invasion, and when not—I sighed,
and across the table she caught it and half-frowned.

I was not alone in thinking that the various dramas and
disasters that had been our lot since Cadarachta might
have served to bring Arthur and Gweniver, our proclaimed rulers that would be, closer together and more in
harmony with one another and with their future task. It
had so far proved not so: Arthur, when he was not occupied with the preparations for war, thought chiefly of
Uthyr, and often, I knew, of Malgan. While Gweniver—
It had been more or less an open secret that Gweniver and
Keils Rathen, Uthyr's chief warlord, had long been lovers; though over the course of the past few years they had
seemed to drift into a kind of closeness that was less a romance than a long loving squabble, now in these frantic
weeks they had grown close again. To the point that messengers sent to find one or the other, late at night, at Arthur's bidding or mine or Ygrawn's or Morgan's, would
look first in the other's bed for the one being sought.

This was held to be no ill thing, mind; Ygrawn for one
made plain her tolerance of the situation, treating Keils as
kin and friend, not simply as a queen might treat a loyal
and trusted advisor, and Uthyr too was known to approve.
But none of that altered necessity: When the time at last
came for it, Gweniver and Arthur would wed as they had
pledged to do, and Keils would then be required to
choose—to end the involvement, or to accept what place
he must, as far-charach, though this was not usual where

royal marriages were concerned, or lennaun, or any of the several other lawful titles and ranks that Keltic law and custom supply in their wisdom for partners-of-love. It might be that when that time came, he would not be able to accept such arrangement; and how that would affect Keils's loyalties, to Arthur and Gweniver both, how that would work upon him personally, none but he, and maybe Gweniver and Arthur, could say ...

It was about that time, in the last weeks before our sailing, that we had our first brush with Edeyrn's hired forces, the galláin mercenaries that had until now been but reported of. And the way of it was this ...

In the course of our preparing for departure—making ready our forces, learning to command our captured ship-fleets, securing Gwynedd against possible attack or counter-rising in our absence—we had not been looking to encounter outworld enemies. So when a scout sloop came limping in at Caer Dathyl's port, with a tale to tell of surprise attack just beyond the orbit of Arianwen, Gwynedd's one small moon, we were inclined to dismiss it as a last stand made by desperate Ravens, a forlorn-hope maneuver ventured upon out of ignorance or suicidal vengement.

"Not so," said Keils, who with Tarian had received first report of the incident. "They were Fomori, Artos, and some of them were flying Keltic ships."

Those who sat round the council table—the usual suspects, plus one or two additions such as Tryffin and a new Companion, Tanwen of Dyonas, who had come into Gweniver's service at Coldgates—sat up at that, as if a spear had flung them sharply forward. Only Arthur still lounged in his chair, sitting on the end of his spine as he did when he wished to think; at his feet Cabal bristled briefly and subsided with a grumble.

"Artos?"

He stirred, but did not respond at once to Gweniver's query, touched as it was with impatience.

"It is a test, surely," said Kei with conviction. "The Marbh-draoi seeks to try us before we come to Tara; and, as Owein Rheged did say, does not wish to spend his own forces to do so."

"Truly," said Arthur, coming to life at last. "And it is

in my mind that Owein did indeed faithfully deliver our message as he was charged to do; else Edeyrn would not be sending these little jabs to vex us."

"Well," said Gweniver, by now vexed herself, "what shall you do about it?"

Arthur grinned at her. "Oh, not overmuch."

His 'not overmuch' proved to be a wave of lightning raids out from Gwynedd in all directions, which netted us, to our great surprise, rather more of the mercenary ships than we had been looking to find.

"Well, you know, Talyn," said Arthur after it was done, "when you see one mouse in the grain-store there are at least twenty more you do not see ... Any road, it was good practice, for as yet we do not have so much experience in space fights as I should like for us to have. And also we have learned much from the galláin ships we have taken in the raids."

"Though not so much, I think, from the prisoners." This last was a sore point: Most of Arthur's closest advisors, seeing that the amassing of galláin captives, as well as that of traitor Kelts, was about to begin on a large scale, had almost as one recommended a course of mercilessness. Some of us were surprised at the apparent bloodthirstiness; but, they argued, we were about to embark on a campaign the scale of which was unprecedented in all Keltic history. Why cumber ourselves with hostage traitors who could most like not be reclaimed, or waste precious resources and troop-strength in guarding outfrenne prisoners?

Arthur heard my disapproval and flushed slightly; his own position was somewhere in between, and he knew I was one of those who held with mercy. Oh, not for any tenderheart motives or even mere disinclination to kill— gods know, I have done enough of *that* in my time, both with my own hands and by commanding the hands of others to be set to it—but rather from a deep feeling that it was always best to err on the side of mercy. Well, so long as it did not cost us the fight in the end, why not? But we had been down this road before, Arthur and I ...

"You know how I feel about that, Talyn," he said quietly. "And have I not ordered camps to be maintained while we are gone? Not here on the planet, true, it would not be safe; but on that Dyvetian moon we took last month. The prisoners will be well kept there, and Dyved was easily retaken, never overinfested with Edeyrn's vermin to begin with. Besides, our own hostages may be more kindly treated do we so."

"Aye, aye, I know." I waved a hand to dismiss his argument; for of course he was right. "So, then. We have Gwynedd, and Dyved, and Powys is about to fall to us. Grehan is on point of winning back Erinna; though Aluinn Douglas has had a harder fight for Caledon, and we must strengthen his arm as soon as we can. But what for us, braud?"

For the first time, I think, since Cadarachta, Arthur gave me his full, unforced smile; that marvellous warm bright blaze across his face.

"For us? Tara for us; royal Tamhair herself."

This, then, was it; it had begun, that to which all this rest, all the torments and anguished efforts of twice a hundred years, had been but prelude and overture. If I had thought we were strung to a pitch beyond mortal bearing before now, I soon saw how very wrong I could be, as every last atom of every last soul of us was bent to the service of one thing only: the readiness to sail, and battle-readiness when we came to our sailing's end.

I saw not so much of Arthur in these last days; as Rex Bellorum he was everywhere, *there* for everyone whether he will or nill, and if he ever tired of it he never let it show where folk could see. Only to us his close Companions—to Ygrawn, to Merlynn, to Tarian and Betwyr and Daronwy, to Morgan and me—did he allow himself to be less than perfect, paying us the very great compliment of being witness to his vulnerability. And we repaid him as we could and as he needed, by undemanding and unquestioning love and loyalty; and also by demanding and questioning and even the odd thump or two where merited ... Only to Uthyr, of all those Arthur held dearest, did he strictly dissemble; and that out of love also, for Arthur would sooner have been dead in a ditch than trouble the wounded King with doubts or uncertainties. Not that he spoke only cheerful lies to his uncle-lasathair—he could just as cheerfully recount tales of woe, but only to make some greater point, never to bur-

den the King with any greater trouble than he had already
to bear.

For Merlynn had Seen and spoken truth: Uthyr's wound
had not healed up, the great wound in his thigh; and though
he had grown but little weaker he had grown no better, and
he was in continual pain. He bore it well, most gallantly
and tranquilly; sometimes as I looked at him with druid-
sight I saw a silver light about him, not the laeth-fraoch, the
hero-light, but the true coron-solais, the soul-veil that
clothes our bodies as the aurora does veil the poles, and silver is the color of faith.

But Uthyr too would come with us to Tara, on that he
had been as iron; and Ygrawn was as one with him in
that. Only Marguessan, of all the royal family, was to remain on Gwynedd; and that chiefly because shortly before Lughnasa she was lighter of a son. It was the first
royal baby of the new generation—well, the first one we
were certain about, in any case; the verdict was not yet
come in on Malgan—and the folk were wild with joy.

"She has named him Mordryth," said Morgan, coming
to me straight from her first visit to her sister and new
nephew. She pitched her cloak onto our bed and stretched
out on top of it, snugging the fur up around her face as
if for comfort.

"A likely name," I said, trying to be helpful.

She snorted. "And you, a bard, to say so! They are putting it about that it is a name of tradition in Irian's family;
but even her husband cannot smooth over its history all
so featly."

"Nay, well, perhaps not." I lay down beside her and
stared up at the ceiling. Mordryth. The name of a remarkable trimmer of old, a gray eminence in the royal family
several hundred years ago; one who wielded a king's own
powers, though he was never crowned . . . I shifted beside
Morgan; this might well be one of the last times for many
days to come that we would have a proper bedchamber
with a proper bed to lie in; once we came to Tara it would
be camp-couches and clochans, if we were lucky perhaps
a commandeered castle now and again—great shame to
waste such luxury just now . . .

But her mind was not running on romance . . . "Talyn,"
she said suddenly, turning and rising on one elbow to
look down into my face, "when we come to Tara, there is

a thing must be done without which all the battles my brother may win shall be won in vain. It is not a thing one person may rightly ask of another—"

I kissed my fingertips and brushed them gently over her lips. "Then do not ask, for the answer is 'aye, and aye again.' What did you think I should say? Who shall come with us? Where do we go?"

She laughed and lay down again beside me. "I think we shall not lack for company! Only let us wait on that until we are there; for the moment, I'd not waste this time on talk, nor yet this bed on sleeping—it will be Fian bedding again for us soon enough now!"

To look back on that morning at Caer Dathyl, when we left the castle in the care of our friend and Companion Ferdia mac Kenver and the planet in the guardianship of my sister Tegau Goldbreast; and, still more than a little dumbstruck with the sheer tremendousness of the thing, took to the skies above Gwynedd where Arthur's ship Carnwen waited for us, to lead the sail against Tara ... Even now, near a century later, tears still sting my eyes at the beauty and the terror and the joy of it.

We had boarded, and settled ourselves, and seen first of all that Uthyr the King was disposed as comfortably and securely as might be, and Ygrawn with him—she had given me a foster-mother's blessing, and Uthyr an uncle's, when time came to leave—and now we had all gone to our assigned posts, for the hour was surely at hand.

From my place behind Arthur, standing on the bridge of this ship he had chosen as his own and renamed Carnwen—'White Hilt,' though in the bardic usage its meaning was more on the order of 'Sacred Claw,' as that of a beast holy to the Goddess or the God—I peered out a viewport and down at the planet below.

That was a sight beyond all brave sights imagined: the planet glowing like a shield of silver; and above it, wherever I looked, like deadly diamonds ships stood out against the stars. I had never seen Gwynedd from such a perspective: It did not look at all like the schoolroom globes on which Arthur and I had learned geography, as lads in Daars. There were all those clouds, for one thing, slashes and tatters obscuring the lands that lay beneath. Then suddenly the tatters swirled and parted—some weather-magic, perhaps, wrought by Merlynn or some other to give what would be for many of us a last clear glimpse of home—and I saw the whole west coast of the main continent, from Caerllyon in the south, past drowned Gwaelod (and here the sea was green, not deep blue, over the sunken land), to the ice-plains north even of Coldgates. That land held my heart, and I was leaving.

I felt a hand placed on my shoulder, and I did not need to turn to know who it was had placed it there. It was Arthur's land too, broken Daars lay there below, tucked away in the hill-folds, though from this height it could not be discerned. *Yet it is there* ... I looked up then, but he was staring straight ahead, out at the stars, across the unimagined distances that no longer barred our path. We were out of the cage: For the first time in two hundred years, Kelts who wore no yoke of Edeyrn's making were about to pass between Keltic worlds. For the first time since Athyn's day, war would come to Tara.

So I looked where Arthur looked, and knew that as it was there with us on Carnwen, so it was with all our Companions on all the ships behind us. Not a one of them but had eyes on that powdered brilliance, straining to distinguish the one speck in thousands around whose brightness turned Tara.

And then I looked at Arthur again. He was smiling faintly, his whole face alight with it, as if he knew some great secret and would not share it just yet with any other. He looked very young, and very happy, as bright and deadly as Llacharn itself. As I looked, even then he raised his hand to his right shoulder and let it fall again, almost casually, to his side.

"Ymlaen," he said softly, which in the Kymric tongue signifies 'Onward!'. And the ship leaped beneath us into space.

CHAPTER
6

From Gwynedd to the Throneworld system of Tara is an eight-hour sail at speed through hyperspace; eight hours, that is, in normal times, which gods knew these times were nothing near. Without question there was fighting to come before ever we reached there, and a greater fight to come after; but first we must cross the great gulf that lay between, and with but a few exceptions amongst the Fianna, and latterly us Companions, we had never made such a crossing before.

Hyperspace—ard-na-spéire, as we call it in the Gaeloch, the overheaven—is a terrifying place, and I did not shame to let anyone see just how fearful I myself did find it. And not that alone, but it made me physically, shamefully, ill: I, who had sailed single-handedly tiny curraghs over the wildest, widest waters on Gwynedd without a single queasy pang, spent the better part of this historic voyage in the confines of the privy, heaving up my guts.

But for all my shame and discomfort, I found this over-heaven lovely past longings: stars like netted gems, with a blackness that seemed softly alive between the knotted light-strands, a faint bluesilver glow over all that seemed to have its source everywhere and nowhere. Even for one who prides himself on ollaveship, it was a hard place to catch in words.

Words, however well-crafted, were not my chiefest task

just now: There was too much else to do of greater import and urgency—preparing and organizing and exhorting and heartening, for Arthur fully expected to emerge at journey's end into the heart of a pitched battle.

"It stands to reason they will be waiting for us," said Tarian. "Edeyrn knows from Arthur's vaunting screed that we are coming sometime, and by now he knows from Owein that we are coming soon. Therefore he will have deployed his galláin fleet across the mouth of our most likely exits from hyperspace, in hopes of stopping us before ever we come to Tara."

"Well, what then, War-leader?" snapped Gweniver. As a rule she did not display open peevishness to or even in front of Tarian, whom she greatly admired, and, a rarer thing with her, very much liked; but demands of duty, and anticipation of battle, and hope and terror of its upshot, and the stretched nerves and sleeplessness that came of all this, had altered her case.

" 'What then'? Then we shall fight, of course," said Arthur, more good-humored even than his wont, though he had no right to be.

But all too plainly too much so for his cousin: Gweniver flushed a little and turned on him.

"If I may inquire of the wisdom of the Rex Bellorum—"

Her tone was a snarl, and I and several others moved swiftly to balk the vicious little rippet that seemed about to break. Arthur ignored us all, and left the room in silence; after a hesitation I went after, catching him up in the passageway. He did not seem unwishful of my company, and we were soon back in his own chambers on Carnwen's main deck.

But once there he did not appear disposed to speak at all, only stood in the viewport bubble and stared out at the streaming stars.

"Artos?" I heard myself asking humbly. "Are we ready? Truly?"

Even then he did not turn. "You have real doubts then, Talyn?"

My patience went the same road as Gweniver's. "Nay, I ask only for sake of breaking silence! *Surely* I have doubts! Do you say you have none?"

"None to speak of," he said calmly.

"What a liar you are, Arthur Penarvon. The dullest

truthsenser in Keltia could hear the sham in *that* from half
a world away."

At that he laughed, and came to sit in the chair by my
own.

"Well, so long as it is only you who hear it, and not the
rest of the army, I daresay I can live with it."

I let a moment pass. "Was it that, that Gwennach
heard, to make her so angry just now?"

"Very like." He regarded me frankly and with just the
faintest trace of a smile upon his face. I returned his gaze,
waiting him out as I had done since our schoolroom days.
"Gweniver thinks I take all this too lightly," he said at
last. "Edeyrn, and Owein who will be waiting for us on
Tara if not before, and again Edeyrn, and the fighting on
Erinna and Caledon, and Edeyrn once more, and Uthyr
the King ... It is not that I take it lightly, but that I must
be *seen* to take it lightly; else the armies will take it too
dark by far."

"Just how dark then is it?"

"Dark enough," said Arthur, rising again and beginning
to pace. He seemed to come to a decision. "Has Guenna
spoken to you, of late, of some—some task there may be
for us on Tara?"

I stared at his averted back. "Indeed ... though as yet
she has not told me what that task may be. Do you know
more of it, then?"

He nodded, still not turning to face me. "We have
stood together in some terrible places, Talynno, but this—
Well, it is not yet, and we will not be alone entirely when
we come to it."

"Then leave it," I said, and we did.

But there was little time to spare for brooding on some
future trial: The trials we had first to surmount were more
than daunting enough.

After what seemed like years but was in truth only a
day or so as days were counted on Gwynedd, we came to
the end of our hyperspace crossing. Before we emerged
into space-normal, Arthur called a halt to all ships, and
with his commanders and closest Companions round
him, with Ygrawn on his left hand and Gweniver on his
right, he stood on the bridge of Carnwen to speak to his
armies. As many of us as could crowded into the bridge-

well below to hear him, while the viewscreens carried his words and his image to every ship in the fleet. Only Uthyr the King did not choose to be part of that grouping, but in his infirmity remained, with Morgan in attendance, in his chambers, and watched as did the rest of us, as Arthur addressed the ages and his Kelts.

What he said is by now part of the loom of legend; what I would now call to memory's eye is rather the look of him, the way we saw him that day, and the way he saw us in his turn.

And what we saw was our King that would be: to speak as we bards speak, the full statement of that theme of kingship which had sounded round Arthur since the night Uthyr had had him proclaimed Prince of the Name, so long since in Coldgates. Then it had been the merest sketch of melody, picked out as it were upon cold harpstrings by a single unskilled finger, no harmony or chording, no concord or consonance or chime.

But now, as he stood there and spoke to us, it was as if the full diapason of royalty were pouring through him, from Brendan long since to kings and queens centuries yet unborn. And the counterpoint was as it has ever been: The life of the land and the life of its ruler are as one; but though they are one, they are not the same, and that is kingship's great mystery.

For so awe-filled a moment, the words Arthur spoke were not what any bard would class as in the heroic mold; they were plain words, for what he saw as a plain hour. Yet as he spoke them, and as we saw him speak them, they became anything but plain, transformed through some desperate alchemy into words of legend, and we stored them up forever in our hearts.

First he thanked us for our loyalty and constancy in service to King Uthyr and Queen Ygrawn; only then to Gweniver and to himself. He spoke of our years together, and the triumphs we had had, and the years and the triumphs, gods willing, that were yet to come. He spoke of his much-loved Companions; he spoke of the many we mourned, Companion or conscript or irregular auxiliar or citizen Kelt, all alike in their dying so that we here might come to this place in such an hour with such intent.

I watched him as he spoke, one part of me the eternal observer-bard, another the loving fostern concerned for the well-being of his foster-brother, and another part still as one with every other Kelt who watched and listened, a participant like any other in this great drama about to be played out on so tremendous a stage. Arthur was one of those annoying folk who seldom allow their faces to reflect their feelings: He looked grave enough as he spoke to us, but it was not so very different from his usual gravity; confident, aye, and even brought us to cheering laughter once or twice, on which occasions he did permit himself a smile as well. But of that inner uncertainty I knew full well he felt, I saw no outward sign upon him; and if I his brother saw none, certain sure no other saw any.

He was clad as he had been at Cadarachta, in battle-dress of black tunic and trews and boots, with a findruinna lorica beneath a surcoat blazoned with the arms of Dôn. The sword Llacharn hung upon a worn brown leather baldric studded with red gold, and his chestnut hair fell past his collarbone. No mark of royal rank did he bear save his father's great ruby seal upon his hand; no more did he need, and not even that for our sakes. Save for the thirty or so added years, he looked soul-stabbingly like that young Arthur who had stood before the folk of Coldgates that long-ago night, when he had flung himself at their hearts like a cast spear, and had not failed of his mark.

Beside him, Ygrawn and Gweniver were for the moment eclipsed; and truth to tell, neither was displeased to be so. This was Arthur's moment; he had fought since boyhood to stand there, and not the present Queen-consort nor the future Ard-rían seemed minded to dispute his place or his right. Or, indeed, his force upon the folk: As I glanced round me, I saw the light upon the upturned faces, the love and loyalty in the shining eyes of those standing by me, and knew it must be even so with all those on all the other ships. What Arthur gave to them freely and fully, they gave back to him full measure; and that was ever the cause of his success—and of his failures also, and his downfall in the end . . .

But such darkling times were far off just then; and though we knew our present state was a desperate one, and that many of those who now heard Arthur's words here as Prince would not live to hear him speak to them as King, still we rejoiced—in him, and in ourselves, and in the great cause for which we had come so far and fared so hardly.

Arthur was coming to the end of his speech now; he spoke again of Uthyr the King (though not of the unhealed and unhealing wound from which the King continued to suffer); of Leowyn Ard-rígh, Gweniver's dead father; of his own dead sire, Prince Amris, and of the death of the only man he ever knew as a father, Gorlas Lord of Daars.

"By the price they did pay, the price we ourselves will pay today and have paid in the past," he was saying, "Keltia will be ransomed back for its people. Not for any great merit of our own has it been ordered that we and not they, nor any of those millions of others who paid a like price, should stand here so; but the gods have made it so, the Mother has allowed it, the Father has confirmed it, the Alterator has set it into being and the Highest has ordained that it should be. All we must now do is that which we must do. And *that,* we can, and shall, and will." He paused a moment, then smiled a smile of the morning of the world, bright, unshadowed, informed by love and joy. "Lean thusa orm!"

'Follow on,' it has been translated; more accurately, 'Follow thou me.' That was the first time Keltia heard the battlecry that was to ring across so many fields on so many worlds for so many years to come. And we who heard it now did as all those who ever heard it would do: We took it up with a great glad shout, and took it to our hearts.

But before that shout had died away, Arthur stepped forward from where he stood, and not one of us there but knew what was to come. Suddenly solemn, without another word spoken we ebbed away like some silent tide, to take up our battle stations, to await the next word that Arthur would speak.

Not long in coming, that: He consulted briefly and swiftly with Keils and Tarian and the captains of the fleet, to verify that all was in readiness for battle, ships and forces alike; had word sent back to Gwynedd, to give Tegau and Ferdia and the rest what might perhaps be the last word they would ever have from us; spoke a few soft private words over the transcom, overheard by no one, to

Uthyr in his chamber; then stepped forward a little, still staring out the viewport, though the screens gave a better view by far.

Gweniver and I, a few paces behind, exchanged grave glances: As soon as Arthur spoke, Carnwen would drop down from hyperspace into space-normal off Tara, and all the other ships would follow her. Into what we would be emerging—enemy fleet or pitched battle or peaceful space—we had no way of knowing. None among us could even say if we had reached clear space or an asteroid belt, as no astrogation charts were available for current conditions round Tara; the best information we had was two centuries old. Even Owein Rheged's captured pilots had not been trusted with such knowledge. But we were here, and we would soon know what we had come to . . .

A movement from Arthur's direction caused our gazes to shift: As before, he lifted his right hand to shoulder height, paused so fractionally that only Gwennach and I marked the hesitation, then—not as before—Arthur flung his arm out and down, as one will do who starts off a race or a duel or a contest. And, again as before, "Ymlaen!" was all the word he gave.

It was enough: The stars reeled around us as we dropped out of the overheaven into space-normal, where time was as it was and ever would be. I glanced at the screens: The rest of the fleet was out of hyperspace and forming up behind us, but as yet there were no signs of attackers, galláin or otherwise.

Perhaps our fears had been in vain? But even as I thought this, and turned to Gweniver to voice my hopeful thought, my sidesight caught swift motion on one of the screens that was mirrored by motion outside the viewport. *An incoming ship, galláin by the look of her . . .*

Arthur had already taken note of the attacker, but so well-schooled was the bridge crew that without a word of command Carnwen's course was altered, weapons were fired, and the enemy craft vanished in a bloom of deadly light. *First blood to us . . .*

But only first, came the thought from Arthur, wry and warning. I spun around as the screens blazed with light lancing from half a hundred attacking craft gyring in upon us.

"Where did *those* come from?" muttered Gweniver, taking her place at a weapons console.

"No matter where they came from; only let us make certain they do not keep us from where we are going." I looked again at Arthur, who at least *seemed* unconcerned enough, and bent my efforts to my communications work . . .

Two hours later, the remaining enemy vessels broke off and raced for one of Tara's moons, where presumably they were based. I scanned for any signs of reinforcements or renewed attack, but the stars were clear. Arthur wasted no time wondering, but ordered the fleet to make planetfall with all speed.

The plan to take Tara had been worked out, insofar as it could be worked out from afar, in our days at Caer Dathyl following the victory below Agned. Taking a leaf or two from Brendan's book, we had resolved to land just east of the entrance to the Strath Mór, far enough from Caerdroia so that Edeyrn's forces must march to meet us and near enough to the City so that we could, with an early victory, roll right through with least cost to ourselves. Not a bad plan, all in all, but no one was entirely pleased with it.

"How many times have I said it?" demanded Tarian. "Moytura may have worked for Brendan, Artos, but I do not think that the Marbh-draoi is going to make the same mistake as did the Coranians."

A ripple of discontent ran round the table, but no one disputed her, not even Arthur. We were involved in one last council before the actual landing; the fleet, still suspiciously unchallenged by any further Theocracy warcraft, was perhaps an hour off from Tara, and here we sat still wrangling about our invasion strategies . . .

Arthur looked up at last; I could tell by his bearing that he was angry and weary, but he allowed none of this to show upon his face.

"Even so, we have little choice of landing-place. Look here"—he stabbed the hologram map with a lightpen—"I do not wish to entrap us by these Cliffs of Fhola, the land is too rough there and the vale too narrow. More to the east, and we will be out of effective striking range of the City. South is only Bwlch-y-Saethau, and there are no passes, or few and difficult ones, by which we may cross over the Loom."

I sat with my chin in my hands, only half-listening to the ancient argument. What *I* was waiting for was the re-action of those who did not yet know what Arthur's *real* plans were ...

I did not have long to wait. One of the new Compan-ions, Alannagh Ruthven, a dark-haired, blue-eyed Erin-nachín who had been seconded to us by Grehan Aoibhell from his command at Errigal, was new enough to our ways still to be in a little awe of most of us, even me, and of Arthur in especial. But she never once had let that awe stand in the way of her speaking her mind; and did not do so now ...

"Artos, after we land at Moytura, where shall the ships be taken to keep them safe? Most like the Marbh-draoi would destroy them do we leave them sitting in orbit, and we shall have need of them after."

Arthur grinned, and I could see that he had been wait-ing for someone to ask just this.

"Not hard, Lann-fach ... But in truth we shall not be needing the ships after, for after we have landed with all our gear I shall order them destroyed. We are here, to live or die; escape is not an option I will allow us. Either we will triumph in our cause, or we will die in it."

Uproar unparalleled. This was news indeed to most of them around the table—though Gwennach and Tari and Keils and a few others of the inner circle of Companions had known Arthur's plan—and judging by the whiteness of their faces and the anger thereon, the news was less than welcome.

"You cannot be serious, Arthur!" Even Carnwen's cap-tain, Bruan Corridon, had not been party to this decision, and he was staring at his Prince as if Arthur had just con-fessed to treason; which, perhaps, at least in Bruan's book, was not so far off the mark.

"Do I look as if I jested?" said Arthur impatiently. "My sorrow if this comes as a surprise to most of you, but it is not a choice I have made easily or lightly, and I will not be turned by aught any of you, or anyone else for that matter, may say."

The small tense silence was broken by, again, Alannagh

Ruthven. "What does Merlynn Llwyd think of this—or, for that matter, King Uthyr?"

It was Gweniver who answered her question, though the response seemed meant rather more for the others than for Alannagh, and carried warning.

"My uncle stands by all decisions of his Rex Bellorum; as for the Archdruid, why, he can speak for himself." She nodded toward the far corner of the chamber, where, all unnoticed in the earlier tumult, Merlynn had come quietly in.

He did not move from his place in the dimness, but somehow he seemed to make himself suddenly visible, and the room fell silent as he did so.

"I am no warrior," said Merlynn, "but this is still my fight as much as it is any of yours; and for all of me, Arthur has chosen the Heroes' Way. No other path will serve us now. Aye, it is desperate; aye again, I am with him in his choice."

Arthur had been watching the faces round the table as our old teacher spoke, and now he stood up, looking as pleased as any man would who has just gotten his way—even a way he did not particularly love getting, for better than any of us he knew what his choice might mean. To invade Tara was one thing; deliberately to strand ourselves here, where the alternatives were victory or destruction, no middle ground, was quite another. But he spoke now as if the whole matter was of no more importance than the choosing of one tunic over another. Perhaps his way was best.

"Then I suggest we each go to our quarters and gather our gear together. We will not be able to come back for anything that may have been forgotten in our haste."

There was little converse in the passageways of Carnwen, and as I headed to my own chambers I thought that it must be the same on all the other ships, where by now Arthur's edict would have been made known to all our forces.

"Well, Talyn." Arthur had come up beside me while I brooded, and now put an arm round my shoulders. "And do you too think me deranged to destroy what may be our only sure way home to Gwynedd?"

Not for worlds would I have let him know what I thought in truth, and thanked gods I was by now a bit more skilled than he at hiding that truth from him ...

"Not a bit of it," I said coolly. "If we win out over Edeyrn, we shall have goleor of ships, and shall not need these ones; and if we lose, why, we shall have no need of any ships at all."

All the same, it was one of the less pleasant moments of my life, standing there on the earth of Tara—Tara!— and gazing upward into the night sky as small spurts of flame flared briefly beyond the Criosanna and went out. Beside me, Morgan sighed and was silent.

Ygrawn stared upward with grim satisfaction. "So much for that, then," she said, more to herself, I think, than to us. Then, as if recalling our presence: "I have ever found it easier to go forward when a way back did not tempt."

And though somehow I doubted that Ygrawn Tregaron had ever in her life found herself tempted to retreat, I loved her too much to dissent.

But we were here now, right enough; we had been landing all night in shuttling aircars from the various ships, and were already settled, even, in a sort of make-shift leaguer. Yet though by blowing up the ships Arthur had announced our presence on the planet in flame and thunder, still no counter had come our way: For all the note the Marbh-draoi had so far taken of us, we might as well still have been tweaking him back on Gwynedd.

"*That* will not last," said Morgan, with a touch of her mother's grim humor. She had been less ebullient than her brother about the choice of Moytura, and I suspected, and dreaded, that she had good cause to be so. With the single exception of Merlynn himself, and even then not always, Morgan could See clearer and farther than anyone in Keltia, and she never failed to recognize what it was she Saw; though it did not follow that she always told others what it might be.

This time, though, I had a thought as to what it might be, and, once our tent was up and we had seen Uthyr and Ygrawn comfortably and safely settled and had gone to our own bed, I taxed her with it.

"It is that mysterious errand you keep hinting at for Artos and me, is it not?"

I had not meant to bring it to bed with us; early in our time together Morgan and I had pacted that we should not

fall asleep with a problem still between us, and by and
large we had held to that, though it had meant more than
a few sleepless joyless nights. But true it is that even
Druid and Ban-draoi spouses do fail, sometimes, to see
what it is that troubles their mates—we are mere sorcerers, not infallible mind-readers—and Morgan and I had
had our share of flaming battle and freezing rage.

But tonight she would not answer my askings, and I in
turn was less than warm to her advances.

"Well then, what would you?" she said at last. "You
are stiff as a sleaghán, and not where it counts, either;
what is on you?"

"On *me*?" I said, annoyed and astonished. "Oh, not
much! Only Edeyrn, and Owein, and Uthyr, and Artos,
and you, and Gwennach and Keils—"

"Gwennach and Keils?" she asked, exasperated in her
turn. "What of them? They are happy with each other,
their work does not suffer for it, they and Arthur seem to
understand one another perfectly—is there a problem in it
somewhere?"

"You tell me. Do you See aught coming from it?"

She was silent so long I thought she had fallen asleep.
When she spoke again I knew I had been right in sensing
trouble to come.

"Much will come from it. Heirs to two crowns. War on
Kernow. Thirteen Treasures restored and lost again. Kin-
strife and kin-slaughter. Faithless love and loveless faith
and loving faithfulness. A triad squared."

She shivered suddenly and burrowed into my side. "Oh
Talyn," she said then, and now her voice was her own
again, soft, unspeakably weary, "and my brother thinks
Edeyrn is the worst foe we shall have to face in this?
Then gods help us all."

Though I held her close and comforting, more than that
she would not say.

CHAPTER
7

If, as Morgan had Seen, Edeyrn was not to be our direst enemy, at least he was our most immediate; and it did not take him overlong to make that known to us in no ambiguous way.

We had set up our camp, as I have said, at Moytura: an ancient place whose name means 'plain of towers.' Once there had been a small city on this site, but it had perished in the wars that had followed Brendan's reign; still, name and memory endured alike, and now it became once again a place of battle.

Arthur had ordered our leaguer so that we might defend ourselves at once should an attack come; and it was well he had done so, because on the third day after our landing we once again crossed lances with Owein Rheged, and this time we did not come quite so well away . . .

Give Edeyrn this at the least: When he chose to move, he moved swiftly and he moved from strength. Though we had the numbers over Owein, he had the inestimable advantages of knowing the land and having a more certain supply train than had we.

I will not afflict you with details of the disaster that was First Moytura, less a battle than a calamity. Suffice it to say that for once Arthur's eye for ground deserted him utterly: Even a grapple-iron cannot hold where the rock it

bites in is no rock but sand ... The same tactics that had
worked so brilliantly against Owein at Cadarachta were
here totally thwarted, the great hinge of the army balked
from swinging free. Our left crumbled like a child's
beach-fort when the tide is running; before we could pull
back far enough to regroup, Owein's horse had disinte-
grated our line completely, and we were scattered and
chased as we ourselves had done to Owein below Agned.

By nightfall we had managed to fall back far enough so
that no more soldiery pursued, back into the hilly country
lying east of Loom-end and south of the Avon Dia, where
Arthur had not wished to go. We lost thousands, tens of
thousands, maybe; because of what came after, the full
count was never known. We were cold, wet, hungry,
many of us wounded, all of us sunk in gloom.

Which gloom did turn to near-despair when a grim-
faced Betwyr and Daronwy, assisted by two tall Fians,
brought into camp an Arthur who seemed all but dead
where he stood.

The makeshift camp seemed all at once to shatter and
re-form around its injured leader: Elen Llydaw appeared
out of nowhere, her healer's satchel clutched to her
breast; quiet messages were sent to Ygrawn and
Gweniver and Morgan; some went to Uthyr's tent to inform the King and others to the lines to tell key captains.

It was not like Cadarachta, this time; I could tell that
from one look at Arthur's face, and more from Elen's, as
she and Morgan carefully cut away the red ruin of his tunic.

As ruined as our hopes ... There was a terrible wound
in his side, from which blood was slowly seeping; other
hurts too, but lesser by compare. He was conscious, but
had not the strength to turn his head; he knew I was there,
though, and his glance flicked sidewise to me where I
stood.

"I asked for a healer, and they send me a tunesmith
—He was racked by coughing; with one casual gesture
across his eyes, Elen put him out so that she could work
unhampered.

"I always liked the way you do that," I remarked, trying to cloak my terror with banter, as Merlynn came
swiftly and silently in to join us.

"Never mind that. Come here and help me." Elen took the dermasealer from her satchel and motioned me to her side. I began to clean away with care the dark beaded blood, saw now the wound's ragged edges, tipped white and red.

"It is a deep hurt—the sutures must be layered in." Elen was talking more to herself than to the rest of us who hovered round; I was vaguely aware of Morgan gently shooing everyone else out of the tent, even her mother, as Elen began to work, Merlynn helping to keep Arthur asleep and still.

I watched with wonder and satisfaction as she drew the laser tool through the deepest places of the wound, stitching with light; saw the lacerated innards seaming together, the smooth shining muscles knitting up where they had been sliced through, nerve and sinew melding before our eyes. It was slow, careful work; but once the blood vessels had been sealed back in place, Elen closed the upper layers of tissue and fused the skin closed over all. The work had taken three hours and more, and we were near as exhausted as Arthur, who was still deep entranced, must surely be, or would be when Elen allowed him to wake.

"That is one miraculous bit of inventing," Elen was saying to Merlynn. "All Keltia will ever be grateful to her whose mind made it real ... No more bleeding, I think, and no real pain; though he has lost much blood, and for about a fortnight he will feel as if a horse had kicked him in the side."

"How did he come to this?" I asked, for as yet there had been no time to learn; I had been too busy, and in any case those who might have told me had all been banished from the tent by Morgan.

"Sheer heedlessness," said Daronwy, who now came back in with Ygrawn and Gweniver. "And uselessness too ... He had no business even being there where he was; but Artos being Artos, who could keep him away?" She swayed a little where she stood, and I caught her before she fell over. "Nay, m'chara, thank you but I am only tired, I promise! Give you goodnight, then."

I saw her to her own tent—she was quite as capable as Arthur of pushing herself to the point of collapse, or worse—then looked in on Uthyr, but he was once more asleep, and I had not the heart to waken him even with word of his nephew's healing; and any road, the King had pain and hurting of his own with which to grapple.

When I returned to Arthur's tent, I was surprised to see Merlynn sitting vigil by the field-couch. He fixed me with a stern gaze.

"If you do not go at once to your bed, Talyn, and get some sleep, I will put you out even faster than Elenna's healer's trick can do ... He is well enough, and will sleep until sunset tomorrow; go do the same. I shall watch him for you."

And I was not about to argue with my teacher.

"My own fault," said Arthur cheerfully; it was just past sunset of the following day, and as Merlynn had predicted, Arthur had just now wakened. He was sitting up, even; eating—rather slowly and carefully—some savory mess from a blue bowl.

I took a seat by the tent wall and watched him for a while. "You have heard of the battle, I take it?"

A muscle leaped along the line of his jaw before he could control it. "Enough to content me," he said carefully. "Or rather, all I need to know, for the knowledge is scarcely contenting ... I have long wondered what defeat must feel like, and now that I have come to it, it does not seem to be so dreadful as I had thought."

"Dreadful enough," I said. "We lost many, and we could ill afford to lose any at all."

The pain was back in his face. "Of the Companions?" he asked quietly.

"None lost," I answered, and his eyes closed briefly in thankful relief. "But Tryffin was hurt near as badly as yourself, and Tanwen and Kei and some others"—I named them—"and Elenna has been busy this past night and day."

"What news of Owein?"

"Surprisingly, very little. He has pulled back into the Strath Mór, and, I am told by the scouts, waits there like a spider to see what may bring us back into his web." I repented of all the ill news, and sought to cheer him. "But, you know, Artos, we did not lose so many as we did fear; and Keils and Tari managed to bring us here to safety, and our store of food and arms is more than sufficient. We are in far less parlous case than we might be, or deserve to be."

"You mean than *I* deserve to be," remarked Arthur, setting aside his empty bowl and leaning back upon piled pillows. "Though you are too civil to say so ... Well, I admit it freely: This is my fault and failing, and I should have heeded those of you who tried to turn me from my course. Is that what you wish to hear?"

"Is that what you wish to say?" I countered. "It does you no good, Artos, and us still less, for you to call hard upon yourself for one mistake—even such a mistake as this. Aye, it is grave; and aye again, it was you gave the order for it. But it is neither the worst nor the end for us, and we need you now more than ever before."

He was silent for some moments, then shifted on his pillows, his mouth tightening in what may have been either a smile or a flinching, and he wishing to hide it whichever it may have been.

"What of the King my uncle?" he asked quietly. "I have not seen him since the day of our landing."

"Methryn looks after him," I said, glad to be able to offer at least this comfort. "He is as he has been, and was feared only for you this day past."

With a move so swift and decisive it took me by surprise, Arthur threw back the light coverlet and, a little less surely, got to his feet.

"Then I must go and show him otherwise." He swayed like a willow in a windstorm, and caught at my shoulder even as I leaped forward to support him. "If you will help me to get there."

When Arthur said he had seen Uthyr the King but once since we had landed on Tara, he spoke knowing that all the same he was one of the scant handful who had done so. Save for his immediate kindred and closest officers, none of us who had sailed with the fleet from Gwynedd had caught sight of the man in whose name we had sailed.

This was as Ygrawn the Queen would have it: Since her lord had been given his unhealing wound at Cadarachta, she had grown a very lioness of protectiveness and guarding, controlling all access to the King's person, restricting even the commanders who came to report to

him of our position. Merlynn alone could come and go as
he willed.

And Uthyr seemed content to have it so: Never robust,
less dynamic than either of his late brothers, nonetheless
he had over the past thirty-odd years that I had known
him exhibited a toughness like a findruinna wire, fine but
near unbreakable, and in all the months since his wounding I had seen no diminishment in that capacity for endurance.

Even now—even as I had helped Arthur, moving
slowly and carefully, into the King's tent, had given him
my arm to lean on as he made his bow to his uncle
(whose protesting dismissal of such obeisance had, of
course, been ignored in its turn by Arthur), I had bent a
sharp glance on Uthyr, to see if aught had altered; and for
all of me I could not see that it had.

So now I sat beside Ygrawn, at her request playing
somewhat upon a rather inferior harp that was the only
one to hand—Frame of Harmony being safely stowed in
my own tent—and pretending, as was she, not to care
overmuch to hear what Arthur and Uthyr were saying to
one another over against the tent's far wall.

Truth to tell, my attention just now was all for my
foster-mother. Ygrawn was possessed of more inner resources than any ten people I knew, but even she had limits; and as I peered surreptitiously up at her when I
thought she was not noticing, I began to wonder if perhaps those limits had not at last been reached; exceeded,
even.

I had thought I was being both vigilant and unobserved, and was most discountenanced when Ygrawn began to laugh.

"Ah, Talyn, you might as well just come out and *ask*
how it is with me, it is no good going on so!"

I muttered somewhat under my breath, then, with red-
dening cheeks, "What gave me away, methryn?"

"Well, that hooded cavebat look you tend to wear
when you would observe and be unobserved as you do
so ... It gave you away as a lad, and it gives you away
now." She reached out a slim hand to silence the strings
of the harp. "A fair cut below your own; let it be still
awhile ... Just let you ask, amhic. I will answer as I
have ever done."

I set the harp aside with a certain relief and looked straight into the clear violet eyes. "Then I will ask: Are you well, methryn?"

"Well enough," she answered at once. "If wearier than I would wish to be . . . Nay, Talyn, it is my lord should be the focus of your fears. Arthur knows this, and Morgan, and Merlynn too; though Gwennach, I think, has not yet seen it."

I felt my blood running cold down to my boots, and against all my resolve glanced over at Uthyr. He was still deep in quiet converse with his nephew; but I could see his face plain where a lamp was casting a golden glow upon it, and in that glow I saw what Ygrawn had spoken of, and I was afraid, and wondered that I had not seen it sooner.

It was the King's face I looked upon, and yet it was also the face of his dead brother Amris who had perished with honor and purpose, and of his brother Leowyn who had died in a pointless drunken brawl. Gorlas too I saw in his face, and even my own father Gwyddno, who had been murdered by the Marbh-draoi's own hand in the hall at Ratherne. It was the face of the Sacred Lord, that ancientest and darkest aspect of rulership: the king who gives his life so that his land might live.

But would even that *sacrifice be enough?* Would *the land live?* I did not know I had sent my fearing thought abroad, until I heard Merlynn speak softly, in the mind-voice, for me alone to hear.

"Aye, Talynno, it shall live . . . But more of royal blood than that shall be required, to restore the land that is waste."

And I looked where he looked, and saw that he looked on Arthur as he spoke this; and I wished to look and hear no more.

While we licked our wounds in the hills of Ossory—for so that region was called—the weather changed dramatically, and perhaps for the better to our purpose.

It had not yet been Samhain when we left Gwynedd, but here on Tara it was full winter. That in itself did not dismay us—from our days in Arvon, when there had been only the choice of fighting or surrender, we had grown well used to winter warfare—but, as the local folk who

now came one by one in secret to our banner did tell us,
winter in this part of the Throneworld could be, to say the
least, various.

And so it proved: Seven days after the rout at Moytura,
snow began to fall at sunset, and by morning it lay two
feet deep with no end in sight. It fell softly and silently
from inexhaustible clouds; it drove against our faces like
fleets of tiny needles, whipped by an east wind glassy
with ice. The temperature too fell, colder than it was
wont in Arvon. It effectively pinned us down in our hilly
sanctuary, right enough; but, as Tarian pointed out, if we
were held immobile so too was our foe, and that just now
was no bad thing.

I did not argue with her reasoning, nor indeed with our
case; but gave private prayerful thanks to Beira the
Queen of Winter, who rules the snows and frosts. Anything that kept Arthur in one place for the moment was
gods-sent so far as I was concerned. And I *was* concerned, more so than I cared to admit: I had over our
years together seen my fostern in many, many moods;
but never before, even in the worst of passes, had I seen
him so downcast, so—quashed. For the inside of a week
he kept to his tent, and Gweniver, Keils and Tari ran the
army.

The thought in camp, which I subtly encouraged, was
that he was simply exhausted from his wound and the demands of the invasion; the opinion among the Companions, which I feared and tried futilely to scotch, was that
Arthur was giving up. Oh, to be fair, not all of them felt
so; maybe not even most. But the feeling was there, and
it seeped into their bright hope and gallant resolve like an
evil mist, to weaken them where they most needed to be
strong.

After another few days of this, I grew sufficiently
alarmed to take counsel where of old I had always sought
it first; and found when I did so that Arthur was there before me . . .

"Come in," said Merlynn, and from his place by the
quartz-hearth Arthur grinned at me, as if he had only
been wondering how long it would take for me to come
there.

"I grew weary waiting for the other boot to fall," I said
sourly, and Merlynn laughed.

"And I am not one to say I-told-you-thus," he replied.
"Well—not much, any road . . . But I have a thing to tell
you both; and you will hear me, and hearing me you will
do as I shall tell you."

Arthur stretched his legs out in front of him and
slumped down in his seat. "That is what I have come for,
athro," he said, and his voice was humble and devoid of
shielding, as it ever was before our teacher; as much a
function of humility, I think, as of his knowing that any
dissembling would be ever in vain.

As Arthur slumped so did I sit up straighter in the seat
I had taken. This was it at last, this was the revealing of
that strange task Morgan had been hinting at for so many
weeks; Arthur knew something of it already, and had all
along, but I had not, and now the full demand was about
to be set out for us . . .

Merlynn saw, and smiled. "Aye, Tal-bach, you have
been patient, and now you shall hear . . . There is in the
Hollow Mountains a place called the Hill of Fare; in its
depths is the Sidhe stronghold of Dún Aengus, where
Nudd the king rules with Seli his queen beside him."

Already I was misliking it: Nudd, as Arthur and I (if
not the rest of Keltia just yet) did know, was the stepfather of Edeyrn Marbh-draoi; and it was that Queen Seli
herself who had given birth to him . . .

"There you must go, you two and Morguenna, as you
three went once before to find a weapon."

Arthur's hand went instinctively to Llacharn's hilt.
"What is it we must seek, athro, when we come there?
And will they receive us, the Shining Folk?"

"For the sake of an ancient kinship, and a newer
friendship, they will," said Merlynn after a moment.
"And also there are other reasons . . . As for what you
seek, before that question may be answered you must
face a sterner inquisitor than I."

The old glint came in his eye at that, but I was no
longer the lad I had been, to be as daunted as I used to
at sight of it—not that I was entirely undaunted even
now. But I spoke my mind to him as ever.

"And is that all the help we are to have? It does not
seem much."

"And do you think you merit more? Well, be assured
more will be given you . . . Nor shall you go unguided:

Whoever will present themselves along the road, those shall you take for guide; and you shall demand of them, and you shall dismiss them, and you shall not thank them for their service. Do not forget this, I charge you both; for if you do any of these things all is truly lost."

I looked at him doubtfully. "It seems gross discourtesy, if naught worse, to do so."

"Do not you believe it! Artos, Talyn, as your teacher I implore you both, for once *only do as I say*! Is that so much to ask?"

All at once Arthur was back again, who had been away for most of the fortnight past. He had not moved from his chair, nor even straightened his deplorable posture, but I could see plain that Arthur had come back to us; his sudden vibrancy made the tent seem small and cramped, and his eyes were alight with thought of the quest to come.

I spoke at once to caution. "Who shall rule the army while we are gone?"

"Why, Gweniver," he said, surprised that I seemed to think it needful to ask. "With Keils and Tari, to be sure; there shall be naught that those three cannot deal with amongst them, or would manage any differently than I should do were I here to do so. As for our enemy, the Marbh-draoi sits in Ratherne, and Owein is cut off from us by the snows. I very much doubt me if either will make any move before our return, and if they do, Tryffin, Elen and Betwyr have grown skilled generals to cope."

"And Uthyr?"

That settled him down a bit. "We must speak to the King ourselves," he said soberly. "And as soon as may be; this is a thing must not be delayed in the telling."

Nor did we delay: No more than an hour later, Arthur and I stood with Morgan before the King in the King's own tent. Ygrawn was there, and Merlynn, but none other had been asked to join us; even Gweniver was kept from this audience.

Uthyr lay as he had lain for so many weeks, on a couch covered with furs, heaped with pillows at one end for ease of reclining. He wore his now-usual garb—a robe of rich if plain stuff that fell to his feet, or would fall to had he been standing upon them. Though it was by no means uncommon in Keltia for older folk to dress so, with Uthyr it had ever been tunic and trews. The robes were worn for one reason only: to keep the unhealed wound in his thigh from the sight of the curious or the pitying; and perhaps, even, from his own sight as well.

But never for the least instant could he be aught but sickeningly aware of it: Though he tried to conceal this as well, the pain of the wound was plain upon his face, coming and going like summer lightning without thunder— what we call a dry-storm—and each time the pain was accepted into his soul. So that, watching him (it would have been the height of indecency not to have looked him straight in the face), I thought that never in my life had I seen anything braver than this, nor would ever see however long I lived; and I was right. Most fitting, then, to honor it by looking upon it unflinching.

Uthyr's pain even so did not prevent him from an awareness of things as keen as ever, or keener, even; so that when we three came and stood before him that night, and made our reverences to him as Ard-rígh, and our loving duties as daughter and nephew and foster-son, he knew well why we had come, and whither we were bound.

"By rights I should as King forbid this," he said, and though he spoke to us all his eyes were on Arthur. "Still—it is not laid by me upon you, but by dán; though in it lies my release as well as our victory."

I spoke unthinkingly from my love. "We would heal you, not lose you, Uthyr-maeth."

The King smiled. "Though I died this night, my son, you would never lose me, and though I were healed a hundred times over still must I soon take my leave . . . I am well content that it should be so; and this"—he gestured toward his wounded thigh with his free hand; the other hand was clasping Ygrawn's—"if this is my part to bear in our fight, then let it be so. Be it dán or the Marbh-draoi's evil working or the will of the Mother, I shall not be healed until you have won what you go to seek, and I shall not die until I have been healed." His fingers tightened on his wife's. "And Keltia shall not be whole until all this has been accomplished. Go then, my dearest children, and do what has been given you to do. My love is with you."

And as I went forward in my turn to embrace Uthyr Pendreic, King of Kelts, I was unsurprised to see that, of all those in that chamber, I was the only one who wept.

BOOK II

Goltraí

CHAPTER

8

A day like an owl's wing, brown, black, gray, white: tones of cold earth and frozen sky blended without seam; heavy clouds, big-bellied with snow and darkening from lead-gray to ink-blue as day faded.

We had been riding for many days now through this harsh country, Arthur and Morgan and I. North and a little east of north was our heading; we had crossed the great iron slash of the Avon Dia on the third day, as far upstream as we could safely make the crossing, for the river ran strong here, with all the swiftness of a mountain stream and already a goodly part of its later wideness.

Of the three of us, Morgan seemed of best cheer: She sang as she rode, lilts of the Arvon hills or strange minor-key chaunts of the Shining Folk, or entertained us with tales of her time with Birogue in Collimare where she had learned those songs; and we were pleased to be ourselves silent to hear her. She had also, by dint of some mysterious process undisputed by Arthur or myself, become the leader of this riding: We but followed where she did lead, and wished to know no more; grateful only to be spared both wondering and deciding, smiling at our memories of another, long-ago, riding the three of us had shared.

The region through which we now were passing was growing ever rougher and lovelier. North of the Avon Dia the land rose steadily, to bare peaks and greengash valleys filled with firs; high above the cold racing streams loomed a long ridge of sharp and serrate stone, like the comb of the Mountain Mother Herself.

On the tenth day we rode through deep pine forests, where sunlight did not fall and the air was thick as wine. I was first in line that day, with Arthur behind me and Morgan riding rearguard. The track was narrow and the light uncertain, and so it was that I did not see just precisely when we were no longer three riders on the path, but five.

I was aware of a horse's nose moving up beside my left stirrup as the track widened, but thought it to belong to Arthur's splendid black mare, Miaren. Then as the beast shouldered in beside my placid bay, I saw that it stood a hand higher than Miaren, and bore a white star and snip on its muzzle where the mare's was solid black. I all but came out of my saddle with the surprise of it, and then as my head whipped sidewise so that I might see the rider's face, I heard her voice from behind the muffling hood.

"Well, Gwyddno's son, you had a better greeting for me the last time we met."

A voice once heard and never forgotten ... I stared speechless as Birogue let the hood fall back upon her shoulders, and a chance ray of sunlight caught the gold of her hair. It flamed to light half the dark wood, and her smile was a torch to the other half: Lovelier than ever she seemed, certainly no whit more aged, and yet somehow she seemed changed; or perhaps it was merely the seeing her out of what I had thought of as her 'customed context, the island-llan of Collimare, the Forest in the Sea.

Her smile widened, and I saw she had heard my thought. And then it was that I had my second shock of that day: As I turned round to Arthur and Morgan—all this had taken no more than moments—I saw that another rode beside them.

I could see no more—the track just then swept down a rocky defile, too narrow to allow for backward glances, even if the footing had been easier—but that one quick sight had been enough to show me that they did not seem distressed nor even much surprised. But who could the fifth rider be? Tall, hooded, upon a mount as white as Morgan's Nyfer ... Just then my bay pecked at a stone and nearly sent me over his head, and I turned all my attention to making our way onto sound ground again.

As we climbed up and out of the little gorge, emerging onto the green open flank of the great hill that stood before us, I swung my horse around and pulled him up hard, blocking the track to those who came behind. Arthur and Morgan halted when I did, but the other rider came on until his horse had brought him knee to knee with me, and I was face to face once again with Perran.

Never in all the years since that day in Daars had I forgotten that face—the face of the one I had blamed for Daars's death, and Gorlas's, and nearly mine and Arthur's as well, that terrible night—the face of one I had held to be Edeyrn's tool, a betrayer Raven—never should I have failed to recognize him, not on a moonless winter midnight in the depths of Corva Wood.

He recognized me too, it seemed, as readily as I did him, and in my fury I did not think to wonder even at that: For I was forty years older, and he had aged not a day . . .

"Nay, Talyn," he said with a smile, "it was not I whom you mistook me for."

I ignored the familiar use of my shortname and did not think to wonder at his words. "Oh aye? Who, then?"

"Oh, I was there that day to spy you out—you and Arthur—but not to aid the Marbh-draoi; I had a purpose of my own." He paused a moment. "What think you Luath feared?"

Luath . . . By now I was in utter bewilderment; to hear this stranger speak the name of our long-dead hound was beyond all reason, and I looked helplessly and wildly at Arthur. For once his face read as baffled as he was feeling, while Morgan beside him bore a countenance both settled and amused. Birogue, behind me, was silent all this time.

And as the stranger spoke a shimmer seemed to have come over my sight, so that I wondered suddenly if I were indeed going mad, or if perhaps the bright mist cloaking this Perran were the harbinger of another of those blinding one-sided headaches with which I had been afflicted of late.

Then I saw that the brightness was not in my eyes after

all, but in Perran, or on Perran, and he spoke from out the glory in a voice it seemed I knew.

"I am Gwyn, son of Nudd," said that glory then. "And though it much misliked me to put fear on you as a child, that you should think me a Raven and one of Edeyrn's creatures, it was ordered that I should do so, and even I must obey."

Gwyn, son of Nudd ... Prince of the Sidhe, son of Nudd the king and Seli that bright wayward queen, heir to the crystal throne beneath the Hollow Mountains—Perran had fled forever, and the face that now looked at me was the face that my faithful Luath must have seen; beasts are not subject to glamourie, as are most of those who call themselves their masters ... I glanced at Arthur, and he seemed as stunned and dazzled as I: Morgan merely looked pleased and enigmatic, not much help *there* ...

Arthur had kneed his mare forward, until he was level with me on Gwyn's other side; in the saddle, he and Gwyn were of a height with one another, and each of the same darkness of eye, though the faerie prince's hair was black to Arthur's red-brown.

"Gwyn son of Nudd," said Arthur on a long wondering note.

"I am sent to be your guide, Artos," said Gwyn in answer to what Arthur had not asked. "And the Lady Birogue too is sent to guide you; will you accept our help as it is offered?"

All at once I felt my shoulders prickling as if a ghostly arm had been laid upon them; and Merlynn's parting words to us came floating back through the stillness: *'Whoever will present themselves along the road, those shall you take for guide; and you shall demand of them, and you shall dismiss them, and you shall thank them not for their service ... If you do any of these things all is truly lost.'*

But it seemed my caution did not go unshared, for Arthur was speaking, and he too had been listening to the words of our old teacher.

"I accept that help," he said. "Now you will take us to Nudd's seat, and having brought us there you will take your leave."

It seemed the height of rudeness and ill manners, and

never in ten lifetimes would I ever have thought to hear Arthur speak so—no matter the mood or the time or the trouble, Arthur spoke fair to all—but Gwyn smiled, and Birogue sighed, and Morgan threw back her head and laughed.

"So even Arthur Pendreic pays heed to his teachers when it suits him," said Gwyn, amusement sparking in the dark eyes.

"Who would defy Merlynn Llwyd must be braver far than I," replied Arthur, in a voice of fervent honesty that spoke volumes of past defiances and their upshot, and Gwyn laughed outright.

"I doubt it not! But come—" Without visible directing movement of his own Gwyn set his horse again to the rising track, and as the tall white stallion picked its way past me I saw that the magnificent animal carried no tack of any sort. No more did Birogue's equally handsome black, though I was later to learn that this was by no means the custom among riders of the Sidhe. Indeed, I saw bridles that were better fitted to be crowns, so richly set were they with jewels and gold. But even those fine fittings were mere headstalls only: Never did mount of the Shining Folk bear bit in its mouth—not of gold or iron or silver—and never was bit needed.

Birogue fell in beside me as we rode, though we exchanged few words, and none of import. It seemed plain to me that she knew well the only words I needed from her, and for my part I knew just as well that time had not yet come for her to say them: words of my mother, Medeni—whose name Birogue had so far spoken twice to me, whose friendship she had claimed, whose saving she had declared beyond even her powers. Much, then, that needed to be known; but I held my peace for the moment, and was happy.

Gwyn, who had led us out of the forest onto the open mountainside, now fell back to ride with Arthur, whether by chance or by design I did not know; and it was, I confess to my mild surprise, Morgan who now cantered up to take his place as leader. With a sidewise glance at me, and a smile I could not read, she set her horse to a gallop; uncommanded by us, the other beasts followed at once.

I was unprepared for the sudden change of pace, and my spine cracked like a whip as my bay Meillion surged forward after Morgan and Nyfer, who were already far down the track. Three strides, and we had caught up to Birogue; glancing back over my shoulder, I saw Gwyn and Arthur galloping as close together as if they rode a race.

It was unexpectedly exhilarating, this sudden thundering across the open hills, after so long a morning's going at a cautious walk through the forest closeness. But as we went up the curve of the first slope, then down another, I stiffened in my saddle, though Meillion did not perceive it—or more like, disregarded it—as his rider's signal to slow gait.

All at once a long-forgotten picture had sprung to life before my eyes: All at once I was far above the ground, as if I rode a falair, one of the great majestical winged horses found of old on Erinna, and no earthbound steed at all. But I did not have even such a mount as that: Rather, I sailed on the air as one of the gray hawks that did soar above my boyhood home of Tair Rhamant; I was heights and heights above the sparkling blue inland sea, whose existence none of us had even known of until now. A sea not so great as Glora, perhaps; but a sizable sea all the same, running down between the great hills that rose now on our right . . .

And from that high place I was watching as in a silent vision five riders came on across the mountain's long green swelling flank. I was a lad again, back in the schoolroom at Daars, caught up in a Seeing of Merlynn's sending: a Seeing that Arthur and I had ourselves called upon us in our traha, though he and I Saw very different things.

I looked now with both visions—the eyes of the body and the eyes of Sight—at the one who led us, her golden hair barely visible beneath the hood. *Morgan, my beloved* . . . It seemed that my heart had always known it, though Sight had been clouded and seeing delayed. *And that other* . . . Perran it was, or had been, and yet not so, never once so: I did not need to turn round to see that face before me, sgian-sharp, eagle-proud.

But we were sweeping now through a break in the hill-line, a pass that led through a natural gateway into a bright and secret vale; I turned in my saddle, last now in line as Gwyn and Arthur passed me, and waved my arm to Taliesin who watched from his high vantage, from his schoolroom stool in Daars, and followed the others into the wild loveliness that was called Glenshee.

The inland sea here spilled over into the valley's foot; indeed, the truth was that the source of that sea could now be seen to be a mighty river that led down from a still-unseen, further source. The valley was not a wide one, and thickly forested on the slopes; a pleasing prospect, I thought, as I stood in my stirrups to get a better view.

Arthur had come up beside me as we paused in the mouth of the pass. "A fair place," he said, nodding toward the landscape spread out before us.

"And a fair folk to dwell within it." I had been looking at our guides, who sat their horses a little apart from us; and the thought in my mind, if thought it could be called, was how in all the hells had Kelts ever thought the Sidhe like to humankind. Some indeed had actually mistaken them for such, and never knew their error; others, knowing full well the difference of the races, had all the same ignored it, or defied it—had wedded with the Shining Folk, had even begotten children with or by them. I had thought the differences most visible when one looked into their eyes: those deep dark wells of a long knowledge and a far magic.

But now as I gazed upon Gwyn, whose face was turned away from us, I saw that the difference went deeper, it was in every pore of his skin and bone of his frame; as if light and not blood did run within him. *And yet his own mother had taken to herself a mortal lord ... had borne Edeyrn to be a scourge upon the worlds ...* With a shock I saw that Gwyn was watching me—he had turned while my attention had been wandering—and now he beckoned me forward.

I gave Meillion a bit of leg, and he willingly ambled up beside the white stallion, whose nostrils widened a little but who was far too aristocratic to otherwise forget his manners. I, less aristocratic but at least as well trained, remembered mine far enough to keep silence until Gwyn addressed me: It is for princes to speak first, faerie princes perhaps in especial.

"This is Glenshee," said Gwyn, "the secretest home of

my people. Yonder"—he pointed to a great gray hill whose top was hid in cloud—"is the Hill of Fare, under whose skirts lies Dún Aengus, where Nudd does reign as king."

I looked where he had pointed: a day's journey on horseback at the least, and maybe two. No great hardship, for the valley was lovely and looked rich in game and other such foodstuffs as might be found in the wild; and even did we choose not to eat of aught within the valley walls we had still the provisions in our pack . . .

But Gwyn was unslinging from his belt a leather-wrapped bundle that had hung there, and now he began to unfold the swathings, to reveal a small gold horn. Ancient of design and of great skill of workmanship, the horn had coelbren letters etched into the flare of the grip, but I could not make out what they did say. A baldric of green silk was knotted to rings at bell and mouthpiece.

Gwyn set the horn to his lips and sounded a single clear note upon it, a note that sent such a weakness through my body that I thought I would die of it, then and there. Such sweetness, and such joy, and such—well, even I, a bard, have no word even now for what was in the note of that horn; and though as the echoes rang and died over the valley and the water I wanted naught more than to hear it sound again, I also wanted naught more than never to have heard it at all.

Strangely, it did not seem to affect the others so: I saw Arthur staring at me as if I had on that instant grown another head, and Morgan with a look of wistful memory but no more than that. Yet I was staggered, I felt as if my bones had been turned to water and my flesh to stone; and still I nearly wept for joy.

I felt the need to explain. "That horn—"

But Gwyn raised a hand, and in his dark gaze I read clear warning, and I said no more.

We rode for two days, as it turned out; Gwyn and Birogue, plainly glad to be once more in their own country, felt no need to push the pace, and the three of us were glad in our turn that they did not, for so lovely was Glenshee that it would have been scorn and insult to have raced through it in unseeing haste.

Toward sunset on the second day we sensed a change in the air, a new softness; sensed a rumbling in the earth, that the horses had earlier perceived, for they had been restless all day, save for the faerie beasts. Then coming round a cliffside, where the path had been cut into the living rock, we saw what no human yet had seen: a ledge two miles wide, over which poured a cataract of waters heavy as marble and light as foam, unearthly white against the darkening sky behind, flaming gold where it caught the light of the setting sun.

Behind that wall of waters there is a great high hall of the Sidhe, and those who dwell within it know themselves safe, for no mortal can unsummoned pass that mighty curtain. The waters fall away into a great stone bowl cut into the gorge below, and from that welling cup the river runs down to feed the inland sea. The sound of the waters' descent, booming off the rocks as they fell, was that distant rumble that had troubled the horses, and, later, ourselves; so tremendous is the power of the force that the sound can be heard for miles—and felt too, if one were at rest upon the ground.

Not only sound but sight of it, the streaming veils of milky white; and its clean, wild, fresh scent, strong as sea-tang but with woods in it, not salt—branches and leaves and dark mossy places—all the inlands it had rolled over before coming to this place.

We were struck into speechlessness; nor did Gwyn and Birogue say aught until we had had our first fill of staring. For me, it seemed that never would I tire of gazing upon this wonder: My eyes moved up the force, past the falls themselves to where the drop began, where the water hung in a curve at the lip of the cliff, clear green above the hidden rocks, white water as a standing wave. Yet it is the rock makes the wave stand so firm and not the racing water, for the water is gone by in an instant and the rock alone remembers that it has gone past, giving shape to the immanent flow. Without the water, dry stone; without the rock, stagnant swamp: But together they make the torrent sing.

Gwyn's voice came clear above the water's roar, and it seemed deeper even than that deep and mighty note.

"This is Sychan, the Dry River."

It seemed anything but dry to us: Even where we stood we could feel the spray upon our faces, the mist drifting up from the boiling white pools below. But Birogue pointed, and we took the meaning of the name, for behind the cataract was a gate that led into the heart of the hill.

"That is the way we must go," she said. "There are other entrances to Dún Aengus, it is true, but this gate is for those who come on such errands as yours. It may not always be so; but for now it is Nudd's law, the first test of those who would come before his throne beneath the Hill of Fare."

This was the first mention anyone had made of a test, and although I had begun to suspect that there must surely be something of that sort in store for us—Merlynn was not the one to send us anywhere a test would *not* have been likely—I was dismayed all the same.

But I followed in my turn, as first Birogue, then Arthur, then Morgan, then I, with Gwyn coming after, stepped out on the narrow stone path, little more than a ledge, that wound behind the force itself. 'Dry river' indeed! The spray that misted the stone, that gleamed upon our hair, that weighed down our cloaks, here turned into droplets of water the size of grapes, flung with such strength as to hit us more like rocks than water; and I was not the only one to flinch a little at the stinging pain of it.

Birogue saw our distress. "Only a few feet more until the ledge shall shield you," she assured us. "It can hurt, I know, for that you are not used to it. But folk have died under those drops before now."

I was *not* comforted; but just then it was as she had said, and the assault from above ceased. We had passed behind the water-curtain now, and here the roar redoubled. The thunder of the falls was in the rock itself; so reverberant that our ears throbbed with it, and to lay a hand on the passage walls was actually to *see* the vibration, so strong it moved one's hand upon the rockface.

We had entered a passage that wound back into the cliff for it seemed miles—our horses had been left on dry land at the force's edge, under Gwyn's assurance that some would come to take them to suitable stabling with the Sidhe's own mounts—and which ended abruptly in a great gate, solid silver and studded with gems and resonant with magic.

Birogue, with a glance at Gwyn, laid her hand upon the worn place at its center and spoke softly in a tongue I did not know. As softly, it swung open for us. I could see Arthur questing round him: He of course had noted their presence as swiftly as I, being Druid like myself, though neither of us as swiftly as Morgan—those hidden watchers who guarded this entrance.

"Lay aside your swords here," said Gwyn. "Cold iron is not master under the hill."

Arthur obeyed at once, as did Morgan, but for no known reason I delayed a little.

"Naught here that cold iron will keep from you," said Birogue with a smile, as she saw my hesitation.

"I know *that*," I muttered, embarrassed that she should see me so uncertain, cheeks flaming that she should think me so ignorant. But in truth I did not know why I held back—indeed, the best surety of our safety in the Sidhe halls was not our swords nor even our magic, but Morgan—and then all at once I was past it. Instead of driving my sword into a crevice near the gate-frame as I had been half-minded to do—there was no wood round this gate to sheathe the iron as the spell required—I placed it gently on the floor of the stone passage, beside Llacharn and Morgan's own sapphire-hilted weapon.

"Well done," said Morgan softly, and stepped with me hand in hand through the gate.

CHAPTER
9

Beyond the silver portal, the passage continued for maybe half a lai. I could see now that the hall was well named 'Dry River,' for plainly it had once been the course of an underground stream, with its many turns and windings. But whether it had dried and died of its own natural shiftings, or had been diverted by hand in the building of this strongplace, I could not say; and how long since either event had happened, I did not care to guess.

But, led now by Gwyn, we were coming to the inhabited regions of this terrifying place; though still we had seen none but those two who were our guides, and neither Birogue nor Gwyn had spoken any word since the passing of the gate. All the same, I could feel the covert weight of many watching eyes upon us, and not a one of them was human; maybe not even mortal. . . .

We were coming to the monarch of the faerie hall. True it was we came in peace and on an errand of state, and had such words to offer as would incline even a monarch to give ear to us; but it was daunting nonetheless, and I tightened my grasp on Morgan's hand.

Gwyn had led us by secret ways, and so it was that all unaware we came to the throne-room of Nudd. Doors opened, and then we were there, standing frozen under the silver stares of Sidhe-folk, those who attended their king as he sat in his hall of state. They seemed as surprised to see us as we were to come so upon them, but if we were too shy and awestruck to rise to the moment, at least the presence of our guides gave us a kind of borrowed sanction, a vouchsafement or warrant that we clutched round us as desperately and as proudly as a beggar does his rags.

And for other of the same reasons, too, as that beggar: defense, and defiance, and challenge; though we had been better advised to have gone more softly, as things turned out . . .

But just then there was little leisure for such considerations: Gwyn had bowed deeply, and the press of folk had parted, and now we could see clearly to whom he had made his reverence. For upon the crystal throne beneath the golden roof sat one less tall, less fair, less—*shining* than the others in that chamber. Not that he was in the least uncomely to look upon—none of the Shining Folk could ever be that—but that by compare to all the rest he did at first glance seem so.

We followed Gwyn's lead at once, Arthur and I making the same bent knee to the faerie lord that we would have made to Uthyr Ard-rígh, while Morgan and Birogue dipped and rose again like ships on the tide. At a sign none of us three could say we truly saw, Gwyn gathered us with his glance and led us down the length of the hall, between the ranks of fair courtiers. Though I tried for wisdom's sake to keep my eyes fixed on him who sat beneath the golden canopy, I dared to steal glances to either side as I walked; and when twice or thrice my eyes met those of the Sidhe, I was sorry I had so dared.

So I strove to keep my gaze on Gwyn; him at least I knew, and though he was surely Sidhe—he was their prince!—somehow he seemed to me less strange and fearsome than those others who clustered round. Or perhaps it was simply that I felt I had known him before—well, I *had* known him, as Perran, true enough, but still. As for Birogue, she was Morgan's teacher, and had called my mother her friend, and was lady to Merlynn Llwyd: To my mind, that made her kin.

Now Gwyn halted, and we did likewise, stopping not three paces from the foot of the crystal throne. At such close distance I dared not turn aside my glance, and with a mighty effort I brought my eyes to the face of the king.

Nudd ap Llyr, King of the Sidhe, lord of Dún Aengus, looked upon us. How shall I tell of him? He had the darkest eyes I had ever seen in living thing, black as sapphires in the cool light; his hair was the black of síodarainn, the silk-iron that is strong and workable and makes the best shields in the world. He was richly clad, though I do not call to mind details of his costume, and bore upon his finger a ring with a golden stone.

He was not looking at me just then, but at his son. Gwyn met his father's glance full on, in silence; and whatever they said to one another then, they said without one word spoken. Then that dark gaze travelled on, lighting first upon Birogue, and lighting up as it did so; moving to Morgan, to whom was given a respectful pause and the barest hint of a nod; then I felt the weight of Nudd's glance, and almost staggered beneath it.

Oh, fairness of face or form had naught to do with *this:* Here was one whom evil could not touch, nor ages alter, yet who had seen both wickedness and time; here was one who had known wisdom, and folly, in all shapes and ways and tempers. I believe I almost went to one knee just then, or both, as a man might before a god; but I was released—and I thought I saw the least flicker of amusement and approval in that gaze before it let me go—and then Nudd looked upon Arthur.

Who seemed to have no such trouble as I: He stood as proudly open to Nudd's glance as had Gwyn, and it seemed Nudd spoke to him as to his own son, and found him as worthy . . .

"Arthur Pendreic ap Amris, stand thou forth."

The words were in the High Gaeloch, that stately ancient tongue, the accent more antique than I had yet heard. The voice was as deep as the silence, deep as the note of the falls without; no question of its not being obeyed. Arthur took two measured steps forward of the rest of us, and waited for the Sidhe king to pronounce.

"I know your errand," said Nudd at last. "And though I do not fault Merlynn Llwyd for sending you, perhaps, when first I heard of your coming— Well, no matter now. You are come in kinship, and in friendship, and in such company as would of itself dispose me to hear you out.

Yet so great and grave a matter must be tried, and an asking be answered."

"Ask then," said Arthur, *not* in the high tongue, with steadiness in voice and bearing.

"Then answer," came that calm deep voice again. "And on your answer stake your life: What are the Four Beasts from the morning of the world?"

My tongue cleaved to the roof of my mouth, and I could only gape in my speechless ignorance, without knowing and without hope. Not even in the halls of the Pheryllt had I ever heard mention of such a piece of lore, and knew—or thought I knew—that Arthur was ignorant as I.

But to my utter astonishment he spoke at once, in a clear and confident voice.

"Not hard: These are the White Mare of the Moon, who dwells in the East and is shod with silver; the Red Hawk of the Sun, who dwells in the South and whose wings are tipped with gold; the Green Hound of the Sea, who dwells in the West and who can run dry-foot upon the wave; the Black Bull of the Mountain, who dwells in the North and whose horns can lift the world."

And silence fell like rain upon that great hall and all within it. I dared a glance upward: Nudd and Arthur were met in gaze, and to my Sight the glance of the one seemed no less filled with magic, no less fenced with power, than that of the other.

Nudd smiled. "Well answered," he said. "But answer me now this: What are those three who are Eldest among all living things?"

Again my ignorance struck fresh panic into my soul; but this time it was Morgan spoke up from her place beside me.

"Not hard: These will be the Stag of Redinvyre, and the Owl of Cwm Cawlwyd, and the Eagle of Gwernabwy; and one there is who is Elder even of all these." But who that was she did not say.

And again Nudd smiled. "Well answered, as befits thy teacher's pupil. But answer me now this: Who is it throws light into the meeting on the mountain?"

Ringing silence; and though none looked in my direction, nor spoke my name to prompt me, nor even it seemed so much as thought of Taliesin, I felt as if the

Hollow Hills above us did shout my name to the stars. And I knew what I must do ... As if I moved through water, I stepped forward as had Arthur and Morgan, and I touched my harp-satchel in the ancient gesture.

A gesture well understood even here beneath the hill, it seemed: A gleam came and went in Nudd's dark eyes, and had it been any less august than he I should have called it a gleam of pure amusement.

"Bold is he who would harp in the halls of the Shining Folk ... But such boldness must be answer of itself. Chaunt, then."

And be damned to me? Well, maybe so, but chaunting was all the answer I knew to make, and answer was clearly called for, and just as clearly was it my turn to reply ... I set my fingers to the strings, hooked them to begin, full ready to live or die by what came next to my mind. But even as I drew breath to chaunt the Awen came down upon me; and even as I gave myself up to it with passionate relief, and gratitude that it should deem me still worthy of its inhabitance, I knew joy that it had not forsaken me, though sometimes it had seemed to me that I had forsaken it.

> "Bard am I to Arthur,
> And my homeland is the country of the
>   summer stars.
> Gwion have I been called, and Mabon;
> At length all kings shall call me Taliesin.
> I was with my lord in the heights of heaven,
> I was with him in the deeps of the sea.
> I was in the galaxy before the throne
>   of the Distributor,
> I was at the court of Dôn before the birth
>   of Gwydion.
> I know the names of the springs in the heart
>   of Ocean,
> I know the names of the stars from south
>   to north.
> On the day of affliction I shall be of more
>   service than a thousand swords,
> And I shall be until the day of dán upon the
>   face of the earth."

If the silence that had gone before had seemed complete, this that now fell was something so far beyond it as had no name for its totality. But the Awen was not yet done with me; it was upon me like a fever still, I could not feel my body around me, not even my fingertips on the strings of the harp. From the tail of one eye I could just see Arthur, and out of the other Gwyn; but my focus was before me, on Nudd in his crystal throne, who looked impassively upon me.

To me, as he had not to the others, he spoke again. "Whence came you?"

And again the Awen took my voice to sing:

"I have fled with fearing, I have fled as a fawn;
I have fled vehemently, I have fled as a fire.
I have fled as a roebuck to a thicket,
I have fled as a wolf in the wilderness.
I have fled as a mare, I have fled as a salmon;
I have fled as a fox, I have fled as a falcon.
I have fled as a boar, I have fled as a badger;
I have fled as a hare, I have fled as a hen.
I have fled as iron in the flame,
I have fled as an arrow in the fight.
I have fled as a spear-head of woe to such
    as have the wish for it.
No man sees what upholds him, no woman
    sees what bears her down.
But the prayers of Keltdom shall not be in
    vain, nor the Highest fail of the promise."

And this time as I sang—as the Awen sang me—it was as if Merlynn's magic had taken me once again, taken me out of my everyday body to a far high place from which I might observe and yet remain unseen.

Many things I Saw: Some were plain to my Seeing, others less so; others still I did not know at all. I Saw holy Brendan, and Nia his mother, bringing thirteen Treasures to Keltia in the hold of the Hui Corra; then Brendan was dead, and Nia bringing the Treasures here to Dún Aengus, to her own people; giving them to Llyr who was king in that time, and he passing them on to Nudd his son, and Nudd passing them on to ... *Arthur*.

I believe I cried out then, but the vision held me fast,

I could not fall out of it: And Arthur taking them out of Keltia, to a dusty foreign world, where they lay in fire and silence until one came to claim them again ...

The world came back around me with a rush of cold air. I was shaking all over, soaked with sweat, and staring at Nudd as if I were possessed, though glad indeed to be back to reality—even such a reality as this. Morgan and Arthur were holding me up on either side—Frame of Harmony had been taken gently from my hands as I stood rigid and convulsed—and Gwyn was wrapping his own cloak around my shoulders.

I had eyes only for the faerie king. "Is it so?" I heard myself croaking, my voice hoarse from the Awen's demands. "Will it be?"

Nudd looked upon me, and in the darkness of his eyes I saw, amazingly, sorrow. *But also exaltation* ...

"Thou hast Seen it," he said, and then that dark glance moved slowly to Arthur who stood beside me.

Well, I may have Seen it, but apparently no one else had: I stared wildly at Morgan and Arthur in turn, and they looked back with mild wonderment, concerned for my obvious distress, but no more than that. *Ah gods,* I wondered bitterly, and very privately, *why is it that I am the one to See these fripping things? Artos has dán from here to evermore, and Morgan more sorcery even than God; I wish only to live a quiet life with my harp and my scribblings and I am the one afflicted with prodigies* ...

"It is not fair," I muttered, as Arthur lifted me to my feet again. "I never had much Sight, or so Merlynn ever told me—"

"Ah well, who listens to *him*?" said Arthur cheerfully. But even his smile faded as we all three turned again to face the king.

Nudd had risen from the crystal throne; he was not so scant of stature as I had thought.

"You have Seen aright," he said, though now he spoke in the vernacular; yet even that was of a more archaic cast than that now spoken. He nodded once to Gwyn, and the prince bowed and crossed to a corner of the chamber behind the throne. There he threw back heavy curtains that had shrouded a niche, and, pausing an instant as if in respect or honor, whipped away a richly embroidered cover of red and gold and blue fringed silk.

Beneath the cloth was a chest of carved dark wood, knee-high to a tall man and of the length of a spear; at each end were set worn gold handles of a curious design, and there was a latch, but no lock to it.

At Gwyn's quiet word, two of the faerie lords set their hands to the chest, bearing it with little effort to the foot of the throne and setting it down. As one we all drew back a little, even Birogue, as Nudd descended the three wide-cut steps and paused before the wooden chest.

Even I could see the many years that were on it, the iron-oak black with age, the dust in the deep carvings, the dullness of the gold fittings. In what time, on what world, had the wood for this been cut, the patterns carved, the panels joined? What was held within it, and whose the hand had placed it there?

Nudd laid his hands palm down on the lid of the carved coffer—a moment only—then withdrew them; and my jaw began to drop as the lid slowly rose of itself, and I do not think I could have looked away had all our lives depended on it.

I could not see what lay within from where I stood, only a corner of yet another piece of rich cloth. But Nudd was beckoning Arthur to come and stand beside him.

"See now the Thirteen Treasures that Brendan brought from afar, that Nia, daughter of our race, brought here to be kept in honor and in safety."

Gwyn knelt to unfold the stiff gleaming cloth—oréadach, as I now could see, cloth-of-gold, heavily embroidered with jewels and tiny pearls—and what lay within the chest was revealed for all to see.

"The Spear Birgha," said Gwyn, lifting a slim ashwood shaft bound tightly about with silver silk. One by one he held up the other sacred things that had lain so long in darkness and in waiting: Fragarach, the Sword of Lugh, serpent-hilted and black-scabbarded; the Stone of Fál, a crystal globe securely concealed within a gilded leather covering; Pair Dadeni, the Cup, a silver bowl with pearls round the rim; oh, and more beside, a cloak, a dagger, a helm, a food-wallet, a silver fillet ... I was too staggered to take proper inventory just then.

But Nudd was speaking to Arthur. "Take them," said the faerie king. "For they are yours by right."

Arthur stared a long moment at the sacred hallows, not

touching any, as if he would learn them by heart and not yet by hand; Morgan and I exchanged a quick thought, both of us suddenly sure of what he would do . . .

"One thing only will I take," said Arthur then, suiting action to word and setting his hand to the hilt of the Sword. "These others have I yet to win; but this I will take now to help me win them."

"With the holy Cup Uthyr's hurt can be healed, his life be spared," murmured Birogue; and though Arthur's eyes closed briefly at her words, I knew he knew it for the testing that it was, knew too that he would not fail.

"Nay, lady," he said. "That *dán* is long decided; my uncle the Ard-rígh would not wish it other than as it is, or must be, and not for me to choose to change what he has freely accepted."

A shiver seemed to pass over those within that hall, an unseen quivering like the wind in the leaves of a willow-wood; and I saw that this too was *dán. Gods, but it ever unhinges me just a little, to see dán's workings made so plain* . . .

Only one more thing remained to be done, and this Arthur now performed: Turning to face Birogue and Gwyn, he gave them words of dismissal, as Merlynn had bidden him; and—again as Merlynn had bidden him—not one word of thanks. For thus it often is with the Sidhe, that mortals may accept their help, even petition for it, but may not thank them in the end when that help is granted; sometimes, of course, they *must* be thanked—and there is no rule that holds, by which one may know which time is which.

But, for now at least, our instruction had been plain: Beside me, Morgan sighed to see it done, and I smiled for that we had managed to do it after all.

Yet as we turned to take our leave, Arthur clutching in his hands the gifted Sword, too shy or too awestruck to hang it from his baldric where Llacharn was used to hang, a stir came at the hall's far end, and we halted where we stood, a little uncertain and more than a little unnerved.

Birogue and Gwyn moved to flank us, and behind us on the throne-dais Nudd rose again to his feet, as a woman clad in red came between the lines of bowing lords and curtsying ladies. Tall she was, her eyes greener than Morgan's and her hair redder than Arthur's; she

walked with a regal stride, and in her hands she carried a
small folded bundle of what looked like white silk.

She took no note of Arthur nor yet of myself, save for
one very sharp, sweeping glance, but stopped in front of
Morgan, who curtsied as she would have done in full
court before her mother the Queen—and I reflected that
even when ritual demanded, Morguenna Pendreic did not
readily bend her knee to any.

Seli the queen—for it could be no other in all her
world or ours—lifted her glance to Nudd where he sat
again upon his throne of crystal.

"I too have somewhat to offer in this matter," she said
in a voice that rang like a clear silver bell, in a tone of
challenge and defiance that announced merely, not asking
leave nor craving permission. Nudd inclined his head to
her in acknowledgment and assent, but said no word of
answer.

Again Seli looked upon Morgan, who returned the gaze
serenely, as was not to be wondered at in one Birogue had
trained.

"To you I entrust this," said the Queen of the Aes
Sidhe then, "and you shall bear it to Gweniver daughter
of Dôn, for her to use or not as she shall deem."

Morgan accepted the white bundle from Seli's hands,
bowed her head but did not speak.

"It is called the Bratach Bán, the White Banneret," said
Seli. "It was not meant for mortals, when first it was
woven; but in part by my own folly this evil has come
upon Keltia, and I would do what I might to lessen what
ills may yet befall. Three times only may it be waved; but
each of those wavings will, in dire need, bring help
unlooked-for."

I caught my breath, for not until now had I in truth remembered that here before me stood the mother of the
Marbh-draoi. *Truly, by her folly indeed* ... Had Seli not
fled court and lord and son, to live among mortals and
bear Edeyrn to Rhûn, Keltia might have been spared the
rule of the Marbh-draoi these many years; only by the
blood of the Sidhe did he attain to such length of life—
had he had a mortal Kelt for mother, we might still have
had him as tyrant and ruler, but not for so very, very long
a sway of time ...

With a start I realized that Seli was regarding me, as if

she had kenned or guessed my thought. I bowed hastily, as much in courtly respect as to escape that green stare, not the green of grass or leaf but the green of balefire. Yet I felt the touch of the mind behind the eyes, and it was oddly warm and well-contriving.

"Taliesin ap Gwyddno," she said, and I stiffened to surprised attention; she saw, and smiled for the first time, a smile like spring across a snow-field. "Look not so feared! Your mother was my friend, as she was friend to the Lady Birogue, and dwelled for a time not far from here, among us all. You favor her greatly." She paused for the space of three breaths. "Ask what you would of me, concerning her."

So—it seemed that I too was to be given a gift of the Shining Ones, to take with me from that palace behind the flying waters ... And yet, now that I had leave to ask freely, all my questions once so mutely burning seemed but embers only, a grieshoch of askings unanswered, and even the need to ask seemed in this time and place a thing unneeded.

"Lady," I heard myself saying, in a voice that seemed not my own, "what you have said is enough for now. I will ask again in time to come, if you allow it."

The green eyes kindled. "There speaks my friend again, in her son's voice ... Ask when and where you will, Taliesin of the House of Glyndour; I will hear and answer."

I could think of naught else to do, sufficient to show my respect and my thanks, and so I bent to kiss her hand; but just as my lips began to brush the cool slim fingers there came a whirling round me like a vortex of light, and a roaring in my ears that outshouted even the song of the great water-force without. Then a sick spinning took me and flung me off my feet, and when my sight had cleared again I found myself lying on the grassy bank beside the falls, and Meillion my horse cropping placidly not ten yards away. I shot upright with a cry and an oath.

Arthur and Morgan were sprawled ungracefully beside me, he still clutching Fragarach in both hands. At sight of the weapon I half-turned back to the hidden gate with a cry of dismay, thinking our own swords lost; but they too lay in a shining tangle upon the warm rough grass, the sapphires in the hilt of Morgan's blade burning blue against the sere green.

They sat up with rather more care than I had taken—and for which I was now paying, with the high king of all headaches beginning to pound behind my eyes—and took quick stock of things. Morgan carefully cradled the white banner against her chest, and smiled at me.

"Did you not then think Merlynn's words of warning applied to you as to Arthur and me? Well that our business had been concluded before you so misstepped yourself . . ." When I still looked blankly on her: "You *do* recall Merlynn telling us that the Sidhe must not be thanked? What were you *thinking* to do, by kissing the hand of the queen, if not thanking her? Thanks indeed, and the grace of the Mother, that the offense was not worse taken, and worse came of it than an overspeedy exit and a pain in the head."

"But—I did not mean to—Well, I did, then," I concluded lamely, sensing rather than seeing Arthur's grin. "My sorrow, cariad, and my mistake: is there great harm done for it?"

Morgan shook her golden head; the three horses, tacked for the journey home, had come ambling over to her, and she was stuffing the faerie flag into one of Nyfer's saddlepacks.

"No great harm, I think, and surely no offense taken," she said, smiling at last. "You did well, though, Talyn, not to ask of your mother just now, though Seli would have told you all you wished to know; but greater good will come of your delaying your knowing . . ." She turned to look at Arthur, and I looked where she did.

He had refastened Llacharn in its old place by his side; but the great serpent-hilted Sword he had bound across his saddle-bow. He was not looking at us, but back at the thundering water that hid the gate to the faerie halls. And I wondered, as I watched him, if he regretted the decision he had made beneath the hill: not to take the Treasures Nudd had offered him, but to earn them with the help of Lugh's own weapon.

He must have felt the question in the air, for he swung about to us, and grinned to see us staring.

"You two look like a pair of baby owls in a hollow tree, all eyes and waiting to be fed . . . Nay, I do *not* regret my choosing; it was all the choice I could make, and I would choose the same again." He laid a hand hesitantly upon the scabbarded blade, as if he both feared and longed to touch it; as undoubtedly he did, as any would have.

"Where now?" I asked. "Back to the campment?"

Arthur stood silent a moment, his head lifted into the wind, for all the world like Cabal as he quested after a scent.

"Aye," he said at last. "But for a small time only, and to leave these precious things with those who are to keep them: the flag to Gweniver, the Sword to Uthyr . . . until such hour as they are needed and their help must be sought." He grinned again and swung up into Miaren's saddle. "But the look on your face, Talyn, in that one moment when the magic began to spin us from the hall—that was worth being so abruptly cast out, and no mistake about it."

"All one," said Morgan, touching her heel to Nyfer's flank just behind the girth. "We have tarried long enough, careddau, and perhaps too long; let us find a swifter way back than the one we followed here."

She turned Nyfer's head west, and we came after.

CHAPTER
10

We found the camp in a new location farther to the east and south, and I could see as we rode up to the outer leaguer that Arthur was not well pleased to find it where we did.

"Little choice, Artos," said Tarian when she met us just outside the leaguer bounds. "The Marbh-draoi sent pursuit not three days after you had gone—no captain of any note. But Keils, Gwennach and I thought that, as a move was inevitable, best to move as far as we could without losing touch entirely with the enemy."

Though plainly cross, and not troubling to hide it from any of the hundreds who swarmed round to greet us, even Arthur could not fault the military judgment of those he himself had left in command; but he said no word, and we rode into the heart of the camp in stony silence.

Here again he surprised us, for instead of going straight to Uthyr's tent as all had expected, he headed rather for Gweniver's, and rather peremptorily motioned Morgan and me to come with him.

There was no way, short of being suddenly stricken deaf and blind, that Gweniver could be in ignorance of our return—the reception had been loud, joyous and all but universal—but, for all the note she feigned to take of it, she might as well have been. When we came to her tent, she was seated calmly at her field-desk, writing out

reports on a small handpad, and looked up with creditable
surprise.

"You are back!" She came round the desk to embrace
each of us—Morgan, then me, Arthur last—and secured
the tent flap behind us. "Sit, have somewhat to drink, tell
me what has passed—"

"In good time," said Arthur, more curtly than was
strictly needful. "There are more pressing matters than
travellers' tales just now . . ." He nodded to Morgan, who
took from beneath her cloak the leather-wrapped bundle
she had been carrying. "This is sent you by the queen of
the Sidhe," he said, ignoring Gweniver's astonished
glance from the bundle to his face and back again, as she
received the gift from Morgan's hands. "It is called
Bratach Bán, you are bidden use it only in the hour of
greatest need. It may be waved three times only to summon help in such an hour."

"But what—"

"As I was told, so I tell you." Arthur was giving her
even less sword-room than was usual with him when they
were at odds, and I—who had not known they *were* at
odds just now—wondered why. "And you may come to
need that help sooner than we may like, or look for. See
now—"

He shrugged off his cloak and took her place at the
desk, where a map had been laid under the transparent
writing surface.

"We cannot come down the Strath to Caerdroia," he
said, his finger following the line of the glen on the map.
"Too many troops, too many fortresses, not to mention
Ratherne—and Edeyrn sitting there like a spider." The
finger stopped beside the notation 'Nandruidion.' "Still,
there are other ways, and sometimes it will be seen that
the surest route is not always the shortest."

"What in all the hells are you talking about?"
Gweniver had regained her self-composure; besides, she
had been 'customed to command of the forces this month
past, and it was, after all, her own tent.

Arthur unbent so far as to favor her with a grin, and
she rolled her eyes.

"You will take the army down to the mouth of the
Strath, to come as far into it as ever you can without engaging Edeyrn—or Owein, or whoever else may be sent

against you. You may keep Keils with you"—his voice seemed suspiciously devoid of inflection as he said so— "and Tari shall come with me, along with some of the Companions. Oh, and a few thousand horse and foot or so; easily spared."

"And then?"

"And then you will sit there in the mouth of the glen— until I join you."

I was beginning to have a very first inkling of his plan—a slowly dawning and horrible one—and I opened my mouth to protest, and then shut it again. *Well, he is Rex Bellorum, after all, not I* . . .

But Gweniver had not yet had any such glimpsing. "And just where, if I may ask, will you be joining us from? Where will *you* have been all this time, with Tari and some of the Companions and a few thousand horse and foot—however easily spared?"

Morgan answered for him. "Taking Caerdroia. From the Loom-ward side." She and her brother met in glance, and he smiled.

Gweniver did not smile. "Did the Sidhe steal away your wits instead of your soul? Artos"—and that alone was clear indicator of her alarm, almost never did she call him by his shortname—"with very good reason is Caerdroia unguarded from the south: because the Loom cannot be crossed by an army in strength."

Arthur grinned, and I ran a hand over my face. *Oh aye, here we go yet another time* . . .

"All the more reason Edeyrn will not be thinking to look for us to make a crossing . . . Any road, he is at Ratherne, and you will be keeping him far too busy for his thoughts to be turning westwards." How busy, none of us just then could have dreamed . . .

Morgan had been studying the map. "Well, Arthur; but there are no passes leading south-to-north you may make use of."

"And none needed, not even at the last." He grinned again at our perplexment, and Gweniver's infuriated stare. "Call the commanders to the King's tent after the nightmeal; I promise, I shall tell you all my plan, and you may speak against it to your hearts' content. But now I must go to my uncle, and to Merlynn; there are things they must hear."

When he had gone, Gweniver stared at the bundle still clutched in her hands, then up at Morgan and myself. I squirmed a bit under that glacial gray stare, but Morgan looked back untroubled.

"*Can* he do this?"

Arthur's sister shrugged. "True it is he has footed trickier measures amid winter hills," she said slowly. "But this is one dance for which I would not myself care to call the tune."

Gweniver laughed then, a little sourly, a little admiringly. "Nor fee the piper when the reel is ended."

No need to give you all the boresome themes of that night's meeting: Suffice you to know that Arthur's plan was gone over in most minutest detail, hailed and hated both; and that he had his way in the end—but *that* you knew already.

As for Uthyr the King—to whom Arthur had on bended knee presented the holy Sword, and who had held it hiltwise against his chest, folded in his arms like a lover or a child, all that day and evening—he spoke no word of aye or nay, only looked on his nephew with shining eyes. Ygrawn, seated beside her lord as ever, was more vocal—again as ever—and put to her son several questions every bit as edged and pointed as that Sword.

Arthur answered her as he had answered all his other inquisitors: with a cool, smiling patience—softsauder even, when it was needed—that seemed to show that, to him at least, the thing was already done. And next morning it began, the armies dividing neatly as if he had been a shepherder sending herd-dogs down a line to part his flocks, like the hair either side of a comb.

Well, more to one side, was that particular parting: Most of the troops were retained by Gweniver and Keils; those who rode with Arthur only a few thousands, as he had said. But for his plan no more were needed; fast and fewer were his watchwords. You must think of a letter Y, lying upon its side; or, better still, the three strokes of the Holy Awen—the center stroke being the line of the Loom, the left-hand stroke the vast open gap called the Pass of the Arrows, and the right-hand one the vale of the Avon Dia itself.

"Gwennach and Keils will draw Edeyrn's forces down the Strath to engage, but will *not* engage," Arthur had said, to murmurous agreement. "When the Marbh-draoi sees that some of us have broken off from the main body, he will send reserves down Pass of the Arrows to bar us, thinking that *we* are thinking to take that way to the sea." His hand moved on the wall-map; that was two arms of the Awen told off ...

"But we will vanish before ever they come in sight of us," he had continued. "We will go up into the Loom and follow the summit ridge, to come down upon Caerdroia from behind. Such garrisons as there are will all be upon the walls and at the gates, and none will be thinking that doom can come also from the hills." His finger traced lovingly the center line of the glyph. "Through here—we shall surprise them."

Above the tumult, Merlynn's voice carried clear as the hai atton, pitched to Arthur's ear but heard by all.

"And may yet find our footing on shifting sands."

And so we did.

Along the line of the Avon Dia, that great and mighty river, right up against the banks at the nearest and perhaps twenty miles off at the farthest, runs the Loom. Not the highest nor yet the grandest mountains on Tara, the Loom holds a special place in the hearts of Kelts, for it was to these mountains that Brendan, saint and astrogator, first did lead his starfarers, in that wide valley called Strath Mór that the Hui Corra beached her boats.

The Loom is then a kind of homeplace, even if one has never been there, never seen it, even, in life but in pictures only: More a tangle of rugged, jagged hills than real mountains, no peak standing more than six or seven thousand feet above the plain save Eryri alone, it is a shaggy, friendly hound of a range. But in winter, the Loom can be as evil as the End-lands of Gwynedd, and that is evil indeed: a very strait country, with little room for ease and none for error.

So, naturally, it was to be over this appalling ground, in the last days before Brighnasa, that Arthur should choose to lead us. Though I love winter above all other seasons save autumn alone, I hope never again to be in such pass; hear me, Goddess! And may a merciful dán forbid it ...

The Dakdak people have a legend of hell as a frozen mountain, where even the air is frosted solid; well, I will tell you, the high Loom in winter is not so very far off it. The ground was iron, the glaze on bare tree and rough stone as slick as silver. Any stream that was not solid white ice was racing black water, the trees and low scrub plated with rime, and we had little to eat, and no way to cook it if we had.

We swarmed up into this dubious safety just as Arthur had planned, barely unseen, only just in time: Our scouts had noted the snow-cloud raised by the oncoming enemy reserves, swift-footing it down Pass of the Arrows, led by one Sennen Vannoch—a competent if none too imaginative captain, one not numbered among Edeyrn's fanatical loyalists; we could probably turn him to our side in time to come ... I shook myself. There was a good deal more to be worrying over just now than the loyalties of Theocracy tools ...

For one thing, the horses; we did not love having to drag the poor beasts on this hell-march—bad enough having to endure it ourselves—but we would need even the few hundred mounts we *had* brought, once we came in the end to Caerdroia. But I felt sorry for the animals even so.

A more immediate worry: I had feared, and was by no means alone in my fearing, that the wake we had left of churned and trodden snow could be read by a talpa. But Arthur seemed unconcerned, and, as ever, he was right: No sooner had we vanished into the tangle of dales and fells that marked Loom-end than a storm came up at our backs, a storm that laid down so much snow so very swiftly that an hour after we had passed, by the time Sennen's column had reached where we had been, there was no mark of boot or hoof or paw. Cabal's paw only; no other hound had been permitted to accompany us, and he bounded along through the snow grinning and happy as only a dog can be.

Not only had the storm risen so auspiciously, but it seemed somehow to *halt* there, spilling out snow, covering our passage deeper into the Dales: keeping Sennen's troops from turning the Loom-end to hit our own main army, and also delaying Owein (as we heard later) in his march from Ratherne. Strange, that; but Morgan, whom I challenged on this matter, merely smiled.

It was so cold that I wept as I walked—we all walked as much as we could manage, both to spare our mounts for the battle at journey's end and to keep ourselves warmer by exertion; though I would prefer even now to think it was but the wind drove tears out of my eyes, and not my own self-pity. Beneath our feet, snow squeaked with the dryness of the air, and made small hard lumps in the shoes of the horses. Even the fine hairs within our nostrils froze as we breathed, and if we moved too fast our lungs stuck such sgians into our sides as to bid us slow our pace.

There was no track what way we were bound, only the sheep-trails; we were relying on guides drawn from the district, stout shepherders of the Dales, who hated Edeyrn for his long cruelties to the folk thereabouts; and they led us along the summit ridge that ran like a knifeback from Skirrid in the east to Mount Eagle that overhung the great bay below Caerdroia, many miles to the west.

That first night's march was torture, plain and simple. The wind was strong enough to lean on, and in our weariness we longed to do so; far westaways, ahead of the storm, just barely visible on the edge of sight, Eagle's three horns were tipped with fire. Behind us, Skirrid glowed weirdly green in that sunset, the Holy Mountain; all the uplands glowed.

We camped that next day in Silverdale; went on night after night, dull and hungry and plodding, to the greatest danger of all our time thus far on Tara. For that camp, a week into the march, was in Deepdale, only a valley ridge away from Nandruidion itself, at whose mouth stood Ratherne where Edeyrn dwelled. In clementer weather all that country might well have been alive with the Marbhdraoi's troops, and we stole glances at Morgan, wondering how long her magic could hold round us like a concealing cloak.

"Long enough, I hope, cariad," she said when I pressed her; she glanced to the north with a distracted air, as if sensing something none of the rest of us could register. "But let us not linger here; I fear time runs short indeed."

But more than that she would not say.

So we went hastily on—or as hastily as might be,

through snow to our knees and rockfaces even a hill-goat might think twice about tackling; and came into Darkdale on the tenth day of marching, before the sun was up; there to lie through the day in secrecy, to gather strength for the final pull.

"Down to Caerdroia from the Loom proper is but one way," said Arthur, as six or eight of us Companions huddled close under the scant shelter of a lichened rock-wall. "And it a narrow and twisting one: the Way of Souls, that leads down from the nemeton of Ni-maen. A small narrow valley with a track passable for horses, and Betwyr, with Tanwen, will lead our horse down that way; some of the foot as well. Tarian will take the most of the foot down beside these Falls of Yarin"—he ran a frost-reddened finger over the line on the map, where, on the far eastern edge of Caerdroia, a stream coming down off Eagle's shoulder falls in leaping cascades over wooded cliffs. "Alannagh and Tryffin, you will second her ..." He paused a long moment.

"And you, Artos?" I prompted, though in truth I dreaded to hear his intent.

"As for me, and the rest of the foot—we will come down into Turusachan itself."

"Not possible!" said Tryffin. "There is no way down those cliffs—"

"Truly; but there *is* a way under them." He smiled at the sudden silence that fell; clearly he had our full attention. "Aye, a secret way into the City from the Loom side. It is called the Nantosvelta."

From out of the mists of my long-ago days at Tinnavardan a memory stirred vaguely.

"The Nantosvelta—Artos, that is of the very first days of Keltia, it may not even exist anymore! Even if it does, sure it is to have lain unused all these centuries—how can you think you will come through?"

"Ah. I do not know, then; I can but try."

"And be entombed under Eagle as the likeliest outcome," I said with some heat.

Before he could reply Tryffin plucked at his sleeve. "What is this Nantosvelta? I for one have never heard it spoken of."

Arthur did not look at him. "A tunnel leading under the Loom; one end of it lies somewhere in Wolfdale, just beyond Black Sail and the Ill Step, and the other—well, the other end emerges in the Keep itself."

A silence even more deathly than before took us all then. I could see why Arthur wished to try this—a band of warriors silently bursting forth in the heart of the Keep of Keltia would shake Turusachan to its roots, and sorely trouble Edeyrn far off in Ratherne—but I misliked it more than I could say. There seemed far too many unknowns for even Arthur's idea of safety . . .

"Nay, consider," he said in a voice of purest reason. "Our spies have told us there is only a force in the City sufficient to keep the population in fear and obedience. All the rest are with Edeyrn or Owein or whoever. Now even after such a march as this we Companions should not find that impossible to deal with, nor the auxiliaries who have marched with us thus far, not so? Crossics to cribbins the folk of Caerdroia will throw their lot in with us, once we have liberated them. They know well who we are, believe it, and that we are here on Tara."

Now this was vintage Arthur, a wine Morgan and Tarian and I, at least, had learned long since to be wary of; too easy could it intoxicate the careless or the willing—and had us, in time past, to our chagrin. But the others were not so proof as we, and I could see how the idea had taken hold of them, firing their minds.

Well, in for a scantling, in for a score . . . I heard myself saying, with astonishing firmness, "That may be, Artos, but you will not be going that way yourself. Morgan and I will take the Nantosvelta; *you* will come down the Way of Souls with Betwyr. We are not risking you another time beneath the hill."

Arthur was silent, and that always boded ill. I had made up my mind to speak again, or to urge Morgan into it, when I heard him sigh and give a little laugh.

"Merlynn said you would do so, Talyn," he admitted. "Though I laid coin you would not win . . ."

"Ah well," I said consolingly. "Did I not hear you once say you would never again enter a town save that you had reduced it first?"

He laughed until he choked, then, still grinning, shook his head ruefully.

"The memory of bards, that my words should so come back upon me—Very well, Talyn, you have me there.

Only take Betwyr with you, and Tanwen and I shall manage very well on our own."

"Well enough, Artos," I said, a little dismayed now that I had won. "But how shall we find the entrance to this road?"

Morgan stirred beside me. "It shall find us."

We spoke no more just then, but settled in for the long wait until darkness fell again, stalking such sleep as we might. We dared not light the quartz-hearths, for fear of being caught out by the heat-traces rising. No hearths of course meant no hot supper; not that there was much left in our packs to serve for supper: only some crumbled pastais, half-hardened cheese-rinds, a little ale. Even the fodder for the horses was all but gone; only Cabal, who had hunted endless snow-hares along the march, had managed to keep his ribs as well-covered as they were when we had started out. But, beast or warrior, if we wished to fill our bellies for tomorrow's nightmeal we must seek our suppers at the tables of Caerdroia.

When dawn struck, so too did Arthur; like something out of a fever-dream, save that it was so cold, the attack began.

We had been moving into our positions since sunset of the previous day: Tarian had brought her forces to the head of the Falls of Yarin, so that by dawn they should have been in position on the water-terraces, hidden deep in the bordering woods. Arthur and Tanwen would by now have begun to lead the horse into the high narrow valley called Calon Eryri, Heart of Eagle, out of which led the Way of Souls, the ancient funeral route of the rulers of Keltia to the barrowing-ground at Ni-maen.

And Morgan, Betwyr and I stood in Wolfdale at midnight, staring at the valley walls and wondering what to do.

Morgan appeared unconcerned, however, and we took our cue from her. She sat now a little distance apart from the rest of us, waiting for the moon to rise; when at last it cleared the great bulk of Black Sail to the east, all Wolfdale seemed bathed in silver light, and as if the light had been a summons, Morgan rose to her feet.

She walked up the valley perhaps half a lai, to the sheer stone cliffs that fenced in that end of the dale. But that was not all that there was: A force, a waterfall, a thin white plume that wavered like pale silk under the moon, fell down those cliffs, into a pool that fed the stream which bisected the valley floor.

I followed after her, gazing up at the loveliness of the water in the moonlight. It seemed to have a strangely musical sound to it as it danced and beat on the rocks; almost a water-harp, it seemed to my fancy. The weather had thawed somewhat in the past two days, so that there was rather more water coming down the force than might else have been; I stooped to cup my hand into the pool, drank a few gulps of the icy water.

When I looked up again Morgan had vanished.

I believe my heart stood still for one long uncomprehending moment; certainly it felt as if my blood had ceased to pump and flow. Then my brain regained the mastery: She had not passed me, she could not disappear (well, she *could*, strictly speaking, but she would not have), therefore she was there *somewhere.*

"Guenna?" My voice croaked like a crow's. "Guenna! Where are you?"

And then it seemed that my mind had deserted me utterly, for her voice came plain to my ear, and it came from the waterfall before me.

"Here! Talyn, come round."

Then of course I saw: It was as it had been at Sychan, the entrance to the Nantosvelta was hidden behind the falls. I picked my way round the edge of the pool, slipped behind the narrow water-veil.

Morgan stood in a little alcove screened by fantastical panels of dripstone; she was smiling with delight.

"It minds me of Llwynarth," she said then. "The passageway begins behind here, and it is wide enough for four or five to walk abreast. Clear but rough, from what I could see, though I only went in a short way. Nay, *what*?" This last to me, now that she saw my face clearly in the reflected moonglow off the pool.

"I could not find you," I muttered, a little shamefaced at my own panicked reaction. "How did you get in here?" Then, "Do not leave me so, cariad—"

"The moonlight showed the way," she said, answering; then, "Anwyl, anwylyd, do not fear! I will ever be with you . . ." She kissed me gently, and I closed my arms convulsively around her.

"Bring the others in," she said then, softly. "We have a tryst at Brighnasa in Turusachan, with the next High King of Kelts."

C H A P T E R

11

Never did I forget that night's march through the deep
places of the Nantosvelta. We had of course brought
with us small handlamps, lanthorns and palmglows and
the like; but their brave beams made scant impress on the
vast and everlasting darkness that lies beneath the Loom.

It was colder and drier in the ancient passage than I
had expected; the floor, though rough-cut, was free of
rubble. No one had passed this way for a very long time,
I thought; how then came it to be so well kept?

"Magic, mostly," came Morgan's voice floating back to
me; she had the hearing of a leatherwing, whether one
spoke or not. "Can you not feel how the magic keeps up
the very walls around us?"

In truth, I had not been noticing much else beyond my
footing and the bobbing lights up and down the column.
But now that it was mentioned . . . I reached out as Druid,
not bard, and instantly I felt whereof she spoke.

"Whose magic is it?" I whispered. "Edeyrn's?"

"Nay!" came back Betwyr's fiercer whisper; though,
with two miles of rock above us, why any of us should
have been whispering to start with was beyond me. "Nay,
no magic of the Marbh-draoi's, but from farther back in
time. Brendan's, maybe—it was his own master-builder
Gradlon who constructed this—or Saint Nia's, even; or
that of others who have kept it since—Raighne, or

Alwen, or Mar. It has served often enough as escape, and will again in time to come; though this I think is its first invasion."

Indeed; there were no known bardic records of Turusachan being invaded by way of the Nantosvelta. But what of after? I thought. Given that the entry had been secret all these years; given too that now some three hundred warriors were privy to that secret ... Morgan and Merlynn and I would need to do some kenning when all this was done, to see how much was remembered, and blur whatever was.

But that was a fear for the future: Just now, our only future was that which lay ahead of us in the darkness of the tunnel, or just beyond it in the light.

It took five hours and more for all of us to make our way to the far end of the Nantosvelta, but at last, we came up to find ourselves in a large chamber cut from the rock, perhaps five times the breadth and height of the tunnel passage itself.

"This must have been a guard-room," said Betwyr, even as he motioned those who followed to take places along the wall and rest awhile. "But how do we get through?"

"And to what?" Morgan moved forward, taking a spare light as she did so and running it close to the thing that blocked our way.

It was a wall of solid findruinna, and the best of our few sensing devices made it ten yards thick. We looked at it in despair and doubt; then Betwyr and I and some others joined Morgan in her search for some sort of key or sensor, to open the gate from our side.

"Well," said Aled, one of Tryffin's Kernishmen, frustrated and baffled and as feared as the rest of us, "so significant a postern-gate could not be left to lesser guarding; thirty feet of findruinna, truly, scarce safeguard enough ..."

Morgan came suddenly erect, as if she had all at once remembered something. "Truly," she repeated vaguely, a smile beginning to break. She turned to me with suppressed excitement. "Talyn, bid them move back a little, back into the tunnel proper. I require some privacy and a bit of help from you and Betwyr, and any other sorcerer who might be down here."

We did as she asked; in five minutes eight Druids and Ban-draoi were standing before the findruinna gate, while the rest of our company had withdrawn to the distance of the passageway entrance.

"It was Aled made me see it," Morgan was saying as I came up to them, after seeing the others safely shifted. "Naught short of atomics could break these gates by force—and bring down half the Loom in the process—but he who built it wished to leave no latch that might be undone by enemies."

Light broke. "No way to open it from *this* side," I said. "But—"

"Aye; from the other." Morgan stepped confidently up to the dully gleaming, monstrous metal slab. "And there are keys and keys—as we learn in our Crafts."

"What will you do then, lady?" joked a new recruit, a bit nervously. "Will you walk through the wall?"

Morgan smiled. "Almost." She laid her hand upon the gate, much as Birogue had done with the faerie gate at Sychan. As one, the rest of us sorcerers joined hands in a loose half-circle behind her; as my old Druid classfellow Betwyr and I closed the linking, a glow began to rise from the floor and seep like groundwater from the walls, and I did not need to repeat my cautioning to those who huddled, watching wide-eyed, in the tunnel mouth.

Come to that, I was fairly wide-eyed myself: This that Morgan was now attempting was by no means a casual magic. Not dangerous, of itself; but demanding, near as much of the ones who supported the work as of the one who directed it. But even in those early times there was none in Keltia like to Morgan . . .

She did not, as had been only half-jestingly suggested, herself physically pass through the wall. But she came as close to it as makes no differ: No word spoken, she seemed to ripple like smoke in a breeze, her form passing through iridescence to incandescence to near-transparency, until it seemed that only a trace of her remained on the air. We reeled a little with the strain of it, but our circle held, our linked hands tightening their grip on one another.

And then, just as it seemed we must burst or die, Morgan was back with us, almost fallen to her knees from her efforts; the great gates began to part before us, and stood wide.

I broke the linking and leaped forward to catch her; she clutched at my arms for support, but her smile was pleased and teasing.

"There now; so much for posterns." She went round the circle, exchanging embraces, quiet words, kisses, with those who had aided her working, coming at last back to Betwyr and me and falling laughing into our arms. We stood so a moment, the three of us hanging on one another in one relieved and happy hug; then Betwyr withdrew himself and bowed to Morgan with a grin, gesturing her to pass through.

"That is surely one very good way to open doors— lady, step beyond."

And with a little curtsy, Morgan did so.

On the other side of the massive findruinna gate was a plain door of black granite set into the rough rock of the mountain. We peered suspiciously round its flush frame, thinking to find some other clever device; but this was, thank gods, a straightforward barrier only, as honest a door as ever could be. No tricks here: The builders had depended, and rightly, on the formidable gate behind us as providing all the defense that could ever be needed. Perhaps none had feared or imagined a need such as ours, or a skill such as Guenna's . . . Any road, this last obstacle was only a granite block that moved on a perfectly obvious track, no art or cunning to it. But before anyone could set shoulder to it, I called a pause.

"Do we know what lies the other side of that?" Wide wondering-eyed faces, chagrined headshakes. "Well, shall we trouble to find out, do you think, before we go leaping through?"

"It felt safe enough," said Morgan, sounding wearied and not at all concerned. "But do so, surely, if you think it best to know."

"It is only that I do not wish us to pop out of here straight into a nest of Ravens," I explained carefully. "We have worked hard to earn surprise; let us not lose it now."

In the end it was a Ban-draoi sorceress named Siara, a Companion since the second Llwynarth, who helped me with the kenning. Perhaps ten minutes later we came back to our fellows quiet and demure; but our eyes were sparkling.

"Well? What is it? Is it Ravens?"

Siara and I exchanged glances. "See for yourselves," I said, with what I hoped was sublime disdain, and thrust the door aside.

Beyond, anticlimactically, was seen only a heavy curtain of rich plain fabric, hanging in dusty folds that looked as if they had not been disturbed for long years. When this was battled aside, a tall chair of curious design was revealed; its back was to us a few feet away, so placed that the chair itself, standing in front of the hangings, concealed the door and the entrance to the Nantosvelta alike.

"Somehow I think this is no ordinary chair," muttered Betwyr; then, as we turned to get a better look, the others pouring through after us, alert for Ravens, one by one we fell silent and still, and stared.

Indeed, no ordinary chair . . . Rising up to the height of a tall man, its front and sides and back and arms carved deep and thick with ancient symbols, its cloud-white marble weirdly pale in the low light, the Throne of Scone peered out aloofly, emptily, over the Hall of Heroes.

Even Morgan seemed awed; as for the rest of us, we crept out like feared mice from behind the Throne, some of us even touching reverent lips or fingertips to the stone as they passed. But there was little time for marvelling; or, at least, not at that . . .

"No Ravens," said Aled, scout's eyes raking the distant corners of that enormous chamber. "Not one—are they flown, then?"

"By no means, Aleddach," answered Morgan. "It is said Edeyrn himself fears and hates this place; no wonder that he would have had it shut up long since."

"They will be outside, then," said Betwyr briefly; he turned to his lieutenants, laying swift plans.

Morgan's hand slid into mine; startled, I turned to look at her, but she was staring at the Throne, and her whole slim frame was trembling. *So, love,* I sent in thought-speech, *so, now . . .* But the sight of that empty throne, bereft for two centuries of its rightful occupant, had shaken me to my own soul, and I could well believe even the Marbh-draoi felt qualms that kept him from this chamber.

But we had no time to waste in moonstruck gaping: We armed swiftly and stripped for the field, all our excess

gear and clothing and baggage left in the tunnel; we had
come to fight, not to carry. Then, going softly and warily,
we fanned out and down through the sibilant darknesses
that filled that great hall. And it seemed to us all that
brave ghosts did watch our going, and proudly did they
send to us their strength and love.

There was not a soul in sight: not a Raven, not a guard,
not so much as a drudge with a broom. Half-jubilant, half-
dreading, we moved deeper and deeper into the Keep, even
as far as where it attaches to the royal palace of Turusachan, and where guards would surely be expected. Still no
one.

What is *this?* I sent to Betwyr, and felt his shrug of
puzzlement; and the bladepoint alertness behind it. Well,
he was right to feel both: Something was plainly happening that had cleared the way for us, and I was having a
thought or two as to what that might be.

Ten minutes, and we had secured the Keep; fifteen
more, and we had penetrated to both sides—to the palace
on the left, and the brehons' former brugh, long closed by
Edeyrn, on the other side, standing between the Keep itself and the entrance to the Way of Souls.

And still no one sighted, let alone fought . . . It seemed,
beyond all reason, that we had all but taken Turusachan,
and that without a single swordstroke. Then from high
above us came three sounds that changed the world.

As the first light began to break far to the east—by
now the snow-clouds that had followed us from Ossory
had gone, perhaps back to Glenshee whence they had
been sent or summoned—the first sound came in the air
above, a sound that brought tears stinging to my eyes, and
the memory of Gwyn's horn leaping exultant to my soul.

But I knew at once that this was different: a kind of
music, as if a great chord were being played somewhere
in the heavens, as if the Loom itself were one vast clarsa.
The chord grew and shifted tone, now ringing, now div-
ing down almost below the range of human ears; but always lovely. Then it died away, moving far above our
heads and out to sea, and I turned to stare in wonder at
the others nearest me.

It was, as I was later to learn, a phenomenon not uncommon here in winter: the heat of the sun meeting the
cold air rising above the Loom, and the granite rockfaces,

caught between, acting as a sounding-board to make the mountain-music by which we had been so enthralled.

But as swiftly as it passed, two other sounds rang out to take its place, and no mistaking the earthliness of either: Arthur's own horn calling from the hillside above, and Tarian's answering it from the Falls of Yarin, seven miles to the east.

That was it, then: We leaped from our concealment like leopards from cover, engaging almost at once with the Ravens that had materialized just as suddenly. I could see Arthur and Tanwen now, with our precious hundreds of horse, down off the hill and forming for the charge, and shouting I have no recollection what I drew off half my company and dashed to clear them a path.

It seemed that the Ravens had had some warning after all—that was why we had encountered no one in all the Keep, they had been needed elsewhere, and no soldier in right mind guards an empty hall that cannot be taken by stealth and holds no strategic advantage—or so at least was thought; but it can only have been a matter of moments, for they were in disarray to begin with, and never succeeded in mounting any real threat to us. Our side-march on Caerdroia, perhaps Arthur's greatest gamble ever, was a triumph of surprise.

We were surging together like magnet and iron, Arthur from the hill and we from the great open square, when down the far slopes of Eagle, faint and clear in the cold Brighnasa morning, floated the strains of the terrible Douglas pibroch that had come from Caledon with Tarian and her Scotans: 'Come wolves for I will feed you flesh.' Even Edeyrn's troops, it seemed, could still rouse to the sound of war-pipes, for they came flooding out of their garrison halls, and we were there to meet them.

In the end it was almost too easy to take delight or pride in; well, almost . . . We went through Caerdroia, and the Ravens' rummeled ranks, like sgians through summer butter, chasing our enemy down through the streets of the Upper Town and into the Stonerows that lie behind the northeast walls. Aye, truly, some did stand to fight, and fought well; indeed, fought like warriors worthy of a nobler cause. But it did not avail them; we were by now too heedless and undeniable, and we pushed them like drifts of autumn leaves right to the walls of the City.

"Follow on!"

The familiar ros-catha carried across half Caerdroia, cried there for the first time: taken up at once by the Companions, then by all who had come with us, that long cold road from Ossory. Indeed, it must have echoed in the hearts of all who followed from Gwynedd ... This had been no fight worth the naming or the chaunting, not until that moment; and then, of course, it flamed. It was a star of combats, a king-stag of battle, a wonder among nations. Ah, Mihangel, thou wert there! Malen Ruadh, thou wert there!

Before noon it was finished: strong points taken and held; captives secured in their own garrisons, now their prisons; our own dead and wounded sped or attended. Then, carefully, quietly, like uncertain frightened wildlings of the woods nosing out of their burrows after a forest fire has roared overhead, the people of Caerdroia began to come out of their housen.

Some, to be sure, had emerged sooner than this, and in no uncertain manner: At the first clash of battle joined, many who saw or guessed what was afoot—for days there had been rumor of Arthur's coming; by the time the tales were told, he was coming to the City on a comet or a dragon at the very least—had roared out of stone cots and tall brughs, shouting for Arthur, Uthyr and the royal House of Dôn. They meant what they shouted, too: Without their help—intelligence work as much as swordcraft—we had never taken Caerdroia so featly as we did, and maybe had not taken it at all.

They came now, proudly, ancient weapons banned by Edeyrn and long hidden away clutched in hands or slung over shoulders, their heads high, some of them leading prisoners or giving urgently needed information, often with tears and blood mingling impartially upon their faces. We were glad of them, and welcomed them as warmly as they did us; but we prayed and wondered all the same, hoping that not overmany should prove turncloaks in the end.

Now, before you think hard on us for thinking so, remember that this was, after all, war to the knife; and we had been cozened before, to our lasting sorrow, by just such dissemblers, who passed as supporters, wronged and persecuted even as ourselves but who were in truth

Edeyrn's creatures; and who wrought great harm before they were found out. Doubtless some of these who now hailed and honored us were traitors of that stripe, spying for their master in our midst; but we felt for them pity as well as the pitilessness with which we would deal with them in the end. They had lived with Edeyrn's hand so close above them for two hundred years, in a kind of oppression we who chose to fight openly cannot know. No surprise, then, if they had gone to his side, for who can say truly what he or she would do in like case? We love to think we shall ever choose the noble road; but that is not the same as knowing we shall do so, or in fact so doing ...

So we kept cautious in the face of triumph, and our joy was not too much tempered. But now the folk those others had fought for came timidly out to us as well, scarcely daring to believe what had befallen: shy, dazed, weeping with joy and fear and fear's ending. Of all the battle-aftermaths I have in my time been witness to, this one was by far the most poignant; if I was not on the verge of tears, it was only for that I was already weeping. Of all those I saw, it was the children and the old folk that moved me most: the bewildered children who could not understand their deliverance, and the bewildered old ones who could not believe they had been at last delivered ...

Scenes all around me of piercing feeling: I saw Morgan comforting a sobbing woman of an age to be her grandmother, who kissed her hands and wept and talked incomprehensibly in confusion and joy; saw Tryffin with a child on either arm, all three of them laughing in purest delight; and all the others, those who stared hungrily at our Companions, who swept our modest auxiliars into delirious embraces; who offered stammering thanks to our overwhelmed commanders.

To me they showed the awed respect and the deference they knew was the due of a ranking bard: I had for the first time today worn my golden star of ollaveship openly upon my battle dress; as Arthur and Morgan and Tarian and Tryffin and so many others had worn the interdicted arms of their outlawed Houses, as so many more had borne their own kindreds' devices openly into the field; it seemed an hour for declaring, did we win or did we fall. Perhaps in especial did we fall ...

But the deference had swiftly altered in the mood of
the moment: Though no whit less respectful, it was trans-
muted into warm loving eagerness, to hear and be heard,
as they crowded round the first true ollave they had ever
known, to tell him of their thoughts and deeds and hopes
this Brighnasa morning. *Brighnasa* ... Had Arthur
planned it so, or had some Other worked it? I wondered;
and resolved to remind Morgan, that we might that night
give proper thanks to the Goddess on Her feast day, for
Her hand had surely been with us in our need.

But now all around fell silent, as Morgan and Arthur
stood out from the host, and, hand in hand, claimed the
City for the High King Uthyr Pendreic. Then, slowly, as
if in a dream from which they prayed they should not
awaken, the folk of Caerdroia went as one to their knee,
before their Prince and his sister.

Now Arthur hated this sort of thing, and Morgan detested it even more; but I sighed with relief to see that
they had accepted the fealty of the folk. *Now is neither
time nor place to assert your dislike of homage,* I sent to
both of them, and sensed their wry assent. In any case,
not to them did the folk offer it, but to that long-doubted
and despaired-of legend called the House of Dôn; and as
such did they accept it.

Arthur spoke to them then, made some small speech
claiming Caerdroia, thanking them for their aid, praying
them to keep their city for him when he rode out—"as
ride I must"—against Edeyrn, who was still at Ratherne
for all anyone knew; spoke of Gweniver, and the fight
that was yet to come, and begged their aid for her;
thanked all gods and avowed his cause anew. Not a long
speech; as for Morgan, she merely thanked the fighters
and blessed the folk, and I was interested to see how rev-
erentially they did receive her blessing. But I think we all
had ever done so: When Morgan blessed you, by gods
you felt *blessed* ... and the people of Caerdroia did so
now.

But longer formalities would have to wait: We were all
too exhausted just then, Companion or Caerdroian, it was
all the same. So much had to be done, too, before Arthur
could ride out as he had said; yet Gweniver and Keils
could not be kept waiting one hour, one *minute*, longer
than must be ...

Still, some things could be dealt with: Arthur swiftly appointed a military governor for Caerdroia, to act in conjoint with a mormaor, last of the City's proud servants, and a council of civil and military officers alike.

As it turned out, there was in Caerdroia a Counterinsurgency presence stronger even than we had dared hope in our wildest ashlings. Warriors, provisioners, armourers, horsemasters, all manner of artisan and artificer, and every one of them keen as wind to do service to Arthur Penarvon. Who, for his part, was a little overwhelmed that so many should be so eager to serve: After so many years of hiding and being hunted, I think all of us found ourselves somewhat daunted, at first, by the unexpected seductiveness of being adored by the folk. Oh, to be sure, the dazzle passed swiftly—being worshipped is hard and thankless work, and leads only to contempt on both sides in the end; much better to meet on equal footing, whether it be one being to another or one to one's god—but for some I fear it never passed entirely, and much sorrow would come of it.

For now, though, we bent all our energies to the relief of the main army, of whom we had had no word since we had gone into the Loom a fortnight since. Time for aught else was scanted; no time even to rest our auxiliars as they so well merited. We the Companions were well used to Arthur's demands, but the regular troops, however battle-hardened otherwise, were not 'customed to such degree of rigor as went with those who went with Arthur. They had shown extraordinary pluck and dash and good humor on the snow-march—which was already legend, a war-tale for the ages (and I had not even had my harp in it; not yet, at least)—but by now they were all but collapsed. Yet there was no slack for any of us: The rope was running taut and swift and near its end, and we must move before the noose caught and held.

There was council that very first night in Turusachan: Arthur, diffident at first, had been persuaded to commandeer the palace for our use, and now we sat—some of us less comfortably than others—in the ancient chamber used for council by Keltia's monarchs for a thousand years and more.

Some had been wondering openly why no galláin had been sent against us, nor yet an attack from space. Edeyrn

still had vast reserves of mercenary outworlders, many
more ships than we had as yet acquired for ourselves;
why had he ventured no throw of either?

Arthur addressed this matter first of all. "Not hard; the
Marbh-draoi wishes to husband his forces for what he
considers the real fight. A space attack would have levelled Caerdroia, and that he does *not* wish, even though
we would surely be levelled with it ... More than that,
such attack can only be made from space; no ships can
fly in air on Tara, save only the smallest aircars. No one
knows why, unless Edeyrn himself knows—but any ship
that tries will crash almost as soon as it clears the ground.
And, for reasons of his own, he chooses not to bombard
from space. So—we fight as we have always fought, and
let us be thankful."

I was only half-listening, as I had heard all this many
times that day alone; but looked around me with considerably more interest. This was a real Council, by gods!
Companions and City folk of rank and consequence all
working together, as had never happened before in all our
years of campaigning. Held in Turusachan's council
chamber, too: Maybe Brendan himself once had stood
where Arthur was even that moment pacing, maybe
Raighne herself had sat in that very chair, Alwen's el-
bows been propped on this very table ...

I came to myself abruptly. One of the City folk, a
woman who had been among the foremost in command,
was speaking to something Betwyr had said.

"You wonder, lord, that the City was so sparse defended? All we here know that had you arrived so much
as three days sooner, you had tens of thousands to deal
with, not hundreds merely."

Arthur nodded somberly. "They have all gone eastwards to the front; well for us, but very hard on our
friends—" He stood up, and the room rose with him.
"Well, though Edeyrn plainly did not think Caerdroia
worth the work of holding, I myself think far otherwise.
If naught else, it will be a sign and beacon to the folk of
Tara and the other worlds. We have taken Caerdroia back
from the Marbh-draoi, and Gwynedd also; and all but retaken Caledon and Erinna, thanks to the efforts of our
Companions Grehan and Aluinn, among others. Who will
soon be rejoining us," he added as he left the chamber.

"They judge those worlds can now be held by their rightful lords, and we need them with us once again. Give you goodnight, sirs and ladies . . ."

I remained awhile, with Morgan and Alannagh and Betwyr and some others, talking to those of our riding who had come to Caerdroia by different ways than ours, acquainting the Caerdroians with Arthur's way of attending to business, simply making friends with the folk of the City.

And so it went, deep into owl-time; but when Morgan and I at last staggered to bed, stupid with fatigue, we saw that the lamp in Arthur's chamber yet burned.

CHAPTER
12

We secured the City for the Counterinsurgency and the High King Uthyr Pendreic in barely five days' time, taking a few days more to rest and resupply ourselves and attend to our hurt and slain; but even Arthur, I think, was surprised at the speed with which things arranged themselves. In truth, though, it was the Caerdroians themselves were chief cause of this ease and quickness, and of the success that followed: Give them the praise, then, for so well did they hold to their own that four separate assaults by Edeyrn's remnant forces were turned away, and not one loss on the side of the defenders.

But that, as I say, came later, after we had marched out: On a cold and cloudy morning halfway to the Wolf-month, Arthur gave command in the City to Betwyr and Alannagh Ruthven, with Aled and a few others of our tried officers to assist. Then, using as much of captured technology as we could master in so short and crammed a time, we led out a prouder and greater army eastwards, to close upon Edeyrn from the rear.

Now any prudent general, when confronted by two perils at the same time, will know it clear duty to dispose first of the greater of the two. Any road, so Arthur had always held; and it was just now by no means certain that Edeyrn even had knowledge of what we had just achieved. But perhaps it was as well for us that the Marbh-draoi was no general, nor even, in the event, particularly prudent . . .

From Caerdroia to Ratherne is twenty-five leagues along the Loom's northern skirts; more, if you take the road that runs by the Avon Dia, a pleasant broad way lined by many country maenors and hill brughs. We took neither, cutting straight across broken country that the two highroads bend to miss, for now it was all our purpose to get to Edeyrn as quickly as we might, and concealment was no longer our concern. We went openly now, and we gathered folk to us as we went; but when we came in sight of Nandruidion, we found to our neverending astonishment that Edeyrn, far from having engaged Gweniver as we had thought he surely must have done—he had had near a month to do it, and all unhindered—was drawn up waiting for us instead.

"Fine for all of *me!*" said Arthur when he saw it, and lowered the spyscope, grinning from ear to ear.

I started as someone gently touched my shoulder; it was Coria Rhikenn, one of the Caerdroian officers that Arthur had permitted to march with us.

"I have not much knowledge of matters in the field," she said apologetically. "Our war in the City was purely strike-and-scurry . . . But Prince Arthur seems *pleased* that the Marbh-draoi has not engaged the army?"

" 'Artos'," I corrected gently, not for the first time, and left it to Tryffin and Morgan to instruct her in our commander's preferences in address. For myself, I was more concerned just now with something troubling in the Marbh-draoi's lines, something strange, something there that should not be, or not there that should, but which in either case was not quite right, though I could not twig it . . .

Then I did, and spoke abruptly, interrupting Tryffin's discourse. "Are we altogether *sure* there has been no fighting here—or anywhere else?"

"Nay," said Morgan, picking up on my unease. "Only that we have heard of none, and so we assumed none had taken place. But we are waiting even now on reports coming in; messengers have been sighted. Why do you ask?"

I shook my head and stared back over the distant enemy lines. "No reason; only that that below"—I pointed to the Theocracy ranks—"looks to me like an army halved, or an army chastened elsewhere."

When the messengers arrived at last, we learned that it was both.

"Second Moytura, they are calling it," said a jubilant Daronwy, who had, with my old teacher Elphin Carannoc, carried the news all the way from Gweniver's own hands. "And *that* is why Edeyrn waits here for you, Artos; we destroyed his galláin groundtroops six days since."

She drank off a quaich of ale someone had thrust into her hands, continued in a lower, calmer voice.

"And 'destroyed' is indeed the word, as Elphin—for all his native bardic caution—will well attest."

Elphin grinned at us all and quirked a brow at me. "Caution is no bad thing, even in bardery; but still . . . We met them at the very same place as our first encounter"— every eye in the room went covertly to Arthur, but his face did not change at this reminder of his first great strategic blunder, or the memory of what it had cost him— "and all that went so wrong for us then this time did go so right that I could scarce credit it."

"Galláin? Of what kind?" That was Morgan.

"Fomori mostly, some Fir Bolg," replied Daronwy. "And I would not be so sure to think we have seen the last of them, Artos, for all we routed them here and now—"

"All in its hour," said Arthur, and I could tell by his voice that he knew something the rest of us did not; though now was not the time to ask him of it.

"Dán for sure," Elphin was saying. "But Gwennach merits all praise; aye, and Keils. Had they not carried the day at Moytura you would now be facing all Edeyrn's massed groundforce here at Ratherne, not merely half as is the case. Which half is still formidable, never think for a minute it is not."

"Oh aye?" came a voice from the rear of the tent. "And whyso?"

Daronwy answered, her dark eyes thoughtful as they rested on Arthur. "It is almost entirely Ravens—and Owein Rheged leads them."

Arthur leaned back a little in his chair, and our glances

met. Owein, our old nemesis—and yet it seemed to me right that it had come to this.

To Arthur too, seemingly ... "Most fitting," he said lightly, "that our first foe should also be our last."

Well enough if that were true; but for myself I was not so sure, and voiced my concern to him later that night, when the last of the staff command had gone and we were alone in the tent.

"You were better pleased earlier, I think," I said accusingly, "when you believed that Gwennach had not even fought the Marbh-draoi, much less won. What is *on* you? Do you still grudge her a triumph or two? She is by no means your equal in the field, Artos, but she has ever been a fine commander. And Keils—"

"Aye, well for them," said Arthur shortly, cutting me off and leaping to his feet so quickly he all but tripped over Cabal, curled up as usual beside his master's chair. Avoiding my eyes, he went over to the table to pour himself some ale; finding the keeve empty, he turned again with a mild oath and looked me in the face at last.

"I wished to have won here without need of Gweniver and the army," he said slowly. "Not for glory! But if we fail here, then they must pull back to safety and carry on; and of all matters in the balance just now, it is Uthyr's safety is the most important matter of any."

"Is it?" I heard myself asking. "*Is* it most important, Artos, and is it in truth as important as you would have us think?" As his angry protest lashed out: "Nay, Artos, this is *I* you speak to, I Taliesin, not a breastling Companion nor yet some green-awed Caerdroian but your foster-brother who knows you *well*! Now I love Uthyr as much and as deeply as do you or Guenna, but let us face facts here: The most important matter is *winning*. We have staked all on this Taran throw—we could have dug in on Gwynedd and fought for *years* from that safety; but nay, we chose the risk of taking war to the other worlds."

"And we have been well repaid for that risk." His tone was almost a question, and it hurt my heart to hear him sound so unsure.

"Aye. Aye, we have," I said after a pause, more gently. "But we have done so for one reason only: to defeat Edeyrn. And it makes no differ how that shall be done, so long as it *is* done. And less differ who it shall be that does it . . . If Uthyr dies for it, if *we* die for it, no matter; and if you must accept Gweniver as your equal on the field, if it is but half an army we now face because of her great victory, then be it so! I had not thought you so small-souled as that, but perhaps I was wrong."

Arthur's face had flushed slow red and paled again as I spoke; now he dropped his glance before mine, and flung himself back into his chair without speaking. Well, it would be he spoke first, I had said all *my* say . . .

When he did not, I turned on my heel and left the tent.

After the snows that had choked the Loom valleys on our westward march, the present weather seemed like Briginda's own spring: Storms had come whipping in all day off the Western Ocean, nipping at one another's heels down the throat of the Great Glen, far inland past Nandruidion. Though the air was cool and fresh, there had been a glint that day in the wind's eye, and now as night fell that glancing light took on visible form.

As I plodded from Arthur's tent to my own, Cabal having taken it into his huge shaggy head to accompany me, the greatest storm of the day was rushing down upon us, so fast that we could feel the breath of its oncoming like fingers upon our faces. I flung myself, not a moment too soon, into my empty tent—late as it by now was, Morgan was yet out upon some errand of her own—and huddled there unhappily, as far back as its altogether inadequate depth allowed, while the storm broke overhead.

It is a shameful thing to have to confess to, but I have a fear of thunderstorms better seen in a five-year-old than a fifty-year-old. A thing left over from some long-forgotten scareful storm of childhood, or maybe from some other life, I do not know; but when the low rolling mutter comes along the valley, or cracks short and tremendous in the height of heaven, I feel a terror such as I have never felt even in the worst battles of my life.

So it was that I huddled and shivered now, flinching at every booming crack, muffled even as most of it was, up in the mountains where the rain still fell as snow. Only a spring storm, I told myself over and over, far from uncommon round Brighnasa here in this northern part of Tara . . . After a while Cabal came to sit with me—dogs hate and fear thunderstorms even more than do I—and I gratefully threw my arm around his warm solid frame, and we shook together as the rain poured down.

The next morning was clear and bright; the wind had dried the rain-soaked ground, and it was colder than it had been, more the cold of early spring than late winter.

I had not seen Arthur since our little brangle of the previous evening, and by the time I awoke he had gone off with Tarian and some others to inspect the lines. As a rule I had ever been included in all such parties, and the fact that—today of all days!—I had not been so summoned stung more than a little.

Morgan rolled her eyes at my complaint. "No great matter! If you are feeling left out, let you come with me on my own errand."

"Where?" I said sulkily. "And whyfor?"

"Well, the 'where' is up the dalehead, to spy out the approaches to Nandruidion; and the 'whyfor' goes without saying."

In spite of my resolve to sulkiness, I brightened at the prospect. Indeed, the going was its own excuse: We had no real knowledge of Edeyrn's dispositions in this region; Ratherne was all we knew for sure. There might well be hidden outposts along the Loom-edge, or high up in the remote folds of the dale country. Or not—we had not encountered any on our force-march, at least; but we did not know, and it would be best for us to learn, one way or the other, and as quickly as we might.

So Morgan and I rode out an hour later, with a word to the watch as to our going, and that we went by Arthur's express command. She waved us off cheerfully; behind us, the campment was as all such are on eve of battle—alert, alive, not merry or pleased, perhaps, but with a sort of vibrancy running through it, a quivering note just below the power of the human ear to sense.

For myself, I was glad to be shut of it awhile, and (most secretly) gladder still not to have to face Arthur just yet. The storm had not blown away my ill humor of the day before; and knowing my fostern as I did I guessed that his mood stood much the same as mine. Morgan, riding easily on my right, was far and away the best companion I could have found for the day; and little did I think how glad I should soon be to have her with me—for reasons I could never have dreamed.

We had been riding perhaps two hours, going slowly and carefully up the length of the little glen, a ridge or two west of Nandruidion itself. It was a gentle, still place—we surprised foxes unconcernedly trotting about in full daylight, fat bramblings, in their patchy winter plumage like rust-splotched snow, swinging on black branches, even a badger humbly crossing the one track that wound up into the very dalehead. A minor place, all but nameless: The local folk called it Butterdale, for the richness of its summer grazing, but it appeared on no map; chiefly of note to us for its proximity to Nandruidion. And, not for the first time, I wondered, and my wondering led me to ask.

"Did Birogue ever tell you why the Marbh-draoi should choose to dwell in so remote a place as Nandruidion, and not at Turusachan? Or even at any other strong place, for surely he had his pick of homes, once Keltia was his to choose from."

Morgan brushed back a wisp of gold hair from her eyes. "There have been prophecies about Nandruidion from the earliest days of Keltia," she said. "Prophecies that a great battle shall one day be fought here, with the strongest magic Keltia shall yet have seen; and whoso is victor that day shall drive out the enemy forever. Therefore did Edeyrn build Ratherne here, so that he could sit in the middle of Nandruidion and wait for it."

"Thinking himself to be that victor," I said, disgusted; was there no end to the man's vainglory? "Well—small hope to him, then!"

Morgan smiled. "Smaller hope than he may imagine: The prophecies Birogue spoke of to me said all alike— that that victor shall be a woman. Indeed, she shall be a Queen of Kelts."

I turned in my saddle, surprised and about to question her further, when all at once the air shimmered and misted and darkened around me. My horse, the everplacid Meillion, reared screaming, and came back to earth to stand four-footed and shivering. I was trembling myself, and not least for that I could not see Morgan at all. Everything looked alike, there seemed no distinction or difference any way I turned, only a haze over the walls of the glen, or perhaps the veil was over my eyes instead.

In terror more for Morgan than for myself I rode forward—with greatest difficulty, as Meillion in his own terror was stiff-legged and white-eyed, and did not wish to stir even under my heels. But the view, or lack of view, was the same in all directions. I shouted for Morgan until my voice cracked like a bell and woke the echoes, but no answer came, and then not even echoes; and when at last the hands reached up to seize me, the unseen hands, I struggled a little for pride's sake, that they should not take me down without a fight. But I was almost thankful and relieved to give in.

When I came to myself again I was most definitely not in Butterdale; that much was immediately plain. I was lying on a softly cushioned couch, in a chamber of what appeared to be a castle. A spacious chamber too, well and richly appointed, judging by what I could perceive from my limited vantage: tapestries, carvings, gilt and furs and plate. And since no castle lay within a day's ride in any direction, no castle save one only—

Ratherne ... I was not aware I had spoken aloud—indeed, I was certain I had not—but whoever it was that now replied had quite clearly heard me, one way or another.

"Ratherne," said the voice, agreeing with my observation; and the voice was deep and pleasant, modulated with a bard's own skill. "Clever of you to see so swiftly—though of course I should expect no less from Taliesin Pen-bardd."

I sat up carefully; my head was pounding and my inner ear was roiled and jangled. The haze upon my sight was gone now, my vision was clear again. *Indeed, all too clear* ...

Across the room, a man stood at the tall lancet window—a keen-cut silhouette against the light, it was yet full day without; then, as he turned and bent his gaze upon me, my whole being seemed to turn to stone. Or wished it could, for the man was Edeyrn Marbh-draoi himself, and we were alone in the chamber.

"Stand up," he said then; and it was less a command than an invitation.

When my legs failed to raise me at once, he snapped an impatient hand at me, and I found myself rising to my feet like a feather on a puff of air. I frankly stared at him, and he smiled a little at my open regard.

He was no smallest whit changed from that memorable night at Caer Dathyl, what was it, fifteen years since. Well, from all reports he had not changed overmuch in two centuries, certain sure fifteen or twenty years were not about to do it . . . Tall; dark hair to his shoulders; eyes of a shade between gray and hazel, deep-set, less dark than I had thought them. And though I tried mightily to keep my mind from that way turning, I found my thought going unerringly to Gwyn ap Nudd (say rather Gwyn ap Seli!), half-brother to this—this—

"Tyrant?" he suggested, still in the tones of utmost courtesy. "Regicide? Duergar-king? Marbh-draoi? I have heard them all before, you know . . ." He seemed to read my thought as easily as if it had been printed upon my forehead in letters of fire; my best defenses, as Druid and bard, seemed no better against him than the littlest un-taught child's; and I would *not* think of Guenna . . .

But if he had heard my thought of Gwyn he chose not to speak to it just yet. A door opened somewhere behind me, though I refused to turn to look. But suddenly it was as if a window had been thrown open in a stifling room and a great fresh clean blast of air was pouring through: With a thrill of joy and terror alike, I knew Morgan's presence, and turned with a cry as she strode past me.

"I could not find you in the mist," I blurted out. "You did not get away, then—"

"I was not trying to," she said tartly. She did not look much like a prisoned princess: Her hair was smooth as ever, her garb unruffled, and she moved with all her own grace and a confidence that was somehow even more than her own—and that own was considerable. With scarce a glance at me and none at all at Edeyrn, she chose the most regal chair in the chamber, seated herself as if by right and laid her arms along the arms of the chair, as would a queen in the throne of her House.

"Pray be seated, Princess Morguenna," said Edeyrn with a slight bow. "And you also, Lord Taliesin; I should not care to have an aer made on me, that I failed of wel-come to an ollave—a true ollave. Your father once sat with me, here, in this room," he added as apparent after-thought, and my breath went out of me as if I had been gut-punched.

"And was it here you killed him, also?" I asked presently, and felt the tiny touch of Morgan's silent warning.

"Nay," said Edeyrn, and he did not seem to gloat over it, though his eyes had gone to smoke-color. "That was in the Great Hall below, before my court. He should not have defied me, Taliesin, he knew well what defiance would cost him."

"And Gwaelod?" I asked, when I could speak again. "Did Gwaelod count that cost too, before you drowned it?"

He looked genuinely puzzled for a moment, as if he did not recognize the name, nor even comprehend my anger and pain.

"Ah," he said then. "I had forgotten—"

My wrath redoubled. "So many drowned provinces you can scarce keep track of them, is that it? And Daars—oh, but Daars was burned and not drowned; did you weary of water and think to give fire a try? What next? A cam-anfa, maybe, to spin Arthur's army down the dale like leaves in autumn, or a—"

"Taliesin." That was Morgan, and I knew that voice of old. I bit back my words only by dint of biting my lip so hard the blood came, but I stayed silent as she did bid me; and Morgan looked at Edeyrn, and Edeyrn looked at her. She did this, I knew, only to gain me time to calm myself, lest the Marbh-draoi grow irritated and think to make a clean sweep of Gwaelod after all. Well, one Glyndour had already perished in Ratherne, no disgrace for me to follow him . . . But the inner hand I closed over my fury was one of the greatest achievements of my life.

When I could see again, hear again, Morgan was conversing pleasantly with our host. Incredibly, it sounded like shop-talk: two master craftsmen comparing notes on their trade in the presence of one less skilled than they, and unlike ever to attain to their level of mastery. (And, of course, they would have been quite right to think so . . .)

"—a stray-sod!" Morgan was saying, with what sounded almost like admiration. "But no other place-magic is like to it. I did not know you had Ratherne so well defended."

Then of course I knew what the strange hazy mist had been, why my senses had been so outraged, back there in Butterdale ... The stray-sod is an old, old magic, some say even from Earth, and the way of it is this: A single piece of turf is cut from the green growing earth of a field, and magicked, then replaced where it was cut; and any living creature who sets foot or hoof or claw or paw upon it has its sense of direction utterly taken from it. All things look alike in all airts; no matter how one may turn there is never a way out, naught looks familiar, all is mist. Even beasts are deceived by the stray-sod, as Meillion and Morgan's Nyfer had been; and there are tales of folk caught by this ill-omened turf wandering for days in the same field, unable even to find their way to a gate in plain view, perishing of thirst and exhaustion within sight of help they could not see.

Edeyrn was nodding complacently. "One of the simpler tricks," he said. "If little used in these less simple days ... But why do we discuss peasant-magics, Domina?"—giving Morgan her Ban-draoi title—"We have other things to speak of, and I did not bring you both here for simple revenge."

I had by now recovered myself, if not my manner. "Nay, let me guess! You have need of us to serve as messengers."

"Oddly enough, that is exactly right ..." Edeyrn was silent a moment, and suddenly I saw the—the *weight* of him, the force, the massive intelligence. Not like Merlynn's, who was quicker, sharper—as the Fians say, a mind like a laighen, where Edeyrn's for all its force was more a mataun. But I saw too (and feared of the seeing) that for all that, the Marbh-draoi's mind was sharp enough.

Nevertheless he seemed unaware of my thought, for he spoke more slowly now. "Out of his honor—or perhaps out of his traha—Arthur Penarvon returned my heir to me. No matter his motive; Owein Rheged is all the son that I shall ever have, and his son shall be my heir after him. Aye indeed do I wish you to carry a message to him; and not to him alone but also to Merlynn Llwyd your teacher."

And then I remembered: how once Merlynn had told us of the Pheryllt, those Druids above Druids, and that the chief of the Pheryllt, the Ro-sai, the Great Teacher, had been one time Edeyrn himself.

He saw that I knew, and smiled; and the smile all but drew me in. "You are wondering, Taliesin, how it was that I turned my back on all that; how came it that I betrayed my once-brothers and my friend and my King. Shall I tell you why? Why I chose to put an end to the House of Dôn?"

Morgan shivered convulsively, once, from head to toe, and I saw that she was only just managing to bear Edeyrn's presence, though she had kept this well hid until now. But—gifted with senses the Marbh-draoi's Sidhe kin trained up to match their own—she was feeling the evil of him far more keenly than I . . .

"Nay," she said with a smile of the greatest serenity, "you have *not* put an end to the House of Dôn."

Edeyrn laughed outright. "True enough! You and your brother and your cousin do still exist, to trouble my peace; the King your father, not so much longer now, I think. That wound of his—"

Morgan had doubtless known all along, but I am slower and stupider, and so it was only now that light broke . . . "It was *you,* by Owein's hand!" I cried out unheeding. "You used Owein, by magic, to give Uthyr his wound—he let us to believe it was his own magic, dearly learned and bought, but it was you all along, not so?"

"So." Edeyrn nodded once in assent. "And before you leave here, there is someone of your acquaintance wishes to greet you, whom you have not seen for long . . ." He sat back in his chair, sent out a silent call. Morgan and I, unheeded for the moment, glanced at one another: What fresh hell was *this*? And whom could the Marbh-draoi be speaking of?

We soon had answer to both queries. For the chamber door opened again, and in the doorway stood Gwenwynbar. By her side was a half-grown boy, tall, thin, wiry, with a shock of red-brown hair.

For once even Morgan was surprised; but I was not so much so, not myself. In truth I had been half-expecting her to turn up: Gwenwynbar had been too invisible too long to have been hidden by any lesser shield than

Edeyrn's own. As to her seeming: Well, she appeared much the same as when I last had seen her, one time at Caer Dathyl, in the hard days of my service to her lord Owein, when I called myself Mabon Dialedd, before Arthur had come to take me with him at last, north to Collimare.

She looked well, even I must say so. Her form was slim as ever, her skin even milkier, but still there was there that same—*overness* about her: the overpainted face and overdone jewels and overflaunting garb and over-red hair and overbearing manner. There is no whoredom in Keltia, we have long since grown beyond that vile demeaning traffic; but if there were, then Gwenwynbar Rospaen would have been a prime exemplar.

She ignored Morgan completely, but looked at me and smiled that old slow smile of hers, the one that had ever made me think of the annic, slim and white, that most deadly of snakes. Though Kelts have ever held the serpent race in honor, calling the wise snake of the rock by a name near to father and teacher, revering it for its prudence and sleight, we find naught about the annic to be clean or good or wholesome, and I ever felt the same about Gwenwynbar. And I marvelled yet again that Arthur had taken her to his bed and to his heart.

My glance went to the boy at her side, and seeing my attention upon him Gwenwynbar drew him protectively closer. He shrugged out from under her confining arm, and took a step forward, unmindful of Edeyrn's amused malice flickering flamelike in the room, his wide dark eyes moving back and forth between Morgan and me. Well, whoever's son he might be, at least the lad was no coward nor milksop either, had a mind of his own and did not fear to show it. I smiled at him, but he remained wary; then all at once some duergar took me, and I spoke in the tones of a herald.

"Hail, kinsman! Malgan Pendreic ap Arthur—" And as I said it I looked neither at the boy nor his mother nor Morgan beside me, but straight at Edeyrn.

It well repaid the risk and the watching both: Edeyrn's face changed like that little lizard, the mankeeper, that out of need for protection and concealment takes upon itself the appearance of its very surroundings. And Edeyrn at this moment was as gray as the stone walls of his chamber ... But the thought that the Marbh-draoi Edeyrn, supreme ruler of Keltia and of Kelts for two hundred years, should feel the need for either seemed too strange even for me to think upon.

Gwenwynbar had not noticed this, but kept her baleful glance trained upon Morgan and me.

" 'Pendreic'!" she snarled. "Not in your brother's dearest dreams, Glyndour, Morguenna! *My* son is Owein's heir of Rheged, heir after him to Keltia, and you may tell Arthur so from me at your leisure!"

Morgan made as if to reply, but Edeyrn, his face now once again the impassive ivory mask it had been for the past hour, spoke first, and spoke mockingly.

"Before you take your leave, guests of my house, tell me of my kin in the Hollow Mountains. Stands Sychan as it did?"

In spite of my surprise to hear Edeyrn speak before Gwenwynbar of his connection with the Shining Folk, I did not answer, and Morgan too was silent. This was yet one more play, still another diversion: But it had come to me in that moment why we had in truth been brought here, and why we were to be let go unharmed. Oh, not for Edeyrn's gloating, nor to be used as hostages, nor to have our thoughts kenned against our will; nor to answer this diversionary query, a shock tactic if ever I had known one; nor yet to carry messages back to Arthur—though all these were of course part of it. Nay, we had been brought here for one reason above all these reasons: to see Malgan and Gwenwynbar. That was the *real* message we were to take with us from Ratherne; and yet—and yet—

He saw that I wondered, and nodded. "Oh aye, Glyndour, there is indeed more! Tell Arthur Pendreic, and Merlynn my onetime comrade, and Gwyn my brother, and Uthyr whom you are pleased to call your King, that there is another: one whom I myself have instructed, one who has sat at my feet to learn skills and secrets, one whom I have raised up so that all they may be thrown down. And even should I be myself destroyed in the fight to come, or all of them perish likewise, this one I have taught may live to rule Keltia in their despite, and raise an heir to follow."

I did not like this one littlest bit, for I heard the truth in it; and stealing a glance at Gwenwynbar I could see she liked it still less. She seemed genuinely thunderstruck by this revelation, or at least by one part of it: the part about this unknown pupil of the Marbh-draoi coming to rule Keltia, and with an heir too. And I wondered very privately just whom was the real message intended for here: No throne for Malgan after all, no matter what his mother had done to win him one? Or was this merely another ploy of Edeyrn's, lest Gwenwynbar should grow too presumptuous in her role as mother of Owein's—or whoever's—heir?

Which of course still left the larger question: Just who was this student whose name the Marbh-draoi would not speak? Plainly Gwenwynbar knew, or at least strongly suspected; but Morgan and I were frankly baffled. Whom could Edeyrn have taught, and how, and where and when, that none of us, not even Merlynn, should have known of it?

But we were destined to know no more of it, at least not then: It seemed that Edeyrn had grown suddenly weary of his little game, for guards entered as at a silent signal, led us away without another word from the Marbh-draoi, put us on our thoroughly unsettled horses and escorted us the short distance down Nandruidion to the mouth of the glen. Here they left us; and, under a white pennon, we made our way back across the debatable ground between the two armies with remarkable haste; the horses just as eager as we to get home.

But something was naggling at my mind's edge, something Edeyrn had said—or maybe had *not* said—there in the tower room; and as Morgan and I galloped knee to knee for the safety of our own lines, in the rhythmic pounding of the horses' hoofs it suddenly came clear.

In his taunting, the Marbh-draoi had spoken of the end he would put to the House of Dôn, had named Morgan and Arthur and Gweniver and Uthyr. 'You and your brother and your cousin,' he had said, and 'the King your father.' And in our confusion and loathing, the aftereffects of the stray-sod and our own long hatred, to Morgan and to me the great omission had not then been apparent.

Well, it was now, and all too plain ... In his enumeration of the Dôniaid to whom he would so boastfully put an end, the Marbh-draoi had not once spoken the name of

Uthyr's other daughter—the Princess Marguessan, Morgan's own twin.

"Nay," said Morgan quietly, later, when I spoke of this to her in the privacy of our tent. Her eyes were bleak and set for distance, as if her Sight beheld some terrible future that could not be averted will she or nill she.

"Nay," she said again. "Nor yet the name of her son—my nephew—Mordryth."

CHAPTER
13

Though by tacit consent neither Morgan nor I spoke our dread to Arthur just then—he had too much already with which to deal, and it had also occurred to us that to speak ill of Marguessan might be precisely what Edeyrn had intended all along, further to fragment the Pendreic kindred—we went straightway to tell him of all the rest; and when we had finished and were looking at him in silence, he steepled his fingers, tapped them twice in Merlynn's old gesture, and looked right back at us.

"Quite an adventure."

I was furious. "Oh, do you not *dare* to take that tack with *me*, Artos, or I shall swat you into the middle of next sevennight! Does it mean naught to you, that we have been in Ratherne, have spoken to Edeyrn—"

"—have seen Gwenwynbar and Malgan," he finished for me, with a sad weary impatience. "Much. It means much." Abruptly Arthur rose from his field-chair and began to pace; from where he was comfortably curled beneath his master's desk, Cabal drew in his paws lest they be inadvertently trodden upon.

"But even so, it is naught for me to act upon just now," he added after a while. "We have Ravens to face, and after them galláin, maybe, and after them Edeyrn certainly. That is enough enemies for the moment, surely. Let it rest there."

All this time Arthur had been careful to keep his face turned away from us, and that too I found significant. I glanced at Morgan, but caught only the tent flap closing behind her and the echo of her thought: *Better I leave the lads to settle it between themselves ...*

Many thanks, lady!, I sent wryly after her, and turned again to Arthur.

He was not ready for me: Terror washed through me at the gray weariness of his face, and, worse, of his soul. Arthur Penarvon, who never had looked so in all the years I had known him, even in defeat, looked beaten, and my fear redoubled.

He glanced up at me, knowing that I saw. "How can I fight with weapons that snap in my hand?"

"What are you saying?" I demanded, with rather more bluster than was usual for me. "Your weapons are far from broken, Artos, and even if they were, still your hand is heavier than most. Nay, braud, you are only weary. So would anyone be, man or woman or Shining One, who has done what you have done since we have come to Tara."

That brought a smile from him. "A good try—but all the rest of you have done as much, and more, and do not feel so."

I took his arm and led him like an unresisting child out of the tent, flinging a cloak round him as I did so and pulling close my own.

"All the rest of us have you to depend upon, that is why we do not feel so and why you do. Walk a little with me."

The walk became a two-hour perambulation round and about the leaguer. By now it was nearly dark, with low gray clouds hurrying by just above our heads, and it was raining again, a hard rain mixed with sleet and snowstones whipped along by a vicious east wind. But for pure shame's sake I dared not suggest we turn back, nor even lag a little as we walked; though the wetter and colder I grew the more the thought of a fine warm dry tent and something hot to eat came uppermost in my mind.

Which Arthur of course knew very well ...

"It was your idea we walked a bit," he observed blandly. "Come along then, ollave."

"To what purpose?" I snarled, for by now I was peevish and frozen and very wet indeed.

"Is it cross, then?" crooned Arthur. "Is it tired? Ah, the poor bodach—"

I turned furiously to meet his eyes, sparkling and warm with merry malice in the flaring torchlight—in that perishing cold rain, quite the warmest things around—and began to laugh in spite of myself.

"By gods but you are a wicked man, Arthur Penarvon, and you will deserve what you shall get."

"Well enough," he answered comfortably, all traces of his earlier mood vanished into the windy darkness. "So long as I get what I deserve ..."

We were passing Uthyr's tent, and the Fian guards outside the door rattled a salute. Arthur absently returned their duty, but it was not until we were once again indoors—my tent, not his; Morgan was not there, though, not at all to my surprise, Merlynn was—that he began once more to speak openly.

"This battle shall be the test of me," he said without preamble. "As both you well know ... All else has but led up to this day and hour: Gwynedd, Moytura, Sychan, Caerdroia, even Gwennach's great victory—all have been but prelude. The main theme is yet to be stated."

"Perhaps that is why the Marbh-draoi sought to distract you," I offered hesitantly. "With Gwenwynbar and with Malgan—it may be his thought was that you might hold from attacking Ratherne, did you know your onetime wife and her son were within."

Arthur laughed shortly. "Edeyrn does not keep them as hostages against Ratherne's investing, nor yet against his own safety; he has deeper plans than that. Besides, I would wager any stake you like that they have already been taken to a place of greater safety far from here. He would not risk them both so near to me."

"And Owein?" I asked presently.

Across the tent, Merlynn stirred, a quiet presence in his gray robes. "His course is all but run; as is his master's."

I stared frankly at our old teacher, and he looked back half-smiling. Since the leaving of Gwynedd, Merlynn Llwyd had taken but little active role in the great campaign; indeed, since Cadarachta he had kept to himself. He had been for the most part silent in all our councils, though Arthur and Gweniver both had consulted him as often as ever in private; maybe even more often than ever, as the fight for Tara took its strange turns.

But as I looked on him now I wondered if the source of his present certainty came from other knowledge; from sources, let us say, less mortal than might usually be ...

"Patience, Talynno," he murmured. "You will know all in time."

"In time, aye," I agreed. "But in *whose* time?"

Arthur laughed. "You sound like Guenna."

"Aye so," said Merlynn comfortably. "And she is one to ask, do you need further proofs."

I glanced up, as if at a sudden absence, or awareness of absence. "Where *is* Guenna? I have not seen her since we came back from Ratherne."

"She prepares for battle in her own fashion." When I looked my need for further knowledge: "She speaks to the Lady, she and her priestesses; to the High Dânu, and perhaps to the Shining Ones also—did you think the storm had come on its own out of the east?"

Well, Merlynn would know about that better than would I ... "And Gwennach?" I asked; but had no answer forth coming.

It was a good and thorny question: I had seen but little of Gweniver since her army, fresh from victory at Moytura, had come up on Edeyrn's other side. She had dared only one visit round the Raven lines, and that a flying one: some hurried speech with her uncle the King, some deep consulting with Morgan and Ygrawn—as priestess to priestesses—and a bitter brangle with Arthur, as to the use of the Bratach Bán in the coming fight.

When I got to the faerie flag Merlynn deigned to reply. "She is doing as she must be doing. But it will be her choice"—this more sternly, and to Arthur—"to unfurl the Bratach Bán. Even though we may stand in deep need of the help it can bring us, may not win without it, even— still it must be Gwennach's choice and hers alone."

Just how much it was her choice, we learned next morning, when she and Arthur met again before the battle was joined.

We had ridden out to join her and Keils and two or three of their generals, on a little knoll well removed from the battle-plain below. Myself, Morgan, Tarian,

Tryffin, Coria Rhikenn the Caerdroian leader: no more than that. Ygrawn the Queen remained with Uthyr and Merlynn below.

We listened as Arthur gave order for battle—he was yet Rex Bellorum, and even Gweniver was bound to obey his commandings—then heard Keils's comment and advising; no surprises there, and Arthur himself modified an order or two according to the advice the longtime warlord gave.

The surprise came from Gweniver herself, and of us all I think that only Morgan, and maybe Ygrawn, had seen it coming . . .

Arthur had spoken of the Bratach Bán, that Gweniver should have it with her in case of need, for need he deemed there would be. "And when it comes time for you to wave it to summon its help—"

"—I shall *not* be so summoning." Gweniver's words, clipped though unemphatic, cut across Arthur's like a sgian.

He took it squarely on. "If you do not, lady, then all we have fought for so long is lost."

"Then it is lost!" she snapped. "But if I do"—and here her voice grew calm again—"then you shall release me from my promise to wed you. The rest of the contract we swore to between the King's hands shall stand as before—that we shall rule conjointly—but this I swear, Artos: I *will* not wed. Not with you; maybe not with any."

Silence then, in which far below us the sounds of the armies readying for the fight floated up to our ears. Arthur flexed his fingers in the old gesture of stressfulness and strain he had had since boyhood, then sighed.

"And if I so consent, and if you see the need or have my order for it, you will employ the flag? I have your royal word on it?"

Gweniver smiled, and laid her open hand over her heart as pledge of her oath.

"Be it so."

"So be it," said Arthur, matching her gesture. He gathered us with his gaze, and we rode with him back to our lines, while behind us Gweniver and Keils and the rest returned to theirs. Though none dared question Arthur as to why he had agreed, and so readily as it seemed, after a few minutes I moved Meillion up to ride leg to leg with him, should he feel the need or wish to, you know, talk.

"If I had not," he said at once, though I had posed no heard query, "she would have kept that scrap of silk beneath her baldric until Beltain came in winter . . . I cannot take that chance, Talyn."

"And the chance you take now? If you two do not wed as Uthyr did bid you—"

"It is the least ill of my ill choosings. This way, we shall win the fight—well, if such is our dán—and still come to rule Keltia as joint sovereigns, if not as wedded mates. It will be no great sorrow for either of us."

He did not look at me as he said this, and I believe it was just then—watching him as he rode, eyes straight ahead, fixed on field and future, that I first knew Arthur Penarvon loved Gweniver Pendreic.

Not that it mattered so much just then: We had a battle to fight. And before that, Arthur had something perhaps even more frightening to face: He had to tell his mother and his uncle of what he had just done.

Standing there before their tent, where the King lay in a litter attended by his Queen—Uthyr had determined to be witness to the battle if he had to crawl to the field, and Ygrawn had relented so far as to allow the litter—Arthur told them both of his promise to Gweniver. He spoke as if it had been his own wish and thought to release her from the vow, and though Ygrawn had eyed her son suspiciously, Uthyr had accepted at once the word of his nephew and war-leader, and spoke no word of blame. Indeed:

"Ah well, perhaps it is for the best after all, Artos. When the time comes for it, both you and she will have the freedom to choose as your hearts will have it. As for the succession, the more branches bear, the stronger-rooted will be the tree—the House of Dôn has need of many seedlings."

Arthur bowed in silence, and left Uthyr's presence; and I went with him. We mounted our horses in silence, and in silence rode down the lines.

"So much for *that*," he said presently.

"But do you not think—" I began.

"Nay, I do *not*! May I not get on the other side of this

small matter with Edeyrn, before I am once more taxed
with what I think or do not think?"

I raised my brows and murmured ironic apology; he
flushed, and after a moment turned to me with an air of
chastenment.

"My sorrow, braud—"

"Naught to sorrow for," I returned. "Though there will
be, soon or late . . ."

Maybe sooner even than I thought; no sooner had I
spoken than Arthur, looking out ahead across the debatable ground between the armies, stood in his irons, then
grabbed a white pennon from a nearby tentpole, impaled
it on a spear and rode forward at a gallop. I went with
him, and as we went I desperately waved a few others to
join us: Coria, Daronwy, Tryffin.

But where was Arthur headed in his mad dash?
Meillion labored to keep up with the far fleeter Miaren;
indeed, Arthur was already some five lengths in front of
us all and pulling away, as if it were a racemeet he rode
in and not to a parley.

Then, as we drew near to the first lines, I saw, and
understood . . .

Owein Rheged, red hair stirring in the light breeze
where he had unhelmed at our approach, looked impassively on me, then slid his glance to Arthur. Save that this
time it was he who stood afoot, and Arthur who had ridden beneath the white flag, it was as it had been at
Cadarachta. Even the words were not unlike, though this
time it was Owein who spoke first.

"Arthur," he said, "forbid thy lions."

And I felt some great galactic balance shift and shudder around me, in that instant; and in that instant I knew
that we had won.

"Owein," said Arthur, "play thy game."

They gazed upon one another for the space of ten
heartbeats; then Arthur had swung Miaren round and was
galloping once again for our own lines. *Was it worth the
risk?* I sent to him with irritation and all the fear of the
last five minutes. *Just to plague him?*

But no answer came.

If you have thought to hear some tale of grandeur and
glory, this account of the fight at Nandruidion may disap-

point. Oh, to be sure, there was gallantry and valor goleor, and on both sides: Owein's Ravens fought with honor that would have been better seen in a better cause, and we fought as we ever fought. The difference here was that though we went into each fight as if it were our last, Owein's Ravens knew this to be theirs. Still, it came not easy for either side; not victory, not defeat.

For one thing, it was purely Ravens we faced here, where in our other battles it had been Ravens and auxiliars together. For another, Owein—presumably at Edeyrn's order—had help from space: The remnant of the hired galláin, Fomori and Fir Bolg mercenaries, had retreated to their ships under Gweniver's goad at Second Moytura; but they had not left Taran space, and now they stood off—again, presumably on order from the Marbhdraoi who had purchased their services—to rake our lines with fire from shipboard sun-guns, space cannon that we, planetside, could not combat.

Well for us that we still had ships not far off that could: Grehan Aoibhell, fresh from his triumph on Erinna, had brought a force in the last week or so, to act in just such case; as they did now. And most effectively, but not before we had suffered many losses.

"Artos," I asked, watching with helpless pain as Companions and auxiliars alike died beneath that fire from the sky, "may we not ask help where it is most needed?" When he made no reply: "Let not your traha win over you, to lose the battle!"

His mouth moved a little at the corners, but still he would not give the order I knew he must give soon, else we were lost: Gweniver must wave the Bratach Bán, to summon help from the Sidhe as had been promised. And so it was that I disobeyed my prince and friend and fostern . . .

Muttering some excuse, I backed Meillion and spurred back through the lines. Had I given any real thought to what I was about to attempt, I should have instead gone screaming into my tent, to hide my folly beneath a blanket or table or pillow; but I did not. Rather, I turned Meillion's head to the Raven lines, and began a flanking movement of my own, that would, with luck and dán riding with me, bring me past the enemy to where Gweniver and Keils were beginning to close in from the east.

Before you say what I know well you are thinking—
before you *think* it, even—let me confess freely that I had
for that moment lost my senses. More, it was a liberating
loss: I never felt so free, before or since, as I did feel riding breakneck past Ravens who struck at me and my
horse. We were wingèd, we were invisible, we could not
be touched—only the grace that shields fools and the
hand of the Lady Herself brought us both through without
a hurt, and when I think back on it now, in cold blood, it
makes my blood go colder still . . .

I was, of course, riding to give Gweniver the order to
unfurl the faerie flag: the order, you will of course be protesting, that Arthur had not given. That was the heart of
the disobeying; for when at the end of the longest hour of
my life I reached Gweniver and Keils, I lied, and told her
that by the terms of her promise, Arthur did order her to
use the Bratach Bán.

"And so that the order carry truth and weight," I went
on lying blithely, "Artos did send me to tell you, and no
lesser messenger."

Now Gweniver was a Domina of the Ban-draoi, skilled at
reading truth and falsehood; and I had prepared myself for
this as I rode: had built up for myself the picture of what
had never happened—Arthur giving me the order, as his
foster-brother, to ride and tell Gweniver of his need and decision to ask for help, by way of the faerie flag; had con-
jured in my mind the image of Arthur's face, grave,
troubled, proud, as he gave me the command . . . bards are
good at this sort of thing.

So I stood there before Gwennach and Keils and spoke,
and they, dear souls, believed me. But now it was
Gweniver's turn to balk . . .

"Well, Talyn; Arthur may so order it, but I it is who
must execute. And I am not sure of the need."

"Lady," I said from the heart of my desperation, "you
have sworn!"

"Truly," said Keils, loyally supporting me in my falsehood, though he knew it not. "Your promise binds you,
cariad, as sure as it does bind Artos—" His voice carried
love and reproof, and she looked away.

So, I thought very privately in this very public moment,
*it is true, then: Gwennach and Keils are indeed beloved
of one another, and not merely bedmates* . . . It would be

most gratifying if I could tell you that at this instant I saw what was to come, saw all the woe and the wonder, the anguish and the triumph ... But I did not; I saw only a stubborn princess trying to avoid the nonexistent order of an equally stubborn prince, and in my fury at both of them I forgot that none of this was real in the first place, save of course the desperate need that had sent me on my lying errand, and I exploded.

"Then if you will not fulfill your word, let someone else do it for you! But in the name of the Highest *let it be done now!*"

"I will wave the flag." The quiet voice in the shocked silence was Merlynn's. I had not noticed him where he stood in the shadow of his own presence, but I was not surprised to find him there. Nor he, me; our eyes met, and more than eyes, and I knew he knew my falseness. But I knew too, as we looked on one another, that he knew the truth and loyalty that had prompted it, and understood.

Understand, aye, came the familiar stern mind-voice, *but, Talyn, I do* not *approve* ...

I sent back acceptance of the reprimand, but asked aloud, "That will not go against the instruction of the Queen of the Sidhe? She said that it was to be Gweniver must wave the Bratach Bán—"

Merlynn's smile was small and his tone dry. "Seli will not object."

In the end, I did not linger to see the actual performance of the Bratach's summoning: Merlynn—without a word or a visible sign, in the old way I remembered so well—indicated I should be gone, and I knew from of old, also, to take my leave when it was so ordered. All the more readily, since my own fraudulent orders were known to him; but I did not miss the moment even so. I knew the thing when it came.

CHAPTER
14

But first did come the fighting, the bitterest swordplay, bar none, that ever I have seen; and that is not to be wondered at, when you consider the stakes for which we fought that day; we, and others . . .

Yet even while I fought, one corner of my mind ran on like a babbling stream amid the tumult, half-heard, half-heeded: What of Edeyrn? Where, in all this final stour, was the Marbh-draoi, and what doing?

A good question, and one that more folk than I alone were asking; yet all no closer to an answer just yet than I myself. And it was to all of us a question of most paramount importance: Since Morgan and I had been his reluctant guests in Ratherne—had it truly been only a day since, it seemed centuries since our ride up that little glen—no news had reached our ears of Edeyrn's whereabouts, or indeed of his actions, and this vast silence, this emptiness where the Marbh-draoi should have been, made me restless and afraid. It had been presumed by Arthur and others that he had merely gone to ground in Ratherne, directing his fight and his forces from the center of his web, like the king spider he was; but I was not so sure, and more others were unsure right along with me. Simple enough for Edeyrn to have escaped altogether, through the postern gate, as it were: back up the high Dales, down along Pass of the Arrows, and from there almost anywhere in Keltia, on planet or off.

"Nay," said Arthur when I taxed him with it in a lull of the battle; said with great authority too, as if he had quartered for Edeyrn like a hunting-dog and had 'found' on some plane past the physical. "Nay. He is near. If not in Ratherne, then nearer still. He will show himself in time. We shall know him when he does."

And so we did.

The fighting had turned toward our leaguer again, the line bending like an overstrung bow, coming dangerously near to where Uthyr and Ygrawn watched from behind a triple fence of the best Fians we could muster, with an inner ring of Companions as well. I had appointed myself captain over those Companions—with Arthur's fervent approval—and lest you think this some soft sinecure of a position, let me tell you we saw more than our fair share of fighting, throwing off in one hour alone three waves of most determined attackers. Clearly Owein Rheged had been set to destroy Uthyr at whatever cost, and just as clearly we were not about to let him succeed in his errand.

I glanced anxiously behind me at my royal charges. Ygrawn caught my eye and gave me a smile of utmost serenity—and I knew that smile from of old, knew that the care-naught was genuine and was heartened thereby. But Uthyr— Though most of his advisors had protested against it, it was by Uthyr's own choosing that he was here at all; and so, of course, Ygrawn's. They had come to do battle in the only way they could, by their presence; it was for them the fíor-comlainn, the truth-of-combat, and if they died for it, well, that then was dán.

Even so, I knew as few others did what it had cost Uthyr to follow us on campaign, as he had done all the way from Cadarachta on Gwynedd. The unhealed magicked wound he had been dealt there had grown all the more painful the nearer its bearer came to its source: Owein's arm may have struck the sword-blow to the King's thigh, but that blade had been guided by Edeyrn, and it was his venomed sorcery that had held sway ever since in Uthyr's blood. Even Morgan and Merlynn had not been able to heal it, only to bate somewhat its

agonies; as for Uthyr, he was a king, and he was King of
Kelts, and he bore his wound as he had borne the wounding of his land.

My attention was claimed by a Raven who had broken
through the Fian ring; I dispatched her almost without
thought, and looked out again over the field. Even the
best-seasoned bow-wood comes at last to the breaking-
place, where it must either snap back to the upright or
else shatter altogether . . . and just now we were not so
far off it.

But for the most part it had been such battle as we
were well used to, men and women, warrior against warrior; even the galláin mercenaries raking us with fire from
space were such as we knew how to fight. Yet now came
an adversary of an order altogether different, and no
shame to tell you that our hearts fainted and fled before
his coming . . .

It was the sorcerers who sensed it first, the Druids and
Ban-dràoi who fought like the rest of us with sword and
bow and spear, as well as with less gross weaponry: a
sense of shadowing, as when on a hot unstable summer
day you turn round at a vague feeling of something behind you, and startle to see towering halfway to space a
black anvil of cloud, on which by Gavida's arm will be
forged the lightning.

It was like that now, that same feeling of sick dreading
anticipation, knowing something frightful is at hand but
not knowing what, nor yet for whom. It was terrible, and
it grew steadily worse: Morgan came to me with a face
gray with unwellness, and I could do naught to help her
for that I was even sicker myself. Even Merlynn seemed
less rock-strong than usual; as for the common run of
folk, they were suddenly adrift, liege and foe alike, pur-
poseless, swords hanging in slack hands, staring mazed,
as if they had all as one trodden upon the stray-sod.

Stray-sod . . . At that my mind leaped back to focus;
the word I had thrown up to the forefront of my brain out
of the sick whirling vagueness gave me something hard
and bright to cling to, leading me out of my fog . . .

I clutched at Morgan's arm. "Edeyrn," I croaked. Then,
louder, clearer, "It is Edeyrn, his doing, his coming . . ."

She started to object, then caught the certainty from me and knew it. "See. He comes now."

And I began to shiver, as below me every Kelt on that field, man or woman, Companion or Raven, was shivering alike. For what came now out of the valley of Nandruidion was no man nor yet wizard, but something out of the deep soul of Keltia, a nightmare legend like the Mari Llwyd, the Ghost Mare, or the Avanc, the frightful water-dragon whose roaring can be heard in the flood; but this was different.

Over the eastern end of the battlefield, down where Nandruidion debouched into the Great Glen, had hung a pall of shadow that was not entirely the smoke and dust of war. Out of it now stalked stiff-legged something tremendous, something black, blue-black, without ears, without a tail; the curve of its back was as a treeless hill, and the bristles of its mane were raised so high and sharp that a horse could have been impaled on each one. It moved slowly, and the ground shook where its cloven feet did set down; behind it came seven of its kind, but lesser.

I believe I made some small sound, for Morgan took my arm; but she too was trembling as she looked. Only Merlynn seemed unmoved; he had come to join us from Gweniver's campment not long since, as if he had known he would be needed.

He it was who spoke its name. "Torc Truith."

It made it no easier, hearing the thing named. "Edeyrn has sent it; has called it up against us," I managed to choke out past my fear.

Even in that moment, my old teacher Ailithir was still, it seemed, alive and well, for the glance he spared me then I had seen often before, in my schooldays at Daars.

"Nay, Talynno," he said gently. "It *is* Edeyrn."

Then of course I understood, and was violently sick; and I was by no means alone. It seemed the end of hope, and what we should all have expected, for Edeyrn to take the shape of the Great Boar to come against us. No other dwimmer-creature out of Keltia's dark soul could have set more fear and horror in us: the Boar who reappears after he has been burned and eaten, to throw souls upon his bloody tusks and lead heroes to hell. I wiped my mouth, and mastered myself, and forced myself to look again upon it.

By now it had lumbered well out into the Strath, and not only our forces but his—its—own drew back before it. I tried, as bard, to objectify the thing, to set words upon it, as if by doing so I could ease the horror and loathing. But words were not enough, and nothing could abate the awfulness of the slow, the terrible stiff-legged stalk that sent it rolling a little from side to side as it came on, like a ship in heavy seas.

Arthur had joined us, with Tarian and Grehan and Kei and some others. I looked round for Gweniver and Keils, but could not see them in the increasing murk that the beast brought with it; Uthyr, in his polechair, was with Ygrawn, still in their ring of Fians, a little way off to my left. I dragged my gaze back, croaked out a question to any who might be still capable of answering.

"Those who come behind it—who are they?"

"They but follow their master as they have ever done," said Merlynn, never taking his eyes off the thing. "They are the four who went with Edeyrn when he broke from Dinas Affaraon, and the three who joined him after. Renegade Druids, traitor Pheryllt—their names are known, but I will not speak them, not yet."

Oh aye, later perhaps? But I took care not to send out my thought; or, at any rate, no farther than Morgan, who pinched my arm but said nothing. By now I was recovering myself, a little, could even shift my horrified gaze from the oncoming shape of evil-working to look at the others around me.

Morgan's face was lifted like the sunrise against the noisome murk Edeyrn brought with him; it was almost as if all his evil had at last taken visible form, clinging around the image of the Boar like muck from some astral pigsty. Uthyr, still in his throne-litter, was whitefaced but calm; Ygrawn looked thoughtful, even judgmental. Most of the Companions had mastered themselves as I had, and their faces had all the same grimness.

But two faces stood out amid the unclean vaporous dimness: Arthur's, keen-cut as the bright steel in his hand, looking as if he had seen some great and final question; and Merlynn's, remote as the moon Argialla, a ghost of a smile in the white beard, looking as if he had seen the answer.

"We must speak with it—with him." I looked around

for the speaker, saw to my surprise that it was Uthyr. The King had taken very little active part in any of the fighting, either on Gwynedd or here, once our war had moved to Tara; for him to order a parley was, at very least, surprising.

Yet Arthur nodded in agreement. "Aye, Lord," he said, and at his gesture Daronwy came up beside him. But before he could give her his command, Morgan stirred.

"She must not go as she is, not to face—that. I will put a shape upon her of protection—" Reading consent and trust in Ronwyn's face, Morgan smiled, and before Arthur or Uthyr could protest, there came a flash and flutter and beat of wings, and where Daronwy had stood now hovered a she-eagle, her fierce gold eye fixed on Morgan's face.

With a high harsh bright cry like a horn or a bell, the eagle was gone, her great wings carrying her steadily toward Edeyrn-Boar, who had come to a ponderous halt a lai or so away. The bulk of him dwarfed our little hill, and the malice and hatred in the burning eyes beat upon us like the summer sun.

Then it seemed as if Daronwy spoke to the thing, for I heard her voice clearly in my head.

"For the sake of Her who made you, come forth as man, to speak with Arthur."

I shook my head angrily, as a swimmer will to clear water from his ears; it seemed not possible that I could be hearing Ronwyn's speech with Edeyrn, but looking round I saw that all had heard, and realized that it was by Edeyrn's will that the words did reach us.

He did not deign to reply, but one of the lesser boars did answer for him; and the name Gwyrch Ereint came unbidden to my mind—he had been one of Edeyrn's disciples at Dinas Affaraon, a gifted Druid who turned when Edeyrn turned, and who was high in the Marbh-draoi's councils and affections. He it was who now spoke, and spoke blasphemy.

"Evil has She done, Who has forced this shape upon us."

The eagle that was our sister-Companion baffed angrily away and returned again, and once more I heard that bright ringing cry.

"You have taken it upon yourselves, by no act of Hers,

and you will sorrow for it, for Arthur will fight, and more with him."

Then Edeyrn spoke, and his voice was an earthquake that laughed.

"Torc Truith will not be hunted until you have Gwyn son of Nudd as huntsman. But he is Master of the Faerie Hunt, and will not be stirred nor spared from his own hunting lands."

Before Daronwy could answer, Arthur had stepped to the lip of the hill, apart from the rest of us, and stared up and across the little distance, straight into the eyes of the Boar, and smiled.

"It is easy for me to accomplish that, though you may not think so."

The red-orange eyes blinked, the vast boar-shaped darkness seemed to quiver a little. But before any other could move, Kei, our hothead, had dashed forward, swinging his sword over his head in bright circles, straight at the Boar's cleft hoofs.

He got in the blow he had so long hoped for—ever since the death of Samhra, his beloved, in the sea-fight on Glora, he had lived only for the chance of vengeance—slicing deep into the sinew of the pastern, even cutting off several of the spear-pointed bristles. But though Edeyrn-Torc shivered as a beast will when stung by a cleggan, he did naught else. Nor did he need to, for a drop of venom, shining like bronze in the dusty light, had formed where the bristles were sheared away; with one flick of the great hoof the drop flew out and struck Kei. He fell dead where he stood; Arthur, beside me, flinched, closing his eyes in pain and loss and farewell, and when he opened them again there was no tear that I could see. But tears were there, I think, all the same . . .

No time just now for sorrow: As if Kei's death had been a signal, the seven boars who followed Edeyrn began to savage the nearby ranks, who still stood rooted in dread; and with horror I saw that they were not tusking and trampling our ranks alone, but those of their own soldiery as well. I looked again at Edeyrn, thought hard and evilly, cared not if he heard: *So, your own tools are to be despised and broken, Marbh-draoi; did they not serve you well and faithfully enough, in your faithlessness?* But I had for answer only the baleful orange stare swinging across our lines, as the creature swung its huge head from side to side, snuffing the air, as if it quested for something, or someone, or sensed something that made it uneasy.

At that thought I laughed in earnest; well, I emitted a ghastly sound, more a strangled hoot than a laugh. What on this earth or indeed any other could possibly strike uneasiness into *that*? His power was great enough to give him the mastery of this shape of terror, to put the same shape upon his creatures, to set them to rout our armies: What could there be to set unease upon him?

Naught much, it would seem; and yet I could sense his—its—fear. Fear for himself? What had he said, he could not be hunted in his form as the Boar until Gwyn son of Nudd came to serve as huntmaster—a thing he clearly thought impossible. I brightened a little: Well, perhaps not *so* impossible, for did we not know Gwyn our own selves, Arthur and Morgan and I, and was he not our—well, perhaps not 'friend,' but at the least not our unfriend. It could happen, that he came to us here ... And with a violent start I realized—indeed, I Saw—that it *would* happen, and how ...

But other things were happening already: Rallied by Daronwy, still in her eagle shape, soaring over the field, the Companions had launched an attack against Edeyrn's attendant boar-things. Our fighters had formed into the all-but-irresistible configuration called the schiltron, and they were methodically slaughtering the sorcerer-swine. Not without greatest pain and loss; but though Edeyrn could not be hunted by less than the Prince of the Sidhe, or so he said, still he had not chosen to make his creatures quite so proof as he against our blades. It was a long and bloody time of it, but one by one they fell. Gwyrch Ereint was first among them, Edeyrn's oldest friend; on the hill called Amman Edeyrn lost a boar and a sow, a banw and a benwic. Soon others heartened and were turned: Kelts all alike, rebel and Raven came together to butcher the Marbh-draoi's evil farrowing.

But even once those minions were dead on the field, returning to their proper human shapes as they were cut to pieces by the desperate armies, still there was the King-Boar to be dealt with; and as I watched him grow vaster and darker and more terrible as each of his creatures perished, I began to lose hope.

But I had reckoned without a number of things: chiefest of which was Merlynn Llwyd. I have said that Merlynn took but little part in the fighting or even the advice in council he had once been wont to give; I see now that this was all part of it. Teach he never so wisely and well, a teacher can teach only so long: At last all his teachings come themselves to be tested, in his pupil, and the worlds will mark how well, indeed, he has taught after all. Merlynn had reached this place with his dearest students: with Arthur, and with me, and with the Companions, and even, I now saw, with Gweniver and Morgan and Ygrawn. He had taught us all; had been prime mover of the Counterinsurgency and the last rebellion we now fought. It had all been on his shoulders, and it had all been carried through to completion; though not without bitter loss and great costing.

I ran over the names in my mind as I looked upon Merlynn now: Amris, Leowyn, Gwyddno, Medeni, Gorlas, so many others, Companions and auxiliars and civilians, all gone to feed that great Boar's evil mawings. I looked down as something cold touched my hand; only Cabal, sensing my sadness and anger, seeking to comfort. He had done battle of his own today, ranging out with the Companion schiltrons, along with Morgan's red-brindle bitch Rhymni and two whelps of their last litter, Atver and Liath, who had come with their mistress on campaign. The other dogs were with Guenna; but Cabal had come to me, rescuing me now, as once I had rescued him, from a trap that had all but closed upon me. I ruffled his ears—silky soft, where the rest of his coat was rough and wiry—and spoke a word to him, and, though he grumbled almost humanly in protest, he obeyed, leaving the front rank on the hillside to take up guard next Uthyr and Ygrawn.

And Cabal's is no bad thought ... I turned and followed him, just as a galloper came tearing up from below, cried out while still ahorse to Uthyr and those by him.

"The Marbh-draoi's creatures are all slain, Lord! His own armies helped hunt them in the end—"

"And Owein?" That was Morgan, her tone oddly urgent.

The rider's own voice was hushed, if harsh. "The Boar himself has slain him."

A stir ran through our ranks; but I myself was aware of at least a handful of emotions. So, Edeyrn killed his own heir and creation at the last . . . There was no love lost between Owein Rheged and the House of Glyndour—since coming to Tara I had lost yet another brother, and my sister Tegau Goldbreast had been wounded sore—but just now I was remembering the man for whom I had harped five long years together. Of course, I had been going by another name just then, or else I might have preceded my siblings to my next life; but strangely enough Owein had been no bad master to me. There had been laughter and banter, a kind of ironic respect even; perhaps because he sensed I was not afraid of him, perhaps for some other reason. But though Owein had been our longtime enemy and bane, and though I was for no sake sorry he had gone to the Goddess, and would have cheerfully have sent him there myself had that been my dán, I was somehow sorry all the same, and gave a brief silent prayer for his speeding, and knew that I meant the words.

Meant them even more, when a few moments later the author of Owein's passing turned his attention again to us, upon our hillock. Still in Boar-shape, Edeyrn seemed more fearful now than before; as he lumbered nearer I could see clearly the broken body of Owein Rheged speared upon one of the bristles of the thing's mane, where the tusks had tossed him. And as if at some unspoken signal all we on the hilltop drew nearer to one another, and closer around Uthyr and Ygrawn, and waited.

Edeyrn spoke again, in a voice that seemed to come from the deeps of the earth, a voice that smelled of smoke and blood and iron, tinged with weariness, edged with the gloat of satisfaction.

"Did I not tell you that Torc Truith will not be hunted by such as you have sent against him?"

Arthur drew breath for an angry response, but before he could utter a syllable Merlynn had stood forth.

"Then, brother, I call a huntsman to suit such quarry. I call *your* brother . . ."

His hand that had been beneath his blue cloak was flung out and up, and from his fingers broke the white folds of the faery flag, the Bratach Bán, the heavy silk catching what sun there was and shining moon-pale through the murk. I had time for one confused thought— *What if Seli is wroth with us, after all, that Gweniver did not wave the thing herself?*— before the hunt was called.

CHAPTER
15

It seemed as if the greatest wind in the world awoke around us. It sent the dwimmer-dark flying, dispersing Edeyrn's sorcerous miasms like morning fog on the slopes of the Loom. Cold and sharp and blessedly clean, it came straight from Glenshee, the sacred, secret valley; the trees and grasses bent low before it, seeming to hail it as it passed.

As did we: It cracked our cloaks like thunder, set our banners streaming, pushed our hair out behind us and made our eyes tear with its force. But it carried joy upon it, joy and the promise of victory; which is why now I raised my face to it, and breathed it in, and laughed for that joy and the victory to come.

I did not laugh long, of course; the faerie wind may have blown away the last rags of Edeyrn's enchantings, but the enchanter himself was still very much with us. Yet somehow the terrible Boar that stood before us, cleft hoofs deep in the trodden turf it had itself turned to bloody mire, was—diminished, lessened. Still powerful beyond all right reason, it was nonetheless palpably smaller now.

And if so, perhaps more vulnerable? ... I looked my question: Morgan smiled, and pointed. Following the direction of her upflung arm, I saw what she had already sensed, and my heart that had been gladdened by the

coming of the wind now rejoiced ten thousand times over,
for sight of what that wind had brought us.

How shall I tell of it: They were riding down the slopes
of the air as a mortal hunt will course over the breast of
a hill. They were silent in their coming, save for the horn
that chivied them on: Gwyn's horn, that I had heard before, and had not forgotten.

I turned from that glorious sight to gaze pridefully on
Merlynn, who had summoned it to be. He was not looking at the Sidhe's rade, but kept his eyes on Edeyrn-Boar,
and upon his face was an expression I had not seen for
nearly fifty years, not since the night Ailithir had shown
the boy Taliesin the death of Gwaelod in the shifting
clouds.

I believe I knew in that instant what was afoot, and was
reaching out my hands to avert it—more fool I, as if *my*
magic could do aught in this compall. Time seemed
slowed, all battle-tumult silenced; on the edge of my sight
I saw Gwyn upon his gold-maned white stallion. But
Edeyrn filled all our eyes and all our thought: He was
changing as we watched, the Boar-shape shimmering and
crazing, vanishing in a direction that we could not understand, going in patches and flakes and waves of darkness.

In its wake stood Edeyrn, as he was; though just now
he seemed but little less fearful in human form than he
had in shape of the Torc. His gaze was not bent on Gwyn,
however, but on Merlynn, his rival, his once-friend, now
his great adversary, and I divined in an eyeblink what he
was about. Not swift enough to stop it; nay, not even my
Morgan could avert this dán . . .

Merlynn Llwyd, Ailithir, Archdruid, met my glance
one last time; looked at me, looked at Ygrawn and Uthyr,
looked at Morgan, looked last and longest at Arthur. Then
he was gone, and where he had stood was a column of—
ice? Too stunned to weep, too confused to think and too
dazed even to try—I could feel no pain just yet, what I
felt in that first moment was, simply, one long wordless
desperate endless No—I stepped forward and lifted a
shaking hand, but did not touch it. Not ice, but a prism-
prison: a crystal tree, trunked and branched and gnarled,
an apple-tree, clear as a diamond where the sun struck it,
milk-blue in shadow. And within it—

But I could not think of him, not yet, not like that . . . And too, there was still Edeyrn to deal with. *Later, then—*

Yet if I had been shock-frozen, others had not had the same reaction: I had forgotten that the fight raged still, and turned at a shout from the place where Ygrawn and Uthyr had so long waited upon the battle's issue.

They waited no longer: The shout that I had just now heard was the triumphant yell of Ravens breaking the leaguer that had protected the King and Queen. Every one of us within hearing, pushing aside our grief for Merlynn, leaped as one to defend our rulers; but Arthur was first of all, Llacharn, earning its name, alight and dancing in his hand.

We fought for all our lives now; engulfed by the Raven tide, I glanced away for the merest of seconds to Uthyr where he sat in his high-backed polechair. He was as he had been all this day, pale and unmoving of face and form, like some stern saint carved in painted wood. The Sword Fragarach was cradled as always in his arms, its blade cloaked by the worn leather scabbard. And then a sound rose up behind me that turned my blood to cheese—a sound part groan, part fear, part warning—and I spun on my heel to see.

What I saw was Arthur standing alone in a ring of Ravens, and Llacharn's blade broken off a foot from the hilt. I think I have never moved so swiftly in all my lives, spinning my own sword point-for-hilt as I ran to him, reversing my grip so that I might flight it to him like the lonna we use in the spear-toss. But before I could get my arm back to throw, I saw that someone else had been swifter.

Uthyr had risen in his place—he who for the past months had not been able to stand or move without another's arm to help him, his own force drained away out of the magicked wound—and now he stood strong in the flood of swords that lapped him, an oak on a wind-lashed fellside. With an arm that trembled no more than the thickest bough upon that oak might have done, he raised Fragarach above his head, and with his left hand he stripped off the black scabbard.

Even I, who am bard and Druid both, am hard pressed to find words for what I beheld, what we all then beheld, as Uthyr Ard-rígh, with the last store of life and strength left to him, with all the love he bore, raised himself up unaided from the chair that had been his final throne, and with one mighty motion hurled the Sword Fragarach to Arthur his nephew.

I say 'sword' only for that I knew it to be so; but in truth I saw only a white fire in the air that came to rest in Arthur's hand. He seemed to have no such problem: He caught the faerie weapon by its serpented hilt, casting down Llacharn—the broken blade-shards were caught up by Companions standing by, and lovingly preserved ever after, though that weapon we had won together, Arthur and Morgan and I, from Collimare was never to be reforged—and it settled to his grip as if it had been made for him, or he for it.

To us who looked on—all this, you understand, happened in a matter of moments, Edeyrn, Gwyn, Merlynn, Uthyr, Arthur, all—it was as if Grian herself had come to Arthur's hand, a blaze of light more silver than golden, so bright that each of us nearby had suddenly a second shadow: a gray and fainter one from Grian above, one of dark and clear-cut black from the Sword below.

It lasted less than moments: Uthyr fell back fainting in his chair and was carried off the field with care and celerity; Ygrawn went with him, and I motioned half our Companions to follow. The rest of us stayed; stayed, and saw.

Even in our desperate defense of our wounded King—though just for that one instant it seemed that Uthyr had been hale and whole and strong again, as he had not been since Owein's dolorous blow at Cadarachta, it was good to see him so once again before the end—we had not forgotten there was still a fight afoot. But now, as that fight closed down hard upon us, and I for one began to think about taking with me to the Goddess as many of Edeyrn's creatures as I could when I went, as it seemed likely I should soon be doing, I sensed a sudden altering, and paused in mid-stroke, as if I had heard a call but could name not the voice that had called me.

I had forgotten Gwyn—never a good or wise thing to do, see you follow not my lead—had forgotten Edeyrn also, in my fear for Arthur and Uthyr and my fight of the moment. Had forgotten even the Sidhe hosting; but as I looked out across the field, I could see plainly that the Sidhe had not forgotten us.

They had lifted not a single sword against a single Kelt that day, though they came to the field as well armed as any of us; yet where they had ridden only our own were left alive. Ravens had fallen like sheaves at harvest—our enemies, though Arthur had never suffered them to be called so, save Edeyrn and Owein only—and though I had striven mightily to compass their deaths I found I could not look upon this. I turned away, shivering a little, trying not to see the dim glitter of that terrible crystal tree, to find Morgan beside me. I glanced down at her, hoping for comfort, seeking solace, but her face was a mask, and her gaze did not waver as had mine, as she looked out upon the slaughter the Sidhe left in their passing. Nay; it was the gaze of a princess and a priestess and a judge, and I began to turn away even from her, my own love, but her voice stayed me.

"Not for naught are the Sidhe called the People of Peace, Taliesin ap Gwyddno."

I did not look at her. "And is *that*"—I flung out my arm to include the scene below us—"what peace requires, lady?"

Her face did not change. "Maybe. See who comes now."

Struck by what the Bratach Bán had wrought, still numb—by the Goddess's great mercy—at Merlynn's fate, I looked where Morgan looked, and saw Edeyrn standing patiently and motionlessly where last I had seen him. *It is as if he waits for someone's coming—and where is my brother?*

No sooner had I thought this, and begun to panic, than one broke off from the van of the faerie host—not Arthur—and came at the gallop straight toward us, toward Edeyrn.

Gwyn it was, prince under the hill, tall in gold mail upon his snow-colored stallion. Unthinkingly I lifted a hand in salutation, but quailed as I saw his face, and drew back; he swept past us as if we had been emmets in the grass, so intent was he on the one who stood awaiting him.

Someone came up on my right—Arthur at last, breathing hard, as if he had been running; but he said no word,

to me or to any. Far across the stricken field I could see
the standards of Gweniver and Keils moving toward us at
snail's gait. But I knew it was only distance made their
coming seem so slow; in truth, they were riding at
foundering-pace to reach us.

They need not have broken their hearts, or their horses',
to do so: The battle here, the fighting in space above us,
Merlynn, even Uthyr—all took a far second to Gwyn and
Edeyrn as they drew nigh each other. And I took a long
shuddering breath as I remembered: These two were indeed
brothers. Not even fosterns, as Artos and I, but born of the
same mother; one half man, the other not man at all but
maybe even god.

And yet it seemed that they were intending to settle
this thing entirely as men, for as Gwyn rode up, Edeyrn
drew his sword. The white stallion checked and crabbed
sidewise under Gwyn's hand and knee, and then the faerie
lord too was afoot, advancing to where his brother
awaited.

I have no explanation, in this life or any other, for what
I did next. But before I could think about it, before any
could hinder me, before even Arthur or Gwyn himself
could thwart my intention, I had rushed forward, straight
at Edeyrn, sword upraised, howling some ros-catha,
seized by purest bloodlust that only Edeyrn's death at my
hands could ease. My father, my mother, my stepfather,
my siblings, Prince Amris and King Leowyn and now
maybe Uthyr as well, my dear friends and my beloved
teacher—nothing would ease my heart save Edeyrn's
blood upon my blade. Well, so at least it seemed, in that
moment; I will not dignify it with the word 'thought,'
even, thought was just then the thing utterly furthest from
my mind.

But this was to be a fight of giants: Edeyrn no more
minded my lunatic rush than that of a chafer buzzing his
head on a summer day, and batted me as easily away. He
lifted a careless hand—I do not think that by then he even
saw me, much less knew me for myself—and when I recovered my senses I found myself sprawled on the
ground a good twenty paces away, not far from where
Gwyn stood.

They paid me no more heed, intent on their own battle.
Yet if it were in truth battle, it was like to no fight I had

ever seen: They stood still as two great trees in the hush before a storm—yet the storm was raging even as we watched.

I looked from the dark glory that burned before me to the white fire at my side. Edeyrn ap Seli and Gwyn ap Nudd faced each other at last, and the thing of most terror in that most terrible of moments was that they seemed one and the same.

A match of equals, then, a standoff not to be broken by even more than mortal means; therefore only mortal ways would serve ... I was not the first to whom this had occurred, for off to my right I saw movement, and it was movement of a nature I knew all too well.

Arthur surged forward like the tide that had rolled over Gwaelod, just as strong, just as invincible, just as inevitable in his moving. In his hand was Fragarach, gift of Nudd the king. It may seem strange that the matter was settled with swords in the end, and not magic; but so it was. To his credit, or perhaps his foreknowledge of dán perceived, Edeyrn gave no blow, as if some strange form must be satisfied, then fell without a groan under Arthur's sword.

It seemed even stranger that all this took place so swiftly: a matter of seconds, to put an end to an evil that had scourged Keltia for two centuries and more. Perhaps only Fragarach could have dealt such a blow; perhaps only Arthur could have dealt it; and perhaps Nudd and Gwyn and Edeyrn, and even maybe Arthur, had known it. Just then I was only glad it should be so; but I think we were all surprised. Well—stunned into silence and disbelief would be more like it, jaws all round the field of Nandruidion were well agape.

I heard myself asking very far away, "Is that it, then? Is there no more to it than that?"

Arthur began to answer me, but Gwyn was there before him. "Much more to it, son of Gwyddno. But, for now, all."

Arthur gave him a long unreadable gaze, then deliberately looked down upon the form at his feet. I take no shame in confessing that I myself would not have had the nerve, had barely the stomach, even, to watch from a distance; but Arthur Penarvon, his face impassive, with the

point of Fragarach flicked back the cloak where it had
fallen over Edeyrn's face.

What was revealed then was not the face of a man of
eightscore years, as he had so long willed himself to appear. Nor yet was it the ageless timeless countenance of
the Sidhe, whose faces in death no mortal in Keltia had
yet beheld but which are fairer so even than in life.
Nay—it was the face of one who had lived unlawfully far
past any natural span, Sidhe or mortal both, a wreck of
bone and leathered skin that looked as if no human had
ever inhabited it. Perhaps none ever had.

And yet, as I stared, revolted and fascinated both, upon
the dead countenance of Edeyrn Marbh-draoi—and how
strange that seemed to me then, to think that, to *know*
that, for it seems strange to me even now—clear upon
that countenance was the strangest and yet most human
emotion of all, to be read by any who looked. Edeyrn ap
Seli ac Rhûn, Marbh-draoi of Keltia, had gone grateful to
his death.

I do not know how long we stood there, Arthur, Gwyn
and I. Moments, minutes or hours, it was all one to us.
Morgan came; Gweniver, Keils, and others of our Companions, though they stood carefully back from Edeyrn's
uninhabited form. Around us, the battle was suddenly
over; like one awaking from sleep or deep-trance, I startled to note the quiet where once the fight had roared.

And all this time Gwyn and Arthur gazed unspeaking
into one another's eyes; into one another's souls as well,
maybe, even—and be very sure that none there present,
not even my Morgan, chose to intrude upon *that* col-
loquy . . .

At last Arthur stirred and drew a deep breath, looked
round him as if mazed at where he found himself, and in
whose company. Then he glanced down once more at
Edeyrn, and his face changed in a way I have no words
for.

Gwyn's dark glance followed his. "We will take him
back with us, to our own place," he said quietly, and I
thrilled to his voice's deep timbre as I had done when
first I heard it. He half-turned from us then, to where his
host circled restlessly over the breast of the hills, then
turned back again, and now his eyes were darker still.

"And he too," he said even more quietly, and nodded once toward the crystal treetrunk that had taken Merlynn. At my and Arthur's uncontrollable jolt of protest: "Nay, it is all dán; never think it is not. Others will need him too in time to come, and he will be there for them; a queen-empress, and a king with a cloak of gold." But more than that he would not say, then or ever.

I stepped forward, and he did not hinder me; after a moment Arthur joined me. The crystal seemed cold and warm at the same time; I could sense Merlynn's life within it, and also a life of its own. Not evil, for all it was the Marbh-draoi's last magic; perhaps he too knew of this future need, and remembered he was Kelt enough in the end to take vengeance only so far.

But gods, how I would miss my teacher; never since my earliest childhood had I been without him, and even when we had by necessity gone our own ways we had never been long apart, and ever we spoke to one another, mind to mind.

And so it seemed now: From an immense distance I caught a faint trace as upon a wind from the future, sensed the unmistakable wry humor Merlynn had been wont to show us, the indulgent affectionate impatience, even the mocking sigh he had so often affected with Arthur and me when another teacher would have caught us both a clout.

Have you heard naught that I have taught you? it seemed to say, and beside me I sensed Arthur startle and smile, as if he too had been spoken to in the old dear way, and through my tears I smiled too, and bade my teacher Ailithir a pupil's farewell.

Gwyn had been watching us both, and when I looked at him again I could see no emotion that I could read upon the fair stern countenance. He nodded once to Arthur, once to me, once to Morgan; then raised the gold horn to his lips. At the sound of the horn's cry I closed my eyes as I had done before, and when I opened them again Gwyn had gone. And with him went Édeyrn, and Merlynn, and all the faerie host.

In the ringing silence I sought Morgan's mind, but she was wrapped in her own thought, and I let my gaze shift to Arthur, then out to the armies below. I looked at their faces, and heard myself say with quiet urgency, "Artos—

they will run mad if you do not calm them. Speak to them. *Now.*"

And this I knew because I myself was not far off it: I was trembling as if I had been too long outdoors in the bitter cold, or had carried too far a burden far beyond my strength. I myself would go mad did not Arthur speak to bid me other . . .

He started violently as Morgan laid a gentle hand upon his arm to underscore my words; glanced wildly around him as if he sought one who was no longer there, and I knew from that how much he himself felt Merlynn's absence, for he would not have let any see even that if he could have prevented it. But as ever with Arthur, the need of others was paramount, and perhaps the terror of reaction and incomprehension in our faces—for we were all a nail's thickness away from breaking point by now—did somewhat to ease his own.

Then his face altered, and he bent to scoop something up from the trampled earth. When he turned round to Morgan and to me, I saw, with a shiver that caught me between laughter and tears, what he had in his hand: the Bratach Bán, plucked from the ground where Merlynn Llwyd had let it fall.

Morgan reached out to take it from her brother's convulsive grasp. "It will be needed twice again before its work is done. Let me keep it safe for now."

He relinquished the banner into her keeping; then, sheathing Fragarach that had hung, unheeded, unneeded, in his right hand all this time, he leaped to the flat top of a boulder nearby, calling out to those who were near to gather in. And, Companion and Raven alike, all of them came at his calling.

I came too, of course, and I have not the slightest recollection, of a single word that Arthur spoke then to us—and for a bard to admit to so egregious a lapse is no easy thing, believe me. Though whatever he said to us, I am sure it must have been fine and correct, for I could see the terror fading out of the upturned faces, felt the fear draining from my own soul as I listened with the rest.

But though that was the most immediately pressing of the duties that crowded now upon us in victory's wake—for it *was* our victory, all seemed agreed on that by now, and Arthur's peace, the Pax Arturus, was already spreading out like ripples in a pond; I could sense the panic vanishing, the evil mists burning off forever, taken away as surely as the Marbh-draoi himself had been taken—it was by no means the most difficult.

That lay still ahead of us, for now Daronwy approached us from the direction of Uthyr's tent, and I knew at once what she had come to say.

And so, indeed, did Arthur.

CHAPTER

16

"Not dead," said Ygrawn my foster-mother; the Queen of Keltia. "Not yet—he waits for you four before he goes." The violet gaze, undimmed as yet by any tear, rested on each of us in turn: Arthur, Gweniver, Morgan, me.

We gave her back gaze for gaze; not for worlds would we have proved lesser at the test than this woman who had been the only real mother all four of us had ever had. But Ygrawn was leading us into the tent's inner chamber, where sconces glowed and the dying King lay, barely there, upon his couch.

The first thing I laid eyes on as I walked through the door was Uthyr's polechair, that had borne him to and from the battlefield this day. And I remembered how like a throne it had seemed for him, this King of Kelts who had not once sat upon the Throne of Scone, high seat of Keltic monarchs since Brendan's day. No matter; he was no less a king for that, and more king than all the rest, again for that . . .

Morgan had laid a hand upon my arm, and with a start I was aware again of my surroundings as she hastened me into my proper position at Arthur's right hand; for I was his fostern, and wife's foster-son to him who lay so still beneath the coverlet.

Uthyr's eyes were closed, his fine narrow face drawn

to a blade-like sharpness, the dark hair and beard seeming even darker against the waxen translucence of his skin. I had, I think, hoped against hope that the King might yet live; but seeing that paleness I had seen so often before, I knew my hope dashed before it had ever risen. It was the light of the withdrawing soul, the blaze of the spirit setting sail, its work completed, free to go home to the courts of heaven.

Across from Arthur and me, Gweniver and Morgan mirrored our mien and stance and thought. Ygrawn, by the bed-head, looked only upon Uthyr; at the bed's foot were Uthyr's closest friends and officers—Keils Rathen, Marigh Aberdaron, three or four others; no more. This was no passing of state, by Ygrawn's wish, and we were glad to have it so.

How long we stood in silence and remembrance I know not; but all at once the tent seemed to hold its collective breath, as Uthyr opened his eyes.

His gaze went first to his Queen. Ygrawn Tregaron did not weep nor flinch nor falter as she returned that loving regard, and I knew from our long shared past that she would do none of those things, not so long as Uthyr was there to see it. Afterwards would be another matter, and her concern.

Then the gentle glance, already turning its focus outward, beginning to make that great shift from physical vision to Sight that comes ever at the end, as the senses are set to higher modes of sensing, moved on to rest on Morgan. Uthyr's younger daughter wept no more than had her mother, but smiled down into her father's face, and whatever was exchanged between them in that moment was too precious and private to be entrusted to spoken speech.

Lifting his gaze to the other side of his couch, Uthyr looked on me where I stood beside Arthur, my hand resting lightly on his shoulder. It had not been given to me to attend my own father's going-out, nor that of my foster-father Gorlas: Both of them had been killed in combat, as it were, and both times I had been in flight for my own life. Now Uthyr would be my third father to whom farewell must be made; indeed he had been lasathair to me since I was scarce fourteen, athra-cheile these seven years past in all but the last vow of law; and I thanked Kelu and all gods that this time at least I was able to make my farewell face to face, on this side of this life.

So I reached out to the King as my Druid masters had long ago taught me in my priesting, and felt flowing back to me the comfort he took of what I gave him, and the love he had ever had for me. For myself, I had comfort in it as well, and felt too the pride and love that came shining at me from Morgan and Ygrawn.

And still no word had been spoken aloud, not until Uthyr turned his eyes at last to the two who were to follow him as rulers over Keltia. Gweniver leaned forward, knelt beside the bed, as if to reach her uncle from across a swiftly widening distance; and from his place beside me, Arthur pulled back, as if to stand away, so that that distance should grow unhindered, and the leaving soul be free to sail.

For it is one of the great pillars of our faith that the liberated soul can be followed out a certain distance, and it is the bounden duty—the joy also, for it is a charge of love—of that soul's nearest to ride escort for as long as may be safely allowed. Never think we go alone, when we come to make that journey for ourselves; they are with us, and unseen guards as well, to ensure safe passage for the voyaging spirit and safe return for the escort soul still bound to earth. Our duties differ by nature of our standing to the journeyer: Ygrawn's chief charge from now would be to companion her lord out as far as she might and her powers permitted; a considerable way, I had no doubt, for knowing her I knew she would go farther than any other could, or would, have done, not turning back to earth again until the gates of Caer Coronach had safely received her consort within.

But the rest of us too had our charge laid upon us: to ride with Uthyr on his road according to our own powers, to protect Ygrawn and help her safely home, to hold Keltia together for Arthur and Gweniver and itself. And perhaps of all these it was this last that would prove most difficult of doing ...

But if Uthyr the King had looked on us others—wife, daughter, niece, adopted son—with love, he looked on his nephew with something nigh to reverence. And yet not for Arthur, not *as* Arthur: The reverence in Uthyr's face now was for the High King that would follow him. That was whom he saw now, not his brother's son, nor the prince he himself had helped to train, nor even yet the warrior-lord who had won him this brief, true reign. Uthyr Pendreic, first King of Kelts to claim that title in truth since Alawn Last-king, was seeing a future that was yet years distant and at the same time all but upon us: the reign of Arthur Ard-rígh.

Yet by Uthyr's own decree, Arthur Ard-rígh would not be alone upon the Throne of Scone but would share it with Gweniver Ard-rían, and this had not been forgotten. He lifted strengthless fingers to Gweniver, who closed both her hands over his; the other hand reached out to Arthur, who came back from his distance, himself falling to one knee to take the King's hand in his own. Some moments the three of them remained so, silent, unmoving; though what moved between them then spoke louder than all words.

Then Uthyr spoke, and the words of the ancient formula came faint and labored; but they came, and they were heard.

"I confirm you both in that rank which has been attested and sworn to, to which you have been called: Gweniver Ard-rían, Arthur Ard-rígh." He continued in a lower, stronger voice, his eyes brighter now. "And until such time as true peace shall come to Keltia, I continue Arthur of Arvon in his place as Rex Bellorum, sole and final master of war in this realm, and charge all Kelts else to obey him and him alone in this task. So say I, Uthyr King of Kelts."

He was looking at his Queen as he spoke, and now Ygrawn moved closer to him, Gweniver giving way for her, and seated herself beside him on the couch's edge. She bent over to him, her hair falling forward to hide their faces; she was talking to him in a low soft voice, saying things to him that none but he could hark to.

At the foot of the bed, Keils Rathen, Uthyr's sword-arm for forty years, said the only thing that could be said.

"Gods save Uthyr, King of Kelts!"

But the King did not hear.

So passed Uthyr Pendreic, King of Kelts. As I stood there behind Arthur, who had not risen from his knees nor relinquished his uncle's hand, I looked across at

Gweniver where she had withdrawn to stand behind the
widowed Queen. And upon her face was something extraordinary. Sorrow that Uthyr was gone, gladness that he
was free at last of his pain—the sorcerous wound in his
thigh had healed just now, as if it had never been—but
also a kind of dazed despair, and a kind of freedom. She
was High Queen now, who had never thought to be, never
dared to dream of being; so that what happened now
came, doubtless, as the most unlooked-for of surprises.

It was said in all innocence, for that I am quite certain;
particularly considering who it was that said it. But said
it was, and so . . .

"Gods save Arthur and Gweniver, King and Queen of
Kelts!" Keils it was who said it, and I knew the hunt was
up.

I felt rather than saw Arthur's whole body go rigid with
shock, and across the dead King's bed I saw Gweniver's
face like a small bright moon that all at once had been
eclipsed. Both of them looked as if someone had thrust a
spear through their hearts; perhaps someone had.

I turned away, unwilling for anyone to see my own
face just then. It felt as if some great claw had reached
down from the sky, or up out of the ground, and had torn
away the scar tissue that had grown over those old
wounds of mine; had stripped away all the poor protection that years and will had made for me, and now left my
soul bare and bleeding again in the cold.

For a moment, as I strode out of the tent unheeding of
questions and clutching hands, I did not think I could endure it; not again. It had been terrible enough before; indeed, it was pain, and pain's aftermath, that had made me
who I now was, who I of force became. I never thought
it was ended, only that I had put it by, had found a place
for it to live so that *I* could live too; but now I knew that
I had only stood aside from it. I had dealt with it, but it
was greater than I, and now *it* dealt with *me* . . .

When I had recovered from grief's first assault—and
make no mistake, it is as savage a mauling as a rape, and
leaves you as ravaged after—I glanced round, with a kind
of dull interest, to see where I had got to.

I seemed to be on the edge of a little wood at the valley's mouth, near the limit of our lines; by straining my
eyes I could just make out Edeyrn's stronghold of

Ratherne a few miles up the glen. *That* would have to be taken care of, I resolved, and soon too; maybe Merlynn— But nay; I had forgotten . . . I shivered again and huddled down inside my cloak. Was there no safe thought anywhere? Aught to think of that did not carry loss and bitter pain with it?

They speak truly when they say be wary of what you wish for: At once, as if my despairing question had been given the grace of an answer, I was given things to See and think of that led my mind off my more immediate woes.

It was not much unlike to what I had experienced after Cadarachta, or in Sychan; but this time the Sight took me far down the road of years: I saw the Crown pass from Arthur's line to Tarian's kindred; a queen around whom holiness blazed like Fragarach's own fire, and a king who might have taken a leaf from Edeyrn's book. Then the road bent sharply, and I beheld the Crown pass again, this time to Grehan's house; four kings and a queen all in swift succession, slain in some civil strife; later, a queen with hair as red as Grehan's, and a tall dark-haired lord who had a look of Arthur and myself, an army of trees, Gwyn's own horn . . .

I cried aloud, and the Sight released me. I thought to see Morgan come to comfort me, as she had done that other time, but the hillside was empty. Nay; she would not leave her mother just now, and besides there were preparations to be made for the ritual sending the family and friends of Uthyr Pendreic would hold that night for him. And before that could commence, I had tasks of my own that called; so I turned from all this Seeing, and trudged heavy-footed, heavy-hearted, back down the hill.

The King's tent was full of torchlight and people and silence; I stood beside Arthur, watching Morgan begin by casting the riomhall, the ritual circle. How can she *do* this, I wondered; then answered my own question—it was her place to do this, as a priestess, and that knowing gave her power, and the joy of rightness in action . . .

"Mar a bha, mar a tha," she said clearly, softly—'So it was, so it is'—and we gave her the response, as softly.

"Mar a bhitheas vyth go bragh." 'So it shall be forever . . .'

I felt the circle form and seal itself, all of us within caught up in its confines; caught the loving touch of Uthyr's presence, and smiled as Ygrawn stood forward.

"What is between the worlds belongs to both and neither," she said, and standing straight and tall and still as a candleflame, she raised her hand. "I invoke the Guardians of the Doors."

Turning sunwise, invoking to the east as was done only at times of birth and death: "The Lady is in the East. This is because from the East do all light and life proceed. Hail, Thou who art Queen of the Four Green Fields!"

And south: "The Dragon is in the South. This is because out of the South do come all strength and valor. Hail, Thou who art blood-red of a thousand battles!"

And: "The Lord is in the West. This is because into the West do all things go in the end. Hail, Thou who art Shield of Tir-n'am-beo!"

And one time more: "The Stag is in the North. This is because in the North is ever the high seat of mystery and of power. Hail, Thou who art milk-white of a thousand magics!"

Then Gweniver stepped forward to join Morgan and Ygrawn, no longer Uthyr's griefstruck niece but a High Priestess like the other two, of the ancient order of Nia the Golden.

"We come in on the wind from the East, we live out our days in the light of the South. We go out from here with the wind from the West in our faces, and we dwell thereafter in the castle that is the Crown of the North. So it was, so it is, so it shall ever be."

Three queens beside a dead king: I knew the moment, and myself stood forth; unslinging Frame of Harmony, I smiled down upon Uthyr's pale chill face—he was not there, but I knew how to reach him—and began my lament for Uthyr Ard-rígh, and ever was it sung after.

> "Thou stag amongst deer,
> Salmon amongst trout,
> Eagle amongst sparrows,
> Tall ship amongst curraghs,
> Uthyr the King, by dán restored . . ."

and so I chaunted for him whom I had loved.

The rest of the ritual passed swiftly; Kelts sorrow beyond the measure of most races for our dead, but we rejoice in their passing in the same measure, for they move now in the Light, in bright and blessed company, and any road they are never gone ... But looking at Arthur as Morgan folded Uthyr's hands over the traditional tokens, I saw only grief—such sorrow in the living as to bring tears to the eyes of the dead. And I knew there was more here than Uthyr for him: There was Merlynn, who if not dead were surely not precisely alive; our lost Companion Kei and all the others dead in the fighting for Tara; all those who might yet perish in days to come. He was King now, it was for him to think so, to grieve so ...

Yet he had taken no part in the rite as yet, though as priest and King there was claim on him that none else could fill. Now, however, he stepped forward, to stand at the foot of the dead King's bed, and put a hand inside his tunic, beneath his leinna. When he drew his hand out again, I saw that his fingers were closed upon a much-folded piece of parchment, and with a shiver of awe I recognized Edeyrn's missive, that mockery of brevity and line of honest warning that had been delivered to us in the days before Cadarachta, and I read it over once again in my mind: '*If thou come,*' it had said, in the formal script and the High Gaeloch, '*and if ever thou come to Tara.*'

And I remembered Arthur's vow upon receiving it, to keep that letter next his heart until the fight was won, or he was dead, or Edeyrn was dead ... Now I watched, as did we all, as Arthur drew Fragarach from its sheath; and that bard's mind was already casting the moment into legend and song, as Arthur, with great deliberateness and no apparent emotion whatsoever, set the Answerer's silver point to the parchment, and Edeyrn's letter was gone in a flash of flame.

And I remembered too Arthur's answer to Edeyrn's challenge: '*And if I go to Tara,*' it had read, in Gaeloch as High and a script as vaunting, '*and if I go.*'

But that seemed to be the last thing Uthyr needed to know done, for I could sense him leaving now, in accomplishment and in peace, and I made my own farewells as he went out. Morgan, working serenely, closed down the circle, and we all relaxed, as was custom, into a celebra-

tion of our loved one's life. The work was done, his and
ours together, and now was the time for warm memory;
his as he went, ours who remained.

But for the new High King and High Queen, there was
more, and other. Though no formal coronation would be
held for many days—by old tradition, not until after
Uthyr's barrowing—and no oaths would be taken until
that time by the princes and the lieges and the folk, nonetheless it was the duty of our new rulers to take oath
themselves; and now that Uthyr was sped we set our
thought to this.

Ygrawn, to whom duty had so long been action's well-
spring, had already considered it, and now she lifted a
hand to Alun Cameron, the Chief Brehon, and to Uthyr's
Taoiseach, Marigh Aberdaron.

"For the law and the governance," she said so all could
hear her. "And for the Orders, let come forward Taliesin
ap Gwyddno for the bards, and Keils Rathen for the
Fians; for the Druids"—my eyes shot to her face as she
checked an instant, but she met my gaze calmly—"since
that our friend and Archdruid Merlynn Llwyd is no more
among us, let the most senior priest stand forward, and
for the Ban-draoi the same."

It was a maimed rite in the end, not done as it should
have been done, full of uncertainty and performed by folk
all unprepared for it; but it was required, and so it was
held, and we were all relieved in the end when Alun
Cameron, improvising desperately for this unprecedented
ritual, charged us in our turn.

"Arthur Ard-rígh, Gweniver Ard-rían, now before you.
Let those who will, obey them and them alone hencefor-
ward, as sovereigns over Keltia. And those who will not,
let them go to serve Nanteos of Fomor or Arist of Alphor
or whatsoever other master they might."

No fear of that: We all swore fervently to Arthur and
to Gweniver; and all the while Ygrawn watched with
composed features and an air of dán met. *She is tired,* I
thought very privately, *we must do somewhat to ease her
burdens; she has carried far too much far too long* . . .

But we were all tired, and had not yet, I think, even
grasped the implications of this day's work . . . Morgan
came and leaned against me, much the way Cabal was
wont to do, and I ruffled her hair as I was wont to ruffle

his ears; she seemed grateful to have it so, and said no word with mind or voice.

The others had left the tent by now for the most part, just family—kin and closest friends—remained by Uthyr's bier. Soon Ygrawn would set the traditional guard around it—a warrior, a bard, a sorcerer, a liege; most like she would watch by her lord all this night, that was a widowed mate's duty and a right not even we her children would dissuade her from. But for the rest of us, it was time to give Uthyr the grace of the Last Prayer, and leave him with his lady.

Outside in the bitter chill, I stretched and flexed my fingers scrabbling at the stars; so close they seemed tonight . . . Waiting for Morgan to join me, all at once I was brought back to earth by a voice just within the tent-flap.

"A word with you—Ard-rígh." The voice smoked with scorn on the title, and I went very still, for the owner of the voice was Gweniver.

Arthur's own voice in answer was the soul of courtesy. "Ard-rían?"

I began to edge away, not wishing to be in the vicinity when *this* battle was joined; but it was not to be, for they came exploding out of the tent together, and I was caught, almost literally, between them, as if between two great feuding forces of nature.

Now you must remember that of late Arthur and Gweniver had not been on the best and warmest of terms; indeed, had scarcely seen one another until they faced off across Uthyr's deathbed. Since we landed on Tara, they had been commanding in different quarters—Gweniver holding the east, while Arthur brought off his spectacular sidemarch over the Loom and the taking of Caerdroia. They had communicated by diptych, third parties and the occasional bolt of mindspeech—and that last usually in moments of wrath.

They could, in truth, hardly be said to have worked together at all on this; and now they were yoked so for the rest of their lives, bound to one another more surely even than by the marriage oaths from which Gweniver had freed herself . . .

Well, I could see they had quite a lot to say to one another, so prudently made as if to leave; but, not even looking at me, Arthur caught me by the collar in a grip of steel.

"Nay, braud, do not remove on *our* account ... Any road, I wish you to be witness to this." He released me, and I stood chastened, not daring to shift position, even. "Like it or loathe it, from this day on we share sovereignty in Keltia, Lady. We have sworn as much, as he who lies now within did wish it."

"Aye? Ard-rígh?" Gweniver, when she chose, could put an edge on her tongue of a sharpness to cut cheese, and chose so now. "And has the Ard-rígh Arthur forgotten so quickly that which he himself did swear to?"

Arthur smiled, and my heart bled for him; how very tired he was, how grief-worn for Uthyr and Merlynn and Kei, how much he cared for this waspish queen, and she for him, though they would sooner die under torture than admit it ...

"Nay, I have not forgotten, and I hold to it; that we rule together, but will wed, if we choose to, as shall please ourselves." His hand rested now on my shoulder, and tightened. "But I swear something more, and freely: Once Keltia has been scoured, the Marbh-draoi's ills subdued, I leave it to you."

Gweniver's control slipped, and she barely caught back a gasp. "And what of you?"

I was echoing her question myself by then; but Arthur looked at neither of us as he answered.

"I have other things to attend to," he said then, and pointed straight up into the blazing night sky. "Out there."

And so he did.

BOOK III

Gráightraí

CHAPTER
17

But for all I tried, I could get no more out of Arthur that night about his future plans, and went furious to my bed, where I tossed and fussed and muttered so much and so long and so hard that at last Morgan set one bare foot in the small of my back and pushed me out onto the tent floor.

"You had no cause to do that," I said, creeping humbly back into the warmth beside her.

"Not? Then talk to me; if you are going to keep me from sleep, and have not love in mind, the least you can do is tell me a tale."

So I told her of what had befallen between Arthur and Gweniver; and she listened attentively, and sighed at the end of my telling.

"I *told* Merlynn and my mother, when first they hatched this ill-found plan, that it would be grave error to harness those two so close, and no hope of free running."

I settled more comfortably against her. "We have been down this road many times before. There was no other way."

"Maybe," she agreed after a while. "But to the best of my knowing Arthur has never before threatened leaving Keltia."

"He told me it is in pursuit of the galláin Edeyrn hired

to fight us; he wishes to punish them on their own home ground—or space."

Morgan snorted. "This is *I*, his sister; let him try a better story on me . . ."

I was as fearful and exasperated as she, but felt a perverse loyalty to my lifelong friend. "Have you any better solution, then? Hu Mawr! If so, I pray you tell us all!" Then was immediately contrite; her father lay dead in the next tent but one. "Ah, cariad, no matter." I gathered her into my arms; she seemed little and simple and small this night. "Has anyone told your sister of the King's—of Uthyr's death?"

She shifted against me. "Aye, I think Tari or Daronwy—I know not. Someone will see to it."

I held her until she fell asleep; by now I was wide awake, and carefully setting Morgan onto her own pillows I lay back and stared up at the tent ceiling. Why had Merlynn to be taken from us just when his vision was needed most? He it was who had been chief architect of all this: to destroy the Marbh-draoi, to make Arthur and Gweniver co-rulers; now, when it came to the working-out, he was not here to guide it. Though, surely, it was scarce his own fault that he was not; or was it?

I glanced over at a small murmur from Morgan; but she slept deep, if not peacefully. Maybe Arthur's intent *was* all for the best; if he were not here, might not things go more smoothly in the transition than they had done otherwise? Still, it seemed the height of folly for the strongest sword-arm in Keltia to be elsewhere employed just when it might be needed here more than ever . . . I smiled in spite of my fears. Gwennach was not like to give anything away, or let aught be taken from her. Besides, she had good helpers: Keils, for one, though that could be a problem right there, and we would have to keep an eye on that union; not to mention Ygrawn and Morgan, and our brother and sister Companions; and new comrades too, who had been of such importance in the victory at Caerdroia and here . . .

For the first time since—well, since leaving Gwynedd, I allowed myself to think on what had in truth happened here. We had won. We had *won*. Oh, to be sure, there was much—a daunting much—still to be done, on other worlds as well as on this one; but the bottom note was unchanged: We had triumphed over Edeyrn; his sorceries and his Ravens had availed him not, in the end, and we had won. Uthyr would be pleased ...

I awoke sweating and shuddering: a dream of Gwaelod, such as I had not had in years, walls of water, green and glassy, roaring over me, yet leaving me unharmed. I turned to Morgan, but the bed was cold and empty; she had slipped away without disturbing me. *Would that she had,* I thought meanly, *I might not have dreamed so else* ... While I hastily dressed—for I heard the camp stirring outside, and guessed it was later than I would have wished it—I ran over the thing in my mind for perhaps the thousandth time, thinking maybe, even now, to find some way of avoiding the pit I saw yawning before our feet ... But for all my thought nothing came to mind; I tied off my last point, threw on a cloak and went out to look for my King and Queen.

I found my Queen first. Gweniver was already hedged round with that indefinable apartness that defines a monarch; since last night she had taken it on, will she or nill she—it was as much in her as it was in the perceptions of those who approached her. She even appeared physically different; taller, maybe, or older, or was it thinner or paler or more remote—I could not name the difference, and as I gave her the formal salute due to the ruler of Keltia, it troubled me that I could not.

But she was still Gwennach ... As I hailed her, she looked up, flushed and gave me a quick kiss. Not uncommon for her to greet me so; we had long history, and a casual affection not unlike to that of sibs. But it was uncommon enough for me to be a little surprised all the same, and I responded with more warmth; it seemed something she needed just now.

"We are readying to break camp," she said, gesturing vaguely round at the chaos. Indeed, I could see for myself: The melancholy business had already begun of preparing to convey the dead King to Caerdroia. It would not be as we had wished, but still ...

"He will be barrowed at Ni-maen," said Gweniver; she had followed my gaze, and my thought.

"And is not that more than we ever dared hope for, back on Gwynedd, at the Bear's Grove, or at Coldgates?"

I asked gently, and saw her wistful smile and slow nod. "But how is it with *you*, Lady?"

She startled at the title I had chosen, quite deliberately, to use to her. Perhaps it was the first time she had been called so, by the address and inflection given only to a reigning Ard-rían. Certainly it was the first time I had called her so; but I had done it for a reason—

"The sooner you 'custom yourself to it, Gwennol, the easier it will be in the end," I whispered for only her to hear.

"Aye," she answered, with a certain ruefulness. "But it is a hard thing to grow used to."

"All the more reason." I paused for a moment. "What will you do, you and Artos? You must have discussed between you how to divide up the needs of rule?"

Gweniver laughed outright. "You mean who shall get to wear the Copper Crown when, or which of us on what occasions shall sit in the Throne of Scone? Nay, Tal-bach, I think we shall let the brehons, as interpreters of the law, and the bards, as masters of protocol, work *that* one out!" The gray eyes danced. "Or not ... I think, Arthur shall get the Crown, I the Silver Branch, no one gets the Throne—we can have two little benches built in front of it instead—and we take it in turns to wear the Great Seal of Keltia. Does that seem fair to you?"

I laughed in spite of myself. "A decision worthy of Sulla vhic Dhau— Or, consider: You might divide the year as do the Goddess and the God; you to rule Beltain to Samhain, Artos Samhain to Beltain ... Gwennach, do you know, truly, what has happened here?"

There was urgency in my voice—did she, in fact, understand?—and caring, as friend to friend. She drew a long uneven breath, and the look in her eyes was something akin to panic.

"Nay, Talyn, I think I have not grasped it," she said in a low rapid voice. "I hear myself called 'Lady,' 'Ard-rían,' speak of Artos as Ard-rígh; but upon my soul I cannot make myself accept it, cannot *know* it! Edeyrn is dead. Merlynn is gone. Uthyr is dead. I am High Queen. We have won. It is so—much." The controlled tone caught, faltered. "But why, *why*, cannot I feel it?"

And I, a bard, her friend, had no answer.

* * *

When we took Caerdroia, there had been other things to think about; none of us had had time really to look around us and *see* the City we had won. Now, as we rode through the Wolf Gate, to the sound of pipes and muffled drums far ahead, following Arthur and Gweniver who followed Ygrawn who rode behind Uthyr's bier drawn upon a war chariot, I glanced about, and marvelled.

Morgan pretended to be unimpressed. "Oh aye—a most defensible rock, to be sure. Small wonder we had to sneak in by the servitors' entrance last time we were here . . ."

We were headed up through the streets of the lower city to Turusachan, the citadel that reared tremendously up at the top of the long rising slope to the foot of the Loom. I tried to cast my mind back to that time only a few weeks since; but all I could recall was utter chaos, a confused impression of battle and a certain frustration at continually finding no enemy to fight . . . This time was better, even though the joy at Edeyrn's overthrow was tempered by grief for the dead Uthyr.

"They hardly knew him, Talyn," murmured Morgan, reading my thought as easily as she ever did. "Those two"—she nodded at the straight backs of Arthur and Gweniver, who rode before us—"are the rulers they have waited for. They will sorrow dutifully for my father, but it is my brother and my cousin whom they hold in their hearts. Do not blame them overmuch."

"And Ygrawn?" I asked presently. "What of the Queen-mother?"

But Morgan only laughed.

The funeral rites were held for Uthyr Pendreic, Ard-rígh of Keltia, at the ancient stone circle of Ni-maen, as was traditional for one who had ruled, however briefly. Not only kings and queens were barrowed here in Calon Eryri, but those of their own kindred as well; even, sometimes, those who had served the Throne, ministers and warlords and diplomats, or those whom the Throne wished to honor, great sorcerers or warriors or bards or lawgivers. A peaceful and holy place in which to leave one's mortal form; but I would not have chosen so, myself.

The rite was but a brief one—all that had been needful

had been done, back at Nandruidion, Uthyr was long since safe on his road—and soon enough we were all filing soberly down the narrow trail again. Morgan, as ever, walked beside me, and I found my gaze going to her in wonder and not a little fear, as I remembered.

The last day before the ride to Caerdroia had seen all manner of loose ends tied off: orders issued by Arthur and Gweniver, separately and conjointly, people arriving in camp from other corners of the planet, from off-planet, even—Grehan Aoibhell from Erinna, Tryffin back from a brief dash to his homeworld of Kernow, Tarian's kindred in from Scota. But it was my Guenna who had bound off the last knot, tied it off with finality too . . .

In the dawn, she had ridden up the dale to Ratherne, with me and Daronwy and a few others; and there as the light broke over that tower of iniquity she had thrown down its walls by the power of her magic. One moment it had stood there, gray and solid in the dawn; the next, it was dust and rubble, all its sorcerous defenses breached by Edeyrn's death, all its resistance withdrawn.

I had been shaken by the thing—this was, after all, where my own father had been slain—but Morgan's face had had no emotion on it at all. Just a face in composure, a face in repose; fair and cold and pale in the early morning chill. But as the walls had begun to crack, the stones to fall like rain, the ground to roll beneath our feet, Morgan's face had stayed so; and that, I think, frightened me more than all.

I had taxed her with it later, but she had looked at me as if I had lost my wits, even asked me if I had. And all at once I had been minded of one I had not thought of in some time . . . Twice, now, in my life had I seen Birogue of the Mountain (and some small part of me knew that I should see her yet again ere all was done); but now, unlooked-for, I saw her there in Morgan's face. And though that face had been never far from my own, sleeping and waking, for the past half-decade, I had looked on it then as on a stranger's . . .

As I did now, walking down the back of Eagle along the Way of Souls. If Morgan noticed, she gave no sign she had done so; but kept her eyes on the notch of the pass below, where Caerdroia could just be seen through the gap in the valley walls. Arthur and Gweniver were well ahead of us; Ygrawn had wished to remain alone at the grave with Uthyr for a while, and would herself come down when she was ready.

My attention was claimed by a most intrusive sound of weeping, and I shifted, frowning, to look for its cause. Not far to look: On Morgan's right and a little behind walked the source of the disturbance: Marguessan.

The dead King's elder daughter leaned heavily (and all for show; she had been lighter of the prince Mordryth for many months now, and she had ever been strong as a gauran) on the arm of her husband, Irian, who looked only solicitous and concerned for his wife's well-being.

I looked away, feeling my gorge rise. None of us had any use whatsoever for either the Princess or her cipher lord; nay, nor for their spawn, most like, what time he should come to be of an age to grate us as much as did his parents ... During the last course of the campaign for Gwynedd, we had not had to much trouble ourselves with Marguessan; her pregnancy had kept her confined to the relative safety of her husband's kindred's lands in the Old North, distant from the fierce last battles before Owein had been overthrown. And, crabjaw though he was, Irian, it was reluctantly acknowledged, *had* contributed to the success of the sail down Glora that delivered our forces to Raven's Rift; but even that small praise was grudgingly offered.

And, no mistake, they both knew it; they might be tiresome, and even evil, as Uthyr himself had warned, but stupid they were not. They were well aware they had been summoned to Tara only because there would have been general shock and appallment if Uthyr's interment had been held without them. Not to mention Arthur's and Gweniver's coronation, which maybe I had better not mention just now ...

Indeed, how Marguessan was going to cope with that would be a sight worth seeing. It was still my private, deeply held belief, you understand, that Marguessan was resentful of Uthyr's gift of the Ard-tiarnas to Arthur and Gweniver; no matter that that 'gift' had been mandated clear as day by Brendan's own law so many centuries since. Uthyr had had no choice in the thing: But plainly Marguessan felt otherwise, as the dead King's eldest child, and, looking sidewise at her now, I had the most terrible premonition that Marguessan Pendreic, Duchess of Eildon, Lady of Locryn, Princess of the House of Dôn, had not entirely resigned herself just yet to the reign of her cousin and her cousin-halfbrother. It was one time, dare I say it myself, where my Seeing was not clouded; but it took long to come to focus—maybe, too long . . .

If I have said little of Arthur in these pages just past, let you know that has been by intent as much as by the chances of the tale. At first there was too much going on, in the tremendous dislocation caused by Uthyr's death and Edeyrn's fall and Merlynn's vanishment; we were both of us simply too busy with detail to have even a quiet moment or two for one another, and after that the mantle of rulership had settled down over him, as invisibly and irrevocably as it had folded itself around Gweniver. But that night at Caerdroia, as I prowled around my new quarters, in a small tower overlooking the sea, unsettled as a cat in a new place, he came quietly in, in the old way, without knocking; just slipped into the room like a ghost, and took a seat by the fire.

After a suitable greeting, I let him sit there awhile in silence before I turned from my contemplation of the moonlit waves so far below.

"I hate heights, you know well, Artos," I said then, in mock complaint. "How did you let the rechtair assign these rooms to me?"

The laugh too was his old laugh. "Oh, by policy, to be sure, did you not suspect?" The smile died away, and he added softly, "Nay—for that this tower connects to my own, and this was the nearest I could get you for just such talks as these—I will have need of them, and you."

"Not if you still plan on leaving Keltia to go adventuring."

I had been watching him keenly, and saw him flush. "You do not approve, I know, Talyn—but I had hoped for you to come with me."

I startled as if he had slapped me. "I had not thought—" Suddenly I leaned forward, put my hand on his arm. "Artos—why are you going? If it is just prudence, to chase the galláin home, let Grehan or Tari or someone do it for you—you are Ard-rígh now, you are needed here."

He would not look at me. "Am I?" he asked presently. "Am I indeed?"

"What—Ard-rígh? Or needed? Artos, you are both . . ."

"I wonder." He stood up, went over to where I had earlier stood, looking through a mullioned window out onto a little balcony. "I miss Merlynn, braud," he said, and I felt tears burn behind my eyes to hear him echo my own thought. "Miss his counsel—*he* would tell me what was my best course."

"Nay, that is where you are so wrong; he would tell you that only you can determine of your best course. Never would he have told you what to do—what is on you, Artos? Truly—this is I Talyn. Speak."

I had tried no bardic tricks of voice or tone on him, but he opened visibly under my words, was again my Artos, my brother and friend.

"Gwennach has said she will wed me after all." He laughed at my goggled surprise. "Surely that does not surprise you so much? My mother was utterly unamazed to hear of it. I think it had been in Gwennach's mind all along, and only when Uthyr died— Well, she has informed me that she will honor Uthyr's wishes, any road, and more to the point, has told Alun Cameron and Marigh Aberdaron that she will do so, and to draw up the fiants."

I was for once bereft of words. That Gweniver should change her mind was perhaps no great wonder; but that she should so swiftly go on record with it to the Chief Brehon and the acting Taoiseach spoke volumes. This was real; this was going to happen after all, and very soon too—

"What of Keils?" I asked after a while. "Are they not—"

"They are." For the first time, Arthur looked troubled. "They are. But that need not alter anything: Keils can be far-charach, or lennaun, as he and Gwennach please; nothing to hinder. There have been royal conjuncts since Brendan's time, and will be long past our day. No great difficulty."

"Is it not?" I asked very gently. "You and Gwennach— Artos, I have seen you together, I know how you do feel."

"Do you? When even *I* do not know how I do feel? I wonder!" He ran a hand over his beard, visibly willing himself to calm. "Gweniver and I, just now, have a duty only to duty, not to love. It may come to that in future, I hope that it may, but for now, not so. We must be High King and High Queen together, by Uthyr's wisdom and the will of the folk; and now she feels, she believes, that if we wed as Uthyr wished us, things will be easier not only for the realm but for ourselves. And I cannot stay: The reiving is necessity if we are to feel safe within our borders—the maigen of Keltia, that I and she must protect."

"And is that it?" I asked, when the silence had grown strained. "Is it all for Keltia? What about Artos? Where is he in this?"

Arthur stirred in the window-seat where he had ensconced himself. "Since Gwenwynbar, as you know well, Talyn, I have linked myself with no one in love; oh, the odd bedding, to be sure, but even those—"

I did know; though I had ever thought his reluctance caused not by a still-flaming brand for Gwenwynbar but by hurt and hate and cold self-loathing. Too, those brief encounters he spoke of had been almost exclusively with women he held as friends, a kind of mutual comforting as much as physical release—he had even been with our old comrade Daronwy twice or thrice, and well I knew there was no romance in *that* ... I faulted none of them, for Gweniver and I had done as much, one time, ourselves—

But Arthur was looking at me, a quizzical smile touching the corners of his mouth beneath the beard.

"I know all about it, Talyn," he said, and I started violently.

"You took long enough to mention it, then," I said. "Well then?"

He laughed. "Well what? I but wanted to tell you, before Gwennach and I wed."

"Did she tell you? It was no matter of romance, Artos—"

"I know that. Gweniver told me, and you would have told me tonight; but it was in truth Gwenwynbar told me first, the night before she left me. I think she hoped to use it to hurt me."

"And did it then? Does it now?" I said very low. "We did not mean to hurt any, and there seemed no reason then why any should be hurt."

Arthur laughed again. "Just so—nay, my brother, I am

only glad you and she found some joy each of the other. It but binds us closer: you and Gwennach, Gwennach and I, you and my sister."

"Well," I said, daring to match his smile—and still I could *not* work out why I felt so guilty—"let us only hope it gets not garbled in the telling, down the years. Else they will be saying that Arthur the King not only married his cousin but slept with his sister."

He rolled his eyes. "They would not!"

But, you know, of course, they did ...

After he had gone, considerably more cheerful than I had seen him for some days, I thought about what he had not said, as much as what he *had* said. It seemed he had yet to come to terms with all this himself, every bit as much as Gweniver: this business of being Ard-rígh. So hard it must be ... For I had risen at his entrance, as I had never done in all our years together, had waited for him to speak first, had addressed him in the first instance as 'Lord,' just as I had done for Gweniver—bards being sticklers for propriety.

And I had seen how it had shaken him, that I did so; though I had returned at once to our old bantering way. But, as I had said to Gwennach, soonest accepted, least hurt; he would have to learn as quickly as she, how best to deal with this new aspect; almost a fith-fath, a shapeshift, even—Artos into Ard-rígh, Gwennach into High Queen ...

As to the wedding, I knew their reasons, and would keep my counsel. Oh, it might be better to delay it, let Keltia calm down after the recent total upheaval before putting the realm through yet another drama. But maybe Gweniver was right, maybe it would indeed be a way of ensuring some kind of rough stability. If the folk were to see their rulers united in flesh as well as in spirit—it might just be the strong center upon which all else could form. By far would it be not the first time romance—or at least the seeming of romance—had saved a throne ...

For the truth here was that Keltia could fall. Edeyrn's hand had been so heavy upon us all these years that the sudden freedom that had come in its place could destroy us, far surer than he could ever have done; and if a wedding could help avert that, so be it.

But Arthur's reasons for leaving, too, had been cogently argued: And Edeyrn was guilty there as well. The galláin he had bought in service against Arthur now knew Keltia's military strengths and weaknesses better than any ought to know them outside our bounds; something would have to be done to alter that case, and it could not be done too swiftly, lest those we chased off come back with friends, and we have to fight them even at the coronation . . .

Leaving Keltia—it was not something I had ever thought of doing, and I found myself shaken to my core at the idea. With the exception of Ravens and other of Edeyrn's creatures, no Kelt to my knowledge had left the Six Nations for many hundreds of years, save on those rare scouting expeditions that now and again some First Lord of War or Taoiseach or curious Ard-rían would send back to Earth, just to see how things stood with our ancient homeworld. This would be something very different: Kelts going out reiving, to make our hand felt in war on other worlds. Was it right, I wondered; was it even clever?

Arthur's parting shot to me had been clever enough, that was certain . . . As he left, he had paused in the door, as if caught by a sudden afterthought.

"Oh, and before we go, Talyn, you know—you and Guenna, you might wed also. Though we should not be gone all that long—"

We were to be gone seven years; but even Arthur would not have believed that if you had told him.

So it came to be that before the coronation, Keltia was to see a royal wedding. Two weddings, as it turned out; for when Morgan and I discussed all this in bed that night—a wonderful new bed in that tower room, carved oak golden with newness and hung about with tapestries—we agreed on it at last.

Oh, we had asked and accepted, turn and turn about, many times before—we had known since our first night that we were wedded already, in soul if not yet in law; known too that one day we would make that last and greatest promise. But, as other things took precedence, it seemed not so pressing; we considered ourselves to be wedded, and that had always been enough for both of us.

At least, until now, when the prospect of leaving Keltia made me wish for something more formalized, something more—

"More real?" Morgan, in her usual annoying way, finished my thought. "Talyn, I ask you, what could be more real than this?" She gestured to us lying there intertwined in the splendid fourposted bed.

But I was not annoyed . . . "Naught, cariad. Never. But I wish it even so. So, if it please Your Highness—"

She laughed, a lovely, silvery sound, and taking my face between her hands kissed me lightly and lovingly.

"It pleases my Highness very much indeed."

CHAPTER
18

So Arthur Penarvon wedded Gweniver Pendreic on the day of Beltain, the first of summer, in the holy circle of Ni-maen, in the presence of Court and kindred, in the sight of all Kelts.

It was a wedding at the stones, a full legal union in the faith; though not, to the surprise of no one, a handfasting. That was different: A handfasting is the true wedding, the Great Marriage, the earthly counterpart of the sacred union between the Goddess and the King; not to be entered into lightly, or without deepest love and firmest purpose, for it lasts not merely until death or the law shall dissolve it but endures beyond death and law alike. Even couples wedded civilly or religiously, blissfully companionate for thrice fifty years, ofttimes never deem themselves ready for the vast undertaking that is a handfasting, or what such faith requires. Small wonder then that Arthur and Gweniver had fought shy of this; it is more than a marriage, it is a union of souls. Even Morgan and I had chosen it for ourselves with some awe; though never once doubts . . .

But that came later. Following straight upon their marriage, Arthur and Gweniver were crowned, right there in the circle, Ard-rígh and Ard-rían. The Copper Crown rested briefly upon each of their heads in turn, the auburn and the ebon; the Silver Branch felt the touch of their hands together. While below, in the Hall of Heroes, Gweniver's jesting word to me had been improved upon: In front of the empty Throne of Scone, not benches but two high seats, scarcely less grand than the throne itself, had been set up, and stood waiting for the new-made monarchs to fill them.

The rings had been a knottier problem. There had been, of course, a Great Seal of Keltia, used by the monarch for all official matters of state; of no particular antiquity, this latest one had been only a few hundred years old—they change often, with a change in House or merely at a new monarch's whim.

For continuity's sake, Arthur and Gweniver had wished to use this very ring; but Edeyrn had defiled it, and it had been destroyed when Ratherne was thrown down. That left us with the problem: Two monarchs, no Seal; and they could not have used the same Seal in any case . . .

In the end, two rings had been cast: Arthur, perhaps not surprisingly, had made them both, glad of the chance to exercise his long-unpracticed craft. For himself, he had chosen from the Crown treasuries a huge flawed emerald that had belonged to Athyn Cahanagh, his boyhood hero. Her lord had given her the stone on their handfasting, and it had never left her finger thereafter, but once only, until the day she died. Gweniver's choice for Seal was a sapphire, blue as Kernish skies or the cornflower that carpets the Loom valleys in high summer; it had a history of its own, having been Breila Douglas's tinnól to Alawn Lastking, and had a strong link to the House of Dôn. Both stones had been newly carved inghearrad with the knot of the Six Nations—undifferenced, naught to show whose hand had made which sealing—and set by Arthur in bands of heavy gold knotwork, and hallowed by the new heads of the Druid and Ban-draoi orders. And I was not the only one who remarked on the fact that both stones had been in their origin gifts of love . . .

Any road, they were wed; and as I stood on Arthur's left, as his supporter or groomsman (Gweniver had wished Morgan as brideswoman, but knew well the outfall if Marguessan were so slighted in public, and so had chosen instead Tarian Douglas, who was so old and close a friend), I could not help but feel a sense of surging hope and joy and optimism, a buoyancy of heart that even all our victories in the field had not managed to bestow upon me.

Why should *not* this work out, after all? They had been through so much together: They shared even their childhood loves and losses, they had so many years of being friends and colleagues and co-workers for Keltia's weal. They understood one another and respected one another; and love too was there, if not yet perhaps admitted or acknowledged, or even truly understood . . . It could happen, that this would be a true marriage, could even come to a handfasting, some time down the way. They would have to work at it, more even than the ordinary pair; but they were *not* ordinary, and still it could be—

With a start I realized that the ceremonies at the stones were over, and we were falling back in line to return to Caerdroia and the far longer ceremonies that would follow, in the Hall of Heroes, where Arthur and Gweniver together would receive the traditional oaths 'of hand and heart,' the fealty Keltia's lieges paid their sovereigns on the day of coronation. As a bard, I had been keenly interested in this aspect of the day—for never had such a thing been before in Keltia, a dual sovereignty—and myself had helped the brehons work out the wording of the new-written oaths.

So that when I myself came to stand before my High King and High Queen—and make no mistake, they were in that moment *not* Artos and Gwennach—there was such a shaking in my chest that it seemed all must see me tremble with the force of it.

But that was merely my perception; Morgan told me later I had stood like a rock in the sea. I myself remember very little: the coldness of my hands, the warmth of Gwennach's enfolding them; the extra pressure of love and friendship and brotherhood that Arthur's hands gave round mine; the love on both their faces, as I looked up on finishing my oaths; the sly glint of humor behind Arthur's eyes; the veiled sadness in Gweniver's.

It was a moment of remarkable solemnity, and it caught me all unawares. I had been expecting something, oh, I know not, something less awesome, less freighted with dán; *why* I should have expected so, I have not the smallest clue—everything else for the past forty-five years had been packed with high purpose, stuffed full of dán from now to Nevermas; why should this moment have been any different?

I tried to explain it later to Ygrawn, as we sat side by side at the great banquet table in Mi-cuarta, the palace's feast hall, larger than Tair Rhamant's entirety.

The Queen-mother—that was the style Arthur and Gweniver had begged her to accept, thinking Queen-Dowager, Rían-dhuair, not precisely suited to Ygrawn's sensibilities—looked lovely on this day; care seemed to have left her, and though loss still shadowed her, those famous amethyst eyes were clear and bright as she looked out over the hall below us.

"I tell you, Talyn," she said in the voice I remembered from my earliest years, "glad am I it is Artos and Gwennach to be sitting in the high seats this night, and not Uthyr and myself."

I glanced at her keenly; but all my Druid truth-sense told me she was speaking her heart. She saw the doubt behind my look, and laughed.

"Aye, truth enough, if perhaps not all the truth—" The lovely face changed indefinably. "I was thinking of Amris today; of how it would have been had he lived, of us together on the throne."

I was astounded, for I had not heard Ygrawn mention her first lord since, oh, our days in Coldgates thirty years ago. But nor did I wish to upset or offend her—

"Do you think of him often, methryn?"

And was again astounded, as Ygrawn replied simply and starkly, "Every hour." She smiled at my discomfiture. "Nay, amhic, do not think I have dwelt unhealthily upon it—But I have never loved any man as I loved my lost prince, Talyn. Had I not had Artos to think of, it might well have been that after Amris I would never have wedded again; certain it was I had no real wish to. Though I respected Gorlas, and I cared for Uthyr—none but Amris ever had my heart, and that is as it is. Perhaps a stronger woman would not have remarried, even so; I am only Ygrawn, and did what I thought was right." Her glance went to her son, who was replying to some shouted pleasantry from the lower tables. "Yet he was Arthur's father, and he would have been King himself in this hour—it is hard not to think on, not to sorrow for might-have-beens."

"He would have been most proud of you, Lady," I said softly, and took her hand to kiss it. "You did well; he would be the first to tell you so. For Arthur, and for Keltia, and for yourself. You would have made him a noble Queen; nay—you *were* his Queen, and are still, and did so."

Ygrawn bent her head. "Wicked lad—you have made me weep . . ."

"Ah, that is naught new for us!" And we both laughed, and so got through the moment together.

But Ygrawn was not the only one to be thinking of the past this night . . . On my other side, Morgan—or, as she had earlier been proclaimed in the Hall of Heroes, Morguenna, Princess of the House of Dôn and of the Name of Pendreic, Duchess of Ys—too had been reflecting, and turned to me with a sudden rush.

"Oh, Talyn, Merlynn—" She could say no more; but no more was needed. I too had been missing my old teacher; this day, this night, were the fruit of his workings, and he should have been with us to feast upon it.

"He knows," was all I could offer; and knew, somehow, that it was true. But it was *not* enough . . .

Of the others at the high table, suffice it to say that they were all much mindful of how we had come there: Tarian, Grehan, Keils, Daronwy, Ferdia, Elen, Betwyr, Tryffin, all of our oldest and closest Companionship; officers of state, such as we had—Alun Cameron, Marigh the Taoiseach, Maderil Gabric our Chief Bard, a few others; and the royal family, by extension and courtesy as well as by blood.

Arthur and Gweniver seemed above it, sitting side by side in the great high-backed carved chairs at the table's midpoint. They had shed the robes of state they had worn in the Hall of Heroes, and were clad now in simple splendor: Artos in velvet tunic and trews, Gwennach in a long silky gúna that showed off her form to perfection. And each wore the tinnól the other had given, the marriage-gift exchanged between partners: Usually given in private, either on the wedding-night or the morning following, tinnól is as a rule something substantial, but also meaningful—jewels or land or titles and such come generally under the purview of the tinnscra gift or the portions arranged by the kindreds involved. Still, a tinnól of jewels was most usual, and so it was in this case: Arthur's shoulders bore a significant and heavy collar of gold links worked with the Pendreic devices of white stag and red dragon; while a magnificent necklace of seastones and rose-cut diamonds, Arthur's undoubted workmanship, graced Gweniver's throat.

I was suddenly sad; these gifts were meant to be private offerings, not shared straightway with onlookers but kept close awhile, between the wedded pair. There seemed to be a statement here, by King and Queen alike, but I was not quite sure, for myself, just what it was that was being so plainly declared . . .

At last Arthur and Gweniver looked at one another, as they had done with sad infrequency over the course of the evening's feast, and as one rose up in their places. We followed suit instantly, and fell silent to hear what they would say to us.

With deference plain to all, Arthur waited for Gweniver to speak first; when she did not, he smiled easily to cover the moment.

"My very dears—my kin, my Companions, my friends—I give you thanks, and blessing, and good even to you all. For the High Queen and for myself—and for Artos and Gwennach, still more so."

He paused expectantly, as if to give Gweniver a further chance to address the Hall; but she simply gave a small smile, to him and to us, and a regal inclination of her head, and left her place beside him. For one moment I actually thought Arthur would refuse to follow her out; but after a plain hesitation he did so, and our cheers and good wishes pursued them from Mi-cuarta.

The festivities bubbled up again; indeed, before the doors had closed behind Gweniver and Arthur, Irian Locryn, Marguessan's husband, had himself risen in his own place at table, to rather drunkenly bid us all remain and make merry, before he collapsed back into his chair.

I shook my head; it *was* Irian's place, strictly speaking, as nearest male relation—he was, after all, husband to the heir-presumptive to the Throne of Scone. Marguessan, not Morgan, was the elder of Uthyr's children; and the mother of Mordryth, so far the only royal child of the next generation. But still.

Marguessan. I drummed my fingers on the wine-stained linen cloth and looked to my left, past the empty chairs of the King and Queen, to the profile that was so uncannily like my Morgan's own. Marguessan Pendreic, for the moment Tanista of Keltia—and a scareful thought *that* was, you have *no* idea—sat sipping wine from a silver cup, listening to some tale being told her by—I strained to see—Ferdia, of all people.

She looked not best pleased to be there at all; and I could guess that there was a fierce tiny war going on just now in Marguessan's—well, what it pleased her to call her heart. Marguessan and I went back many years in unfriendship: back to a time when I had thwarted her working ruin, for her own amusement, on a helpless sailing ship off the Gwynedd coast. She had never forgiven; and I had never forgotten ...

As if all at once she had become aware of my scrutiny, she suddenly turned those strange eyes of hers on me—blue-irised, black-rimmed, most unsettling. I inclined my head to her in politeness to a princess, lifted my own cup in salute; she flushed a dull angry red, and turned away.

"You and my sister should just fight it out one day, Talyn, you know," said Morgan, amused; for all Marguessan was her twin sister, Morgan stayed clear of her as a cat does of water, with something of the cat's same finicking distaste too. Even now, I could almost see Morgan shaking figurative paws at the idea of having to be in such proximity to her elder sib.

I was a little chagrined. "Does it show as much as that?"

"You must be joking! All Keltia probably knows how cordially the two of you do mislike one another—"

"Never mind. Where is Mordryth?" I looked around. "Surely she would have had him here for the ceremony?"

"Oh aye, he was up at the stones, and Irian held him for the oath-taking in the Hall; did you not see? I think the nurses have taken him away; he is not yet a year old, remember."

I remembered, right enough; but said no more of it. After the coronation festivities were over, Marguessan and Irian and their spawn would be going back to Gwynedd, to their lordships there; I could endure her presence at least until that happier day.

But as we two quitted the banquet a few hours later,

and strolled hand in hand down the endless empty carpeted corridors of Turusachan to our own chambers, I could not, for all my regard for propriety, keep my thoughts from going to Arthur and Gweniver. And though it is no part of my duties as bard and historian to indulge in revelations of the marriage-bed, I could not help but wonder, and hope, all the same.

The next morning saw no prodigies or astonishments: Arthur and Gweniver, looking just like themselves, appeared for the daymeal in Mi-cuarta, and vanished afterwards to their separate offices and shared Councils. All of us who had been hoping for some fireflaw of revelation to have blasted them both in the hours between middlenight and morning were doomed to disappointment: They behaved to one another as they had ever done, with courtesy and humor and respect and friendship. And all of us were sick about it.

"Nay, come!" said Morgan incredulously, when she had finally stopped laughing. "Did you truly think they would take one look at each other across the pillows, the scales would fall from their eyes and they would be instantly and evermore in love?"

"I must admit," I said with tremendous dignity, "that the thought had crossed my mind. And not I alone, Guenna!" I hastened to add, for she was laughing again. "I lay you odds ten-tenths of Mi-cuarta last night was hoping the same—"

"Then more fools all of you. Can you not accept that Arthur and Gwennach are wed where once we never thought them to be, will rule together, have a close and enviable relationship, yet still need not of bounden imperative be in love with one another? They can be a perfectly good King and Queen without it, you know; maybe even a better King and Queen without it, who can say?"

I muttered something shamefaced and savage all in one, and Morgan relented.

"Ha-yaud! Listen, Talyn, while I try to put this as delicately as I can for your bardic sensibilities: Gwennach told me earlier that she and Arthur last night fulfilled in every particular their function as monarchs; and too, that neither of them found it precisely the onerous chore both of them had thought." Her mirth renewed itself as she saw the look on my face. "Not that I think they will make a pleasant habit of it, mind! But aye, they have lain together, and not for the last time, either; so the succession will be direct, and all you old wives of both sexes can stop fretting, and none of us need worry about my sister or her brat stepping in."

"Well. I am chastened as well as instructed— Perhaps that is all we can hope for, after all," I said after some thought. "An heir in time, and two monarchs who have care and liking and respect for one another; that is not so bad a bargain."

"So my father thought when first he made it," said Morgan at her driest. "Let us go now to Council, you and I, if you are done looking under other folk's coverlets. The real work is about to begin."

Lest you think Morgan was one of those extremely tiresome folk who are always right no matter what (I mean, genuinely right; not just thinking they are in the evidence's despite), let me hasten to add she was wrong on this occasion. The real work, as she would put it, had in fact begun long since.

From Edeyrn's overthrow and Uthyr's passing to the crowning of Keltia's first double sovereignty had been six weeks or so, from the spring Daynighting to the coming of summer; and in those weeks we had not yet even begun to make the tiniest of inroads on what had to be done in Keltia. Only think: Two hundred years of Edeyrn's rule to make right again; the Fainne and the representative bodies of governance to be re-established; the clann system to be restored to its old smooth functioning. Not to mention ridding the realm of the worst (we could hardly hope for it to be the last) of Edeyrn's lackeys and marplots and turncloaks, and setting at naught any lingering magics the Marbh-draoi or his spoiled priests may have left us as surprises, and rounding up any Ravens that may have eluded the great sweeps Grehan and Elen and Betwyr had been conducting.

Those last were a thornier problem even than the seal rings: They were traitors, of course, and as such drew sentence of death; but really now, could we truly call them traitors to have gone along with a ruler who had been at his evil-doing before their grandparents were born? They could, it is true, have chosen the Counterinsurgency, the life of exile and hiding and fear that we ourselves had elected; and perhaps they should be made to answer for that they had not. But death? I am not the gentlest or most forgiving of souls, not by a long road; have done my share of slaughter. Yet when it came to this I found myself gored by the horns of that familiar beast Dilemma (and it never has only two, you know); so pointed were its jabs that I brought the matter up in one of our early Councils.

Now Arthur and Gweniver were already ruling conjointly, and the first thing they did as one was to choose themselves a working Council; and one of the first people they named to it was Taliesin ap Glyndour. I was not surprised to be so named—indeed, I would have been devastated had I *not* been chosen—but had misgivings all the same. Then again, so did most of those who were ordered to the Council, even (or especially) those who had best deserved it: Keils Rathen, Arthur's—aye, Arthur's, not Gweniver's—first appointment, to the post of First Lord of War; Tarian Douglas, to take over from the weary and ailing Marigh Aberdaron as Taoiseach; Grehan Aoibhell, as Earl Marischal; Scathach Aodann, teacher to Artos and me at Daars, victor at Ravens' Rift, as Earl Guardian; Elen and Daronwy and myself as common or garden Councillors. The rest of the positions were filled by veterans of Uthyr's service, or mutual choices of the High Queen and High King. All in all, a likely lot; and so when I made my halting protest, it was scarcely as if none of them had heard it before ...

"Death," said Tarian unemphatically. "It is Elen's opinion and Alun's that they cannot be successfully reclaimed. Our new Archdruid, too, and our Ban-draoi Magistra agree with this course, Talyn. My sorrow you cannot see it so."

Across the table, those she had named looked back evenly at me: Alun Cameron, Chief Brehon, my old dear friend Elenna, the Magistra Becney Vechan; and sitting apart a little from the rest, Comyn Duchray, Merlynn's successor. And that was part of the problem right there, for I had violently opposed naming anyone to the post just yet, though doubtless this Duchray was as worthy as any, and had been loyal to us since the Coldgates days—

indeed, he came from the same country as Irian, Marguessan's lord.

I shook myself and looked away. No doubt it was just
the resentment of grief, that any at all should sit in
Merlynn's chair, and certainly not so soon after his—
going; but I could not rid myself even so of a vague feeling of unease.

Arthur rolled right over me, as he knew from long
experience was the only way; and so it was that we began
our rule in blood, not the hot blood of the battlefield but
the vein-ice of execution. No help to think that, as
Gweniver reminded us all, Edeyrn would not have been
slow to do as much to us and ours had we been the van-
quished; and I knew in my heart it was grim necessity.
But thousands died, perhaps rightly, perhaps not; and it
was not forgotten.

It was Arthur's resolve to leave Keltia by Samhain at
the latest, for his reiving against the Fir Bolg and Fomori
and the other galláin mercenaries who had hired out their
swords to Edeyrn's last-ditch throw. Though this plan was
not yet common knowing—Arthur deeming, and quite
right he was too, that the folk would be dismayed at his
going, and they still so unstable and rattled by all that had
happened to take his departure out of all proportion—in
the circles of the new Court it was well known, and not
at all liked.

But I knew from of old that Arthur with his inmost
mind made up could not be turned—as well try to stop
the planet from spinning. And so I went quietly about my
own business, setting my personal affairs in order, doing
what I could to order Keltia's affairs, before the year did
turn; and what I wished first of all to do was to wed. And
my lady being for once of that same mind, we set about
it.

CHAPTER
19

Gweniver and Arthur may have wed in civic splendor at the stones—they were, after all, Ard-rían and Ard-rígh, and as such owed a certain show to the public, who as a rule loved royal display—but despite our own rank and position, Morgan and I were not so bound, and had chosen for ourselves a different way. And so it was that some eight weeks after the double crowning, upon the day of Midsummer, we found ourselves climbing Mount Keltia hand in hand to accomplish it.

We had determined, as I have told you, on a handfast wedding in the ancient tradition; but Morgan herself had suggested Mount Keltia, and the great bluestone circle of Caer-na-gael that crowns it, as the proper place for so significant a rite.

She was most correct to choose so: Caer-na-gael is the oldest and holiest of Keltia's many nemetons. Its origins are lost to even our careful recordkeeping—or perhaps it is that they have been deliberately obscured, for what reasons I know not—but it is commonly believed that the stones were raised below the Gates of the Sun by Saint Nia herself, mother of the great Navigator; what is known for fact is that when Brendan came to die Nia laid him to rest beneath the huge tablestone at the circle's hallowed heart.

But that was all we knew. We had been effectively

barred from the Holy Mountain ever since Edeyrn's rule began; he feared the place, and with good cause too, for it was of old a haunt of the Shining Folk, his sundered kindred. Those who dwell near Mount Keltia whisper in awed tones that on bright nights one can see, if one dares look that way, the whole top of the two-horned mountain aglow with shifting lights, as the Sidhe meet there for purposes of their own. But no one knows for certain.

Mount Keltia, for all its height, is an easy mountain to scale; there is a pilgrims' road sweeps up the western face that a child could manage. We were surprised to find it in perfect repair; but, as Morgan pointed out, no one had been up it for two centuries or more, and perhaps the Shining Ones kept the paving-stones intact—though the thought of faerie roadwork was too much for me, and I grinned about it halfway to the top.

Caer-na-gael sits in an upland plateau where the mountain splits, flattens and then climbs again, rising in two jagged horns to the peaks called Gates of the Sun, first summit on Tara to be touched by the rays of the rising Grian. You come on the circle by surprise: The road takes one last turn, through a cutting of gray granite where the walls are always wet with groundwater, and then Caer-na-gael is before you.

We stopped as if by instinct; stopped and stared.

"It looks as if it had grown here," said Morgan at last. "None had hand in its making but the Goddess Herself. She called the stones up out of the mountain's deeps; they broke the turf like shoots in spring."

I was rapt. "Who knows? Who can say they know?"

We moved forward together, like children in an ancient story, holding hands for comfort and caution, passing through carven gatestones, dolmens thrice the height of a tall man. We sensed presences other than our own, but dismissed it: The place was hedged thick with magics, Brendan himself was barrowed here, small wonder we deemed ourselves not alone ...

Until we came to Yr Allawr Goch, the Red Altar at the circle's heart—it is neither an altar nor red—and saw that we were not.

From her place beside the huge stone chair that stood on the eastern edge of the sacred space, Birogue smiled on us both. She looked as fair and untouched by time as she had when first we met; or when last we met—under the hill, behind Sychan's great pale of waters. Morgan ran to meet her, with all the eagerness of a child long parted from a beloved kinswoman; and their greeting, if wordless, was eloquent even so.

"Well, Talyn? What then?"

I turned slowly at the sound of that voice: deep, amused, so familiar. Turned to look at him who sat in the stone seat just within the trilithon ring: And Gwyn son of Nudd looked back at me.

He was smiling as warmly as Birogue, and even as I gave him the bent knee I would only have given Arthur in full court—he was a prince, after all, to be in his time king over the Sidhe—I was wondering furiously what in all the seven hells these two were doing here . . .

Morgan's delighted laugh pierced my bemusement. "Why, Talyn, did you think we would wed ourselves?"

And then it finally dawned: Birogue and Gwyn were here to handfast us, to witness and seal our union; and I was even more awestruck than before.

I mumbled and shuffled a bit. "Well, you know, we might have—" This was true: Morgan and I, as priestess and priest, were well able to conduct our own wedding rite—it is not an uncommon choice, among those who serve the High Dânu—and so I had expected we would do, when we went alone to Caer-na-gael. Now, though—

Gwyn was smiling even more broadly than before, and I sighed; vain to think I could keep aught in my mind hidden from him and Birogue. But truth was, for all our past associations and common cause and even what I in my traha should like to call our friendship, or at least comradeship, these two were—well, they were not *like* us, were they, and they were mighty among their folk.

"Taliesin? Is there a problem here?" That was Birogue, and I turned to her and bowed—not the king's reverence I had given Gwyn, but one suited to Morgan's teacher and my mother's friend.

"Nay, lady," I said at once, with again a little sigh to find myself so easily read. "Only a small daunting, to think that the Prince of the Shining Folk and the Lady of the Loch shall stand for me before the God and Goddess at my wedding."

For that is a deep part of handfasting's mystery: The man and the woman are God and Goddess to one another, both in the wedding circle and ever after; but also they are wedded *by* the Goddess and the God in the persons of those who conduct the rite. The priest and priestess act for the divinities; but the couple *become* the divinities: action and indwell ing. It is a solemn and exalting way to wed, and so we had chosen it.

We had chosen too to wed for all time: The vows taken at a religious ceremony such as this can be as the couple do wish them—for a year and a day, for a lifetime, for all lifetimes yet to come. This last Morgan and I had chosen: We had done so before, after all, and we would do so again.

Birogue seemed to understand me, and held out her hands.

"Glad your mother would have been to see this day; Taliesin; my everlasting sorrow that she could not."

"And mine." I was about to ask her, point-on, what had it *been*, this matter of my mother that none had ever yet dared to tell me; but Gwyn had risen from the stone chair, and I had other things to think on.

So we were wedded on the day of Midsummer by two of the Shining Folk, Morguenna Pendreic and I: were censed and asperged, passed our right hands through the sacred fire and had our foreheads smudged with ash from the thirteen sacred trees. We made the third of the Three Cuts upon our wrists, drank the few droplets of our mingled blood in the consecrated wine, spoke our vows, set rings each upon the other's hand: gold rings in form of interlaced snakes, an old, old style of marriage ring (some say even from our time before Earth) that bespeaks eternity, a bond that is ever new yet never dies.

And through it all it never once occurred to me to wonder if Birogue and Gwyn even had the right to wed us; for it came to me that their right and their power, coming from a different spring of the same source as that which feeds our mortal faith, are every bit as true and valid as our own. So when Birogue at last pronounced us wed before the Goddess and the God, and Gwyn joined our hands, bidding us live and love in the name of the Highest, I looked at my wife, and she at me, and we were con-

tent. And it seemed at one and the same time a new thing
and something we had known and been forever; and this
too seemed just as it should be.

When we returned from the Holy Mountain to
Caerdroia, it was to find preparations well advanced for
Arthur's reiving; and those who had been for it were for
it still, and those who had been against it were more
against it than ever.

As for the two principals, it seemed that both were for
and against together. Gweniver could see and approve the
military necessity, could think Arthur's absence a debatable thing for Keltia, and could, by turns, be delighted or
indifferent to have him gone. While Arthur, for his part,
had doubts about leaving the folk so soon after his rule's
commencement, but plainly chafed to get himself gone as
soon as might be.

For myself, I partook in equal parts of all arguments
and feelings; but chiefly I regretted the separation from
Morgan.

"All those years on campaign we were no more than a
pillow's breadth apart and not wed," I complained one
evening. "And now we are wedded, and I must leave and
go gods know where on Artos's sleeveless errand."

"Sleeveless, maybe; bootless, never," said Morgan
calmly. We were sitting in the solar of the chambers that
Gweniver, when she heard of the wedding, had ordered us
given. Tremendously more opulent than my old, preferred
rooms, indeed than anything Morgan and I had heretofore
shared, or so they seemed to me; Morgan, with her usual
equanimity, had merely taken them as given—but then,
she was a princess. But now, I was a prince, and not yet
sure I liked it: Keltic marriage law dictates that in a union
of two partners of unequal rank, whoever ranks the lower
is raised to the title of the higher and takes the higher's
name (as do any children born to the union), and which
is man and which woman has nothing whatever to do
with it—not as it is in some societies I could name.

But we were speaking of the reiving ... I turned the
topic. "How does Gwennach feel about ruling here alone?
Is she daunted, or cross, or does it please her, do you
think?"

"Why not ask her yourself, Prince Taliesin?" came a

voice from the doorway, and Gweniver came in with Ygrawn, both of them showing all the signs of intending a cozy family midnight chat.

I kissed them both in greeting, and offered them places to sit and wine to drink; Ygrawn took the proffered chair, but Gweniver disposed herself on a heap of rugs and pillows in front of the fireplace, pulling off her low boots and curling her bare toes luxuriously in the furs.

I studied her covertly as she sipped her wine and talked softly with her cousin and her aunt. She seemed, in the firelight, but little changed from the maid I had met nearly four decades since: the same face and form, the same cloud of dark hair. But now she was High Queen; and, I tell you, that made a difference. She had always been royal; but now she ruled, and you could see that every time you looked at her.

"Well then," I said after a while. "What about the answer to that question I was asking when you came in? How does the Ard-rían feel about the Ard-rígh's reiving?"

Gweniver laughed, and shifted to lie on her stomach. "Artos will do as he feels he must—you know this perfectly well, Talyn, since you will be going with him to protect him, I trust, from the full extent of his folly. We three"—she indicated Ygrawn and Morgan—"will manage well enough without you. Nay," she added, sitting up tailor-wise, her mood perceptibly altering. "I have something to speak of that concerns us all, as family; and especially does it concern you, Lady." This last to Ygrawn, whom she often still addressed by her queenly title.

Ygrawn for once looked at a loss for words, so Morgan found some for her.

"Well then, let you tell us, Gwennach."

"It is to do with the Duke of Kernow."

"My brother?" said Ygrawn, more puzzled than ever. "Marc'h? But he is such a switherer—naught but riding and hunting and dicing and drinking, no care for governance. Tryffin will do better at managing the dukedom when it comes his turn."

Gweniver looked even more uncomfortable than before. "That is just part of the difficulty—Duke Marc'h wishes to wed again, and as liege he has petitioned Artos and me for leave to do so."

"No surprise there," remarked Morgan. "My uncle

Marc'h and my good late aunt Senara had been at odds
for years. The succession is assured with Tryff; why
should not Marc'h choose to remarry?"

"Oh, no reason not, but it is the lady his eye has
lighted on that causes the problem. She will not have him
at any price, and moreover is yet too young to decide for
herself."

I was interested deeply by all this—bards often serve
as marriage intermediaries for all ranks of Keltic society,
and we are most well versed in the laws and customs ap-
pertaining thereto—and poured out more wine all round.

"Well, do not keep us in suspense! Who is it, Gwennach?"

"The lady is the daughter of the Lord of Arrochar; his
only child and heir."

"I know her well," put in Morgan. "We studied together with the Magistra Ildana, back at Coldgates. She
was clever and funny and fair, and suffered no fools,
gladly or otherwise. Her name is Ysild."

"Aye, well, this Ysild is giving your uncle Marc'h a
good many sleepless nights—and not for that you are
thinking, Talyn," she added swiftly.

But I was wondering about something else ... "If you
two studied together, Guenna, she must surely now be of
age to choose her own mate."

Morgan shook her head. "Nay—by the time she came
to the Ban-draoi to be taught, I was already done with my
first training. Still, she cannot be less than thirty, and in
another three years or less she will be free to choose for
herself."

"Unless her parents sell her off first." Ygrawn had spoken evenly, but we all of us looked up in some surprise
at the bitterness behind the words.

"Would Marc'h be buying?" I asked after a moment.

Ygrawn laughed. "Marc'h is always buying." She cut
her glance to Gweniver. "What will you decide, Ard-
rían?"

Gweniver looked a little startled; she was still not used
to the title, and especially was she not used to hearing the
former Queen so address her.

"Artos has given the decision entirely into my power,"
she said then. "But I think that 'The Ard-rían shall take
it into advisement.' "

I hid my grin behind my wine goblet. That was the old
courtly evasion practiced by monarchs since monarchs
were first thought of; Gwen learned quickly. But she had
been watching masters all her life . . .

"At least, for the next couple of years," she added, getting to her feet and brushing off her tunic. "Naught will
come of delaying a match for which the bride is so reluctant, and Marc'h may well find another choice."

But, of course, he did not, and much did.

But we had more to do in that time than force unwilling heirs into marriage with lords thrice their age: We
were securely in possession of most of Keltia by now—
between Grehan and Tarian, every single one of Edeyrn's
warlords and creatures had been accounted for, either
dead or turned or prisoned on the inhospitable moon
Teallach—the Anvil, named long ago in grimmest irony.

There had been executions, as I have already mentioned; too many, some of us thought. But they had been
killings of necessity, of those too deep in Edeyrn's councils and workings and affections ever to be a tenth part
trusted in our own. The rest—the spear-carriers and
trimmers—were cast in durance, with Druids and Ban-
draoi to work on them in hopes of their being reclaimed
for us.

There had been some famine, and some epidemics, and
some fierce bustle about resettling those made homeless
by Edeyrn's depredations—Artos and Gwennach worked
day and night for longer than was good or healthy—and
for the Council of Keltia, work of our own. One of the
first things that had been done was to restore the Fainne,
the Ring, the supercouncil of the six system lords, the
viceroys and vicereines that ruled the Six Nations in the
name of the Ard-tiarnas itself. As it had been two hundred years since the Ring was broken, and no general
agreement that the positions had been hereditary, Artos
and Gweniver reckoned that they could with impunity ap-
point whom they liked; but in the end they had left this
to us of the Council to effect.

Oddly enough, all our appointments were well received, save for one; even more oddly, that one was the
viceroyalty of Kernow, and it was Ygrawn's brother
Marc'h who claimed it loudly and insistently for himself.

When the Council denied it him, on the reasonable (to us, at least) grounds that he stood too close to the Throne and our granting him the post would smack over-much of family favoritism, he took it ill indeed—though *how* ill would not be made apparent until years after.

But, as I say, that was the only thorn in our collective paw: The rest went more smoothly and happily than it seemed we had any right to expect. So much so that by Lughnasa—and a fairer, finer time we had of harvest that year than any could have hoped for—Arthur was already revising the departure date from Samhain to Fionnasa, a month earlier than his first decree.

I taxed him with it. "Why is it you hasten so to get us gone? There is so much yet to be done, Artos—"

"—and Gwennach to perform it perfectly, and our mother and your wife to help her," he countered. But something in his voice, or not in his voice, caused me to look more closely on him as he sat there at his cluttered desk, Cabal snoozing in the patch of sunlight that crept along the floor behind him.

Since Nandruidion, since his crowning, even, Arthur Penarvon, as he still insisted on styling himself, had changed both subtly and grossly, in a way that I could not put my finger on. As with Gweniver, of course now the aura of the Ard-tiarnas had closed round him, the invisible crown sat firmly upon his head; indeed, the very visible Seal gleamed green on his left hand. But there seemed something more ... I knew Arthur's face as well as I knew my own, since my fifth year in this life; and yet it seemed, now, that I did not know it at all, and I wondered.

Arthur had been watching me as all this went on behind my eyes, and now he gave me the old grin, that at least unchanged since our schooldays.

"Leave it, Talyn," he advised me kindly. "I know what you are seeking; but I do not know myself what it is. At least, not yet do I know."

"And will you?" I asked as forthrightly. "Shall you?"

He nodded slowly. "Oh aye. When there is need, braud. When there is need."

On the night before we left Keltia on our reiving, I stood alone with Morgan on the little terrace outside our new rooms. It faced the great bay below Caerdroia, catching the sunset full on, and had quickly become one of our favorite places simply to sit and be together.

Morgan was uncharacteristically restless tonight, though that was scarce unexpected. On the morrow, her brother and King, her husband and very many of her dearest friends were leaving Keltia on a dark errand from which they might well never return. No surprise that the dubhachas had come upon her . . .

For myself, I confess I felt a shameful elation. Oh, I was as distraught as my lady at our parting, make no mistake; but there was a not inconsiderable piece of me that was secretly thrilled to be on the war-trail again with Artos the Bear. Though it was not so much 'Bear' these days, as it had been at Llwynarth—Arthur now bore as his arms the crimson dragon from which the Pendreics had their name, though he stubbornly kept his foster-father's name, and used alternately the arms of Gwynedd and the arms of the House of Dôn, as did his co-ruler . . . I shook myself. Heraldry, while my wife paced up and down the tiny terrace like a caged lioness, and in the next tower over the Ard-rían of Keltia was doubtless little calmer of heart . . .

Morgan seemed to have reached her goal, for the pacing suddenly stopped and she stood quite still. Then all at once she vanished into our bedchamber, returning a few minutes later with a silver-bound leather casket that I had not seen before.

"A wedding gift?" I teased; the leather was worn and papery with age in places, the deep chasing of the silver hasps rubbed almost smooth.

"Strangely enough, that is exactly right . . ." She set the thing down on a bench in a little niche against the western wall, and opened it carefully.

I craned to look inside. Only some scraps of worn velvet—then Morgan turned back the velvet and lifted out what lay inside, and I gasped.

It caught the sunset light and blazed like firegold in her hands; but it was silver, and of far more ancient workmanship than the hasps that had bound its receptacle. Carved and incised with symbols even I as Druid and bard could not decipher, knotwork panels framing cut stones, round studs of rock crystal, clear and cold as snow-melt off the Stair ...

"What is it?" I breathed. "Whence came it, who gave it you?"

"It is the marriage-gift of Nia the Golden," said Morgan in a voice hushed as my own. "The Sidhe gave it to her, and she gave it to Brendan, and so it has come down to us. Birogue and Gwyn bestowed it on us when we wed."

"I do not think so!" I said incredulously. "I *think* I had remembered that!"

She smiled and tilted the lovely thing in her hands, so that the light flared and ran along it.

"Even so, Talyn ... This is our tinnscra from those who dwell in Glenshee—ours in truth, yours as much as mine."

I reached out a tentative finger to brush the silver, then, much emboldened, rested my first two fingers on the center stone—larger than the other crystals, faceted antiquely, there was something different about it ...

"I wish you to take it with you on the creagh-rígh," said Morgan then. Hearing my immediate protest, "Nay, none of that, Talyn, I am in no mood for it! You may have need of it where you are going, and for my part it is my best assurance that you will come back to me."

Her vehemence silenced me, and for a few moments I did not look at her but only at the fillet—cathbarr, is the old word for such a thing.

"It will never fit me," I said presently, and at that Morgan laughed.

"You think so? Come—" She took up the fillet in both hands, and I bent my head as she raised it up and set it around my brows. I felt the cool touch of the silver, smooth and light and utterly comfortable. Then Morgan had lifted it off, and set it upon her own head; and it fitted her as closely and conformably as it had fitted me. I took a little sharp breath at the awe of the thing.

"It was made by one who knew how to take a measure," she said quietly. "He made it to fit, and he made it to last ... Though women wear it most and best, men too have borne it on their brows; and this is not the first time it has been given in protection at parting, nor will it be the last."

"But such a treasure—"

"*You* are the treasure, Pen-bardd"—I startled at that, for never had I told Morgan of that name Elphin had prophesied for me so long ago—"and, had you forgotten, you are a prince of Keltia, full fit to wear greater relics than this."

"I think little can be greater than this," I said humbly, and bent my head again for her to place the cathbarr upon me. "But to look after so valuable a thing, on the war-trail—"

She smiled. "It will look after itself, I think you will find; it has a way of staying hidden, and will add not a crossic's weight to your pack . . . But let me look at you."

She turned me to face into the sunset, stood before me gazing up into my face. What she saw there I know not—my love for her, my fears for Keltia, my resolve and pledge to Arthur, very like, for I saw all these in her own face as she looked up at me—but Nia's fillet was upon me, and I Saw, suddenly, the years that would lie between us before I lay again with her . . . But I said no word, and no more did she; and we stood so until the sun had gone, and then we went within.

CHAPTER
20

In the end our going was not so bravely taken: It was, as Arthur insisted every chance he got, a workaday expedition, a punishment, not a riding for vaunt or show—there would be no grand send-off with pipes and drums and banners. To that end, then, he had assembled a hand-picked band of professional captains, and they in turn had chosen their war parties. The muster that met on the plains below Caerdroia was purposeful and single-minded; for we went to chastise those who had made war upon us in the hire of Edeyrn, and to discourage them from repeating that mistake.

Therefore our success would lie in secrecy and speed, not in numbers; indeed, we sailed in one ship, only one. But such a one ... Now Carnwen, Arthur's flagship for the invasion, had been destroyed with all the other craft, burned in space. So in one of his first acts as Ard-rígh, Arthur had ordered built a new ship to be his own.

Prydwen was it called, 'Fairface', or 'White Shield' in the bardic speech—a name that carried both protection and implication. It held some three hundred warriors, a manageable war-band, yet sufficient to accomplish our purposes—we were not intending invasion, after all, only strike-and-run raidings, merely to remind outworlders that Keltia's fist was still mailed, no matter that the hand within belonged now to another.

Strangely enough, the folk supported Arthur in this thing; I and others had thought—hoped, even—they would not, had cherished a vain dream that the people would rise up as one and require their King to remain at home. But this did not happen: They seemed as eager as Arthur himself to work a bit of requital upon the galláin, and they cheered us off like heroes, though it would be otherwise upon our return. But you shall see.

So we set out from Tara on the feast of Fionnasa, an omenable day, which auspicious nature was not lost on any; and steered course first of all for the other planets of Keltia, to look in on matters there. No surprises: The Fainne had taken up its old authority, the planetary lords had resumed their old jurisdictions—at least, the loyal ones had. Those who had cast their lot with the Marbh-draoi had been removed, one way or another, and new chieftains of our choosing—well, Arthur's and Gwen-iver's choosing—set in their places. Not, perhaps, always without strife and difficulty; but by now pretty near all had seen whose hand was on Keltia's bridle, and those who fought against the bit were reined in speedily and firmly.

The last place we stopped was Erinna, to bid farewell to Grehan's Aoibhell kindred, restored to their ancient princedom of Thomond; our old Companion's father, Durric, met us with Fidais, his Princess, and feasted us royally before we took ship again next morning and headed out past the orbit of that planet's three moons.

Once past Banbha, the outmost satellite, we were into space proper; technically outside our Keltic borders, for Erinna is the fifth and final planet of that system. I stood at the helm viewport and stared ahead into the starry dark; not yet was I brave enough to look behind me to the stars I so loved. After a while, Arthur came up beside me, put his arm through mine and followed my gaze outward.

I cut my glance sidewise to his face: He had that old look I knew so well, of a questing hound that scents new airs, new hunting lands, new quarry up ahead. And I was both heartened and dismayed to see it . . .

"We have left Keltia," he said then. "None of our race has been out among these stars since first we came here, maybe. And it is we, Talyn, we three hundred, who go so."

"Aye?" I said flatly. "Ard-rígh?"

He grinned and shook his head. "You have used that voice on me since we were five years old; do you not know by now how it never works?"

"Oh, sometimes it has been known to do so, no matter your protests to the contrary." I was silent a while, staring out at the rolling heavens. "Where do you have us sail? Or do we just go stravaiging round all the known worlds until we die?"

"Well, now, if you had looked at the charts and maps Grehan and Tari and the others drew up for us, you had had no need to ask ... But since you ask, I will tell you we go first to pay a call of courtesy on our nearest adversaries."

"Those would be the Fir Bolg—"

"They would be, and their home planet of Kaireden is—see, Talyn, it is over there. We have only to go."

It sounded simple enough; but then, everything ever sounded simple enough when Arthur said it. I know what you are thinking; and you are of course right in thinking so—I should have known better than to be taken in so featly by my brother's honey words. And, as a rule, I say in my own defense, I was seldom so snared. But as we stood there, looking out upon stars no Kelt had seen since Brendan's day, I was suddenly seized by the riachtanas, what bards call 'memory's grasp,' the demanding recollection that surges to the forefront of one's awareness will you or nill you ...

And what I was remembering was a thing Merlynn had told us, Arthur and me, back in our Coldgates days: a thing we had not understood in the least when he had pronounced it, and which had lain, in the manner of such memories, sleeping and silent, until its time had come to be remembered.

We had been discussing a magic Merlynn had performed at Arthur's importuning—nothing of significance, just a small pishogue—and then Merlynn had suddenly gone away from us as he sat there before us in his great chair. A brief journey: half a minute there, half a minute back again. We had stared at him, a little fearfully, and then he had looked straight through us both as if our bodies had been glass.

"When the last battle comes, you shall take the treasures with you from Keltia," he had said, in the most terrifying voice I had ever heard. "And though most of what Arthur wills shall be won, it shall be for another to complete the work, another's dán to bring them home."

And Arthur had leaned forward then, as he leaned forward now, straining sight and Sight alike to see his future. "How shall this other know of us, athro, and of these treasures you speak of?"

Merlynn's gaze, that had been set for distance, lengthened beyond all measure, and I shrank back, suddenly cold, for I knew what he would say.

"Gwyn shall give the word. The Sidhe do not forget."

I had shivered with the awe of it, as indeed I shivered now in remembering, and had met Arthur's eyes, and each of us knew in that moment the other's thought: Gwyn son of Nudd, prince under the hill, lord of the Shining Folk. We had not yet come to know him at the time of this pronouncing of Merlynn's, and when we did, the memory had chosen not to be revived; but now, as Arthur and I stood arm in arm and Prydwen beneath us ran on to our reiving's first meed, it came rising up out of the past like a ship out of deep water.

"Nay," said Arthur then, his eyes still on the stars. "Not yet, not now. Another time. We shall see it, you and I, and some of these who sail with us today. It will come."

And he said no word more that day.

The sail to Kaireden was uneventful, the raids we made on the Fir Bolg manufacturing outposts—little planetoids, a space station or two—more successful than we had any right to expect. We struck fast and hard, as we were wont to, and were gone before any counter could be launched against us.

I had had my doubts until that moment about the wisdom of our entire venture—what if the galláin nations we struck at took this not as retribution for prior damage but provocation to war? We were well enough set up at home to turn back chance raids, or even a civil uprising or two; but we were not in posture to throw off a determined invasion, and these peoples we now went against were fighters for hire, their swords never far from their hands.

Arthur listened gravely to my litany of doubts, as he had ever done since our boyhood; but when at last I ran out of fuel, and came to an uncertain stammering stop, he smiled and nodded slowly.

"I take the point, Talyn," he said. "But you see how easily Kaireden was breached—too easily, you think. Well, perhaps; but do not forget, Edeyrn chose galláin mercenaries not so much for their skill and heaviness of hand as for their cheapness. The Fir Bolg are worthy enough fighters, as we Kelts know from of old, but they are not wont to strike back after such a strike as ours; they will be resentful and ill-disposed, they may even seek to ambush our vessels once we have re-established trade with the outworlds, but they will be cowed by to-day's work. They are not, after all, the Coranians, you know!"

"And thank all gods for that!" put in Betwyr, who had been listening with an expression that grew more and more distraught as we talked.

Arthur favored him with a quick smile, but said no more, and the others who lounged round the common-room for this casual war parley turned to other matters. I looked at them with the eye of friendship: Companions almost to a one—not only Betwyr but Daronwy, Ferdia, Alannagh Ruthven who had wrought so well for us on Tara, Tanwen Farrach, many of our oldest Companions from the Gwynedd days, many more of newer kindred-in-arms, who had proved themselves on every world of Keltia in the fight against the Marbh-draoi. We were well accompanied, Arthur and I ... And yet we had left at home friends as dear and warriors as accomplished: Grehan and Tarian, above all, to work beside Gweniver; Elphin my old teacher, Tryffin, Keils, Scathach, Elen, Berain —the Company was there, too. And that was to prove well for us all, in the end ...

But for now the reiving went most smoothly: True to Arthur's assessment, the Fir Bolg—the name means Folk of the Belly, a childish taunting nickname, they were a tough race and deserved better—came not after us, nor visited Keltia with punitive raidings, but merely withdrew within their borders to lick their wounds and hope for vengeance to come. It never did, at least not against us;

but that was not ours to fret about, for we had now greater matters to occupy us ...

"The Fomori," repeated Alannagh, expelling the word on a long sigh of disbelief.

"They did more harm to us in the fight for Tara than all Edeyrn's other hired help combined," said Tanwen flatly. She but stated the obvious, as all there well knew; indeed, I would even say 'understated.' The Fomori were at the time of which I speak the greatest mercenaries in the known worlds: We knew them, too, from of old: Brendan had had some savage dealings with them in his day, and down the centuries our paths—and our swords—had crossed with theirs more times than a few.

"But a raid on Fomor itself—" protested someone at the back of the common-room; a newer Companion, one not so well used as the rest of us to Arthur's little ways.

Ferdia and I exchanged looks full of meaning and memories, but did not speak up. That was for Arthur to do, and just now he was not yet ready to do so.

I looked at him nonetheless. The Ard-rígh of Keltia was sitting on his spine in the chair he favored at such meetings, halfway down the far side of the long table. As was his custom, he wore the same plain brown uniform as the rest of us, the flightsuit of the Fianna; only his was undifferenced by any mark of rank or standing. *Well, when one is High King one can afford to be modest,* I thought; and heard in my mind Arthur's inner shout of laughter. I blushed—I had not known I was sending—but remained unrepentant as Arthur straightened, the faint grin on his face echoing his mental mirth, and leaned forward to end the debate.

"Only a raid," he said, and laughed at the massive disbelief he saw registered upon our faces, for we had all heard that song from him *many* times before ... "Nay, truly! You shall see." He called out the holomaps in the center of the table: Fomor spun in black space, ringed by its six moons. Arthur's light-pen touched the second outermost.

"That is the one to beware of," he said. "It is Launius, their chief defense against outworld invasion." He touched a keypad, and data began to flow across our placescreens: armaments, weaponry, strength both offensive and defensive. I was not best pleased at what I saw, and said so.

Arthur shrugged. "King Nanteos has become lax these days; or so the spies have told us. He has approved a manufacturing colony on this small moon here"—the light-pen flicked out, then pointed at a most hospitable-looking planetoid, third out from Fomor.

I could scarcely believe it. "It is Talgarth all over again!" I shouted, ignoring the baffled looks on the faces of some of our newer Companions.

"Aye, and well, what if it is?" said Arthur equably. "We came cleanly away from Talgarth with what we needed, then . . ."

I waited him out; it took more than a minute, but in the end he capitulated.

"Well, then, it is not like Talgarth, not entirely. We will make a diversionary raid on this moon—Meroke—but our main thrust will be at Fomor itself. There is a thing I would reive away, that might be of use to us to haggle a treaty."

I closed my eyes, took a deep breath. "And what might that be, Ard-rígh?" I asked, very carefully, for already I had a fairly good idea—

Arthur waited until I was looking at him again before he spoke, and even then he kept silence a beat longer.

"King Nanteos his own self."

Just so . . . I said nothing, for it seemed there was nothing to be said; but the others in the room found quite a lot to say, and it took the best part of ten minutes before they fell silent again. Or for the most part: Daronwy was still furious, and I leaned back with interest to watch her battle it out with Arthur.

"Sheep led by a goat!" Now she was challenging the rest of us, most of whom were already worn out from their earnest entreaties. Her eye fell on me; I gave her no more than what was needed to convey helplessness, between such friends as she and I, and she shook her head angrily.

"What is *on* you! Artos—speak to me! Tell me how such a loon-brained scheme will serve our purpose! Now!"

Daronwy in a rage was not someone I should myself care to go up against: And I speak as one who knows. Of all our old Companions from Gwynedd, I had ever held her, with Grehan and Tarian, as the cleverest, and perhaps she stood alone as most creative. In any number of our desperate situations, more often than not it had been Ronwyn who had cut through the brush and led us to the highroad of the solution we sought. Her mind was brilliant, and did not work as ours did; very often she was miles ahead of even Arthur, and could thwart his path with ease and logic, or at the least could turn it onto a more useful and reasonable track.

But not, I think, today ... "Lady, you speak to your High King," I murmured in mock cautioning, just to goad her a little more and enjoy the fun.

"High King nothing!" she snarled. "I speak to an idiot! Was this ever what you had in what it pleases you to call your mind, Artos, or did it just now fall in through one of the many holes you seem to have bunged in your own head?"

Alannagh and some of the newer Companions flinched a little in their alarm; but they had only known Artos from the Taran campaigns, mostly—they had not seen his stupidities on Gwynedd, had heard report only of his blazing triumphs. Quite naturally they would be shocked and surprised, to hear Ronwyn rant so against him. We could have told them how little good it would do in the end; but more instructive to watch ...

Ronwyn ran down like one of those ancient timepieces that work by spring-tension, and stood at last staring at her friend and King. Arthur looked back at her, a faint grin just grazing the edges of his beard.

"I love *you* as well, Ronwynna," he said smiling. And we all knew it was not the love of man and woman he meant, but the love of friend and friend, and dear friends at that. Still, it looked as if that love had done naught to change Arthur's course ...

Ronwyn rallied for one final throw. "Arthur," she said carefully. "*Ard-rígh*. Tell me this one thing. *Whyfor?*"

Arthur leaned forward again in his chair, all merriment gone from his face. "Because we can do it, Ronwyn, and because we need to do it. We need a bargaining chip to secure the Fomori, and since we cannot win one by arms we must try to earn one by cunning." He stood up, began to pace, and with that I knew he was by no means as sure about this as he made out to be.

"If we take Nanteos," he said at last, "we can use his safety to negotiate a truced pact with Fomor, something that will hold for more than a season or two. If they see that even their own king is not safe from the Kelts' cleverness and bold chancing, they will go slow before they go again on the war-trail against us."

"Or so at least you think," muttered Ferdia; which only showed how far had spread the misgivings Daronwy had given voice to.

But before Arthur could draw breath to answer him, Daronwy herself had cut swiftly in.

"Nay," she said, with the resigned open honesty of one who has done her best in opposition and now must form ranks upon her leader will she or nill she, "Artos it was who got us here in the first instance. Whether through luck, or dán, or policy, only the Goddess can say; but the fact remains, we *are* here, and it was his hand that brought us with war out of Gwynedd." She paused, looked over at her King as he stood by the viewport staring out into space. "Artos, I hate it more than I can tell you, but I think perhaps you are right in this as well."

It was a handsome admission, and Arthur bowed to her from where he stood. And suddenly I caught something in their posture, or in what they had said, or had not said . . . I all but blurted it out then and there, but controlled myself, and when Arthur and I were alone after the council's ending, in the corridor leading to our quarters for the few hours of rest we would most like never get, I turned on him.

"That little scene with you and Ronwyn—you cooked it up between you, not so? To lull and gull the others—Artos, answer me!"

"If we had done," he said presently, though he would not meet my eye, "do you not think we had good cause?"

"Well. But you might have told me, at least. I am not so bad an actor, that I could not have played along."

He slipped his arm through mine. "Nay, braud, you and I are too close for it—we have been playing such scenes so long together that they would have twigged in an instant. Daronwy is the last Kelt on Tara they would have suspected of such connivance."

"And so the logical one to help you connive." I was silent for a while, then, as we came to the door of my small chamber amidships, I looked my fostern full in the face.

"And if we fail?"

"Then Gweniver will be sole monarch over Keltia." He repented at once. "I know what you are going to say—that I am not an ordinary Kelt who may please himself with risks and adventurings. But, Talynno, that is just why I *must* do this thing—" He glanced at the chronodial in the wall, then drew me farther along into the corridor and into his own chamber. When I had taken the chair he waved me into, I folded my arms and waited for him to speak again.

He was sitting on the edge of his couch, toying with something he had taken from a small carved box in the bedhead niche. As it flashed green in a sudden ray of light, I knew it for what it was: his Ring of State, the huge emerald that had been Athyn's tinnól, now set in the band of gold knotwork he had crafted with his own hands. I had not known he had it with him.

"You should make things more often," I heard myself saying.

He smiled. "Ah, the tongue of a bard; never one meaning where three will do better . . ." With sudden firmness he put the ring once again on his finger, closed his hand to a fist around it. "It will make a fine song, will it not; glad I am to have so high and gifted a bard with me, a *prince* of bards."

"Ah, do not," I muttered; for still I had not managed to come to terms with my princely status, and it was well for me that such things counted for naught among the Company.

"Is all well with you and Guenna?" he asked, almost shyly. "You seemed so happy when you came back wedded from Mount Keltia—no surprise, but even so . . ."

I opened my mouth to speak, all of my great love for my wife and how it seemed to us that never had there been a day we had not been wed, but much to my own surprise I found myself saying very different.

"What of you and Gweniver? Do the High King and High Queen of Keltia go strong together now, or is it Coldgates come again?" Coldgates, where there had been no peace between the two royal cousins from morn to middlenight, even the vast shieling had not been vast enough to contain them both . . .

But he shied away from the question like a frightened colt. "Well enough . . . But, Talyn, this reiving—"

I understood. "I will make a fine song of it," I promised, "and I will sing it to you in Turusachan."

And with that Arthur seemed content.

CHAPTER 21

It fell out *nothing* like to anything we had plotted, of course. We should have known, things being what they were, Arthur being what *he* was ... Still, it all *began* perfectly according to plan: We fell upon Fomor like the wolf from the stars. It was only after that falling that everything changed.

You would think that I might have guessed it, when it all began to seem a little too easy, that dán was only lying in wait for us. At the time I had been only grateful: We laid our diversionary trail at Meroke, the small moon—and the Fomori went for our lure as a salmon goes for a fatling grub—then slipped round the postern, as it were, dashing past Launius (our flesh flinching every instant, dreading to feel the bite of sun-guns into Prydwen's síodarainn hide). But we flashed past before we ourselves, even, could quite believe it; though I do recall thinking uneasily when would the Fomori drop their other boot, and how much would the hobnails in it pain us when they did.

But it never happened! We came to land, and hit the planet running, and that is where all Arthur's wagers were suddenly called back in ...

* * *

Before we came into Fomorian space, we had received certain information, from our extremely high-priced spies, that the King of Fomor himself, Nanteos, would be travelling to a remote corner of his throneworld; under a false identity, with few guards and no state, on an errand the nature of which required that the king go in stealth.

Which suited our purposes well: Our plan was to intercept Nanteos as he disembarked at his destination (where, we fervently hoped, they would not have the defenses that the spaceport at Tory, the capital, could boast), and to bear him off as hostage to Prydwen before we ourselves could be hindered. Not the best plan, you are thinking; and you are so right to think it. But it was the best plan we had.

And at first, it worked unbelievably better than any of us had any right to have hoped. Running right under the noses of any number of Fomori tracking stations, we landed at the small, undefended spaceport—a few miles out from a country town called Zennor—just in time to meet Nanteos's ship coming in itself to land, all unsuspecting of our presence.

The fight was bitter and brief and sharp; but even that went better than our expectations. We killed a few Fomori, for which we were sorry; but, mindful of what they had done to us in Edeyrn's hire, we managed to set our sorrow aside.

But the great shock came when, having fought our way through to the king's cabin, we found within not the monarch of Fomor we had sought to find but a very frightened fourteen-year-old boy, who was trying very hard to be brave.

"Melwas," said one of the guards we had captured; he would not have spoken if he could have helped it, but Tanwen had prodded him with something rather sharper than a sgian—a nice magical goad. "Nanteos's grandson and heir."

Well, well ... I reached out to reassure the lad with a thought-touch, and jumped back as if my mental hand had been clawed by an angry kitten. So, the heir to Fomor was a sorcerer in training, and a most promising one too ... That made things easier all round: I reached out again, much more firmly this time; and with a little gasp the young prince folded up like a roosting heron, falling tranced and unconscious into Betwyr's arms.

It was all over within moments: We were back aboard Prydwen with the sleeping Melwas and racing back out past the now thoroughly wide-awake Launius defenses. We took one or two minor hits from the sun-gun emplacements, but our shielding held and we got out into the relative safety of the scallogue belt between two of the outer moons. I saw our young hostage safely bestowed, on a comfortable blastcouch in one of the empty cabins, under bedside guard; then I hastened to the bridge, where I found Arthur standing like a dolmen, calm, immovable, impassively watching the vain hunt on several of the viewscreens.

"They could well declare war on us for this, Artos," I said evenly, when he showed no immediate signs of conversational intent.

He flexed his shoulders. "Aye," he said after another moment, "but they will not."

I closed my eyes in brief annoyance; why was it he was ever so *sure* of things?

"Oh aye? You *know* this, do you? It goes well beyond the reiving we said was all our cause for coming here. Just to prick them, you said; just a reminder that they would attack Keltia at their peril, just a small payback for their aid to Edeyrn. Not—this." I gestured helplessly, but he made no answer. "What do we do now?"

Amazingly, he grinned. "Why, we wait, of course. What else?" He lifted a hand, and at the helm Tanwen and Ferdia did something I had never before seen. Prydwen seemed to shudder beneath us; and as I looked to the viewscreens for an explanation, any screen that showed an exterior image of Prydwen itself went suddenly dark.

I felt as if some great gauran had suddenly kicked me in the belly, drew my breath in to croak, "Artos? What has *happened* here?"

Arthur did not reply at once, but seemed to quest round him, in that way he had; finally, apparently satisfied to some standard of his very own that all was well, he turned to me with a smile.

"It is called a tirr. It is a kind of cloaking spell, more magic than artifice. I learned the way of it from the

Pheryllt, what time I went to study with them at Bargodion—oh, long since, back when you were tramping the roads of Gwynedd as a spying bard."

I stared at him. "You never said."

"Did I not?" His face was all innocence. "Perhaps it slipped my mind in the press of greater matters. All the same, it is a useful thing! We cannot move while it is at work—something the Fianna must improve upon—but while we remain at rest we are hidden from all view, sight and probes alike. Only if some ship were to sail straight into us would any know that we were here waiting."

I had recovered some of my wits by now. "And just what do we wait here *for*?"

"Why, for Nanteos's answer; what else?"

The King of Fomor's answer was not long in coming: The long-range scanners showed warships quartering the space between the moons, so many they looked like tiny silver minnows in a peat-dark lochan. I knew we were safely hidden—well, I did not *know*, just so, I had merely taken Arthur's word for it, as ever—but all the same, as I watched those moving needles, any one of which could have taken such a stitch in Prydwen as to sew us all into our shrouds, I was fearful and doubting of my fostern as I had seldom if ever been.

For his part, Arthur seemed pleased and confident. He had sent a hail to Tory some time since, and presently it was answered by someone who could only be Nanteos himself. Arthur moved to the center of the bridge to take the message, and all at once he was the Ard-rígh of Keltia.

"I love what way you do that," I muttered, and a quick grin flashed over his features before he schooled them to a more kingly expression.

Nanteos of Fomor was older than I had expected, with long white hair, a carefully trimmed white beard forked into two plaits and a stately bearing that minded me at once of my dear lost Merlynn. He was plainly angry; but behind his wrath, and his concern for his grandson, he seemed almost amused: the amusement of a skilled fidchell player at the utterly outrageous and unconscionable, unexpected move of a novice opponent. But he was no dotard and no fool, and he fixed Arthur with a very grim glance indeed.

"I could declare war for this offense, Arthur Pendreic," he said, before greetings had even been thought of; an uncanny, and unnerving, echo of my own words to Arthur not an hour since.

Arthur's mouth quirked at one corner as he read my thought, but he addressed himself gravely enough to the Fomori monarch.

"And I upon you, Nanteos, for your hiring-out to the Marbh-draoi," he answered. "Consider this a small return on your services."

There came a subtle shift in Nanteos's features. "Edeyrn is dead, then? We *had* heard somewhat ... And it is you who now rule; we have heard of you, too—a little—even in Tory."

Arthur permitted himself a smile, and Nanteos's face changed yet again. "I do not doubt it; not even a little. But I rule conjointly with my royal cousin, Gweniver Ard-rían; so do not think that if you destroy us—if you find us—you will be ridding yourself of yet another Keltic sovereign; a lawful one this time, I might add."

Nanteos snorted. "That might be argued! What of my grandson, Pendreic? If you have harmed him—"

"No harm has come to him, nor will. Melwas son of Tisaran is safe and sleeping."

Across the star-miles, Nanteos seemed to quiver and grow still again. "And what will it take to keep him so?"

"Only a little small thing; you may think of it as honor-price, an éraic for your work against the Counterinsurgency, which is now the lawfully constituted Ard-tiarnas of Keltia." The smile vanished, and the steel flashed. "You will pact with me, and with Gweniver Ard-rían, and with our lawful heirs and successors, never to come in arms against Keltia again. And this you will swear to, before the High Justiciar at Ganaster, so that the pact be known."

I looked at Arthur in wonder, as indeed did all others who were just then on the bridge with us. The Justiciary on the planet Ganaster was an old, old institution in the settled galaxy: It had often served in the past as arbiter and mediator in planetary disputes short of war, and sometimes even in cases of war. Of late, or so we had heard even in our isolation under the Marbh-draoi, Ganaster's power had waned from its onetime high prestige, its authority diminished by repeated floutings. But a pact signed, sealed and settled by Ganaster was still the galaxy's best surety; for Arthur to ask it now of Fomor showed—well, I was not yet sure *what* it showed. But it seemed that Arthur was.

Nanteos seemed as surprised as were we. "That pact would bind Keltia too, I take it?" At Arthur's curt nod: "Well, then. But what surety do you have, that Fomor will hold to this pacting?"

Arthur looked back at him and moved not a muscle. "Hostage-keeping has been a tool of Keltic statecraft for ages past."

Nanteos had gone very pale, and abruptly cut off the voiceband of the transmission, to consult with some who had remained out of view all this time. When he cut back in again, his voice carried more uncertainty than it had yet done in this parley.

"He is but a boy. You would return him safely to us?"

Arthur laid his hand over his heart. "Once the pact is made on Ganaster, he will be sent back with honor. Until then, he remains our guest."

The white head slowly nodded. "And that is a sacred status among our folk as well as your own, Keltia . . . Who shall negotiate for you, cousin?"

I sensed the great wash of ease and relief that flooded out from Arthur just then, but he gave no sign of it as he spoke.

"In another time, I had sent my fostern, my sister's lord, the Prince Taliesin Glyndour ac Pendreic." I startled to hear this, glad that I was out of scanner range to Arthur's side, then realized the focus had shifted, and I was in plain view to the Fomori king. I bowed with as good a grace as I could manage, sending evil thoughts to Arthur behind deep shields.

"He is ollave, a master-bard," continued Arthur suavely and serenely, "well versed in diplomacy. But he is needed with me, and I will send instead whomsoever seems good to me to send. You will be informed."

With that he terminated the link, and closing his eyes blew out a long deep heartfelt breath, and half-collapsed against the bridge railing.

"My gods, Arthur Penarvon! What a chance you took here today!" That was Daronwy, but she spoke for us all. "This is very like the worst day's work, with the best result, that you have ever done! How dare you risk yourself so!"

For once Arthur seemed quite content to be publicly humbled, listening with a chastened air to Daronwy's tirade and making no attempt to defend himself. When she tired, others took up the theme; as for me, I sat and watched and listened, arms folded, eyes on Arthur.

When at last all the Companions had had their say, and left the bridge, Arthur still remained leaning against the railing, head bowed, not looking at anyone or anything but, apparently, the floor in front of his feet. I began to move away myself, but still without turning his glance to me Arthur spoke.

"Well, Talyn? Have *you* naught to flail me with? You generally have had enough to say all other times I have been in such error."

I closed my eyes against the—the *smallness* in his voice; then I went to him, took him by the shoulders and led him off the bridge. He came with me unresisting; it seemed as if he had no will of his own left, as if the encounter with Nanteos had drained him like a dulcaun's glut.

"Nay, braud; you have already said to yourself all that I would say to you, I think ... And anything that might have been left out was surely said by Ronwyn and the rest. Silence has many tongues."

"If thrawn ears can hope to hear them." He stumbled as we went, leaned on me for support, and I was a little alarmed. Was he well? Why did he seem so wearied?

"Never mind." We had reached the door of his cabin, and I half-carried him inside. He flung himself onto the blastcouch without so much as another word, and was asleep as if someone had slain him.

I watched beside him for an hour or so, concerned for his state of mind, reading it, as far as I might, while he slept unmoving. He had pushed himself harder and farther and more harshly than we had realized these past weeks since leaving Keltia; the same mistake, I realized with ruefulness, that we had ever made on Gwynedd and on Tara—he might be Arthur, but he was only human after all. He might forget it from time to time in Keltia's need, but we ought never to forget, and surely not those of us who so loved him.

So I kept watch, and gave him what healing I could, and hoped that whatever he had in mind to do next would be kinder to him than his actions of late had been. And knew, of course, that I hoped in vain.

We sailed on, still on Arthur's reiving, which he yet adjudged to be insufficient to his purposes—whatever those might be. Once we had worked out a preliminary agreement with the Fomori, and had seen them take it to Ganaster, we sent our own representatives there also—Alannagh Ruthven, Betwyr and some others, escorting our young hostage prince.

Oddly enough, Melwas seemed reluctant to depart our company; in the weeks of his enforced guesting he who had been at first hostile and angry as only a wronged child can be had reversed himself, to where he honestly grieved to bid us farewell. I knew better than most what had in truth happened here: Like so many others before and so many yet to come, Melwas had fallen in love with Arthur Penarvon, with all the adoring hero-worship which only a fourteen-year-old can muster.

Arthur, of course, knew very well that he had a worshipper on his hands, and dealt with the lad kindly and firmly, as he would have done with an awestruck nephew or the son of a friend; as, indeed, I was well used to see him do. Though, perhaps, the kindness and firmness he exerted here had as much to do with the smooth running of the future as of the present ...

"And aye, why should it not?" he admitted to me on the evening we had packed young Melwas off to Ganaster, as promised. "He may well come to rule Fomor one day; better it is he is better disposed to us than his grandsir has been. Any road, he is a likable lad; and kindness costs nothing, and is well seen in anyone."

"A king still more," I agreed blandly, and laughed when he glared. "But, Artos—"

"Before you even ask, Taliesin"—he had flung up a warning hand to forestall further speech—"the answer is Nay. I have *not* done with what I have set out to do."

"My question was not if, Ard-rígh, but when."
Again the glare. "When I say."

And Arthur did not say, not for many months: We were
hunters, living off our raids, systematically tracking down
and punishing as we could all those allies who had sold
out our true Keltic order, all those worlds that had traded
for profit in Keltic blood, all those mercenaries who had
hired themselves out to the Marbh-draoi against us over
the years the Theocracy had ruled in Keltia. It made a formidable list: After the Fir Bolg and Fomori had been duly
chastened, we went on to fetch a sizable swat to people
as far-flung as the Thallo and the Parishen, the Hadulin
and the M'drani. Even the Dakdak, far away on Inalery in
the icy strongholds they so love, took a thump or two as
reminder: Not wise the thought, to try the Bear's paw.

Indeed, it seemed that Arthur these days was as sore-
headed as his namesake wakened too soon from winter
sleep: Prydwen was large as ships go, but we all went in
fear of its master from time to time, and were glad of the
raids—at least they got us off the ship and, for a while,
out of reach of Arthur's moodings.

It was in the course of one of these raids that we met
the Yamazai, and the manner of that meeting was in this
wise . . .

We had been pursuing a vessel belonging to the Duvan
Cheteri, yet another of the many folk on Arthur's list to
be chastised, when all at once we blundered across the
track of a greater battle, and perceived that it would be
well for us to intervene.

As a rule you do not do this in space warfare, but when
on occasion—as on this occasion—an unarmed civil craft
is being pounded by the guns of a dubious-looking in-
truder ("Smuggler if I have ever seen one," said Arthur,
and that was all he said until after), rules are often broken.

Even so, we were more than a thought reluctant to intervene. Could be a matter best steered clear of, could be
a trap . . . But when the cruiser sent out an agonized call
for help, and the smuggler ship began closing in on it like
an orcaun on a wounded seal caught in the shallows, we
knew we had no choice.

Knew still better, when Daronwy, who had been monitoring the smuggler ship, told us who the attackers in truth were.

"Fomori?" That was Arthur, for once discountenanced. "Are you sure, Ronwyn? They are very far from home."

"When did that ever stop the Fomori? Nay, they may be sailing outside the law, or under Nanteos's own letters of marque, I know not; but certain sure they are of Fomor."

"Then whom do they attack?" I asked.

"Their enemies," answered Arthur. "And the enemy of my enemy must be my friend . . ."

"Ah, but are we not ourselves now not Fomor's friend?" I countered, and was dismayed to see on Arthur's face that smile I knew so well.

"And if we are, who is to say these here have not heard word of it just yet? Ganaster is a long way off, messages take time . . ."

I shot him a hard look, and I was not the only one to do so: He seemed almost too unconcerned, even as the crippled cruiser's hull began to bloom with fireflowers, seeded by Fomori guns.

"Artos—" That was Daronwy, moved by the strangers' plight; whoever they might be, nobody deserved this. And if the Fomori were attacking them, all unprovoked as it did seem, almost certainly they were folk we should wish to have for friends . . .

"I know," said Arthur. "Take us into it."

Prydwen leaped ahead before he had quite finished giving his order.

I tell you now, we had nothing but the grace of the Mór-rían Herself to thank for that we ourselves were not blown to spacedust right along with the ship we went to aid. Though we both came away unbroken, we were both mauled more sharply than we might have liked; but the Fomori smuggler ship was the one to die.

We had scarcely drawn a breath upon our victory before we were hailed by the captain of the rescued ship. Arthur took the hail himself: Our viewscreen blurred, then cleared to show the image of the cruiser's bridge, and the captain who stood there.

She identified herself, in the Common Tongue, spoken by one clearly used to its quirks.

"I am Sastria, first officer—now captain—of the ship Aloyu, out from the planet Aojun. May I know who has saved us?"

I came up beside Arthur, staring openly at the screen. Oh, not for that the craft's officer was a woman—a commonplace in Keltia, if perhaps not in all cultures we have encountered; but for another reason. The thing that had caught my attention most and first was the mark she bore ·upon her forehead, between her fine brows: a crescent moon, tattooed in blue ink, intersected by two angled cuts in shape of the letter V.

In my astonishment I heard Daronwy's little gasp of surprise; but I was no less surprised myself: This foreign officer—how could she carry on her own flesh the sign of the Ban-draoi of Keltia?

"No surprise at all," said Sastria later, sitting very much at her ease in my own quarters and inhaling appreciatively the fragrance of the herb tea I had prepared. "We who serve the Mother are a sisterhood on all worlds, and the sign is not so uncommon as you might think, lord."

"I daresay not." I held out to her one of the pottery cups, filled with steaming brown tea, and she took it eagerly. "And your people are, as mine, children of the Great Mother?"

"And of the Allfather." She made a curious sign with her left hand, and I started violently, for out of my Druid training I recognized that too, and made it back, as casually as I might. "But He is for the men to follow; on Aojun it is the women who deal most with outsiders."

Daronwy stirred in her chair. "With us it is equal; we find it more harmonious."

Sastria laughed. "Not in our midst! We have found it better for the men and the women to go their separate ways most of the year's turning, and we have cast our lives to order it so. With us, the women live in the towns and cities most of the year, and the men stay out in the hills and woods and herdlands, out in the campments. Women, *I* think, have chosen the better part! But the men are herders and growers; women are makers and traders and artificers."

"And warriors?"

She met my eyes, and in hers I saw amusement. "Oh yes. And warriors. Rulers, too."

"Who then rules your folk?"

Sastria drew herself up, with an air that partook in equal parts of formality and eagerness and respect.

"The Jamadarin, who is Dar Majanah, in the sixth year of her reign. You will meet her."

My start of surprise was not lost on the Yamazai captain, and she smiled again.

"Has your captain not told you?" she asked. "We sail now to Aojun. Your ship needs repairs and refuelling and resupplying, and you have some few injured to tend to, as do we. Aojun is not far off."

Daronwy looked down into her cup. "Why were the Fomori raiding so close to your home planet?"

A good question, and I looked expectantly for the answer. But Sastria only smiled.

"Ah, that is a thing the Jamadarin herself can answer better than I . . . in good time."

After she had gone, Daronwy and I looked long and hard at one another, and went as with a single tread to seek a swifter answer. Arthur, when we found him in his cabin, was less than forthcoming.

"Aye, well, where could we go else, save but to Aojun? As Sastria did say, it is near at hand, and it can supply our needs. What is more, it is happy to do so, to discharge the debt of honor they now have to us. They take such debts as gravely as do we."

"Indeed," I said, trying vainly to quiet the great rising groundswell of doubt and dán I now felt coming over me. *Aojun* . . . "And how long do you mean to stay there?"

Arthur shrugged. "Why, Talyn; just long enough."

Perhaps we stayed *too* long; but I outpace the telling.

CHAPTER 22

"What a fair world that is below us."

Daronwy it was who had spoken so, but I would have said as much myself given the chance. We were in orbit off Aojun, readying ourselves to follow the Aloyu in; to help us in the navigating, the Yamazai captain Sastria had left us two of her deck officers, and they both smiled proudly and shyly on hearing Ronwyn's remark.

"We have tried to keep it as we found it," said the senior of the two; a man, for all we had been told men did not go for warriors so readily as did the Yamazai women. He was called Mahago, and he had been helpful in the days of our slow journey to the planet Aojun. Slow for that the Aloyu had been too badly damaged to sail the overheaven; so we held back for our new friends, and paced along in straightspace.

It had been an interesting and instructive journey: Daronwy had already made fast friends with the woman officer, Julitta, and I with Mahago. He was, like me, a bard, though he was also quick to modestly inform me he was but a 'summer-poet,' as he called it, an amateur who makes but for his own pleasure. Still, shop-talk is always enticing, and from them both I learned much of the culture of the Yamazai.

Though the name of that nation has ever connoted a

woman's world to outsiders—and women warriors at that, the ferocity of the Yamazai is a byword in matters of the sword—it seemed the race had as ordinary a civilization as any other, structured along the familiar lines of trade and industry and agrarianism.

Like us, they lived under a monarchy; but with them, the crown descended in the female line only: The Jamadarin, as the ruler was styled, had her throne by right from her mother or aunt or sister, from the women's side alone, and brothers, whether elder or junior, were forever barred from the succession.

They did not seem to mind much, at least according to our new friends: "It has ever been so with us," said Julitta, who was a distant cousin, in fact, to the current monarch.

"Is that not perhaps something unfair?" I asked gently.

She seemed surprised. "On your worlds, perhaps so; but every time the law has been put to a vote of change, it is the men who choose to keep things just as they are."

We were sitting in the common-room of Prydwen—Daronwy, Julitta, Ferdia and I—waiting for the call to the bridge that would signal our descent to the planet's surface. Mahago had some time since been himself summoned, as it seemed Arthur needed him to communicate with certain of the planetary authorities.

"We will be setting down, I think, in Mistissyn itself," said Julitta, appealed to. "I am not sure if Dar Majanah has yet spoken to your leader, but she has been informed of all that has occurred, and is most grateful for Keltia's help. You saved a civil craft from an unlawful attack by Fomori warships, and that means much to her, and to us all."

"My enemy's enemy—" murmured Daronwy in a tone just the tiniest bit edged with skepticism, and the Yamazai laughed.

"Aye so ... But I think you will find Janjan—Dar Majanah should have been a friend to Keltia in any case. And I know she will find Dar Arithor the same."

Dar Arithor ... That was how they turned Arthur's name in Aojunese; the royal title 'Dar' was the same for him as for their own ruler because the Aojunni had no provision in their tongue for anything else.

I mulled this over in silence for a while, playing with

words as bards will, when Mahago craned his head around the common-room door.

"Dar Arithor's compliments, and the honor of your presences upon the bridge. We go down now to Aojun."

I knew we were in trouble as soon as I saw her. Some things you just *know*, so, and there's an end to it . . . But to his credit, so did Arthur.

She was not much like to his usual partners: Chiefest, she was a queen, and that alone was something greatly new. Oh, surely, she was beautiful—well, not beautiful maybe, but handsome in a way I had seldom before encountered. Strength shone out of her, strength both physical and mental; and spiritual too, she was together with herself, she was all of a piece. But she was lovely as well: a lion-colored woman from head to toe—dark gold hair of many shadings, golden eyes that could darken to clouded amber with anger or passion, even her skin gleamed like the sun's metal.

But that was by no means all of it: Something there was about Majanah, Queen of the Yamazai Nation, that explained everything, and excused much.

We had been received as honored friends by the first minister to the Jamadarin, a tall dark woman named Saldis, who looked as if she could give our own Tarian lessons in elegance and guile. But we were too busy staring about us—gazing up like ducks in a thunderstorm—at the wonder of the city that rose above us on the hill.

Mistissyn has much in common with Caerdroia: It sits in the lap of a most picturesque mountain range, low wooded hills rising in ranks to bare crags against the sky. Walled, too; but that was only prudent . . . But that was where the resemblance ended: Caerdroia was built of stone, every color and texture of stone from every quarried cut in Keltia; this city was a town of wood.

And wood worked into every fantastical shape a wright could think of: gables and step-roofs and fabulous carved porches that looked like the stern cabins on sailing ships of old. There was the odd stone building here and there, poking through the wooden roofs like a tor in the middle of a forest, and looking just as out of place; but Mistissyn had all the charm of a great capital and a rustic village at the same time, and we all of us fell in love with it on the spot.

If not, perhaps, quite so quickly as our King fell in love with its Queen ... If I had thought Arthur instantly taken with Majanah, it seemed plain to all that she was as caught by him. Plain to see neither of them gave a cat's-lick for formalities, not in the aftermath of that first slamming blow of the grá-tintreach— But they both kept to their public faces, at least for the moment; they were princes both, and knew how it should be done ...

We had been presented in a formal ceremony, had received the thanks of the Jamadarin and the Yamazai Nation, had been given assurances of alliance to come— welcome news to Arthur, I knew; we could use all the friends we could find. Now we were escorted with no small degree of pomp to the Great Hall of the royal palace, for a banquet that seemed to my feast-familiar senses as if it would go on until morning—launa-vaula with a vengeance.

I was sitting at the high table, of course, as befitted my rank as a prince of Keltia and matebrother to its King; my dinner partner was one of the Jamadarin's officers of state, who did her best to keep me entertained. I was grateful for the effort, but as the evening wore on and my mood soured, I found myself wishing fervently to be just about anywhere save where I now was; by preference, in the Well of Ashes that lies seven miles below the seventh hell ...

I started violently, as someone took my hand and drew a finger over my palm; and started yet again to see that it was Majanah herself. She had in the lull between courses left her place beside Arthur several seats away, and sat now where my previous companion had yielded place to her.

"Your hand is full of stars," she said smiling.

I must have been staring open-mouthed at her, for she laughed out loud, and it was one of the most delightful sounds I had ever heard: not some silvery tinkling giggle, but a clear arpeggio of real amusement, and it won me over then and there.

"Do you not have the art in Keltia?" she asked. "Dar Arithor has been telling me of your skills of sorcery—"

I recovered myself. "We do," I said, adding hastily,

"madam." For such, I had been told, was the respectful address used here in conversation ... "But it has been long and long since my hand was read for me."

"Then allow me to do so now. I am not so skilled as once I was, but—" She bent my fingers back, turned the palm first one way and then another so that the light fell on the fine lines and the clear ones alike. "You are a thousand years old, Prince Taliesin ... You have always been of the priesthood—you have been a priestess also, the mark is here of the Goddess's daughters"—the polished oval nail traced stars and triangles, the great irregular M that crossed the whole of my right palm—"you are wedded to one who is your true mate from all time, and who will ever be so."

I must have shown my skepticism—she could have had that from Arthur over dinner, or from any of the three officers who had been aboard Prydwen—for she smiled again.

"And as proof I have read it here, I tell you a thing only you and she do know: She has crowned you with ancient silver, and you bear that crown upon your brow."

I pulled my hand sharply out of hers, but she was not in the least offended as I stared blankly at her. How had she seen that? The cathbarr of Nia, that sacred fillet Morgan had bestowed upon me, was hidden away on Prydwen, in its place of concealment where none save me could come at it or, indeed, even knew of it. Involuntarily I glanced at my hand; where was it written in those lines I knew so well? And how could this foreign woman know a secret that was purely of Keltia and things Keltic?

As if she knew my confusion and unsettlement, Majanah reached out again, and I flinched a little. But her fingers only touched the back of my hand, with gentleness; then she made me a salute with cupped crossed palms, and slipped back to her seat beside Arthur.

I have little recollection of what followed—my mind was whirling with questions and fears—so it came as a considerable shock to me when I noticed all eyes turn my way with expectation. I glanced at Arthur, found him smiling and beaming with the rest, and deduced from my dinner companion's subsequent delighted questions that Arthur had apparently promised them all a song from his brother who was Pen-bardd of Keltia.

I leaned across my partner, rudely, and muttered something savage to Arthur in Vallican, our old Arvon dialect. I half-expected Majanah to intervene, but she only smiled again.

"What tongue is that? It sounds like the bones of the mountains."

I would gladly have enlightened her; but Arthur at once engaged her again in intimate converse, ignoring my outburst, and I resigned myself to my performing stint to come. At least there was a bit of respite first . . .

As is the custom among most civilized peoples, the visiting poet was entertained first, before being required to perform; that way, he could decline gracefully if he did not feel up to following the resident talent. But considerable face would have been lost tonight had I done so, and, cross as I was with my fostern, I could not in good conscience back away from the challenge. Nor did I particularly wish to: So after some remarkably fierce atonal drumming chants from Majanah's court poetess, a dark-skinned wonder named Tamikka, I rose obediently at Arthur's nod and began to tune Frame of Harmony—brought to the hall against just such need—to its liking in this new clime.

Then I heard Arthur call to me, "And let it be something we have not heard twenty times over since we left home, Talyn!"

I shot him a glance full of venom. He was a few parts drunk, to be sure, and more than a few parts intoxicated with Majanah, but even so . . . We have a saying on Gwynedd that it is death to mock a bard (the other two parts—of *course* it is a triad!—tell us it is death to love a bard and death to be a bard); well, not death for my King and brother, obviously, however he might mock me, but certainly a pointed little stinging . . .

For a half-buried memory had stirred just now; a song heard once and never forgotten had come rushing to harp and hand and tongue. A bard of the ancient Scotic house of Douglas had made it for his lady, upon her teasing complaint that he never wrote lovesongs for her, could compose only obscure poetry and impenetrable, if haunting, chaunts. She had wagered him that he could not produce for her a ballad in the gráightraí mode, with simple words and many verses and a turn to the refrain. He took up his wife's wager, and wrote her this song I now recalled to mind. I do not know what was her forfeit—she had been an Aoibhell, of all people, another redhaired scion princess of the House of the Wolf—but I know she must have paid it with joy.

For all his lady's loving chaffing, he had been an elegant and accomplished songsmith and poet. For this song, though, he had deliberately chosen to write in a primitive vernacular; and I hastily translated as I went, to make his carefully casual idiom sing in the Common Tongue we used tonight among us, for I would for no sake lose the lovely melody, nor yet the poignant chimes the Douglas bard had made.

> " 'My love in green came down the meadow
>   Let it follow, let it follow
> My love in green came down the meadow
>   Long time ago.
>
> She hear my song, she come to find me
>   Let it follow, let it follow
> She hear my song, she come to find me
>   Long time ago.
>
> First she smile and then she touch me
>   Let it follow, let it follow
> First she smile and then she touch me
>   Long time ago.
>
> She shake her hair, she jar the river
>   Let it follow, let it follow
> She shake her hair, she jar the river
>   Long time ago.
>
> She steal my heart, I let her take it
>   Let it follow, bound to follow
> She steal my heart, I let her take it
>   Long time ago.
>
> She save my truth, she heal my laughter
>   Let it follow, come and follow
> She save my truth, she heal my laughter
>   Long time ago.
>
> She put a ring upon my finger
>   Let it follow, time to follow

She put a ring upon my finger
    Long time ago.

She lay with me, she give me kingdoms
    Let it follow, love will follow
She lay with me, she give me empire
    Long time ago.

My love in green is mine forever
    Let it follow, I will follow
My love in green is mine forever
    All time from now.' "

When the song ended, and I had played out the little musical flourish that rounds off the mood, making bearable that sometimes jarring transition from entrancement back to reality, I looked up, and saw through suddenly blurred vision the upturned wondering faces, heard the rapt quality of the silence before the applause began to roll from wall to wall.

For my part, I preferred the deep rapt instant of silence; but I too had been unexpectedly shaken by the words and the burden of the song. Not a great song, as songs go; but a loving one, and a moving and honest one, and it had called up my beloved so vividly to my inner eye that I wondered now had it summoned such a picture for its maker, of his own lady. Surely it must have done, for her portrait is in the song itself. But he had died young, that maker, slain not many months after the song had been made. His wife, herself a bard, had lived on long years alone. She never wed again, or loved another, even; yet with such songs I think she can never have been without him . . .

Perhaps I myself would share her state in years to come, I mused, as I put Frame of Harmony carefully away in its leather-lined case. It was not something I could honestly say I had ever before considered, and the thought had a strange and sobering touch. Did I die first, Morgan would be the one to bear the loss, to grieve and mourn and suffer, and that I could not bear to contemplate—to leave her so! But if she went before me to the Goddess, I should be the one left grieving, as alone as that long-dead Douglas's mate had been. If such should be my dán, I knew I could comport myself as she had done; there would be no other love for me as there had been none for her, and how could it be otherwise, for we say in our marriage rite itself that death shall *not* part us ... But such pain—still, better I to suffer it than Morgan, I would spare her if I had the smallest choice in the thing. Which was worst, to die first or to follow? And do we ever really choose?

"Oh, follow, to be sure," said Majanah, when, prompted by her quizzical questioning look, I had finished telling her of my reaction to the song. "And sometimes, perhaps, I think it can come to be in our power to choose ... But though it is a most selfish wish, if choice *I* should be given, I should ever choose to die before my mate."

But Arthur, when the Jamadarin taxed him, shrugged the question off, and I wondered belatedly if I myself had chosen aright here, to sing these two a lovesong, and one with such a weight behind it ... Shortly thereafter, or so it seemed to me, Arthur excused himself, and retired rather abruptly to his rooms. Majanah did not seem offended, and sent some of her courtiers to escort us—for of course we went with him. When I knocked gingerly upon the door of his chambers, having given him a quarter hour to settle himself, his voice from within curtly bade me enter; and then he said no other word to me for a full two minutes.

"She never listened to his songs again, you know," he said without preamble. "That bard's wife—"

"I know," I said softly, for it was true: She never did.

"Because she did not love his songs, or him, enough?"

"Because she loved them, and him, too much," I said, still softly, and closed the door behind me.

Alone in my own suite of rooms on the other side of the wide sconce-lit corridor, I flung myself upon the huge bed fully clad and stared up at the ceiling. Arthur was not a stupid man; though he often did stupid things, just as often there were quite good reasons for his doing them, and those reasons made his actions come right in the end. My bard's ear had called up that ancient music tonight for a reason, and that troubled me; there was something deep here, I had not sung that song just for that the lady it sang

of had worn green for her lord and love—green as
Majanah had worn tonight.

Nor, at heart, was I even sure of the message I had
wished to convey. Arthur and Majanah were already well
smitten: that much had been plain to half the hall. And
what if they were? Who were any of us so pure or perfect
as to toss caltraps?

All unbidden, my mind sent up a picture of Gweniver.
Well, she had Keils, did she not; no disgrace to her or to
Arthur, and none here. It was no great matter in Keltia for
a king or queen, or anyone else, to take a sanctioned lover
in addition to a duly wedded husband or wife. So long as
the thing was amenable to all parties, and the brehon marriage laws observed with respect to rank and property,
and the permutations spelled out so there can be no
misunderstanding ... And somehow I very much doubted
that Gweniver, when she came to hear of it, would mind
overmuch; and besides, she might not ever hear of it at
all.

And too, I thought drowsily, as I pulled off my boots
and prepared to fall asleep in my trews, this one is a
queen herself. Even Gweni can take no slight at that. And
if she does, that is, after all, why honor-prices were invented. Though that for a queen would be, well, queenly
indeed ...

"They have a union here not unlike to our céile-
charach partnerings," explained Arthur. "My daughter
could be Jamadarin of the Yamazai herself one day."

"Daughter?"

He had the grace to blush. "Not yet ... But only
daughters can succeed, as you know, and an heiress is
needed."

I was furious, and oddly hurt. "And you just the one to
supply such."

Arthur would not look at me, and perhaps it was best
that he should not. We had been on Aojun eight months
now, and the companionship between Arthur and
Majanah was by this time widely known; and just as
widely approved of, at least to judge by what our
Aojunese friends did tell us.

"Tell me again how that works," I said, rather sulkily,
when the silence had grown obstinate behind me—how

well I knew *that* silence from of old . . . And spun on my heel when the voice that began at once to tell me was by no stretch of any imagination Arthur's.

"Aojun was settled by several humanoid races," said Majanah, who was standing in the doorway, and now came forward to dispose herself upon one of the low soft couches. And again I was reminded of a lioness, draping herself in the crotch of a tree to watch for prey . . .

"We call ourselves all Aojunni, but the Yamazai people are pre-eminent, and the Jamadarin is always one of our daughters. It is not unknown for a Yamazai heiress to wed a man of different race, but although it has happened often enough, it is not encouraged. Men who are not of our blood cannot always understand the—necessities of union with one of us."

Was it my imagination, or did she so carefully refrain from even the tiniest glance at Arthur as she told me this? I was not prepared to let her off just yet.

"How is it that the women of the Yamazai became the fighters? Are the men so soft and coddled that the War-Goddess favored them not?"

The golden gaze met mine equably. "They are tough enough, when such toughness matters most. Nay, the women are simply better at it than are the men. Surely it must be the same on your worlds, in certain things?"

Before I could sink further into the pit that had been slowly opening up beneath my feet, Arthur stepped in to save us both.

"In more ways than it likes me to think on . . . But I doubt you came here to lecture my brother on Aojunese history?"

Majanah laughed and uncoiled onto her feet again in one sinuous movement.

"Not so—I came to tell you that my officers have finished drafting the treaty we have been working on. It waits your inspection."

Arthur smiled. "That *is* good news—with luck, it can be sent back to Keltia before the spring is out, so that our two nations will stand in formal alliance."

I was unimpressed. "And what do you think Gweniver Ard-rían will make of it when she sees it?"

"She will accept it, as I would do with any treaty arrangement of her making. You know this well, Talyn," said Arthur crossly. "That was, after all, our agreement."

"Oh aye," I agreed. "That *was* the agreement . . ."

Majanah, no slothel when it came to nuance and mood, was already moving toward the door.

"Artho, I will leave you to speak of this with your brother—it seems you have somewhat to discuss with him, and with the rest of your folk."

She was gone, and Arthur turned roundly on me before the door had closed behind her.

"And just what was *that* all about? You *know* how hard we have worked on that treaty, how do you dare misdoubt it in front of her to my face? And when you *know* how it stands with Aojun and Fomor, why the Aloyu was attacked—"

"I dare because that is my job, braud," I said with coolness. "That is what I am here to do—what I have always done for you, if you care to think back on it."

The very air twangled for several exceedingly long and discomfortable moments; then all at once it broke, and Arthur began to laugh.

"And so well you do it, too . . . Ah, Talyn, what is it you would truly say to me?"

"Only this." I fixed him with a very level look. "Do not let this treaty become more of an alliance than is strictly required. What of your bond with Gwennach? You are a married man, Artos, lest you have forgotten."

"And married folk, even in Keltia, are not forbidden lesser unions, the which I am sure *you* have not forgotten, from your days in bard-school those many hundreds of years ago . . ." He was silent for a time, and I did not press him. "I love her, Tal-bach, and she loves me; it is not a mere matter of princes or power, or even plain desire. Any of those could have been dealt with in other wise . . . Besides, you like her better than you liked Gwenwynbar?"

That last sly dig caught me like a well-placed foot to the ribcage; I stuttered and fumphered, for once bereft of words. Which of course was his intent . . .

"That was most unfair," I said when I was again capable of speech. "And, since you ask, aye, I like her very much indeed, she is not difficult to like or respect— But does that mean you must—ally yourself with her so far beyond a treaty?"

Arthur laughed again. "Nay. But it means I want to. That is fair, surely."

And with that I could not dispute.

CHAPTER
23

Majanah bore Arthur a daughter in the time of winter Sunstanding. In accordance with the custom of Aojun, they had had a ritual of joining some months before, when the Jamadarin first knew she went with child, and from all my best information the people were well pleased at the news.

For myself, I was not so sure: It seemed to me, when first they told me of the coming birth, that they were asking more of the Aojunni than perhaps either of them realized, to give Majanah's people a future ruler who was half-outworlder. And though the thought of a Jamadarin with Keltic blood was not without a tremendous appeal, at least to me and to the rest of us who had come to Aojun a year since, I could not seem to rid myself of this faint far unease at the prospect.

"Truly, Talyn, the folk rejoice for Artos and Janjan." That was Daronwy, who herself had astounded us by taking up with a Yamazai warlord named Roric. Still more astounding, the union appeared to be a serious one.

Janjan ... I began to laugh at the incongruity, and Daronwy looked her question.

"Oh, nay, not at you, that is, not truly—it is just that it takes a very forceful person to dare call another very forceful person by such a byname and not get swatted for it ... 'Janjan' is *not* how *I* think of her, I promise you!"

Daronwy was not offended. "Perhaps you should. Morgan would like her, Tal, you know."

"Aye. Aye, she would." I paused. "What does Roric say about it all?"

She shrugged. "He thinks, as does most of Aojun, that it is purely the Jamadarin's business whom she chooses to sire her heir; that she should have chosen an outworlder is a little surprising. That she should have chosen a king, not surprising at all. Besides, the folk genuinely like and respect Artos for himself; the army, so Roric says, think he is some kind of war-god come to Aojun in mortal guise. Do you know, they call him Artho Kendrion among themselves—which means the Young Lion."

Now that did not surprise me: Over the past year, Arthur had, with Majanah's eager blessing, been gradually reforming the Yamazai military structure. True, he had had impressive material with which to work, and some might have said, with great correctness, that no improving was needed. But gradually even the critics had come to admit, ungrudgingly, that Artos had had the right of it, and had been grateful in the end.

"How long do you think he means to stay here?" I heard myself asking, and had an answer of sorts when I saw Ronwyn's start of surprise.

"I had not thought—"

"Well, I have thought on little else." I tried to soften the aggrieved tone I heard creeping into my voice. "We came out of Keltia on a reiving; we have been gone near three years already, and it looks to me as if—"

"As if?"

"As if Artos would choose not to return home, if choice he had."

Daronwy squirmed in her chair. "Well, but he *has* no choice, not unless he renounces his title, gives up being Ard-rígh. Do you think he would do so? Have you spoken to the others about it?"

"I have waited—you and I are the closest to him here; and Ferdia, but policy has never been *his* strong suit."

Daronwy blew out an indulgent laughing breath. "Nay, not since Caer Dathyl! I will never forget how cross I was with him, even in the midst of my terror watching Edeyrn come down the hall at us— Still, Talyn, we should at least speak to Feradach and the others, before we tax Artos with it. And too, there is the child."

The child ... "Aye," I said slowly. "I have not forgotten. But I cannot help thinking that Artos might have done better to get an heir for Keltia before he chose to get one on an outfrenne queen. Much ill may come of it in years to come."

But in that, as in so much else, I was dead mistaken.

From the first, Donah was a forward infant. Almost as soon as she could focus, she included me in that circle of family she chose to recognize and respond to; and with her pointed chin and brown-gold eyes and silky red-blond hair, she was utterly impossible to resist.

Arthur was proud of her to a degree that quickly became very near tiresome; Majanah, though plainly she loved the child, had a bit more distance on it, as was the custom among her folk. There were shoals of nurses and fosterers and milk-mothers to care for the tiny princess— whose official title was Heir of Aojun and whose style was Jai Donah, for those who like to know such things— but Arthur continually set palace discipline all through-other by swooping down on the nursery to carry Donah off on what soon became unofficial progresses.

When the babe was thirteen months old, Majanah ordered that she be named heir in formal ceremony; which of course required that Arthur be acknowledged as the child's father and given the Yamazai title appropriate to such station. There were some grumbles at this, and not all of them emanating from the Aojunni: Some of our own Kelts were not best pleased at such public commitment, by their Ard-rígh, to a foreign sovereign and a foreign succession, and for the first time since we came to Aojun, they were not shy to let Arthur know it.

He took it well, for the most part, delivering himself of his annoyance only in private, and only to Majanah, Daronwy, Roric and me. The five of us, with Tanwen, and Ferdia, Julitta the Queen's cousin, and a few other officers of the Aojunese court, had formed a—well, aye, I *would* call it a family. Certainly a clann, as we Kelts understood the thing, or a tribe, as the Yamazai were wont to name it— Our friendship was the focus; that, and Donah, who at the age of a moon-year was tall and bright and well-grown enough not to disgrace a two-years'-child. Her hair had darkened to a shade midway between each parent's, and her eyes had lightened; I had already begun to teach her some little songs, and she loved Frame of Harmony beyond any toy or trinket she possessed.

But the ceremony troubled me, and the more so because I could not determine just why; and when Arthur first spoke to me of it I flatly refused attendance.

"But why?" he had asked, genuinely distressed and sorely puzzled.

And I had not been able to answer, not even when he went away at last angry and hurt; and some time later, Majanah herself dropped by my rooms, as if by merest chance. She had Donah in her arms, a thing somewhat unusual for her, and I could only think she had brought the child along to shame me into reconsidering.

"Artho says you will not come to the rite." She never wasted words, this one; gods, how I liked that . . .

I was equally blunt. "I'd sooner eat my own toes."

Majanah laughed. "There speaks the Talvosghen I have come to know and respect! May I know the reason for your refusal? I would not command you, you are not of my own folk to order—but my daughter loves you, and I should like you to be there for her, if you cannot find it in you to do so for my lord and for me."

I stared back at her, hearing my name as the Aojunni turned it, seeing as if for the first time, though of course it had always been there since I had known her, the crescent moon tattoo that rode between her brows. And, as clearly as if she had been beside me, I heard Morgan's voice in my ear; and what she said to me was simple and to the point: *Idiot*!

Outside a peal of thunder rather dramatically punctuated the sulter and the silence; it was unseasonally warm for the time of year, and, for all its temperate clime, Mistissyn had been plagued for the past two days by storms more appropriate for high summer than deep winter. On the carpet where she had been deposited to amuse herself, Donah looked up at the sound.

"Sky-drums, my kitling," whispered Majanah, and the baby favored us with a smile and an enthusiastically undecipherable comment before going back to her play.

I looked at her, then up at her mother. Majanah was not

watching either of us, but gazing out the tall wood-
framed windows at the oncoming storm; and on her face
was such an unguarded expression of vulnerability and
weariness that I dropped my eyes before it. She was not
feigning this to gain my pity and acquiescence; this was
how it was with her just now. And she seldom showed
such openness; she was a strong ruler and a very clear-
minded woman indeed, but not wont to display even to
friends her uncertainties ...

"You need not fret yourself about Gweniver," I said
impulsively and out of instinct, and was rewarded by her
reaction. She whipped round to stare at me, open-
mouthed with astonishment.

"Sometimes I think it is you, not Artho, who are the
true wizard amongst your kindred! How did you know?"

"The truth? You will think it strange—but my wife just
now told me."

Again the look of utter confoundment, to be replaced
by deep amused suspicion. But it was true: Morgan *had*
told me, as plainly as she had called idiot upon me a few
minutes past.

"I feel I know her," said Majanah, choosing to ignore
the rest of it. "From Artho, and you, and the others of
your folk ... According to our law, she is now my sister,
being my daughter's nearest womankin on the father's
side; and you too hold a special place as father's brother.
But my lord has another sister—"

"Oh aye," I said with grimness. "He has that ... But
Morgan would like you; as would the Queen-mother
Ygrawn. You are all three very much alike; no surprise—
Janjan—that my brother should love you."

She blushed, and I felt abashed. That was perhaps the
kindest thing I had ever said to her in the two years and
more of our stay on Aojun; I was shamed it should be so,
for I honestly cared for her. And not just as Arthur's foreign ban-charach, or Donah's mother, but as a true friend.
Now did I regret that churlishness anew, and was only
glad it had not cost me something real.

"Tell me of the rite," I said smiling. "I would know
what it is that I am to witness, if I am to witness it aright,
as bard, and as uncle to the Heir of Aojun."

Her face shining like the sun that had just broken
through the clouds without, Majanah embarked upon a

description of the rite that was to take place on the morrownight. It was in form and spirit very like to our own rite of Keltic saining, and I said as much.

"Not only that, but it is a rite of the Goddess," I added in faint protest. "And I know from Morgan that the Mother's holiest ceremonies are for her daughters only, not her sons. As the rites of the Lordfather are for men . . ."

"True enough," answered Majanah. "And here too the deepest mysteries of the Goddess and the God are reserved each for their own. We who serve the Mother share with our sisters of Keltia that deepest ban and bond: that men are not to witness the Great Mysteries. But for this we make exception, that the male kin of the child be named for the night to the ranks of women, and permitted to witness. So you and Artho, as closest kin, and your friend Ferad should you wish it, may attend, as well as the ladies of your company."

I was humbled by the concession, and deeply ashamed of my previous resistance, and not too proud to say so; Majanah accepted my apologies.

"No matter." She hesitated. "How will this, think you, be taken in Keltia? Will your folk hold it against Artho on his return?"

"I see no reason why they should. Artos does as he sees fit to do; I have known him, have been with him, since I was a child of five years, and never have I known him in all that time to do aught he did not wish to. His great gift is that so often he can make others wish in accord with his wishes, and think they wished so of their own will. You will have naught to fear from any Kelt."

"Not even from the Queen Janfarie?"

Janfarie . . . "Gweniver? Surely Artos has explained to you their situation—they are wedded, and rule conjointly, but they are not partnered, not consorts as are you and he. Any road, Gwennach—Janfarie—has a consort, a lennaun of her own; or at least she did when we left Keltia."

"The lord Keils; Artho has spoken of him. But how if in time to come I were to visit Keltia, bring Donah to see her father? How would we be greeted there?"

"The people will see you as Artos's beloved," I said honestly. "And Gweniver Ard-rían will receive you as befits a queen and sister priestess."

Majanah laughed. "No answer is also an answer."

"Then let us wait until the question is asked in earnest." I looked again at Donah, who had fallen asleep on the soft carpet under the windows, curled up like a little red cat. "I pledge you both this, though: When you come there, you shall find kin who love you, and a bloodlink that shall not fail while we remember."

She looked at me and did not smile. "The rite itself can promise no more."

And that was where we left it.

During the time of our sojourn away from Keltia, communications from home had been of force few and terse: Transcoms were not effective at such distances; carrier waves, even subspace ones, could be tapped into; and couriers could be waylaid. Even telepathy, generally reliable between those who were trained to it, was not entirely to be trusted: Others who were also trained to it could intercept the focus, catching the echo from the psychic trace such mindspeech left, almost as a wake in water where a ship has passed.

So we had had little news of Keltia's faring in our absence, save for matters of urgency that required Arthur's awareness, if not his action. It seemed from the couriers who managed to reach us at odd points in our reiving that Gweniver was managing most well, with Ygrawn and Morgan and Keils and Tari to call upon for strength and advice. There had been some incursions by, aye, you have guessed, the Fomori—at least before Ganaster stepped in, and our arrangement with Nanteos took effect. (And Melwas had been safely returned to his planet and his people; though not, Morgan gave me to understand, without real reluctance—perhaps Arthur had made a future friend for us in that young princeling after all . . .)

On the domestic front, things had been rather frighteningly tranquil. Cleaning up after Edeyrn had been a task worthy of Ercileas himself, or even Fionn the mighty; but the people were eager and glad to tackle the work of rebuilding, and despite setbacks—and there were many—remained of unceasing good cheer and high spirit, grateful beyond all measure to be free of Edeyrn's long yoke.

But it was the private communications that Arthur and

I had every now and again which told a somewhat different story: of tranquillity's end.

"We knew before we left that there might well be trouble out of that quarter in time."

Across the table, Arthur shrugged off my accusation.

"Well—we knew Marc'h was cross at not having been chosen viceroy over Kernow. But Gwennach and I told him plain as salt he would not be getting the seat on the Fainne because the family had not held it by right; and also because he was too closely kin to the Ard-tiarnas, through Ygrawn his sister. But mostly because we did not think he deserved to get it."

"And just as plainly he did not hear your telling . . ." Tanwen flung down onto the table a palm-sized crystal block: a coded message to Arthur and me from Ygrawn.

We looked warily at it, but made no move to take it up and play it. All those present knew very well the message contained therein: that Marc'h Duke of Kernow had tried to get his duchy to take the planet out of Keltia altogether; had tried, in truth, to secede.

"But what can he have hoped for?" asked Ferdia. "Surely he must have realized that no other worlds would go along with him into secession; and what could independence have meant to him, any road? Kernow is not self-sufficient, it could never have supported itself; and no other Keltic world would have dared supply a secessionary planet, at least not openly."

"And covertly would not have been enough—" Arthur was fiddling absently with a small toy Donah had left lying about, after her last visit to her father.

"Then what must be done? What shall you do?" asked Daronwy, who had been uncharacteristically silent for most of the meeting.

But Arthur kept turning the little plaything over and over in his hands, as if fascinated by its making or purpose. Covert, half-despairing glances were thrown my way by the others at the table—a typical staff session, such as Arthur held at least once a week without fail. No Aojunni, significantly enough, were invited to these councils but Kelts alone—not even Daronwy's mate Roric or Ferdia's Jennica—which meant, in practice, those dozen or so closest to Arthur.

And of those dozen, it was I who was perceived as carrying the greatest influence with him: charged, therefore, with the often thankless task of reminding him that he was still the High King of Keltia and would do well to keep in mind that he had been absent from his sphere of rule for nigh on seven years.

Seven years! It seemed scarce possible—nay, it was maybe a sixmonth, a year at most—but it was so, and we knew it. Seven years away from our homes, our dearest ones; seven years hunting a foreign ground, tilling a foreign soil. We had come to care deeply for Aojun, and the Yamazai way; some of us had come to care so for individual Aojunni—not least, as I have said, Ferdia and Daronwy, who had both taken mates from this world. As, indeed, had Arthur himself . . . But what of the rest of us? If this news was not enough to make them press for return of the speediest, what then would be?

"It is not as if Aojun cannot maintain itself without our help and presence, you know, Artos. This world ran along fine enough before we came here, and will again after we leave. Better, even, for that you have wrought so well with its armies and defenses . . . Majanah and Donah are secure upon the throne; and it is not as if you shall not see them more—they can visit us in Keltia, or we can return here some time to come." I paused for breath, and to calculate the effect this speech was having upon my fostern.

Not much of an effect, it would appear: Arthur continued doggedly at the work he had at hand—crafting a necklet for his daughter, in garnets and gold. But I could tell, from long experience, that he was hearing as well as merely listening: The set of his head and angle of his shoulders gave me the clue.

"*And* from what we hear," I continued, heartened by his apparent not-unwillingness to be instructed, "it is time for us to go home. You are High King; Keltia needs its Ard-rígh no less than its Ard-rían. Gweniver has been forced to rule alone too long; this is not what Uthyr meant to be. Artos—we must go home. We must go home *now*."

I ran down at last, and looked uncertainly at my matebrother where he worked so patiently at the gold gaud. It was more than a month past the meeting where we had discussed the news of Marc'h's attempt at secession: Only this very day we had received an urgent pleading communication from Ygrawn, begging us to return with speed. You would have thought such a plea, and from his own much-loved mother, who had been in her time Queen herself and well able to gauge political necessity, would have done the trick; and when I carried Ygrawn's message to Arthur in his workshop I had had every confidence that this, surely *this* would succeed where so much else had failed. But I was wrong, it seemed; what was he waiting for?

"A sign," he said at once, when I put it to him just so, looking up at me with a face as frank and open as water. "Just—a sign."

And all at once I knew what sign to give him.

"I never knew you had this, much less had it here with you."

Arthur reached out a tentative hand, glanced at me for permission, then gently touched his fingertips to the glowing silver of the cathbarr of Nia that I had taken from its hiding place that evening, and, well, begged its permission to allow itself to be used so in our extreme need.

We were in the small chamber off my solar that I used for meditation and such magical workings as I still kept up. For magic is different on all worlds, or differently powered—the mechanics are different, if the source and grounding is the same for all; and, whether out of respect to the gods of Aojun or no, though they were in many ways the same gods as our own, or merely out of laziness and sloth, I had not been as assiduous in my Druidry as I would have been, or should have been, at home.

But I had commanded Arthur here tonight; he and I only, not even Daronwy who was closest to us of all our comrades was with us here. This was a thing for Arthur and for me; and now I turned to him as he beheld with wonder the marriage gift made to the Pendreic kindred by the kindred of the Sidhe.

I would not have revealed it even now, even to him, had it not been made quite clear that I had no other choice. This was a thing apart from policy and politics; I was loath to sully it so, to use it as a means to even so imperative an end. But once again, as so often of late in times of stress and need, I heard Morgan's voice—and before you scoff and scout and call hard on me for delusions and fancies, I would bid you remember my lady's training and teacher, no less than her skills—and I knew I was right to do so.

But it was still a hard thing to do: The cathbarr was so lovely, and the knowledge of its giving so precious to me, so bound up with my marriage and my love for my mate; it had been so great a comfort to me over the past years of our exile.

For all that, though, I had not once set it upon my brow since Morgan herself had set it there, back in Turusachan; I had held it, meditated upon it and with it (oh aye, sometimes it seemed more sentient than I was entirely at ease with), even fallen asleep, once or twice, with my hand upon it as it might have been upon Morgan—it made her and home seem somehow closer. But I had not worn it, and, to be quite honest with you, had been feared to try.

I still was; but watching Arthur's face as he beheld the cathbarr, seeing his hesitant wonder as he touched it, I knew that try I must—if only to see, or to See, what might be seen. Or what needed to be Seen . . .

So I cast a circle in the usual manner, Arthur standing as my second what way he had so often done in time past; then, having purified one another as was customary, with incense and candleflame, water and salt, we seated ourselves before the hearth, cross-legged and facing one another, touching palms briefly in ritual gesture. And then I took the cathbarr from its cushion between us and set it upon my head.

What I was attempting was known as cailleach-na-luaith, the divination of the embers. I do not recall what I had been expecting; indeed, now I think on it, I am quite sure I had been expecting nothing at all. But the silver of the fillet had not even grown warm against my skin when I was suddenly no longer in Mistissyn, no more on Aojun, even, but back on Keltia, in a hall it seemed I knew . . .

It seemed I walked unseen, a taish among my own people; my own kin, even, for I had realized by now where I was, and who were the others in the room with me, the

ones I beheld but who could not see me: Marguessan was
one, and she was the angriest and the most speechful. But
there were others: Irian her lord, who had aged ungracefully and who seemed only eager to humor his raging
wife; Marc'h Tregaron, Ygrawn's brother, of whom we
had recently been hearing so much that was so unsettling;
and one other, a woman, whose face I could not quite
make out—

I touched my fingers to the great cushion-cut crystal at
the frontlet piece over my forehead, and jolted upright as
if someone had pulled a string in my back. The woman
was none other than Gwenwynbar, Arthur's first wife,
who had repudiated him so long ago and turned to his
great enemy Owein Rheged; and not only could I see
what passed here, I could hear as well . . .

What I heard I did not understand: It seemed that
Marguessan and Gwenwynbar, far from being the adversaries one would have expected them to be—both had
sons, you will remember, who could be held to have some
claim to the kingship; that is, if you accepted that Malgan
was indeed Arthur's child, not Owein's as the public had
been led to believe—were somehow in collaboration with
one another, cat-of-a-kind.

What they were now so angrily discussing seemed to
be to do with Marc'h: his abortive attempt at secession,
and how it worked on their own plans and schemes. Once
Marguessan made reference to Ysild, Arrochar's daughter, whom Marc'h had been vainly seeking to wed before
we left Keltia; it would appear he had not abandoned his
purpose, and the Princess was roundly berating him—
though whether she taxed him for his intent or for his
failure I could not make out.

In all, I was more profoundly unsettled by the feel of
the scene, rather than by anything I could hear: the sense
that here lay treason and real trouble, here were the seeds
of evil. And yet they had been sown long since: Even
Uthyr, back at Cadarachta, had warned of Marguessan
and Irian; had later included Mordryth, their sole progeny,
in that dire prediction.

The picture wavered before my inner sight and began
to vanish like smoke in a high wind. But the voices lingered a moment more, and through the gathering dimness

I heard a woman's voice speak clear: "So now will boar be set against bear."

It struck me with terror and confusion all in one; I did not know what was meant by it, or even which of the women had spoken it. But when I came back to plain everyday awareness—with a raging headache splintering my sight and a dull throb where the cathbarr bound my brows—and looked across at Arthur's face in the firelight, I had a feeling that he might know better than anyone.

I had not imagined eyes so dark could look so cold. His gaze that was usually warm as the sun on the bark of an oak tree looked now like the wing of a stooping hawk, like a black diamond under a snow-moon at midnight; and I shrank back in real, if momentary, fear.

He saw this at once, and reached out to seize my hands in comforting; and for my part I clung to his grip unashamedly, and stared and stared, for I could not speak. And I knew that at last, at long last, he *had* seen.

He saw this, too, and smiled; that old warm smile that for fifty years and more had meant a brother's love.

"Ah Tal-bach," he said. "Time it is we went home."

But when he had left, and I sat on alone, the cathbarr removed and resting next me on a velvet cushion near the hearth, I stared long and unseeing into the leaping flames. *Home . . .*

Then I reached beneath my tunic, beneath my leinna, and tugged gently on something I had worn so long I had ceased to notice it was even there. And into my fingers, out in the chill of the room, came that thing so familiar its weight and presence no longer registered around my neck: a fine, strong gold chain, and on it, a slim gold locket carved in likeness of a hawk's feather. The bright metal, mellowed with age though the fineness of its carving was as sharp as the day it was made, was warm from my body, and I raised it to my lips but did not spring it open; I did not need to.

The locket had been made for me by Arthur himself, oh, it must be near forty years gone now, and I had never taken it from my neck but once. It contained, behind a crystal cut from water-clear sapphire, that which its shape denoted: a hawk's feather, silver and black and gray, unfaded since the day my mother found it, since the day my father passed it on to me six years later. Arthur had crafted the gold casing as a birthday-gift, and the thing had become my chiefest talisman and signature.

And all at once I was hit by a wave of sadness and joy conjoined, so that when the tears came scalding to my eyes I did not know whether I wept for good or for ill, but knew only that I wept for change unalterable. And was not that a strange thing for me to do?

BOOK IV

Fíortraí

CHAPTER
24

"So, then. We are back."

It was a bright blowy spring afternoon, fresh with recent rain, the wind down the Strath still chill with the last edge of winter. I looked round at the long-absented landscape and drew into my lungs a deep draught of Keltic air that went to my head and my heart.

And, given it was so with me and with all the rest of us, you had thought Arthur might have said somewhat of more resonance than merely the unadorned observation recounted above. After all, he was High King of Keltia, and it was incumbent upon him to do so, and he was back after seven years away, and his wife and Queen, with what seemed like half the Court, had come to meet him here on the landing field of Mardale. And all he could do was lamely observe that we were back. Not 'home,' you will note; merely 'back.'

Not only that, but he had actually checked for just an instant, in the doorway of Prydwen, almost as if he were half minded to turn and go back inside and head again straight out to space: Nay, nay, all a mistake, never meant to come back so soon, sorry to trouble you all, farewell until later ... I gave him a sharp and unsubtle shove in the small of his back, and he straightened up and descended the steps to where Gweniver awaited him.

Who gave him for first greeting a look so chilling it

would freeze a flame. What in all the hells is going on
here? I wondered privately, and was still shivering from
that glance of hers when she turned on me. But me she
gave a kinswoman's full warm embrace of gladness; and
then, royal protocol satisfied, Morgan and I were free to
run into one another's arms.

Which we did, as soon as Arthur and Gweniver had de-
parted side by side. We clung together wordlessly, heed-
lessly, utterly uncaring of the many watching eyes and
indulgently smiling faces who were witness to our reunion. Well, it had been seven years, after all, surely she
and I were entitled to a bit of a public display . . . and certain sure it was that Gweniver and Arthur had not met the
need folk had for clips and kisses.

When I finally prised myself apart from Morgan, I
leaned back and just—*looked* at her. And marvelled how
it could be that something human could be so little
changed in seven years: Oh, there was a bit more of slim-
ness in her face, perhaps, a new depth in the deeps of her
eyes, if that was possible. But otherwise nothing: the
same gold in her hair, the same cream in her skin, the
same steel to her carriage. What she saw in my face I
knew not, and it seemed to matter not at all.

Under cover of the spaceport's noise and clamor, I
whispered to Morgan as we followed Arthur and
Gweniver off the field, "There is so much I must tell
you—"

And she whispered back, smiling all the while for the
benefit of the watching eyes, "Not so much perhaps as
you might think."

We had but a brief hour or two together in private—in
which time, I grant you, little was actually *said*—before
we were required to present ourselves in the Hall of Heroes for the formal welcoming.

As I came in with the rest of the family, I glanced
around at the well-known faces. Again, I was struck by
how little changed they seemed; it was almost as if some
rann had been laid over Keltia in our absence, so that our
return wakened them all from an ageless sleep. Ygrawn
looked not a day older; Gweniver, now that I could study
her at greater length, seemed, oh, I know not, taller,
maybe? Of our other friends, Tarian Douglas, still

Taoiseach, had wedded; Berain, captain of Ygrawn's guard, who had comforted me in her arms when I was five years old and newly orphaned, had died, which saddened me immeasurably; others had assumed lordships or taken new postings or been granted titles and dúchases and rule, all at dán's decree—or Gweniver's.

As for the folk themselves, they seemed—well, they seemed sullen, is what they seemed. Grudging, even; not unmixedly glad, in any case, to have their Ard-rígh returned. And I wondered why this should be: True, they were probably still haunted by Edeyrn's long legacy, and by the necessity of dealing with the outfall from those years. Yet Gweniver and Ygrawn and the rest should have been able to help them over that jump; you would think that in seven years— Or perhaps that was it right there: They resented Artos for leaving, going off on his own personal reiving and abandoning Keltia to struggle on without him.

But were they no whit pleased that he was back at last? I glanced round, and found myself doubting, even as my glance came once more to rest on Arthur where he sat beside Gwennach, in the carved oak and gilt chairs set side by side, in front of and one step below the Throne of Scone.

He looked both utterly in the moment and utterly absent, all in one; and I forced myself to examine him as a healer might, seeking clues to mood and health and resource. He was dressed more royally than the occasion strictly called for, in a gorgeous new blue sith-silk tunic embroidered with pearls and tiny sapphires; around his neck he wore a massive torc that had belonged to his father, Prince Amris. Ygrawn must have given it to him in welcome, glad for his safe return . . .

I let my gaze travel on to Gweniver. Now here was a nice contrast: If Arthur had clad himself unaccustomedly like a king, Gweniver Ard-rían had just as deliberately dressed down, and as a result drew all eyes to her. She sat quite quietly in her tall-backed throne, wearing the plainest and simplest gúna I had ever seen on her. No jewels save only her Ring of State; not even a fillet bound the cloud of black hair. I nearly laughed out loud; and Gweniver seeing my small convulsive catching cut her eyes my way, and I saw one corner of her mouth flicker.

Still, little enough else to laugh at: The ceremony was brief, and deathly solemn, and then we were all free for the hours till the nightmeal. Arthur and Gweniver vanished like asrai after a rain, presumably to closet themselves with their high officers of state—I had seen a look in Tarian's eye—but as a mere Privy Councillor I was excused for the moment. Which was well for me, since Morgan and I had plans to spend the next month or so in bed, with orders for meals to be left outside the door at judicious intervals. But since we both knew that plan unlikely of fulfillment, at the least we could hope for the next few hours, and maybe even the next few nights as well.

"I am so hungry I could eat the moons," I boasted later, as Morgan and I left our chamber and hastened down to Mi-cuarta, Turusachan's great banqueting-hall. I am no watchpot usually; but Guenna and I had loved hard and often in our short span of privacy, and now we both were famished.

"Well, at the feast, then." She did not look at me as she spoke, and I shook her arm where it was slipped through my own.

"What?"

Still she would not meet my eyes. "You and Arthur have been long away," she said after a moment. "Matters here have long been decided without you—without the Ard-rígh. He must find his own way back among us. That is all."

I thought about that as we came into Mi-cuarta and threaded our way through welcoming friends. "Will not Gwennach work with him to do just that? That is, after all, the arrangement."

"It *was* the arrangement. I think my brother will find that the case has altered in his absence."

Just how much that case had altered was made plain when we took our seats at the high table: Arthur and Gweniver side by side, of course, in the two great chairs at the table's center; but plainer still was the silent message that sat at Gweniver's left hand—Keils Rathen, First Lord of War, tall and lean and sardonic as ever.

And apparently most unwilling to be displaced, even by the High King of Keltia . . . Nor was there any reason, in law or in love, why he should be: After all, Arthur had wedded Majanah according to the way of the Yamazai, had fathered Donah—what wonder that Gweniver, in her co-sovereign's absence, should not have grown even closer than formerly to her longtime lennaun?

I shifted a bit uncomfortably in my chair. I had always borne Keils great and loving friendship, and respect for his merit as a warrior, and honor for his devotion to Gwennach. But I could see unquiet roads ahead, and not just us to be riding them.

As for Keils, tonight at least he was behaving as a knight and a lord of Keltia might be expected to do: He had borne himself to Gweniver in public with the courtesy due to the Ard-rían, and to Arthur with the deference due the Ard-rígh, and only the tiniest touch of frost on each. Not so much as one not close to any of them would notice; but true it was that Gweniver had entered Micuarta on Keils's arm, not Arthur's; and, at feast's end, he was also the one on whose arm she left.

Morgan and I stayed on awhile, enjoying ourselves with our friends, for of course all our old Companions were here this night; and it was deep into owl-time when we quitted the banquet-hall and went upstairs to bed. I watched Morgan as she divested herself of her gúna and the heavily bejewelled overtunic and seated herself before her mirror to unpin her shining hair.

"Not so much as a touch of silver," I said, to tease her.

She would not rise to it. "Indeed, why should there be? What point in being a sorceress if one cannot keep the gold in one's hair? Though I have noticed a snowy strand or two atop your head and Arthur's . . ."

"Aye, well, I am not surprised." I lay back on the piled pillows and linked my hands behind my head. "You know about Artos and Majanah, I take it."

She nodded, looking only at her reflection in the glass. "He sent us word when it happened, you *will* recall?"

"And what was the thinking on it here?"

"I would guess much the same as yours there."

"How did Gwennach take it?"

Morgan turned at that to meet my gaze. "In truth, I think she was glad of it, Talyn."

"You mean because of Keils." Well, I could hardly say I was surprised, or that I blamed Gweniver for a very human reaction. Arthur's taking himself a ban-charach doubtless lifted from Gweniver not a little of that which she had plainly been feeling about her union with Keils—not guilt, but a kind of unease, perhaps even a sense of divided loyalty. It was all a mystery and wonder of impatience to me, for I knew as only a bard can know that Arthur and Gweniver loved each other. The impatience was for that both of them were too bone-stubborn to admit it, to the other or to themselves, and certainly not to the rest of Keltia.

"They will, you know, in time." Morgan had shed her chamber-robe and slipped into bed beside me. "In the meantime, there are far knottier problems with which we all must deal; thank Goddess you are returned to do so."

But what they were, she would not say that night; and after a while I was not of a mind to press her.

The next morning Arthur and Gweniver summoned us all to a Council meeting, and those problems of which Morgan had spoken were laid out plain for all.

"There is no easy way to say this, Arthur." Gweniver had risen to speak as soon as Tarian Douglas had called the session to order, and every single soul in the room strained forward to hear.

"Then say it the hard way." His voice was calm as ever, unstressed.

Gweniver looked straight at him down the length of the Council table. "Your uncle of Kernow is working treason. Marc'h has taken the planet to the brink of secession; he has armed against the rest of Keltia; and—"

"And?"

"He has kidnapped his son Tryffin's lady, and would have her for his."

The room was very silent, though most of those present had known all this for months. Even we, far away on Aojun, had heard some of it, and it was that which had caused us to come home again when we did. But this surpassed in evilness aught that we had heard heretofore, and I was not the only one to gasp aloud with the shock of it.

"You might have warned me," I muttered fiercely to Morgan. But Gweniver was speaking again, as Arthur had made no sign one way or another.

"You will recall, Artos, that some years ago—before

you left Keltia on your reiving—Marc'h your uncle had wished to wed Ysild Formartine, heir of Arrochar."

"I remember." The voice seemed to come from a far cold place; the face was unmoving, and yet it seemed as if a beam of light hit Arthur's eyes, leaving all the rest in shadow.

"Then you will also remember that Ysild rejected him out of hand. What you will not know, as it had not yet come to pass, is that Tryffin your cousin, Marc'h's heir, has himself fallen in love with Ysild, and she with him."

"A complication." I felt the need somehow to shift a focus from Arthur, a focus I did not like.

Gweniver did not even bother to glance my way. "As you say, Glyndour . . . Any road, when Ysild and Tryffin went to Marc'h to seek his blessing on their marriage, your uncle reacted—poorly. He cast his own son into imprisonment, seized Ysild against her will and, almost it seemed as afterthought, announced to me and to the Council and the Fainne that Kernow was breaking away from Keltia."

Arthur made the nervous gesture I had known him make since boyhood in times of stress: a graceful flexing of his swordhand fingers, a double ripple from smallfinger to thumb and back. But he betrayed no other hint of his mood.

"What has been done about it?"

"What we felt in conscience we must do." That was Keils, and the currents in the Council chamber shifted yet again. To me it seemed that the Councillors, save for those who had been away with Arthur, were better disposed and fuller willing to listen to the First Lord of War than to the Ard-rígh; and I liked it not at all that it should be so.

"And that was?"

"We have put Kernow under siege. Blockade, to be more precise about it . . . No ship gets in or goes out: No commerce is permitted, no supplies can be landed, no reinforcements can be had. Marc'h stands alone."

"Ah, but does he?" whispered Morgan, and several heads turned nervously.

"What is the news of Tryffin?" asked Daronwy from her seat near my own, and I sensed her concern in all the rest of our old Companions. I was sore concerned myself:

Tryffin had been my friend and comrade from our days in Coldgates, in Bargodion——he and Arthur and I, and Grehan Aoibhell who sat now across the chamber, and Kei who had died under the Boar's hoof at Nandruidion, and Betwyr who had been with us on our creagh-rígh. We loved him dearly: He was no great thinker, was Tryff, but he had a high heart and a caring soul, and there were few better sea-lords in all Keltia.

"No news," said Ygrawn, and my gaze shot to her at the note of wretchedness in her voice. And well might she be feeling so: Marc'h was her brother, Tryffin her nephew, and the High King her son—a hard knot to cut through, even for a queen.

I looked steadily at her until she felt my glance and met it. Ygrawn was the only mother I had ever known, my own having died in my faunthood; she had been my methryn since I was scarce six years old. More than that, she had been my Queen for all the years of her marriage with Uthyr, and she was my matemother besides. There was nothing I would fail of doing did Ygrawn ask it of me, and even did she not ask . . . She read all this as we held each other's eyes, and after a moment she smiled.

"He holds Tryffin on Kernow," she said then, and her gaze shifted to Arthur, but his head was bent to the computer-pad inlaid in the table before him and he did not see. "In the fortress of Tyntagel, on the headland of Penguiron."

I knew the place, and a harsher, harder, more unassailable prison was not in all Keltia. There had been some talk, even, of using it as durance for the Marbh-draoi, should it have fallen out that he had been taken alive, so strong and defensible a place it was.

"And where is Ysild?" I asked.

"Marc'h keeps her close with him at Kerriwick," said Gweniver. "And therefore have we held off from besieging either place, confining ourselves for the moment to the blockade from space."

"And has that been as—effective as you could have hoped?" Arthur seemed to be back among us, and on his face now was that old look I remembered from the days on Gwynedd. He had a plan, and it was naught to do with anything that had yet been done . . .

"It has kept Kernow to a standoff," admitted Keils. "If

they will not remain with us, still they cannot be quit of us, not in any real sense. And it is in my mind, Ard-rígh, that the most of the Kernish folk wish not to be party to Marc'h's secession. They will not rise up against him; not yet, that is. But neither will they give him the support he has been counting on."

"Then whence comes he by such arrogance and imprudence—such traha—to so defy us?"

Gweniver looked Arthur straight in the eyes. "For that you were not here to hold the strong hand uppermost upon him. I am Ard-rían, and Keils is our First Lord of War, yet he did not fear *our* hands as he would have feared your own. But you were not here."

That last was spoken with more of a snarling snap than I had ever in all my days heard Gweniver use; not even in the worst times at Coldgates, when she had been thrawn for every reason and no reason, had I known her to put such bite into her tone.

If Arthur heard it, he gave no sign, but addressed himself to the chamber at large.

"Well. My sorrow that my uncle has seen fit to·act so ... But, kin or no, he cannot be permitted to go on what way he has chosen. And, more importantly still, Kernow cannot and shall not be let to go its own road apart from Keltia. I took oath as Ard-rígh of the Six Nations, and by gods I say I shall not preside as Ard-rígh over five only ... But, Lady"—this to Gweniver, who startled visibly at his use of both tone and title—"I would speak of this with you in private. As for you others, keep yourselves to hand; I will be summoning you for counsel as you are needed; and the Ard-rían and I shall address the High Council and the vicegerents of the Fainne again in session tomorrow forenoon. But now my wife and I must speak."

"That is the first mention Artos has made, since our return, of the fact that he is wed." I set down my mether and leaned back in my chair.

Ygrawn laughed, a little grimly. "And yet, amhic, I do not think he ever once forgot it whilst you were gone ..."

"Be that as it may," I pointed out, "he did take the Yamazai queen to him, and got a child by her—"

My foster-mother waved dismissive fingers. "No matter to us, Talyn, and I say a boon to Aojun that their future ruler shall be half a Kelt."

"Aye, well, there is that." I lapsed into uncertain silence. "She will come here, you know, methryn; when the child is old enough to make the journey."

"And I shall be glad indeed to meet them both—nay, truly! The Kelts and the Yamazai go back long centuries in friendship; this is no unfitting thing my son has caused to be, and a queen is hardly an unsuitable ban-charach for an Ard-rígh to choose. What is she like, this Majanah? A hawk? A helianth?"

I laughed in spite of myself. "No flower she! Unless she be that firerose I have heard of, that grows on Alectyn Vair—the one that to breathe the great fragrance of is to perish where you stand."

"Then she must be dangerous indeed."

"Oh, aye, like enough—" But I was still working out what Majanah was like. "She is more like a hunting-cat: not wholly biddable, can claw and purr at the same time. I like her well."

Ygrawn nodded. "And the child?"

"A bright and bonny lass, as you will see." I looked up sharply. "Ah, nay, you do not think what I sense you are thinking—you *are* thinking it . . ."

"It must be thought of," she said reluctantly. "If Artos and Gwennach do never contrive an heir between them—this Donah is Arthur's firstborn."

"That we know of." Morgan's four little words dropped the ground out from under us; all the more, as she had been silent since we came to her mother's rooms.

"It has never been proved," I said after a while, "that Malgan is not Owein's son."

"Nor has it been proved that he is not Arthur's. Oh, I know you were at Caer Dathyl all those years, and even you, my beloved, could not say for sure. So let us not now assume one way or the other if we need not."

I was no whit annoyed by Morgan's jab, but following a thought of my own.

"Where is Gwenwynbar these days? For that matter, where is Marguessan?"

"My sister is back on Gwynedd with her lord and son. She and Irian came to the title last year, when old Strahan died. They have two more whelps, by the way, a girl and another boy, born while you were gone—Galeron and Gwain."

My thought was rising to panic, and yet I did not know why. "And Gwenwynbar?"

"No one knows," said Ygrawn, who had cordially detested her son's first wife and who had been hated every bit as well in return. "Not that I care if the ground has opened up to swallow her, save that she will surely trouble Artos's path somewhere up the years—but it seems suspiciously impossible to me that she could have vanished so completely, and stayed so hid for so long. But so she has, and the boy with her."

And then all at once it came back to me, broke in upon me like the sea that had once broken in on Gwaelod, just as strong, just as whelming . . .

"On Aojun—when I put on the cathbarr—"

Quickly I told these two dearest ladies of mine what had happened that night in Mistissyn, what I had seen and heard while the fillet of Nia was on my brows. And, sorceresses both, they understood as perhaps no others could, or would. I saw by little signs in their bearing— little things that were, littler things that were carefully not—that they were deeply alarmed by my tale and Seeing, and I was afraid; as I had not been before.

CHAPTER
25

When I went to Arthur's chambers later that day, at Arthur's summons, I found his solar empty. Only Cabal, snoozing in his 'customed spot in the window-nook, who swept his tail over the stones as I entered but was too lazy elseways to bestir himself . . . I went over and scratched his soft ears, and he sighed and leaned his huge head into my hand.

Through the mullioned window just above the hound's little niche, I saw Arthur outside on the turret walk, and giving Cabal one last scruffle I went out to join him.

We had not been alone together since our return, and I glanced curiously at him as I came up alongside. He was not looking at me, but out at the unparalleled vista before us: the great Bight of Caerdroia below, the huge curving half-moon bay that stretches from the ridges of the Dragon's Spine, far out of sight to the southwest, all the way past the City cliffs and the mouths of the Avon Dia up to the feet of the Stair.

Indeed the view this hour was more dramatic even than usual: Sunset was rolling up banks of cloud in the lift westaways, humps and hillocks of blue and purple and gray edged with burning lines of gold, and the wind that often got up in late day was chivying the clouds along.

Arthur was looking at the sky as if it spoke to him, as

perhaps it did, and I would for no sake be the one to interrupt their converse ...

"Gwenhidw's flocks are going home to pen."

"And Aengus's wind to drive them like a sheepdog of the skies. Artos, what is on you?"

Still he did not turn to me, and I was sharply minded of Morgan standing just so, what time she gave into my hands Nia's fillet. They did not often show sibling resemblance, these two stems of Pendreic, but when they did it was startling to behold.

"Artos?" I asked again, gently, as I had been asking it for fifty years and more.

"To speak as do you bards, Talynno, I have ever loved counterpoint above harmony, and the undertext to the plain gist of the song ..."

I let that pass; soon enough he would come to what he had to say; though what he had just now told me was the thing he had wished me most to hear. But the sheep of Gwenhidw were all safe penned in their starry fold below the skyline before he spoke again.

"I must go to Kernow, Taliesin. Go in force."

"To rescue Tryffin."

"And Ysild; but also to give my uncle Marc'h a lessoning I had never thought to give him. What he has done cuts at my authority and Gwennach's, no doubt of it, but more: It cuts at the fabric we have woven here in Keltia since Brendan first set up the loom." He laughed. "*Beside* the Loom—But Marc'h must be stopped."

I leaned on the stone coping, still warm from the long afternoon's sun. Since our return two days since, and often on the road home, I had boxed my mental compasses to puzzle out just why it was that Marc'h of Kernow, by all history and opinion an unimaginative and dull-brained trimmer, a gutling and a rake, should so suddenly and spectacularly turn his cloak. Kidnapping Ysild and imprisoning Tryffin I could almost understand; but treason seemed a thing so far beyond Marc'h's line of country as to be more plausibly laid to temporary lunacy than any other more usual cause.

"I know what you are thinking," said Arthur then. "I have been shadow-fencing with it myself since Gwennach first told us ..."

"And?"

He closed his hand over his Ring of State, stared at the green stone as if he had been a jewelsmith appraising it for flaws.

"In Mistissyn," he said haltingly. "Who was it you saw when the crown of Nia gave you the Seeing? Do I need to mind you of their names? Or their goals?"

I ran a hand over my new beard, grown three years since on Aojun. "Nay—would I could forget."

"And I. But this did not begin with our denying Marc'h the place he sought in the Fainne, the lordship paramount of Kernow, though he claims that now as his right and justification. It did not begin with Gwenar, even, nor yet with Marguessan. It is rather the last working of the Marbh-draoi Edeyrn. His arm is long, and reaches out to us even from Annwn; it is he who pulls me into kin-strife."

"You are not the one did begin it."

"As Ard-rígh, and kin to Marc'h, I must be the one shall end it. And to do that—" He drew me inside the solar and latched the turret door against the night. Cabal, too lazy to budge for me, leaped frisking upon his master, as if they had been parted another seven years, and I grinned to recall the frightened four-months' puppy I had rescued from the ruins of a murdered town.

"To do that," Arthur resumed, when we were sitting beside the hearth as so often we had done down the years, methers in hand and toes to the grate, "I must walk a line notoriously difficult of treading. Many others have come to grief over such a path in time past."

"You have ever been neat-footed enough when it counted. But see, Artos," I said suddenly, leaning forward, "see how it may be done."

And I spoke as if Midir himself, the lord of plan and meaning, had taken command of my voice and tongue and brain; and when at last I ceased to speak, Arthur nodded, simply, once, and said only, "Aye."

The system of Kernow was the fifth of our seven to be settled, and like Vannin and Tara it has but the one inhabited, eponymous world. A small planet as planets go, it is a surpassing fair one, rich in mineral wealth: mostly ocean (hence the great sea-skills of the Kernishfolk), with two continents and a vast number of island groupings of varying formation and size.

Perhaps because of the sparseness of its population and the distances between settled regions, Kernow had ever been one of Keltia's more peaceful planets, Ruling House succeeding House in orderly, lawful turnings. The Tregarons, Ygrawn's family, were the seventh ducal kindred, and eleventh overall, to claim the lordship of Kernow, and held sway from their ancient seat at Kerriwick, twelve miles down the iron-fanged coast from Tyntagel.

Dynas Dau Gell, the Twice-dark Stronghold ... It was the most unassailable castle on Kernow, one of the most fearfully tenable in all Keltia, and never once in all our history had it been reduced, by siege or by straight attack.

And we had no hope or indeed plan of so doing now ... I sat in my chamber aboard Prydwen and studied what tapes I could find. Tyntagel had been built in two sections; a weakness, I hear the strategical architects among you already crowing, but let me assure you it was not so. The main ward was on a high rocky peninsula so narrow at the join as to be as near an island as might ever be; the Carrai, the tiny neck of land was called, the Thong. The lower wards were on the Penguiron headland proper, and were operable, and defensible, on their own.

It was in the island ward that Marc'h had imprisoned Tryffin his son and heir— I ran the tape forward and back until it flickered of itself to the place I wished it; after a long time I froze the image and slumped in my chair, staring unseeing at the screen, confidence all but dead within me.

How in all the seven hells had I allowed my traha to pull Arthur into so mad a plan? Bad enough that we had come home to face treason and kin-rift so near the Throne; worse still that it had come so hard on our return, before Prydwen's hull was scarce cooled from our crossing. This, though ...

"Second thoughts, Pen-bardd?"

That was Morgan, who had entered all unheard; Daronwy was with her. I smiled, and waved a hand at the tapescreen.

"As you see, lady ..."

Daronwy laughed and seated herself across the table.

"It grates me that we must work this against Marc'h, who seems more stupid, I think, than evil; but truly, does it not feel like the old days come again!"

In spite of my deep misgivings, I smiled back at her. "Good days, ill days both, Ronwyn."

"Never mind. Tryff will be glad to see us, any road."

"And Ysild?" I cast my glance sidewise to Morgan. "She is your friend, after all. How think you it will work on her, raped away by Marc'h?"

"Marc'h has made several mistakes here," said Morguenna Pendreic. "Any one of which were sufficient to cause his downfall; but taking Ysild may well prove to be the worst day's choice he ever made."

I reached over and pressed a button or two; the picture on the screen suddenly changed, to another castle, this one inland, the country in which it was set rolling downland, few trees and no other habitation in sight. This was Kerriwick, an ancient seat of the Tregarons, twelve miles from Tyntagel and perhaps five lai from the sea: Ysild's home of force, for the moment.

Now you must not think because I use such words in my telling as 'taking' and 'raped away' that I mean to suggest Marc'h committed any violence against Ysild's person. Rape of the body is a thing of the past in Keltia: There have long been deep-encoded, soul-stamped prohibitions against that vilest of crimes, which shames only its instigator, never its subject. Of old on Earth, the punishment had been death, no questions, no quarter; though before so irreversible a judgment was brought to bear, of course, the thing was most carefully sifted by truthsensers of the highest degree, kenning both accuser and accused. Too, rape was still on the brehons' books as one of the Three Rank Offenses that required submission of the accused party (and again, the accuser as well) to the proof of the Cremave, that fearful instrument of perfect, and immediate, justice.

But in our days since coming to Keltia we had evolved past such gross evil; and, on the rare chance that we had not, women were taught by the Ban-draoi, or by their own kinswomen, a method of dealing with potential rapists that was both painful and effective, and which carried its own safeguards against possible vindictive misuse. Nay, I knew Ysild was safe enough in that respect. Still, she had been spirited away by force and was being held against her own most clearly demonstrated will; and the body is not the only thing that can be violated.

"Talyn?"

I came out of my musings to see Morgan and Daronwy, and Ronwyn's mate Roric, who had come with her to Keltia and who had just now joined her here. All three were watching me indulgently and curiously.

"Marguessan," I said, with all the certainty of a Druid oracle. "As I saw on Aojun. Marguessan, and Irian, and— and one other."

"Gwenwynbar," said Morgan quietly, and I gaped, for I had not told her of Arthur's onetime wife figuring in my vision. She saw my surprise, and laughed. "Did you think I did not know?" She reached inside her leinna, drew out a thing I had seen but once before, and then in Arthur's hand: a clach, a small sphere of purest rock crystal, bound by silver hoops incised with runes half worn away. I smiled, and reached out to take it as she undid the chain upon which it hung.

"I remember *this* . . . Arthur had it at Caer Dathyl, what time we went to dine with Edeyrn and Owein Rheged— you were there, Ronwyn."

"Indeed." She leaned forward, as interested as I in the magical jewel. "It was this saved all our lives, if I recall aright."

"Birogue and I worked on it together, in Collimare." All at once Morgan looked as if she were a six-years' child struggling not to weep. "I wish to the Goddess that I had not seen in it that which I have seen—but it was this clach first gave me to know that my own sister stood behind Marc'h's astonishing new mode of treason and secession."

"Marguessan has long been suspect," remarked Daronwy. "I mind me that Uthyr Ard-rígh warned us Companions, before Cadarachta; and then of course after—" She broke off, unwilling to call more vividly to mind that scene in the High King's tent; not to herself, all the more not to Uthyr's daughter and her mate.

"That goes back long before," said Morgan quietly. "My sister has ever thought she was our father's right heir, and her son after her; could not, would not accept the succession as it stands by law and might. But I had not wished to believe her envy and hatefulness of Arthur and Gweniver would ever lead her to such a pass as this."

"You are certain, then, she is behind Marc'h's actions?" I asked, though I had my own reasons, old reasons, for not doubting Marguessan's bent to evil.

"You have Seen it yourself, beloved . . ."

"Will they be at Tyntagel, do you think?" asked Roric. "Or at Kerriwick, even?"

Betwyr came in hard upon his words, slung himself into the one remaining empty chair.

"Marc'h will be at Kerriwick, certainly," he said with conviction. "It is a strong fort, and the country roundabouts better far than that near Tyntagel."

"Aye, well, how *will* we come to take Tyntagel?" asked Ronwyn. "There is but the one road to the cliff-face, and then that scareful outside stair cut in the stone, and only two may go abreast. It is like Sword-bridge, Bridge of Dread, in the lands of Dobhar and Iar-Dobhar . . ."

Silence fell upon the chamber: All of us here were sorcerers, we knew that place whereof Daronwy spoke, felt that bridge's bright blade-edge bite through our feet . . . I shook myself.

"There is a plan," I heard myself saying, and across the table, Morgan's glance met mine: She knew well whose was the plan I spoke of.

"He generally has one," was all she said, and there we left it.

Prydwen sailed on toward Kernow—it was one of the more distant systems from Tara, but even at our less than urgent pace we would come to it in well under a seven-night; Arthur did not wish, for reasons of his own, to force the approach with haste—and as I watched the planet grow in the ship's ports from an indeterminate gray blur to a sharp-cut blue and white orb, I reflected on the plan that we had made, and I wondered anew.

On the sixth day we joined the flag vessel of the station force that had been maintaining the blockade for the past few months. Called the Dawnsio, she was one of the larger craft inherited from Edeyrn's Raven-ruled fleet, and was commanded by none other than our old friend Elen Llydaw—she who would soon be known to all Kelts

as Elen Llydawc, Elen of the Hosts, for her generalship
both against the Marbh-draoi and the galláin who would
come after. So we had a brief happy reunion before Arthur put his plan in train.

Thus it came to be that I found myself on foot, cold
and frozen, in thunder snow and a howling wind, staring
up through the whitened dark at the walls of Kerriwick
castle. Daronwy and I had come ahead to spy out the
land; even though we had scanned it from space and
scoped it on the way in, Arthur still held to his old habit,
and had sent us on to see for ourselves. Again that giddy
feeling had seized us both, that feeling Ronwyn had spoken of on the way here: a sense of having been down this
road many times before, and a gladness for having done
so, for doing so now. And, of course, it *was* no new thing
for us: Back on Gwynedd, we had often journeyed round
the provinces as Counterinsurgency spies, Companions
under Arthur's command, and had enjoyed ourselves no
end while we did so.

But none of us here this night loved freezing in the
gale off the waters of Galva Sound, a few lai to the north
of Kerriwick; and our moods were not improved by the
knowledge that it would be even worse at Tyntagel, and
that naught could or would be done to work the weather
into something more clement. The worse it was, the better for Arthur's purposes: Indeed, I suspected Morgan and
some others of sorcerously coaxing the storm from gray
rain to this white beast, this strong cold power that ri-
valled the húracán.

I brushed vainly at the sharp stinging needles of sleet
that the wind was driving into my skin, squinted up at the
wet slate walls. Kerriwick had originally been built as a
hunting lodge; only later had one of the early ruling families felt the need of fortification, making up the perceived lack with a thoroughness that struck me now, nine
hundred years later, as cause for hatred. How were we going to deal with *that,* even by so clever a plan as ours?

Daronwy touched my arm, and I turned to follow her;
we slid on our bellies like otters, down through the snow-
slicked hillgrass into the woods at the bottom of the
combe. I ran my mind over what I had just seen, again

and again, as a tongue will push and prod a broken tooth. But we spoke no word till we were away.

"It is bigger than I thought," said Daronwy judicially. "And that glacis off to the left will hinder Arthur's maneuvering if he allows himself to be led in so close—" She went on cogently and at length about the shortcomings of the strategy—"Where is Tari when most we need her!"—but I was only half listening, my thought running on a track of its own.

Arthur's strategy was, for him, most unusual: We were not going to win, or even to give true fight, if we could avoid it. Oh, Marc'h would be looking for some show of force, he had seen our shuttles, had noted Prydwen's arrival on blockade station. He would be waiting; but what he would *not* be doing was allowing himself to be caught inside Kerriwick. A siege was not to his interest, or so he would think; well, he would be wrong, and we knew that at the first sign of Arthur's imminence Marc'h would ride out to meet him.

And we would join battle: But Marc'h was not to know that it would be a sham battle only, a feint, a lure to get him away from Kerriwick. While he was gone, Morgan was to enter the castle and bring away Ysild. We did not know how she was to accomplish this, and we did not ask. She said that she could do so, and we accepted her word on it.

After that—well, then came the hard part.

"What does methryn think of all this coil?" I asked Arthur, once I was safe and warm and dry again in the shuttle we were using, instead of battle tents, as commandery. "Have you told her what is toward?"

It was a question I had not dared ask him before. True it was that Ygrawn Tregaron, Rían-dhuair of Keltia, and her elder brother had long not been on loving terms of kinship—plain hunt, she thought him a wastrel, he thought her a queenly shrew—but even so . . .

"I have," said Arthur evenly. "And she agrees with me as to what must be done."

"I may assume, too, that Gweniver Ard-rían—not to mention the First Lord of War—is in agreement with you on this."

"Assume as you like—but aye, they are that." The dark

eyes had begun to grow a touch warmer, and I knew of old what that foreboded. But I pressed on regardless.

"And you are prepared to slay your own uncle?" I asked, with a coolness I was far from feeling.

Arthur very deliberately paced across the shuttle's tiny bridge and seated himself in the command chair before he spoke.

"I do not *wish* to slay him, nay, Talyn; but if that is what it comes to— He is guilty of crimes against the Ard-tiarnas, crimes that of old have carried death as punishment. Even does he survive this night, I may yet have his blood on my hands. But, Pen-bardd"—the irony was savage here, his voice almost a snarl—"is not that what it means to be a king?"

"I would not know; if ever I was one in a life gone by I remember it not." I reached across to put my hand on his arm. "Besides, is not that why the brehons have given us honor-price? All to avoid such choices?"

"Maybe, but there are some things even honor-price cannot buy back." He ran his hands over his face, left them cupped to hide his features for longer than perhaps was warranted, then lowered his hands and looked straight at me, through me. "Do you not think it the least bit strange, Tal-bach, that Gweniver should have let this go on so long as she did, and yet told me of it so hard on our returning? Almost as if, do you see, she wished me gone again from Tara before I had fairly come home ..."

I had thought just that, of course, but had foreborne to speak of it to any save my wife. As I did now; but something else came unbidden to my tongue.

"Are you prepared, Artos, to find Marguessan here? Or Irian? Or—" But I could not say it, and he said it for me.

"Or Gwenwynbar ... Aye, I have thought much on it, you know. Ever since she left my bed for Owein's, ever since you saw her at Ratherne, before the fight at Nandruidion—in the joy I had with Janjan, even, never did I forget to wonder what Gwenar might be working. And there is the boy."

Ah, the boy. So Malgan ap—Owein?—still lodged as a notable thorn in Arthur's heart. I saw the trouble in his eyes, and spoke, I thought, to help him. But help is not what came out of my mouth ...

"Your heir will be of Gweniver, not of Gwenwynbar: a

prince for Keltia, and a princess his sister; and another who shall be queen in a far country, and who will not forget her kin."

I was as astounded as Arthur, for that had *not* been what I had planned to say. But my fostern was looking at me with the half-smile of surmise.

"You sound more like Merlynn every day, do you know that . . . What *has* my sister been teaching you?" Then, before I could reply, Arthur swung up out of his chair with all the old grace of eager action. "And speaking of my sister—give order to break camp, let Daronwy and Roric see to it. Morgan will be at the gates of Kerriwick by now, and if we are not timely to her arrival, she will have our guts for greave-straps. And I for one would not grudge her them."

CHAPTER
26

I shall never forget that charge on Kerriwick in the driving blizzard, that wild night so soon to become wilder still—a night out of legend, that itself became legend before day dawned.

As all our strategists, even the notoriously exacting Tarian, had agreed, our hope here lay not in force of arms but in surprise and cunning. If mere military victory had been all our aim, we could have reduced the entire planet to glowing cinders, let alone two castles only, and stayed warm and dry and safe aboard ship while we did so. But Arthur had decided on this as our best and most prudent way, the one most likely to leave fewest scars after; and we took his assessment on faith, now, as we had taken it all those years of war. And he, and we, were mostly right . . .

So we had a small force of foot, perhaps a thousand, just enough to lure Marc'h into the path we had planned for him; and also a small cavalry wing, its riders not imported with the rest of the troops but scouted up from distant Kernish districts loyal to the Crown, not to the Duke. They were mounted on fell-ponies, clever shaggy beasts, whose footing on their native hills was nothing short of a wonder.

In the end, it proved absurdly easy; the first part, at least. At our approach to Kerriwick, Marc'h, whom none had ever either accused or acclaimed as a master of war, emptied the castle and trailed after us, as biddable as if he had been a pig on a string. I looked up toward the castle gates a mile or more distant, hoping for a sign of my wife, but all was still, and no figure showed. Which was, I hoped, a good thing.

Our purpose down below was, as I have said, not to give real battle, but only to keep Marc'h busy while Morgan brought out Ysild; and, later, if that went well, while we went to Tyntagel for Tryffin. Though I tried to hide it, I was full of fear: Morgan had gone alone into Kerriwick; not only that, she had laid heavy geis on any who tried to follow her, thinking to 'help'; and she had been cold and inflexible as findruinna upon that point.

Not that any was so inclined, to disobey Morguenna Pendreic when she stood in her power as sorceress. Even I, her mate, had flinched a little when she emerged from the tent of the Goddess, where she had been preparing herself and her magic, when I saw the light in her eyes, and the look upon her face, even though the plan she now worked had been of my own devising . . . But we bent to our tasks, and she to hers; and when after three hours of us playing at pig-i'-the-wood with Marc'h's troops, in and out amid the mist-thick downs and twisting combes, Morgan was suddenly there among us as if she had flown there, and another beside with her, we all froze where we stood, and stared, and were more afraid than ever.

She dispelled that at once by breaking into a grin that warmed us all, and drew forward to Arthur and me the pirn around whom all this coil did wind.

I must say, she did not look like the damsels of legend who had been carried off for love or lust or simple politics. Then again, little about Ysild Formartine was usual; and just now, the prevailing mood with her seemed to be fury. Not at us, this rage of hers: Ysild made Arthur the reverence due the High King, gave me a courteous nod of recognition, glanced round at each of us with eyes like sapphire lasers and said, "Where is Marc'h? I wish to kill him."

Even Arthur was a little shaken. "All in good time, lady. I take it you had no trouble?" This to Morgan, who grinned again.

"*We* were not the ones who had the trouble, Arthur, this I can say in all modesty! As for the rest of them up at the castle, well, you would have to ask of them yourself."

Ysild laughed. "The Princess Morguenna is more modest than you know: Never have I seen aught like it, magic wielded so featly against so many."

"But what did you *do,* Guenna?" burst out Daronwy, unable further to endure the curiosity that was consuming us all where we stood.

"Played them a sleep-strain, a suantraí, such as my lord himself might have done—" Morgan cast a wicked glance at me, her eyes brimming with mirth and the pleasure of a thing achieved.

"They are all asleep?" asked Arthur.

His sister nodded. "And will stay so until, oh, about sunset tomorrow, if all goes aright. If not, they will snore on another day; no more. And will take no harm of it, save maybe for a raxed neck or arm here and there; some of them dozed off in less than ideal or easeful attitudes. I found Ysild, who had helped me cast the spell, and we walked out the main gate, got on our horses and came here."

The utter everyday plainness of her voice and mien did little to dispel the awe everyone was feeling—myself included. Oh, it was one thing to know Morgan's gift, even to have seen some of it at work; but this was of an order entirely different, and we knew it.

"The fith-fath may have helped too," added Ysild casually, and she and Morgan laughed together like two schoolgirls.

"What fith-fath would that be?" I asked warily.

"Oh, the one where I made myself into Marc'h's image," said Morgan, with a becoming modesty. "You and I must speak, Arthur, before we go on to Tyntagel, for you will have to do the same to get us in there, and I must use my own power to keep them all snoring at Kerriwick."

"That was the plan?" asked Roric. "To use magic? But will not the defenders at Tyntagel be aware of it? And what of Marc'h himself?"

"My uncle is no sorcerer," said Arthur. "Yet I have sensed—I know not, something, someone, at Tyntagel whose strength is set against our own. If you insist, we can discuss it as we go, though it will not alter our plan. But the night is wearing on, and I wish to be clear of Kernow, Tryffin safe with us and Marc'h safe in keeping, before the sun is up."

We all raced back to the shuttle, which lifted off the ground almost at once, under Daronwy's piloting, to make the quick hop down the coast to Tyntagel. We flew barely skimming the down-crests, and saw below us the progress of the 'fight' with Marc'h's troops. They would not trouble us.

I took Ysild to a small private cabin aft; after she had changed into garb more suitable for the night's work yet to come, she joined me in the common room and gratefully drank off the shakla, well laced with usqua, that I gave her.

I watched her as she grew calmer with the realization of safety. She was above averagely fair, yet no bard would have sung her in the role of captivator on her face alone. But as I watched her, I saw at once what Marc'h had seen, and what Tryffin loved. There was a sweetness in Ysild of Arrochar, a great gentleness of spirit that I have known in no other being. She was an unstinting giver of kindness unpoisoned by pity, a generous soul; and it was just this generosity that Marc'h had so greedily snatched at.

She was not, however, looking very generous just now. And that too, I could see, would have had its attraction for Tryff and Marc'h both: Ysild may have been the sweetest of ladies, but she could snap. And, my Goddess, was she ready to snap this night . . .

And what blame to her if she did? She had been beset with unwelcome offers from the besotted Marc'h for the past eight or nine years, though she had given him no encouragement and had, indeed, actively repudiated his suit, even to the point of insult. Marc'h's efforts had only redoubled when Ysild fell deep in love with his own son and heir, and Tryffin with her; according to Morgan's account on the way here, the Duke of Kernow's wrath had been fearful to see, although it was her considered opinion that his outrage was due more to wounded vanity and disappointed hopes (Ysild was after all a notable heiress) than to thwarted passion.

She flushed a little under my regard. "I truly do wish to kill him, Prince Taliesin," she said then. "He did not lay so much as a hand upon me, all the time I was kept in Kerriwick, but for prisoning me, and for what he has done to my Tryffin, I will have his blood."

"If dán allows, lady," I answered, still watching her face. "And if Arthur permits it; not otherwise. And it is just 'Taliesin.' "

Ysild laughed. "So Guenna said you would say. We were great friends of old, you know, in Coldgates, she and I. You will not remember me, I was a child skittering round the caverns, but I recall *you* well: Morgan's brother's fostern. I used to hide sometimes near the bards' practice-rooms, so that I could listen to you play."

"You must have been very quiet."

"Oh, aye, I was that! But the music—I have no gift that way, and to me it seemed the purest magic." A light of gently wicked amusement gleamed in her astonishing eyes. "I think I was a little in love with you, even; as a girl-child will be with a young man. But then you were gone to be a spy for Arthur; I wept for a week, and promptly fell in love with the Master of Cameron— another older man, I think he must have been all of fifteen."

"And Tryffin? Where does he come into it?" I held out to her a baldric and gorget, and she buckled them on.

"I met him eight years ago; strangely enough, at a ceili that Marc'h had hosted for my parents, thinking to win them to his wish to wed me. It was the grá-tintreach for both of us, as if some sorcerer had put a drench in the quaich we shared. I used to tease him, after, that one must have done ... But we have loved so long, and would have wed, save that Marc'h would have disowned Tryffin, and my own parents would have been ill pleased."

"You are of age, and surely you are of firm intent, to decide these matters for yourself."

Ysild paused in her arming to look down at me, and her gaze was sober. "I think you must yourself have experience of such a coil; you wished to wed the High King's daughter, but for many years you, and she, chose not."

"Oh aye," I answered, unruffled. "But that was not for Uthyr's opposing the match."

"Even so, you know how it feels to have your marriage put off. But that is not why I shall kill Marc'h—*if* it is permitted me," she added with a mocking half-bow. "I shall kill him for the injury, and for the insult, and for the violence he did me and my beloved. Marc'h is a soulless clod, and does not understand the pain he causes others with his cloddishness."

"Are folk to be slain for being clods?"

"How are they to learn if they are not?" But she was smiling as she said it; and in the end hers was not the hand to strike Marc'h down.

Tyntagel stands, as I have already said, on a headland that is all but island. The only landward way to reach it is down a needle-thin ravine through which a small stream threads its racing course to the sea. On both sides of the tiny valley the rock walls rise up sheer and holdless; we would be like fish in a keeve if Marc'h's soldiers came to the edges above. We did not dare send up the shuttles to cover our venture, even; they would have spotted the craft in an instant, and may well have slain Tryffin out of hand.

So we did what Morgan had said all along that we would have to do, and counted on magic ... Perhaps three hours after Ysild had been returned to us, eight riders, cloaked and hooded in heavy sheepskin against the flying sleet and snow, picked their way down over the ice-glazed stones toward Tyntagel. Had any marked their faces in passing, he would have been surprised to see the Duke of Kernow, Marc'h himself, riding lead, with a lady close behind him who seemed, incredibly, to be that very same one he had kept for the past twelvemonth mewed up in Kerriwick. As for the others, they too bore faces well-known in Kernow: Brychan, the Duke's right-hand man; Demelza, a cousin of Marc'h's late wife, Senara, who had served as lady-in waiting to Ysild in her captivity; other warriors and household lords.

It was not true, not a word of it: Morgan was 'Demelza,' I 'Brychan,' and Arthur himself was 'Marc'h'; Daronwy and Roric, and two newer Companions, Lioch and Sherrun, made up the number. Only Ysild turned her true and unveiled face to Tyntagel.

It was more than glamourie, less than fith-fath; not true change, but an illusion deeper than surfaces—on that Morgan had insisted, and Arthur had seconded her unstinting, as if they sensed more than simple tricks would be needed here. And, as usual, they were right.

I pulled my hood closer around my face and ran my tongue over lips cracked with cold; to my surprise, the taste was salt. Straining to see through the whirling whiteness, as we came around the last bulwark of rock, I suddenly knew why. Sand began to mix with the wind-whipped snow, tiny flakes of shingle lifted off the stony beach that lay at the track's end. I dismounted, holding my snorting pony close under his muzzle, and stared at the scene before me.

The cove that lay below Tyntagel was a roaring cauldron this night, the water lashed by the vicious wind out of the north. Thickened with falling snow, the seas looked like milk on the boil; tremendous even in the shelter of the cove, they were running far up the shingle with a sound like a thousand drums. What it must be like out on the open ocean I did not wish to think, and muttered a brief and heartfelt prayer for the fisherfolk along that coast this night, that their curraghs had all come safe to land.

Ysild came up beside me. "The path lies up there; it is narrow and very steep, and only two may go abreast. We must leave the horses here."

I looked where she had pointed, and am not ashamed to tell you that I whimpered just a little; which unmanly sound was thankfully lost in the wind's scream. What seemed a track no wider than my body clung to the rockface, ascending at an impossible pitch; and so huge were the seas by now that every tonn-mhór, the mighty ninth waves that are kings of the eight who go before them, climbed clawing up the path we must now set ourselves to tackle.

Add to that the wind that tried to prise us like winkles off the cliff, the grit that bit into our skin, the sleet likewise, the spray that soaked us and then froze in hair and beards and crimbeuls—the only good thing was that the gale's fierceness kept the snow from building up on the

path beneath our feet. And then there were the guards we
would have to deceive when we came to the gate at the
clifftop, and the folk within the castle . . . I moaned again,
and followed Arthur and Ysild up the track.

At the top of the approach there was a two-towered
gatehouse with a small faha before it; to either side the
castle walls were smooth and unbroken, looking as if they
had been hewn from the headland's rock, not builded—as
perhaps they had been.

Now came the first test of Morgan's magic: Glancing
in turn at me, at Morgan and at Ysild, Arthur turned his
back on us and hammered on the gate of Tyntagel with
the hilt of his sword.

A port was opened in the gatehouse and a light shone
through. "Who comes?"

"Marc'h." Arthur's voice was gruff and clipped, altogether unlike his own. "Open up, man."

"My lord!" The guard seemed about to weep. "Her
ladyship has given me orders—I must ask you for the
password."

My heart nearly stopped right there, and no mistake. A
password was a problem, to be sure, but there were always ways: At worst, Morgan could lift it out of the
guard's mind, as a cutpurse might filch a laden pouch,
and as unnoticed. But who could be this 'ladyship' the
fellow spoke of? Senara, Marc'h's only Duchess, was
long dead; and to our knowing he had taken no other
lady, being too besotted with Ysild to look with favor on
more willing candidates.

But before any of us could do anything, Ysild had
stepped forward, thrown back her hood and lifted her face
to the yellow light. Snow swirled round like moths at a
cold flame.

"The word for today is 'tenaigin,' the forced-fire," she
said in a clear calm voice. "Now let your master in, and
the rest of us; it is scarce Beltane weather this side the
door."

The light vanished, and we heard both a torrent of
apologies to the supposed Duke and the gate mechanisms
being activated—which latter concerned us more, and as
one we blew out sighs of relief. Also as one, we turned
to stare inquiringly at Ysild.

She shrugged under our gazes. "I did not think to mention it—but Marc'h told me every day what the password was to Tyntagel. He did it to torment me, that I should know the word to unlock the way to my lord but not be able to use it." Her smile blazed. "But now I have."

The gate swung wide, and we crowded inside out of the storm. But Morgan stepped lightly and warily, as a cat will on a narrow planking, looking round her with more than eyes.

Arthur muttered some curtness to the guard, strode past through the six or so others who watched from their benches near the fire. I held my breath and followed after, escorting Ysild with great show of solicitude. Let them think we are bringing her to see Tryffin, as torture or inducement . . .

And apparently that was what they did think, for saving their salutes to Arthur as their supposed master, they showed no further interest in any of us; not even in Daronwy and Roric, who unobtrusively took up places near the doorway that led into the castle proper.

Which, since Lioch and Sherrun had been left below with the horses, made us four who went after Tryffin. We kept silence as we went; Arthur knew the castle well, he had spent time here in boyhood with his uncle, and Ygrawn had given him detailed reminders before we left Tara.

"He will be held in the upper castle precincts," said Arthur as I moved up beside him. "The ones built into the cliff behind, with only the sea below the windows—"

He broke off abruptly, as the sense of danger came to all of us at the same instant. Morgan was the first to react.

"The power that is here—" she whispered. "The wards—but I cannot tell—"

"Ah, Princess, can you not?"

The voice had come from the top of the stair ahead of us. Though all was dark but for the small palmglows we carried, and the sconces along the walls at long irregular intervals, I could discern a figure there, on the landing that, presumably, opened upon Tryffin's place of internment.

I knew that voice, but could not place it—a rare and troubling thing for a bard, whose trade is all in voices—

and daring a quick glance at Morgan I saw that no more could she. But Arthur seemed to have no such difficulty.

"Gwenar," he said, and stepped forward to face her.

Gwenwynbar, once Penarvon, came down the wide shallow steps and halted on the lowest riser. No one doubted for the smallest instant but that she could perceive our true faces through our fith-fath: She flicked a very seeing glance indeed over each of us, laughing outright when she saw me beside Ysild, ignoring Morgan. All her attention was for her onetime mate, yet for long she did not speak even to him.

She was as lovely as I had remembered her, perhaps more so. Not so showily attired as once was her wont, she stood there in a simple gúna, her wonderful hair more red-gold than ever, her face white in the glow of the sconces, so white that the sunspecks sprinkled like stars across her paleness stood out like ugly brown scorches.

I felt Ysild tense beside me, sensed Morgan's power firmly held in leash. As well it would be: This was no equal opponent, not for my lady, and Morgan had more reason than most to know that a fair fight was the only one worth having. Gwenwynbar's, then, was that power we had all earlier sensed; but how had she come by it, whence learned it, at whose teaching?

Then I had it, as Morgan and Arthur, and you too, no doubt, had seen it already. I remembered Ratherne; I believe I tried to cry out, to *scream* it out, just in case they did not know; but my voice was all at once as frozen as the night without. I raised a hand helplessly to my mute throat, and Gwenwynbar smiled.

"How feels it, Glyndour, to have that which you prize most taken from you? Think how I felt, and know it a fitting punishment for a bard who dishonored my lord's own halls." If my voice was stopped, hers held the hiss of nathairs. "Oh aye, I know all about it! Pity it is I was not 'ware of you back there at Caer Dathyl; you would have harped to my calling, chaunting all before you died."

The terrible pressure on my throat slackened long enough for me to rasp, "Even Owein, Gwenwynbar—a better lord than you knew, or deserved—knew how bards should be served. See how *he* was served, in the end, by the master he had chosen—as you will be by yours. Such masters ever abandon their tools in crucial moments."

My throat closed up again, tighter than before, but I saw that my words had struck. Saw too that Arthur and Morgan knew what I now knew: Back at Ratherne . . . Gwenwynbar had not sought the Marbh-draoi for refuge alone, had not gone to him only for protection. She had gone to him to learn magic.

And magic he had taught her, magic she had learned, I could see that as I looked at her now. Magic of a kind, at the least: At the bottom of it all, Edeyrn had still been Druid, and knew well enough the quality of this pupil. Even in his utter bentness, he would not have entrusted any true thing of power to one who was never to be more than an unskilled laborer. He would have taught Gwenwynbar such magics as any industrious student could learn with reasonable effort; but the higher workings, the greater lore, these were not for such as she. No more than they had been for that other dupe of Edeyrn's, Owein; borrowed powers, borrowed plumes . . .

Arthur had said no other word since he spoke her name—the shortname only he of all our Company had ever called her. He stood still as wheat on a windless night, never taking his eyes from her face; and it seemed to me that he had expected to find her here. Oh aye, we had guessed and wondered, but the rest of us had thought it more likely to encounter Irian and Marguessan here, not Gwenwynbar. But Arthur, it seemed, had known.

Morgan now stepped between me and her former sister-in-law. She could destroy Gwenwynbar, and Tyntagel, and perhaps all Kernow, with a word did she so choose; and well they both knew it. Well they knew, also, that she would not.

"Nay," said Gwenwynbar, eyes fixed on Morgan's, "that would bring you down to my level, would it not, and that you could not endure. Nor would your traha allow it: Hard it must be, to be so noble, so pure, in use of one's great gift. But what good is a gift, I say, if it is too good to be used in need? Such need as now, perhaps—"

She lifted a hand; and though it was I who flinched, expecting to feel the stroke, it was Arthur who staggered, all but fell to his knees in what looked like stabbing pain.

And Morgan did nothing.

CHAPTER
27

Well, if she would not, I, perhaps, *could* not; but it seemed at the least that I might try. For I was Druid, you will remember, and no untalented one, though I say it who might more modestly let others do so.

I saw well enough, though plainly Gwenwynbar did not, that Morgan did not act because she had, simply, not yet come to the place where she would. To use magic was grave business for her: It was not that she held herself above it, as Gwenwynbar believed; only that for her the balances had not yet evened out. When they stood level, when the price of using magic equalled the cost of not using it, then, and only then, would Morgan act from power. Arthur knew it, too; it was why he took the pain of Gwenwynbar's spiteful cantrip. And never would he strike back himself at his once-wife.

I, on the other hand, had no such compunction; if truth be told, I would have gladly given Gwenwynbar a dint to knock her into next fortnight. But that seemed not the best choice here, and though I still could not speak, I did not need my voice to work my other craft. Nor would Gwenwynbar be expecting any such attack from me, but was concentrating all her force on warding off Morgan . . .

I wasted no more time—Arthur, no stranger to pain, was by now all but prone on the slate floor at Gwenwynbar's feet—but lashed out sharply with my mind, and was inordinately pleased to see Gwenwynbar stagger and collapse in her turn.

Arthur got unsteadily to his feet; and, after a moment, Gwenwynbar did also, giving me a glance of unparalleled balefulness, with some grudging respect mixed in.

"Well, Taliesin. I had not thought it of you. But now I think on it, it was you, was it not, that night I was here with the others?"

If I had not already been unable to speak, that would have taken away my powers of utterance right there and then. She could not have known, could not have felt my presence that night . . . But it seemed that she had.

I felt the chokehold ease again. "You," I croaked. "And Marguessan, and Irian, and Marc'h—all here—"

Gwenwynbar seemed amused. "Aye, and you were here as well, it would seem. How?" That last word fierce as a dirk-thrust.

But I would have taken a hundred real dirks sooner than tell her of Nia's cathbarr, to besmirch that clean and holy thing with the touch of Gwenwynbar's mind; and though she pressed me sore, I said no further word, and after a while she left off trying.

"Well. Howsoever you came to know, it makes no differ. You are here now, all of you, and I am here, and Tryffin is here, and Marc'h is coming. Aye, he rides down the cove path even now, and when he arrives you will be seized for the marplots and trespassers that you are. There are many in the guardroom below, and you will not leave Tyntagel."

Morgan shifted beside me. "Nay," she said, in a voice of infinite sadness, as if she looked on a terrible mischancing mishap from a very long way away, "it is you, and Marc'h with you, who will not leave Tyntagel. My sorrow that it shall be so."

Gwenwynbar laughed, but there was a note now of doubt creeping into her confidence and defiance.

"Marc'h!" she said jeering. "He played well enough the part I allowed him, and thought he ordered the piece himself. A cat would laugh: Marc'h the leader of secession and revolt! Marc'h the lackwit . . . He was possessed of a grievance, and I needed one with such a grudge through whom I could work my will. The fact that he was kin to all of you made it all the more delightful in the working out; indeed, he believes to this moment that we are true partners in this enterprise—and he will think so, until it is in my interest for him no longer so to think."

"And then?" asked Morgan.

"And then I will deal with him as he will soon deal with you."

"And Tryffin?" That was Ysild, and I closed my eyes at what I heard in her voice.

But Gwenwynbar did not hear it. "Another tool," she said. "Or a bargaining chip— Do you know, lady, you are much to be commended? He is still yours alone, though it was not for my lack of trying."

Ysild smiled, and Gwenwynbar actually flinched—a sight that gladdened me beyond all measure. But she said nothing more just then, and in the silence I could hear the noise of the storm outside redouble, the wind slamming into the castle so hard it seemed the walls did shake. After a moment, Gwenwynbar took up baiting Morgan again, though she took care not to try any more magical tricks, at least for now.

It occurred to me that she was buying time for herself, until Marc'h should get here and could deal with us. It would never happen, of course: Morgan would have acted long before that; and Marc'h had first to get past Lioch and Sherrun down below at the stairfoot, and then there were still Daronwy and Roric in the guardroom . . . I had a thought, and trying an experimental cough found that I could speak again.

"Tryffin," I husked, then found my real voice, and called more strongly. From the chamber on the landing above came a glad shout.

"Talyn? Is that you? A long way from Bargodion, braud—"

"As you say. But we are all guests this night in Tyntagel; you, and I, and Artos. Morgan is here, too, and Ysild—"

I omitted to mention the other four of us, lest I tell Gwenwynbar somewhat she was not yet 'ware of; but though I paused, she gave no sign. Perhaps all her attention was focused on us here, and she could spare none for matters farther off; much as Morgan herself, who, we all knew, had the most of her power already committed, to keep them all napping at Kerriwick. Oh, one or two folk under a suantraí, the thing can run itself; but it takes a good deal more than that to keep a whole castle slumbering, and that was another reason why Morgan delayed any strike that she might have to make.

Gwenwynbar was taunting Arthur now; it seemed that she was enjoying herself greatly, that this was a moment she had long savored in fantasy, and now it was here at last. She would make the most of it, in her old, mean little way . . .

I did not trouble myself to listen to her weasel-words, but was wondering furiously just what part her co-conspirators had played here: Gwenwynbar had earlier boasted that the plan was hers, but I—well, I knew Marguessan, knew her ways of old, and I would have laid crossics to cribbins that whatever Gwenwynbar may have believed, it was merely what Marguessan had pleased she should believe, and no more.

Too, I wondered what should befall when Marc'h arrived and found us all here in his upper halls. But we were never to know, because just then Ysild of Arrochar came at last to the end of her spancel. Gwenwynbar's gibing, Arthur's pain (the pain he had not let us see, not merely the temporary pangs he had suffered here tonight), Tryffin's desperation, her own long frustration and captivity, and above all Morgan's seeming impotency: All came together, no word or work did spark it off, and Ysild, quite calmly, snapped.

Without a word of warning, without a hint of intent, without, even, a whisper of mood, so swiftly that I scarce saw her motion begin and so soon completed that I hardly saw it end, Ysild drew her shortsword, reversed her grip on the hilt and fired it like a javelin, like the great Spear Birgha itself, straight through Gwenwynbar's slim body.

No one could have halted it, it happened much too quickly for that. Too quickly even for Gwenwynbar to suffer much: She raised one hand to the blade, as if to pull it from her chest, then looked straight at me.

"Taliesin," she whispered, "you heard. Tell them. The boar has yet to come against the bear." She closed her fingers round the blade, shivered once, gasped and died.

Ysild was the only one of us who could move: She

crossed almost casually to where Gwenwynbar had fallen, and with one tug pulled free her blade.

"Well," she said, looking down at her handiwork. "That will teach her to be more careful whose man she tries to meddle with, and whom she seeks for playmates . . . Better judgment to you next life, Gwenwynbar Gerwin's daughter."

I stared open-mouthed. This was a side of Ysild I had not guessed; nor, I would wager, a side that Duke Marc'h had ever dreamed of. She met my look, her face remote and terrible as the bansha's that is said to keen for the Name of Formartine.

"I did not so to Marc'h, Talyn—much though I did wish to—for the same reason that Morgan did not so to this here." She nudged Gwenwynbar's dead body with the tip of her boot. "A fair fight, and a foe worthy of one's blade: Aught else is simply dán's scutwork."

Morgan looked at me then, and I read in her eyes the same message Ysild had just pronounced, if perhaps differently phrased. We are all instruments of dán, make no mistake, all of us tools of our own devise, and you may rail against it as much as you please; it will avail you less than nothing when it comes to it. But know, too, that sometimes your dán is worked out for you by others, though it be yours still, as truly and deeply as if you worked it yourself. For, in a sense, you always do. Another lesson Gwenwynbar would not have learned from Edeyrn . . .

Well, she would learn now, and that too was dán. Learn how better to choose her teachers— Any road, it was out of her hands, and now out of ours as well. I could not say I was sorry she had ended so—Gwenar was ever an evil piece of goods, and what Artos had ever seen in her scheming, shamming, leeching little soul I could never in all my lives imagine—but if I felt for anyone here, I felt for him. And so had not dared to look at him.

I dragged my glance his way. He was standing quite still, gazing down at Gwenwynbar's face. Upon that face of his I knew so well, I saw only regret that it should have ended so meanly; not the least regret that it should have ended. Perhaps at last he saw her as she truly was, not as a shining projection of his hopes or reflection of what was good in himself. We do that more often than we like to admit, to those that we say we love: We profess to love *them*, their true selves, but what we are sometimes loving, in cold truth, is merely the mirror we have made of them to reflect our own souls. Not wise; but most human. Even Arthur had done it, and even I have done it, and even you; or if not yet, be very sure you shall. And you will never know it when you do; as none of us know.

Just now, though, we had other things to concern us, and Ysild was the only one sufficiently in command of herself to do them. Once she had satisfied herself that Gwenwynbar was dead, she had flown up the stair to the landing, and was now struggling vainly with the door behind which Tryffin was locked away. She was scratching at the wood and metal with swordblade and her own fingernails, and she was weeping, and talking to Tryffin in a dreadful choked voice that in all likelihood even he could not understand.

Arthur took an immediate hand; this was something he knew he was at last permitted. He stepped past the body of his onetime wife, came up beside Ysild and moved her gently to one side, laying his right hand on the door.

"Tryff, step away." The oak slab, a full foot thick, began to crack and shiver before he had finished speaking, the findruinna hasps beginning to glow darkly red. And still Arthur kept his hand to the door: It took less than a half-minute before there was a sudden explosion of splinters of metal and wood; and then Tryffin was through, and Ysild was holding him as if she would never let him go.

Not even to let him embrace the rest of us, eager to greet our friend; though after a minute or two she did so, still clinging to him herself. We longed to talk and tarry, but if Gwenwynbar had spoken true—and it was always possible that the streppoch had not—Marc'h was perhaps already here at the castle. And as soon as the guards below laid eyes on him they would know that the 'Marc'h' who had gone up to the tower rooms an hour since was a lying fraud. They might even know that he was the High King; and they might not care, even, if he were or were not.

So we disposed Gwenwynbar's body with dignity, on the canopied bed in her own chambers, the sword-wound, which had bled hardly at all, scarce visible now against the velvet gúna. Morgan said the speeding prayers for her, spoke her name to the Goddess; no more could be done for her, and we were not inclined to do any more than this, any road.

But this we did is the due of any dead Kelt, no matter what the Kelt may or may not have wrought in life. Even Edeyrn had been given this bare necessity of sending; now we gave it to his pupil, and prayed, in all honesty, that both would learn from the errors they had made in these lives now closed, and took comfort that they would. For that is the grace of the Highest, Kelu's gift to us all: that in facing our own errors, ourselves sitting in judgment on ourselves, we learn more truly and judge more rightly than any god there is. Too, we judge by the best that is within us, not the worst; not by sin or crime but by good, and by high purpose. The best thing we have done in the life just past: That is what determines of the soul's choice for the life next to come; and this is as it should be. Evil is all very well when we are in the imperfect body; but it bows to good in sorting the road of the soul, and faiths which claim it does not are telling lies. Remember that.

Our mission, now, was of the simplest: Get out of here. We had accomplished our main goal, the rescue of our friends; Arthur's remaining intention—to bring the High Justice of the Ard-tiarnas to bear upon the Duke of Kernow—could be accomplished presently. At the moment, we thought it best to get out of Tyntagel undetected. Tryffin and Ysild could pass themselves off as unwilling captives being taken back to Kerriwick; a deception we trusted the guards would fall for. The thing now was to save ourselves.

Arthur turned at the door, and gave one last look at Gwenwynbar; I could not see his face. Then he turned to me.

"Everything passes," he said with firmness, and led the way down the stairs.

As I said, our plan had been to slope off unnoticed; or at the least as unnoticed as we could contrive it. So when we heard from below the sounds of fighting, we knew our plan had been altered.

Marc'h and his small escort had apparently overcome Sherrun and Lioch down at the cove—only at great cost to themselves, as we later learned—and were now in the guardroom, where our subterfuge had been discovered. Now were the buttons off the bladepoints, quite literally: Roric and Daronwy were holding off the entire garrison in the one doorway that led into the castle precincts. Thanks to Marc'h's futile effort out of Kerriwick, the garrison here tonight numbered only some dozen; more seemed hardly needed to hold so defensible a fortress, and of course Marc'h had counted on Gwenwynbar to do the rest. All that was changed now, as we have seen; but he did not know it just yet.

We came down behind our friends, who were even more pleased than they might ordinarily have been to see us, and joined in the fight. Ysild in especial seemed possessed of battle madness; with her flying black hair and eyes flaming blue, she looked the very incarnation of the Mór-rían, the War-raven Herself. Tryffin, too; but that was understandable, they were taking out in battle all that they had endured at Marc'h's hands the past months and years. The rest of us were just fighting for our lives; and, for the Companions, that was no new thing.

Arthur kept inching his way toward the door at the far end, the door that opened on Kernow, and freedom. Marc'h's hasty arrival had left it ajar, and through it, as I followed close behind Arthur fighting all the way, I could see the ferocious night outside. The moon had broken through the clouds, but it was still snowing, and the wind had fallen off not a jot.

Before we were more than halfway across the guardroom, though, Arthur found himself blade to blade with his own uncle. The fith-faths we had used to get into Tyntagel had dissolved just now in the fight—no one can keep a magic in place while fighting to save himself; well, Morgan maybe, but very few others—and we all now bore our true faces.

So Marc'h knew his sister's son, the High King, his nephew Arthur, and cared only to slay him here and now. Arthur seemed unconcerned—his uncle was even less a swordsman than a sorcerer, and his own supremacy in both arts had long been a given—but it suited him best to take Marc'h prisoner, not kill him here in this mindless desperate squabble. There were things only Marc'h could answer, and answer for, and Arthur was resolved to see to it that he did.

In the fury of the press I found myself out in the snow-choked faha beyond the gatehouse, much, much closer to the cliff-edge than I liked. Roric had already started Ysild and Tryffin on their way down the stairpath to the cove, and daring a glance over my shoulder I saw that Morgan was just following them down. That left Daronwy, who at last sight was holding off three Kernishmen at once, putting forth not half her strength and enjoying herself immensely, and Arthur still inside Tyntagel. Of Marc'h I could see no sign; besides, I was too busy to look more closely, fighting with Brychan, my own other 'self' this night. He had seen the fith-fath, had seen me wearing his face, and he was angrier than a shorn ram, and intended to take it out on me.

He was doing very well, I am sorry to say. He had beaten me back nearly to the palisade that runs round the cliff top—at one point I even felt it digging into my back, and prayed frantically to whomever might hear me that it would hold under my weight, not break and send me down into the heaving waters below—but I managed to slip under his guard, and ran unheroically for the stair.

Marc'h saw me shoot past him, and came hard after, himself eager to get out of Arthur's rain of buffets. The Duke aimed a few cuts at me from behind, which I tried to parry, but suddenly I felt a searing fire, pain like a whip across my shoulders, and I stumbled on the track.

He was on me immediately. We had come to one of the several rough widenings in the narrow pathway—little landings, where those who climbed to Tyntagel might pause a while to catch their breath—and here there was room for real swordplay. I could see Arthur, still too far above us to be of any help, and Daronwy farther up the cliff than he; below, Roric and Ysild had turned at my cry of pain, and were toiling up again. But they were weary, and far below, and the path was half-drifted now with mingled snow and seafoam, from blizzard and waves alike.

So I raised my weapon to meet Marc'h's attack. If he had been a better sworder, it would have been over for me right there, and some other bard would have been tell-

ing you this tale—and, it is to be hoped, telling my part
in it aright, not to mention well. But I was wounded, and
he was older and less skilled, and so we were equally
matched.

We swung a few ringing touches, the swords striking
sparks in the charged snowy air, then we grappled together, using sgians for the close work. I was so tired, and
my shoulder hurt abominably; but even so I got a few
scratches in on Marc'h, and was just beginning to feel
something confident of victory—he was weakening, Arthur was nearly here, Roric only a few steps away—when
Marc'h lunged too far out. He went over the stairwall
without a sound, and he took me with him.

It seemed that I fell for miles. Bards have sung for centuries that in such moments you see your life pass before
you at speed—you can see the same when you die naturally, of sickness or old age, only then you see it more
slowly—but I am here to tell you that you see no such
thing.

Or maybe it was just that it was not yet my time to die,
so I did not see what I should have seen; I know not. But
something in the feeling of falling brought a long-
forgotten poem leaping to my mind, and I chaunted it all
the way down, singing myself out like a true bard, until
the water came up to take me.

I was not afraid of death, no Kelt is, that is not our
way; but like most of us I was a little feared of the actual
dying—would it take long, would it hurt very much. Neither did I have any hope of surviving the fall: The coast
below Tyntagel is deep-watered, but it is floored with
fanged rocks, and the currents that thread them would
carry my body far out to sea, long before my friends
could find me. This did not seem to matter, somehow, nor
even greatly to distress me; but I had not yet finished my
poem when I hit the water, and that, strangely, did.

The impact must have knocked me briefly unconscious,
for I have no memory of the actual moment. Still, my
senselessness can have been of the instant only, for I did
not drown, and I came to myself in the midst of lashing
water, hills of glassy gray and white crashing together. It
was Gwaelod: The sea-doom that I had escaped five decades ago had come at last to claim me. Already the cur-

rent had me in its jaws, for I was clear around the other side of the castle crag, far from where my friends would be looking for me.

My friends . . . Aye, I remembered them now. Saw Arthur's face as I went over the edge, felt Roric's lunging desperate grab for me that caught only my cloak, heard Morgan's wordless anguished mindcry. It no longer seemed to matter, any of it, and after what seemed a long time I came to the end of my song, and began to consider my situation.

Well. I was not dead of the fall from the cliff, so that must count for something. But I was here alone in the sea, and I knew that I had very few minutes left. I am not an especially strong swimmer even at the best of times—few Kelts are, for all we like to live so near the waters—and the freezing seas and bonebruising waves were fast draining away my strength with my body's warmth. The coast was too far to reach, and none could find me in the wild wastes.

All at once I panicked, almost as if by reflex, thrashing my arms and legs, shouting, in a frenzied struggle to turn myself to the land, to catch someone's attention. But it was of course no use, and after a few minutes I could no longer remember why I had even wished to bother. Manaan's white horses would come galloping for me across the wavecrests, or the crystal ship in which he sails the Otherworld oceans would part the billow and take me safe aboard . . . I knew I could hold off the end for a few minutes more, did I choose to. But I cared not: Warmth was stealing over me from my neck down, and with the warmth came a delicious sleepiness, up from my toes. So that when the waters closed over my head at last, and silence sang in my ears, the loveliest sound I have ever heard, I remember only smiling, and closing my eyes to better hear the silence's song . . .

Then a hard-muscled furry body thudded into me, startling me awake and shooting me back to the surface—which was very much farther away than I would have thought. I broke the water into cold booming noisy air, and retched hideously, struggling to breathe again, already a half-forgotten art, pulling air into lungs all but finally filled with water.

It was of course a silkie who had propelled me up from

drowning; the Sluagh-rón, the seal-folk, love to live along just such rocky coasts as these, and Kernow has ever been a favorite world of theirs. While I was thinking all this, my rescuer was joined by two more, and together they pulled me easily to shore through the towering seas.

We came to land just to the east of Tyntagel's own cove, and while two of the silkies helped me clamber over the streaming rocks, the other slipped back into the water, arrowing through the breakers, round the giant headland to the castle cove, to tell my friends I had been found.

The rocks were slick with spume-ice, and sharp as knives; my clothes were cut to ribbons, and my feet— bare, I had kicked my boots off during my one attempt to save myself—were bloodied on the stones, and purple with the cold. I pulled myself up beyond the surf's reach and collapsed weeping, and by all gods I cannot tell you if I was glad or sorry to be there . . .

When I could speak again, I rolled over onto my back and looked up into the furry faces that were watching me with such concern.

"Thank you, my friends—" I was racked again by coughing, and they waited politely for me to recover myself. "You move marvellously in the waters."

"And you in the airs of heaven—are you well enough, that you might sit up?"

Strong brown four-fingered paws helped me to a sitting posture, and I leaned gratefully against the glossy-furred side of the silkie nearest me, for the air was bitter cold through my drenched clothing, and I had begun to shiver violently. They saw this, and huddled me on either side, to warm me with their own bodies until help arrived, singing softly in my ear—or perhaps that part was hallucination, but it seemed most real to me just then, a strange wild song of life below the ocean's green salt roof.

Then, long before I had thought to, I heard voices, and twisting to my left saw lanthorns bobbing toward us over the rough shore. The silkies drew back a little, shyly, as Morgan threw herself on me weeping; I had never seen her weep like that before, and I was distressed for her sake.

"I knew you were not dead, Talyn, I kept my hand on

you all the while, but Mighty Mother, it was a near thing—" She hugged me closer, and then Arthur and the rest caught up with her; so great had been her haste to get to me that she had left them all far behind.

They had brought dry clothing, and boots—too big for me, but I cared not—and Morgan cast a scallaun round us while I changed my soaked garb, now almost frozen stiff by the winds; Arthur himself struck fire from the sea, to warm me while I drank some usqua from Roric's flask.

After a quarter-hour or so, I was feeling remarkably better, and thought I could venture back round the headland to Tyntagel. But Arthur had other plans, and once he was sure I was well enough to be moved, he sent out a call for a shuttle to come land on the beach and take us all aboard.

I turned to the silkie who had saved me. "May I know your name, my brother?"

He ducked his head along my arm, unused to all the attention. Morgan reached out a hand, touched his shoulder, and he turned to her, his huge soft dark eyes brimming with astonishment as he felt her mindtouch on his own.

"I am Hoen," he said. "My sisters are Joruth and Laan. We dwell in the—" He made a strange musical trill, like to that of a mother cat calling in her kittens, and gestured out to sea, to the great Sound behind us. "I cannot say its name in your tongue, how we call it amongst our kin. But we heard your calling that one was lost from off the—" Again an untranslatable melodious chirrup, a different one this time, edged and somehow rougher, and I guessed he was now naming the Tyntagel castle rock.

Forever bard! I was instantly lost in visions: seeing all Keltia as named from a silkie's perspective, an interspecies placename book, a silkie-to-Gaeloch primer . . .

I came back to myself, caught by what he had said. "You were 'called'? Well—by whom? Who called?"

"I did," said Morgan, and I laughed.

"Now I wonder why that does not surprise me—but I thought only bards had the secret of the silkie-singing."

Morgan smiled, but I could see what that kind of smile cost her. "Love can find out more secrets than that—when there is need."

There was a gentle stirring among the silkies as they murmured to one another in their own tongue. Then Laan, the younger female: "We heard the call, and also we heard *you*, lord, as you sang in the sea. We found you by your song; that is all we needed. A small thing."

"Not to me!" I spoke fervently to them then, tendering broken thanks, pledging friendship. Arthur too bespoke them, though they knew he was the High King and were even shyer than they had been with me. But they listened gravely; then, plainly anxious at being so long upon the land, turned to slip back into their homewaters.

Hoen lingered last, ducked his sleek head against my side once more, and then he too was gone, going as easily and joyfully into the thundering waves as a child goes through a springtime clune. They all three were vanished in seconds; but I looked after them even so.

We did not tarry longer: Morgan, suddenly all commands and concern, ordered me lifted up to the hovering shuttle in an invalid's litter, and saw to it that I was bestowed comfortably for the brief trip up to Prydwen.

But once I was settled in my own familiar cabin, that had housed me all the way from Aojun, and had received the ministrations of *three* healers, who all agreed that I had suffered but would take no lasting harm from my ordeal (Marc'h's swordcut was healed already, by skinfuser), I demanded an account of what had happened after my precipitous exit from Tyntagel rock.

"We could not quite believe it," said Arthur happily, in that tone of strange enjoyment that seems almost to relish the horrors of the past that have turned out unexpectedly well. "I saw you go over, Talyn, and I do not think I believed my own eyes, that you could be gone. Now Guenna"—he nodded smiling at his sister, who sat holding my hand on the other side of the couch—"*knew* you were not dead, but it was hard for the rest of us to credit. Roric, I think, has not yet ceased to blame himself for not being swifter to seize you."

"He came close enough, tell him it was well done." I snuggled down into the pillows. "But, cariad, how did you know?"

Morgan considered a moment: how best to impart knowledge to the unknowing.

"There is a kind of magic the Ban-draoi have," she said at last, "like a hand that reaches out to touch the ones we

love. We call it the 'hand of the heart'; it is a touch of the
spirit, a sensing— I would always know where you were,
Talynno, if you were in the next room, or in your grave,
or a million light-years hence, or in your next life. Perhaps it is a woman's magic. Any road, I reached out, and
I knew you were not gone. So I called the silkies and told
them where to bring you. They had heard you already,
singing, and so when you went under they were only
yards away."

She shivered involuntarily, and I raised her hand to my
lips and gently kissed it; I had not meant to make her re-
live that moment.

"I knew it was not your dán," she resumed. "But it was
hard even so! The rest—well, as it was."

I was restraining my impatience with difficulty. "Aye,
but the rescue? Marc'h? Tryff and Ysild? The silkie—
Hoen—said but *one* had fallen from the castle rock into
the sea. What of Marc'h?"

They were all silent for a moment, and I caught the
picture from Morgan's mind. Then Arthur spoke.

"Marc'h did not fall into the sea, Talyn. He fell on the
rocks of the Carrai; there was nothing anyone could do
for him."

I closed my eyes, feeling again Marc'h's arms around
me, pulling me over the coping. Only the Goddess's
mercy had spared me from his fate, had sent me into the
sea; and only dán had sent Marc'h of Kernow to his death
on the stones of his own land. Dán, and Marguessan . . .
And Gwenwynbar too had met her fate here, at the
Twice-dark Stronghold— I put a hand over my eyes, for
cold tears were seeping down my cheeks, and all at once
I had begun to shiver with reaction to my own ordeal.

Morgan's arms slipped around me, and I clung to her.
"Save for your unpredicted swim," she said, in a tone calculated to give me heart, "it all worked out to your plan. Ysild
and Tryffin are safe in the next cabin, the troops are safe returned, Kernow is once again loyal to the Crown and restored to the Six Nations. Marc'h and Gwenwynbar—well,
that too is plan, if not perhaps yours or Arthur's. And we
know Marguessan to be behind it all."

Though still not how . . . I raised my face to Arthur,
who saw recovery in my eyes, stretched and stood up.

"We will watch her," he promised. "Now that we know

what is toward ... For the moment, and I expect the future as well, since Gwennach and I will so confirm him, Tryffin is Duke of Kernow, with the soon-to-be Duchess Ysild. The rest can wait the telling. Sleep now. Guenna, make him do so."

He kissed us both and was gone. Morgan looked after him as the door closed, and gave a gentle laugh.

" 'Sleep'! Easy enough for him to say so, I have seen him nod off in the midst of battle—but I do not think I shall ever sleep again, save it be beside you."

"This couch is wide enough." I shifted myself to one side; she stretched out beside me, above the coverlet, careful not to jostle any of my scratches or sorenesses, and spoke to dim the cabin lights to a soft warm glow.

"Artos did not speak of Gwenwynbar," I said after the silence had grown long and sleepy.

And Morgan answered after an even longer silence, "Did you truly think he would?"

CHAPTER
28

The very first thing Arthur Ard-rígh did when we came home to Turusachan was to send for Malgan son of Gwenwynbar to come to Court.

"So much for not speaking," I observed to Morgan when I heard of it.

"When my brother is not speaking, we know he is doing."

But this he did now was a thing that would reverberate long after the first shock and surprise had subsided; and none of Arthur's close friends could let it rest.

"Is it guilt, do you think, Talyn?" asked an exasperated Tarian Douglas. "Or it is just another of Artos's imprudences, yet another of his everlasting challenges to dán?"

It was perhaps six months after Tyntagel. Tarian, Daronwy and I were sitting in my wife's solar; Morgan herself was across the castle square, at the Ban-draoi brugh up against the foot of Eagle, near the mouth of the Way of Souls.

In half a year, much had changed, and much had changed not at all. Malgan ap Owein had come to Turusachan, this was true—arousing astonishment in all who saw him, so like was he to Arthur himself at that age. Gossip was rampant, you can be sure. But the lad conducted himself impeccably, and if anyone knew for sure that his patronym ought to be altered, none said so aloud.

"Guilt, surely," said Daronwy, when it appeared I would be making no such comment. "Why else did he forbid Ysild to make honor-price payment to Malgan, but took care of the restitution himself?"

"He did not order her to kill Gwenwynbar," I pointed out. "That was all her own idea. I was there; I know."

"Maybe," said Tarian, unimpressed. "But I daresay he did not deny himself a small little jig of despair when Ysild put that idea into train."

"Nay, well, he may not have sought Gwenwynbar's death," I conceded. "And he may not have been overly grieved when it was accomplished ... But she was his wife once, Tari, and there is the boy—"

"Ah. The boy again." My old Companion Tari Douglas was gone, and the Taoiseach of Keltia spoke in her place. "Do *you* think he is Arthur's? You Taliesin Glyndour Pen-bardd, now; not Talynno who has wed the High King's sister, not Tal-bach who has been the fostern of Artos from a five-years'-child. But the Bard of Keltia— what does *he* think?"

I shifted uncomfortably in my cushioned window-nook. Gods but I did *hate* that title ... Yet since our return from Aojun, and latterly from Tyntagel, it had begun to be applied to me more often than not. And, aye, in some sense of course I was proud, for I knew I had earned it: In our long absence, word had begun to go round of what my labors had been in the Counterinsurgency's cause; how all those songs that folk so loved, that had kept hope alive in Edeyrn's blight, were songs born of my harp; word too of the Hanes Taliesin, which had become a benchmark of bardery amongst my peers, perhaps the one thing I had done that I knew for sure would live on after me.

Still and all, it was hard to be hailed so, to be praised for things that I knew were no choices of mine at all. I had not decided to make the Hanes; it had been a gift from the gods of bardship. Had not studied to make those songs; they had chosen to come to me, and I was humbled and honored that they should choose so. To be called Pen-bardd, the title of Plenyth himself: Well, the praise was not to me, and I tried in pride and humility to pass it on as was fitting, to those to whom the praise was rightly due.

Tarian was still waiting on my answer; so I shrugged—what else could I do?—and found myself repeating a word of our dear Kei, dead at Nandruidion.

"If he is not Arthur's, no matter. If he *is* Arthur's, we shall all know soon enough."

And Tarian had to content herself with that. But more folk than she were asking, and not content to let it rest there . . .

I have never believed in coincidence; all is dán, and though things of dán may be altered—we are creatures of the Highest, but creatures of order are still free to choose for themselves—I do believe that matters love to run in pace with one another much as mortals do, so that what may look to some like coincidence is in truth but part of a larger pattern whose weave we have not yet grasped.

So I was thinking, any road, when I returned to my chambers from that afternoon's converse with my friends, to find waiting for me Malgan ap Owein. He leaped to his feet as I entered the room, flushed a little with shyness or presumption; and politely deferred for me to speak first.

"Greeting to you, Rheged." I had quite deliberately used the patronymic, and noted that he did not flinch or flicker. I gestured him to sit, and took my own usual chair by the hearth.

He was, as I have said, a well-grown lad, tall above the average run, his hair more red than brown, his eyes a shade between blue and hazel; I had heard from my spies among the Fians that he was talented of fence, though but little gifted in the unarmed combat forms. He was still a minor under Keltic law, which posits a full legal age of thirty-three and gives limited privileges when a citizen reaches twenty-seven. But Malgan was not near either age just yet; and so Arthur, exercising his right as Ard-rígh—indeed, his duty—to succor orphans and the kinlorn, had summoned the boy to Court, and made him a royal ward. That, at least, was the reason given out; but all Keltia knew that Arthur had taken Malgan under his protection for Gwenwynbar's sake alone.

And that seemed to be what the lad was here to address this night . . . He took the seat across from me, clasped his hands nervously over his knees and looked me in the face at last.

"Prince," he began.

" 'Taliesin,' " I said as if by rote; why was it I had ever to explain my discomfiture at my royal title? "Please, 'Taliesin' only."

"Well—my lord, then ... I have need to say a thing, and I find I cannot say it to the King or the Queen; nor can I tell the Lady Morguenna, and so it falls on me to speak of it to you."

"Speak, then," I said, but I said it gently, putting sooth ers into the tone and the emotion I sent with the words, and I saw him visibly relax.

"It has been a sixmonth since my mother was killed—no fault of any under this roof," he added hastily. "Indeed she brought it on herself—I tried to persuade her otherwise, always, but she would not— Well, it is only that I would let the High King know I am grateful to him for taking me in, knowing as he did who were my parents. I cannot say this to him, lord, truly I cannot"—here he looked up, and I saw that tears stood in his eyes—"so I would ask you to do it for me. It is something I want him to know, and maybe some time to come I will be able to tell him myself. But, please you, do it for me now."

I did not answer at once, but continued looking at him, and though he flushed again under my steady regard (and under the kenning he doubtless knew was behind it), he held my eyes and did not shift away.

What he had just done had taken courage and honesty; traits of Arthur's, to be sure, but neither were they inconsonant with Owein Rheged, who though he had been utterly wrong in his allegiances had nonetheless been utterly loyal to his chosen master. Loyalty misguided is yet loyalty all the same ... and loyalty cut adrift may justly seek a new lord. As, perhaps, it did now ...

When I continued silent, Malgan with immense dignity rose up from his chair, bowed to me and bent his head.

"My sorrow to have troubled you, Prince Taliesin; I thank you for your courtesy."

I let him turn to go before I spoke. "Malgan." He halted but did not turn back to face me. "That was a hard thing for you to say, and a brave thing. I served your father for five years in Caer Dathyl, and though he was the enemy of all Arthur stood for still I served him with respect; even, sometimes, with liking. Sit and share some wine, and we will talk."

At that he came round on his heel, and I saw that he bit back tears. And I felt a stinging in my own eyes; was this the first time that anyone here had spoken anything but unkindness to the boy? If so, I was shamed for us all; and felt, even so, that some balance had been tipped, and that this was good. So we sat and drank our wine, and spoke.

That was not the only thing, nor yet the greatest by far, that had changed since our return from self-imposed exile—well, Arthur-imposed exile. The change that had all Keltia mouthing in secret, and, sometimes, not so secretly, was how Arthur and Gweniver had changed with one another.

Oh, mistake me not, Keils Rathen was still very much part of the picture—and what outworlders may find it difficult to countenance or credit was that he continued a close friend of Arthur, as well as Gwennach's lennaun—and most of Turusachan knew that Arthur spent hours in composing communications to Majanah or choosing gifts to send to Donah. But somehow, somewhere along this track of tricky footing, Gweniver and Artos had begun to learn how to pull in double harness, as Ard-rían and Ard-rígh; and this, be very sure, was no small triumph.

And, as time began to lengthen—a year, seven, twelve—other triumphs came along as well: Morgan and I became parents—a son, Geraint Pendreic ac Glyndour, never to be called anything else but Gerrans.

He was a droll, obstreperous infant—Morgan called him her hedgepig, for the way his hair grew spikily around his fat little face, and for the prickliness of his disposition. But by the time he came to faunthood, he had turned into a placid, sturdy, handsome lad, who seemed, most distressingly, to have interest in neither music nor magic. But Morgan was unconcerned, saying that very often gifts show late, and no doubt our son's would make itself known in good time.

She was a casual, though loving, mother, giving Gerrans the kind of affection more often seen in men to their children than in women. When I questioned her on it one day, she shrugged.

"I never told you this, Talyn, but if ever it came to a choice between you and the bairn, I would choose you every time, without hesitation and without regret." I must have looked shocked, for she smiled. "I have ever known I was a woman for my mate before I was a woman for a child. Oh, I love Gerrans well, do not mistake me, but more for that he is yours than that he is mine. I am too jealous of you, want you to myself again, want us to be each other's and none between, not even our son."

And she proved a woman of her word: sent Gerrans off to his fostering with scarce a tear and turned to ourselves again with a kind of hunger and relief. So my son was brought up chiefly by, of all folk, my sister Tegau and her lord Eidier, with their own brood of five; and I think he grew up all the better by that than had we had the raising of him. Morgan was more right than she said, or maybe even knew: She and I were man and woman for each other, first, last, ever, before we were parents for a child; and she at least had had the courage to admit it to herself and to me. Perhaps we should never have bred him at all; but things would have been very different had Geraint never been . . .

Still, he thrived in the happy household of his aunt and uncle. Tegau and Eidier, once peace had been restored, had gone back to Gwynedd, and built a maenor on the shores of the Western Sea, as near the ocean as could be contrived. As near to Gwaelod . . . I called vividly to mind my first meeting with my sister after returning home from our long sojourn away: I had caught her up in a bearhug of an embrace, still faintly surprised to find myself so much taller, still in my mind the slight fourteen-year-old who had come to her at Coldgates after the flight from Daars . . . Then I had seized her by the shoulders, and held her away a little, and stared, both of us smiling. For the breast of gold from which she had taken a name of legend was gone now; both her breasts were soft and warm again, she had fulfilled her vow to Keltia and to herself—and though it may sound strange to say so, it was by that one thing I knew at last that we had had in truth the victory.

Any road, my son was growing up amongst kinfolk, in a place not unlike to my own calf-country, with cousins to play with and fight with, for all that he was royal. In

Keltia, children take the status and style of their higher-ranking parent: I was, after all, but the youngest child of a minor lord, a provincial chieftain; while my son's mother was a princess, a royal duchess, who would in time pass those titles on to her only offspring.

And what of that highest title of all, you ask? Well you may: Despite their new peace and ease and friendship, Arthur and Gweniver—to put it as delicately as I might—had not yet seen their way to securing the direct succession, and all Keltia was wondering.

For that deficiency left Mordryth, Marguessan's eldest brat, as heir of line after his mother, followed by his brother Gwain and sister Galeron, and they by our Gerrans. Enough heirs to ensure a throne, you would think; well, perhaps, and the royal line had hung on slenderer threads than this. But we had that dreadful memory ever present, of Edeyrn's all-but-destruction of this very House; and though the Marbh-draoi was gone, still the fear remained.

Besides, it was natural and human enough to want an heir of Gweniver and Arthur to rule Keltia after them; no one was pleased when the Crown was passed sidewise, as it were. In truth, had they not come to power after the Theocracy's interregnum, even Gwen and Artos might have faced some grumbling displeasure—for you will recall neither was direct heir to their immediate predecessor. But folk were so glad and grateful to have the Dôniaid restored, they cared not a whit how the descent was reckoned.

I diminish them in so saying: The folk were well pleased to have the rulers they had been given, and let not that be discounted, ever. Gweniver was Leowyn's daughter, and the people had loved him well, the Sun-lord; while Arthur was Amris's son, and if anything he had been loved even better, not least for the breathtaking romance of his union with the Lady Ygrawn. That these two scions had become heirs to Uthyr, first monarch of the Restoration, and had wed each other, too: Well, it seemed a miracle of dán, and what wonder that the folk wished the miracle, and, indeed, the dán, to continue?

They were luckier than they ever knew. For Keltia could not, in this time of change and chance, have done better for rulers than Gweniver and Arthur. We who knew them and loved them had long known this would be so, once things had settled down and they came into their lordship; but the great run of Kelts had had no idea. Only now, as the years drew on, and the reality of peace began to make itself felt even by those who had been wounded deepest, did the people come to see and trust and believe, and to thank all gods for what they had been given.

If Arthur had won the wàr, it was Gwennach who had won the peace; she had managed magnificently while we were away, and it may well have been due to her alone that Arthur had a kingdom waiting for him, and a kingdom in such good order too, when he deigned at last to return. To speak in military metaphor, she had held the center, while Arthur had done the flanking work he had deemed necessary; and though Ygrawn had been a powerful symbol of continuity with the past, and Morgan an equally inspiring image of continuity to the future, and Companions and Councillors together had turned hands and minds and souls alike to the tremendous task, still it had been Gweniver who at the end of the day had been Queen *and* King to Keltia, until such time as the King returned.

But once he did return, that King brought to his kingship all the old verve and flair and force that once he had brought to our desperate campaignings. Nor was the one so very different from the other in the end: To restore a nation to its former state and station, to restore to it its own self and soul—this was the task before Arthur now, and he took it on in the old way.

All the same, I do not think any of us, not even Arthur and Gwen, had had any real idea of just how much was in need of healing. Uthyr had had some inkling, but he had been called upon to heal Keltia in a different way, and to his imperishable glory he had risen to the task. But what had to be done now was very different, and though Gweniver had made a heroic start, it would take an Arthur—it would take *our* Arthur—to bring it to completion.

Nor was it to be done overnight, nor even in a matter of a few years. It was an ongoing process, and it took decades. It began with Arthur's re-establishing the ancient houses of government, as Brendan had originally ordained should be for all Kelts for all time: the Senate and the Assembly. The House of Peers, as the most easily reconstituted, had already been convened by Gweniver during Arthur's absence, and it had been governing conjointly with the Ard-rían and the Council until the elected bodies could once more be called to Turusachan, as they had not been for many hundreds of years; aye, even before Edeyrn had they been abolished, most unwise. But both Arthur and Gweniver thought it crucial to Keltia's survival as a lawful kingdom that the common folk should have representatives to defend and advance their interests; and so Brendan's ancient system was revived. And, very like, not a moment too soon.

For the rest of us, our lives had changed with Keltia. Peace meant many things, some great and eternal, others little and small, unnoticed save by those to whom the difference was made ... It meant that Elphin and I and the other master-bards could now wear the star of ollaveship openly, the mark of our calling and accomplishment. It meant that Ban-draoi and Fians, too, and true Druids, could go about in openness without fear. It meant that the brehons returned, bringing the law with them, that most honored glory of our folk.

Grimmer realities too: A standing army was established, such as we had not had since the days of Athyn Cahanagh; and, perhaps, the lack of which had led to Edeyrn's rise to power. If Alawn Ard-rígh had had a loyal force behind him, it might have been that the Marbhdraoi could not have suborned so many to work his evil will, and the Theocracy might never have been ... But to think in the way of what-ifs is to court madness: It went as it went, and goes as it goes, and is for us to deal with; then, now, evermore.

It was not just Arthur and Gwennach, though, who were caught up in the Keltia rising out of Edeyrn's ashes: All we of the Companions suddenly found ourselves honored and exalted above all others, our deeds extolled and 'broidered upon, made into legend even while we lived who could discount it, falsified in a way we loved not at all. To be idolized for what looks like courage and daring to those not present, and what was, in plainest fact, merely common integrity and love of our leader beyond our own lives: Well, it sat strangely upon us. We passed it off, for the most part; none who had been down the roads we went with Artos could succumb to easy adoration; we were all too well-seasoned for that, too tempered in the real.

But the romance, the glamourie, even, that the folk insisted on clothing us in—those persisted, and endured, my sorrow to say. We were *Companions,* of the Company; that was our prime identity. We had been with Arthur, and all the rest had not. We would never be able to escape it; and in the end we gave over trying. For there are worse fates by far, than to be known to Keltia forever as one who rode with Arthur the King. But it would breed evil even so, and that not small ...

My sorrow to have gone on so; but needful it is that you see the actors in this play against their proper backdrop. As bard, I would be remiss in my art and duty did I not set it out for you: It is my job to put the truth into the tale, and it is yours to find it; that is the bargain between bard and hearer. Nowhere is it written that I must make it easy for you, or that I must do all the work! Let us take that as sung, then, and go on with the story.

So almost thirteen years had passed since our return from Aojun, near twenty since the downfall of Edeyrn. Things were much of a sameness: Arthur and Gweniver still in their old dance, counterpoint if not harmony; the Companions still seated around our old table of friendship and storms weathered; Morgan and I still caught up in each other and in our arts. Malgan ap Owein was still at Court, now grown to young manhood; he had made himself quietly liked and respected, and if any still wondered about his paternity they never spoke of it aloud. Arthur himself treated him as a deminephew, which was just about his true and correct status in brehon law, as the son of a deceased former wife; but not even the most avidly curious could have said that Malgan was favored as the High King's own son.

I myself liked him well, and we had come to be friends, our dealings almost those of an elder brother to a younger, even. It may seem perverse to you, that I should so care for the son of one who had caused so much death that had touched me so nearly; but the son was not the fa-

ther, and even that father ... I had served Owein myself,
those five years of spying for Arthur at Caer Dathyl, and
had seen a different man than merely Edeyrn's tool. If
that inner Owein had ever been allowed to rule in place
of the other, if he had met Arthur young, say, and they
had become friends—well, again, what-ifs are no fit pursuit for anyone. But, all the same, even if only sometimes, I could sorrow for what might have been; and did.

Of Marguessan, the heir presumptive to the Copper
Crown, we heard little and were glad of it. She and her
lord and their children kept very much to themselves, on
their lands in Gwynedd's Old North; and though we kept
a certain discreet eye on her, as I had long ago promised
Uthyr Ard-rígh, not a breath of scandal or treason or even
dubious politics seemed to be stirring. Perhaps she was
aware that we were watching—I for one had not forgotten
my vision under the cathbarr, nor yet my long-ago inter-
vention at Coldgates—but for the moment she was putting on a good masque as the country lady busy with her
husband and children and lands, with no thought at all of
the throne that might one day be hers, or theirs.

And, should you have wondered, Tryffin and Ysild
wed not long after our return from Tyntagel; Arthur confirmed them as Duke and Duchess of Kernow, and indeed
gave to Tryff the rank he had denied Marc'h, that of viceroy over the planet, the seat in the ring of the Fainne that
the elder Tregaron had coveted enough to bring his planet
to the brink of civil strife. Their child, a boy called
Loherin, was born the year after our Gerrans, and the two
became friends.

But for the rest, all was well; so that when Gweniver
summoned me to her office one summer afternoon, I
racked my brain to think what I might have done of late
to annoy her. As a rule, close as we were, Gwennach and
I did not consult officially. We saved our policy discussions for informal sessions, as we had done since our
days at Coldgates, and held it best that it should be so.
But it was not so today.

She was standing behind her desk when I came in, and
was reading—for what seemed not the first time—a message diptych bound in silver and sealed in gold, such as

monarchs are used to send one another on matters of state.

I made her the brief salute I always made my rulers—not that either of them insisted on it, ever, but *I* insisted; it was a thing I felt both they and I did need to be minded of, whenever possible, and I never neglected to do so—and sat down without waiting to be asked. Gweniver started, as if only then noticing my presence, and without hesitation handed me the diptych.

"Advise me, Pen-bardd."

I scanned the message, and was already shaking my head and lifting a hand in denial and protest before she had spoken.

"Not I, by gods!"

"Talyn—"

"Ard-rían." I took a deep breath; she waited me out.

"You knew her well, Tal-bach. I need to know."

I ran my hands over my face. Well, we had all known this day would sometime come, I expect even you have been awaiting it—we who had been on Aojun with Arthur. We who had known Majanah . . .

"I have already sent back by the courier who brought this my invitation to her, that she should come here. And bring the child with her."

Ah Goddess, why me . . . "Perhaps Daronwy or Tanwen can better serve you in this, they are women themselves—or Roric, even, he is of the Aojunni." Though maybe not so much, not these days: Daronwy's lord, who had accompanied her home to Tara, had chosen to stay, becoming, as we called it, more Keltic than the Kelts.

But Gweniver only laughed. "This is *I* you speak to, Talyn," she reminded me derisively. "We have nothing hid between us—nay, how could we?"

I blushed at the reminder of our onetime, *long*-ago bedding; which I remind you had been more out of curiosity and mutual comforting and need than out of any real passion—though it had been the door to the long and loving and utterly honest friendship we had shared from then on. I muttered something lame and excusing.

"Not good enough! What must I do to get it out of you—ask Morgan?"

In the end, I got through it by pretending it was a tale I was telling her as bard: that Majanah, and Arthur, and

the child Donah, and all the rest of it, were but part of a
chaunt like any other. And the High Queen listened, and
heard; and when I had finished she sighed and straightened in her chair and looked anywhere but at me.

"Well. That is what I needed to know. Thank you, Tal-
bach. As ever, thank you."

I stood up, uncertain if I was being dismissed; but she
waved me back into my seat again.

"There is no reason why she should not come, you
know. We—Keltia, that is—have been friends and allies
with the Yamazai of Aojun since, oh, before Athyn's day;
indeed, she was the one who brought our folk closest.
And the child *is* Arthur's; he will want to see her."

"Are *you* not curious, Gwennach?" I asked quietly.

She laughed a real laugh this time. "You mean am I
jealous? Well, aye and nay to that, if you must know.
Artos and I have been wedded all these years; we share
each other's rank and power and thoughts and goals, and,
sometimes, beds. So nay, I am not jealous of this
outfrenne queen. But aye, for that she has had with Arthur a thing I have not had, and maybe never will: love,
and a child out of that love. I am not sure, even, that I
wish it; but I think I *wish* to wish it, and sometimes that
makes me—"

But she did not say how it made her; and I leaned
across the desk to kiss her gently on the forehead.

"Ard-rían," was all I said; and, just then, I think all she
needed, and wanted, to hear.

CHAPTER
29

So the Jamadarin of the Yamazai, with the Heir of Aojun, came to Keltia, and I was delegated to meet them at Mardale.

Very like you are thinking that after all this time surely Arthur might have managed to be there himself to greet his ban-charach and their child; or, if naught so personal carried weight with him, then at the least as Ard-rígh of Keltia receiving a galláin monarch. But that was not how Arthur did things; and so I found myself, on a brilliant spring afternoon, shifting nervously from one foot to another as I watched the shuttle come in from the orbiting Aojunese flagship.

For all my training as bard and all my years as prince, I did not do this sort of political chore well or gladly. I have ever loved and studied to be a watcher, not a worker; to observe great events, not to do them myself. It is the maker's way: One must be distanced from the thing one wishes to make into art. Chance and dán, of course, had arranged things otherwise down the years, as here recounted; but when I had the choosing I preferred to stand back and let others do, so that I might watch and, later, write of it. But that choice was not mine this day.

The shuttle door opened, and then Majanah was standing there, the Keltic sunlight on her gleaming hair, looking exactly like herself. Beside her was a tall, shy, coltish creature who seemed more an asrai or annir-choille than a princess ... I acknowledged Majanah's smile of greeting—her relief on spotting a familiar face had been very visible, not to mention flattering; but it was as much joy at seeing an old friend as discovering a known countenance amid the faces of strangers. Even queens can be daunted by the unknown; but she came forward with stateliness uppermost in her bearing.

I had performed this very chore on many another occasion—when one is fostern to the High King, and husband to his sister, one generally comes in for more than a fair share of ceremonial drudgery—and now I ran off as by rote the platitudes of diplomatic greeting, 'In the names of Arthur Ard-rígh and Gweniver Ard-rían,' you know how it goes; and Majanah, who had herself endured her full share of similar occasions, responded duly in kind, 'In the name of Aojun of the Yamàzai,' and all that. But she and I held each other's gaze gravely and desperately, as if we feared that if we let down our ceremonial purpose for an instant we would be shouting for joy and laughing and hugging promiscuously in front of both our escorts. And, very like, we would.

At last I came to the end of my mouthings, and Majanah to the conclusion of her parroted formal responses; then, as we settled into the chariot for the ride to Caerdroia, we were free to greet each other as long-parted friends.

"Ah me," said Majanah, after we had spent quite a few minutes kissing and weeping and laughing, "but it is good to see you again, my fox."

And that was a name she had given me of old on Aojun; but she turned now to her daughter, who had said no word so far and who had not taken her eyes off me since we met.

"This is the Lord Talvosghen—Taliesin—who is foster-brother to your father the High King and mate to the King's sister the Princess Morgauna. You and he were great friends when you were a child, but you will not remember; he is your uncle, by his law and our own, so greet him thusly."

Donah regarded me gravely and shyly out of eyes near as dark as Arthur's own but flecked with gold that came to her from her mother, and still she said no word.

"I remember *you*, Princess," I said, to help her over the moment. "Though you were scarce three years old when last I saw you . . ."

I faltered, for her gaze was *most* unnerving; then all at once she smiled, and she was there again, Majanah's kitling, the charming child with the pointed chin and the joyful heart, and spoke softly, shyly.

"Do you still have your harp?"

"Indeed I do so, and you will hear it tonight." Turning to Majanah: "Arthur and Gweniver will receive you when we come to Turusachan, and there will be an aonach and feast this even, as befits the arrival in Keltia of a reigning queen and her lovely heir"—here I bowed to Donah, and she giggled like the lass she was. "But that will be all of ceremony; Artos, as you know, does not go in much for state."

"And the Queen Janfarie?"

'Janfarie' . . . gods but the one word took me back in an instant, back to those days in Mistissyn, city of wood—

"No more than does Artos," I said with great firmness. "As you will see."

Suffice it to say that Artos and Gwennach had not favored their own coronation with such state as they both seemed to think Majanah's arrival merited . . . I was well and truly shamed, catching the look Majanah shot me on our arrival in the Presence Chamber. But how was I to know? We speak here of a king who preferred to patch his own tunics and a queen who thought naught of wearing ragged trews to her own Council meetings: But that afternoon for their first, informal meeting with Majanah, and that evening, at the aonach, they had positively glittered with jewels and silks and silver.

At first dismayed sight, I thought perhaps it was to honor the Yamazai queen; and too, it was the first sight Donah would have of her father in conscious life, no surprise if he should wish to appear in kingly splendor. But that did not seem right either, somehow, though I did not know whyever not.

Then, as I watched Arthur and Gweniver at the aonach, doing their social work as effortlessly and smoothly as they did their political chores, moving amongst the guests, one or the other of them at all times by the side of their royal visitor, it came to me that they had chosen to appear so as a message to our own folk, not to the visiting Aojunni nor yet their Yamazai queen: that Gweniver and Arthur were Kelts; of Keltia, rulers; and no galláin queen nor half-Kelt issue could alter it.

But messages of one sort or another were thick on the ground that night ... For one, the Princess Marguessan had actually deigned to come to Court for the occasion. She did not as a rule honor us with her presence more than once a year or so—for which we all of us were ever profoundly thankful—and she had been to Turusachan already once this season; so her attendance this night was most beyond norm and custom. Added to that, she had brought her heir with her, the Prince Mordryth, almost unprecedented; and the crosscurrents of query and speculation were running strong and counter from one side of Mi-cuarta to the other.

I was watching them both particularly closely, Mordryth maybe even more so than his mother. He was not a stupid young man, that I knew already; not so tall as Arthur had been at his years, a touch stockier too, having more a look of Uthyr to him, or of his father Irian, than of Marguessan or Ygrawn. His uncle though I was, I seldom if ever spoke to him, and tonight was no exception.

But it seemed to be a night of scions: Malgan ap Owein was here as well, looking altogether more prepossessing than his princely coequal. He had long since ceased to wear the red of mourning for his late and unlamented parents, but tonight by some chance, or perhaps no chance at all, he was clad in garnet-colored velvet, which should have jarred against his red-brown hair but somehow did not. In truth, he looked quite handsome; but the dynamic that was running between him and Mordryth like a shuttle on a loom had more to it than mere appearances, and was, indeed, baffling and hard to read.

They two had met often enough before, of course, over the years; indeed, for two young men so much of an age and so near in rank, it would have been stranger still had their paths *not* run together now and again. People thought them cat-of-a-kind, but that was not so. They were not friends, but neither were they antagonists; wary, respectful acquaintances was about the weight of it, and I thought I knew why ...

But I was hindered from further speculation by Morgan's elbow in my ribs and her voice in my mind; and I had felt both voice and elbow often enough to know that never did their owner employ either without excellent cause, so now I looked obediently down to see what she would have me notice.

"See how Malgan looks on Donah," was all she said, and nodded across the chamber, where the young Heir of Aojun, completely at her ease, was conversing happily with a group that included Tarian Douglas, Alannagh Ruthven and Grehan Aoibhell's niece and nephew, Fidelm and Rhydian.

I looked again: Malgan Rheged, too shy to go across and be presented as was well within his right to do, was staring at Donah as if she were the first girl he had ever beheld, or the fairest.

"It is but the novelty of the thing," I said, hoping to gods I was right. "An outfrenne princess—and so fair a one, what lad would not take notice?"

"She is a child," said Morgan coldly. "And not only that—"

"Say it not! Nay, cariad, do not even *think* it too loudly!" I glanced wildly around to see if any had heard—Morgan had a lovely carrying voice when so she chose, and a lovely clear thought-voice that was if anything more carrying still. She could throw her thought or her mood over all this gathering as easily and completely as a blanket; and I knew all too well her thought just now, for I had had it myself—that young Malgan might well be looking with gogglement on his own half-sister.

I reminded myself of a few facts, and was consoled thereby: Apart from *that,* even if the youth *were* smitten, Donah was too young, being but half his years, for him to do aught about it. Though Malgan might well entertain calf-love or wild hopes, such feelings would scarce withstand the decade's stretch before Donah could consider them, or even be considered eligible. And never would they withstand the long star-miles between Keltia and Aojun; not to mention the stance of Arthur and Majanah in the matter.

Then it came my turn to employ the elbow of significance, and Morgan who must perforce frown and consider. Marguessan, her twin, was standing off to one side of the great banqueting-hall; and plainly she had either forgotten Morgan's presence or discounted Morgan's magic, for she was looking at Arthur with such a look of hatred as took my breath away, made me reach as if by instinct for my belt. But my sgian was not there—this was, after all, a party, one does not go armed to a feast in one's own home—and I was all the more unsettled that I should have felt I might have need of it. And the worst thing of all was that Marguessan was smiling.

Otherwise, it had been so far a most pleasant and successful evening: The Jamadarin could charm the badgers from their winter dens did she so choose, and tonight she had set herself to be as enchanting as even she could be. I perceived easily what some plainly were thinking: that she hoped thereby to win back Arthur for hers; but I can tell you right off that she had no such intention. That was not why she had come to Keltia; and the truth of it was attested by the fact that Majanah was paying Gweniver every courtesy and attention and deference that she was paying Arthur, to the tiniest measure, to the smallest degree the same. Nay, she was here for precisely the reasons she had claimed that afternoon in the Presence Chamber: to foster the friendship between our two nations, and so that the Princess Donah might meet her father and the other half of her heritage.

That last intent, at least, had been an unqualified success: Both Arthur and Donah had fallen instantly in love with each other, as a father and daughter should, as if the resumption of their long-abeyant bond were as easy and natural as breathing; as if, indeed, that bond had never been suspended at all. They were astonished and enchanted with each other, and few in all that hall looked on them with aught but benignity and smiles.

But in the midst of all these dynamics of mood and place, like tiderips of the soul and senses, the dynamic I noted before all others, and had been vainly trying to disbelieve all night long, was the one between Arthur and Gweniver. As I have said earlier, they were utterly in concert as King and Queen these days, had been for many months, even years; but what I saw tonight when I looked on them together, or, especially, apart, was that at last, at long last, Arthur and Gweniver had fallen in love with each other.

Now whether it had taken Majanah's arrival to bring this result about, had precipitated it like that one last crystal added to a supersaturated solution, or whether it had been just about to happen in the normal road of events—Keils and Gweniver had drifted apart some time since, though still friends—and had only chanced to fall out so tonight, naught to do with Majanah at all, I have no smallest idea. I neither know nor much care, and leave it to those more suited to the graíghtraí than I to harp about, even. But it was past mistaking, though so far I seemed to be the only person, save Majanah herself, who had seen it.

And I rejoiced to see it, had been waiting for it to happen since our long-ago days on Gwynedd; had known too that it would come, and that it would come when it would, when it determined to come, and not a moment sooner. But it seemed too that with Majanah's coming to Keltia, all Arthur's past had suddenly been put into perspective; as if all the women in his life had been mere aspects and forerunners of Gweniver, who was his Queen and his wife. Gwenwynbar, Majanah, the ladies of Court and Company with whom he had enjoyed dalliance or romance over the years: All had come together in one woman, and she neither stranger nor incomer but one who had been friend and challenger and equal and goad, for long; and now, at last, his mate.

And now, it seemed, Arthur knew it as well, and Gwennach also ... I was very happy, and turned to Morgan to tell her all this, thinking to boast a little at having perceived the truth of it before she had. But a small commotion on the other side of the hall caught my attention, and I cut through the crowd, Morgan close beside me, to see what went on.

Surprisingly—or perhaps not so, considering Marguessan's smiling evil look of an hour or two since—it was Mordryth seemed to be at the heart of it. He had approached Gweniver and Majanah, who had been talking together animatedly in the center of a knot of friends—Tryffin and Ysild, Daronwy and her Aojunese lord, Roric, glad to see once more his friend and Queen, Betwyr, a few others. He had somewhat in his hands, and stood now before the two queens, as if to proffer both or either that which he held so close.

I cannot tell you what a feeling washed over me then: a cold tide, the shadow of the wing of dán, disaster breathing in the room like the coming on of a cam-anfa. But I shouldered brutally through the last few folk who barred my way, pulling Morgan after me, coming to stand just on the edge of the little circle that had formed, near enough to see and hear what passed, and, maybe, prevent the worst . . .

Small chance! Looking back, I see that Marguessan must have had this planned for a long time, had been biding her moment, cherishing her ancient hatred. This was not a thing of yesterday with her, but something that had root in the far past. Though all of us had long been 'ware of Marguessan's resentment and ill will to Arthur and Gweniver—as you will recall, she had never ceased to deem herself the rightful heir, as Uthyr's eldest child, no matter the law or the will and wish of King and folk alike—what we had all failed utterly to note was the slow cold nature of that will, that had let her wait in strength unwearied and patience unceasant, until she should judge her time had come to act; as now she had.

And it was Mordryth who was to be the instrument of that acting . . . I was close enough now to see what it was he held in his hands: a cup, a quaich of ordinary design, made of silver or perhaps white gold, its rim edged with knotwork and black pearls. And it troubled me strangely, for it seemed that I had looked on just such a vessel once, or one very like to it, though I could not say when or how or where.

But the cup seemed inoffensive enough in itself, as Mordryth held it out to the two royal ladies; and then he said, in a light clear voice that seemed higher and shriller than usual, "This is the cup that belonged once to Olwen White-track, and came from her to Llariau, and on down."

And then of course I knew; but it seemed that I could do naught to stop what I was full aware was about to happen, and beside me Morgan seemed as deadened and incapable as I, and we could but watch as the coil played out.

Majanah's face bore only polite puzzlement and interest, but Gweniver well knew something was amiss and awry, and I could see her gathering herself up to strike even while she sent out fingerlings of her power, like little spies of magic, to see what mischief was here, or about to be.

Her sole question came warily. "What nature is to it, and what peculiarity may it possess?"

I threw back my head with admiration and joy, for that was a ritual question if ever there was one; now, *now,* the thing was cast, and every sorcerer in Mi-cuarta that night well knew it.

Not being Ban-draoi, Marguessan did not, and she smiled to make eager answer to the Ard-rían. It must have seemed to her that the moment of her triumphing was come at last; for she answered Gweniver at once, and in so doing she convicted herself before us all. At the time, I thought it a grave mistake; now I am no longer so sure . . .

"The nature and peculiarity of this cup are these: that only a true mate may drink from it; and that any who drinks, man or woman, who has done violence or violation to the bonds of marriage or union will find in the cup not wine but ashes and shame. Or worse, perhaps—but do *you* fear to drink?"

That last question was delivered with a smiling snarl only Marguessan could have given it; I well remembered that snarl, had heard it aimed at me by the child Marguessan at Coldgates, not yet twelve years of age and already possessed of all the spite and malice we saw displayed here this night. She looked well pleased at the consternation her words had struck: Plainly she had calculated this ploy with Olwen's cup as having most potential for public obloquy and dishonor to her intended victims; knowing as she did the state of her cousin Gweniver's marriage, hoping the worst of Majanah. Across the empty space between us I saw Arthur go black as thunder, and Keils Rathen, who had come late to the feasting and now stood at Arthur's shoulder, white as steel.

Then Majanah laughed to break the silence, and reached out to take the cup from Mordryth's hands. Sunbright she looked in that moment, warm and golden as the nooning as she raised the cup to her lips.

"May the Queen Janfarie forgive me," she said, "but I will drink first, to pledge her and Arthur the King, who is Arithor of Aojun." And she drank deeply of what the cup held for her.

I have never heard such a hush as fell then; it seemed as if all the City, all the planet, all Keltia even, held its breath as one. What ought to have happened, at least according to Marguessan's vile design, was simple and terrible: Majanah should drink; the wine would choke her as the magic deemed; and she would stand accused before all—leaving her and Arthur shamed, Gweniver with further shame to come, perhaps even the alliance between Aojun and Keltia in ruins. Not a bad night's work even for Marguessan; but what did happen was very much other wise . . .

So Majanah drank; and when she raised her head again to look at Mordryth she was smiling.

"A strong vine to make so rich a pressing." She turned then to Gweniver, and in her bearing was only courtesy, though a certain glint now stood in the golden eyes. "Lady, will you drink as well?"

Gweniver took the cup, for it could not be refused, all the time holding the other's gaze. And she must have trusted well what she read there, for without a moment's hesitation she lifted the cup as Majanah had done, gave salute to the Yamazai queen and drank off the rest of the cup's contents. When she lowered the shining bowl from her face, her eyes were closed, and as they came slowly open again I flinched where I did bide, for the look that stood in them was terrible, and it was bent wholly on Marguessan.

Who was staring at the cup as if it had suddenly turned to a mass of noisome writhing crimmocks: For some reason Marguessan could not comprehend, the magic had not worked as she had willed it; and her mind, if not numbed by the magnitude of her miscalculation, was surely wheeling frantically amongst the possibilities, like a horse in a burning stable.

I could track her thought as clearly as if she had blazoned it out upon the walls of Mi-cuarta in letters of fire: What had happened? The wine should have been ashes in their mouth, should have choked them where they stood as false to their vows of union with the same man. But clearly they had

drunk nothing more nor less than good Arvorican red . . .
Had the quaich itself been to blame? Or had other magic,
more powerful still, thwarted Marguessan's aim, balked her
throw? Had it been Arthur, perhaps, or maybe Morgan, who
had foiled her, or even, gods forfend, that graceless tunesmith who fancied himself Druid as well as prince—
meaning me, of course. As I say, her thought was plain for
me to read; but I was wondering just as hard myself how
she had been so featly parried out of hand.

Arthur had come up beside me, seemed about to speak.
But again the Yamazai queen was too swift for any of us:
By some means—and the Yamazai are by no means unskilled as sorceresses, let me tell you—she had determined, just as had Gweniver, that Marguessan was the
author of the insult that had just been played out, that
Mordryth was but a tool. So now, stepping forward before
any of us had an inkling of her intent, Majanah slapped
Marguessan across the face, thrice; left, right, left again.
No word spoken, and none needed; the clear print of her
hand showed red and mottled against the sudden ugly pal-
lor of Marguessan's cheek.

But it did not end there. Again, before any of us could
move—we were rooted like trees by now, sunk knee-
deep, seemingly, in the marble flooring—Mordryth
stepped forward in turn, and struck Gweniver Ard-rían in
the face.

The silence screamed in our ears as the slap echoed off
Mi-cuarta's walls. The moment seemed unbearably, im-
possibly long, stretched and endless and timeless: We
were no longer living breathing folk here but tiny painted
figures, and the sound of the blow that Mordryth struck
went on forever and forever, never had it not been, never
would it cease to be . . .

Yet end it did, and in no manner we could have
dreamed of, for in the midst of the silence and the intol-
erable shrieking tension and the reeling impossibility
came a high singing sound, like a silver wind in the room.
It seemed to come from all directions and no direction,
and was of a great and lovely sweetness of tone, such as
even I, a bard, had never heard before, or would have believed could be.

And with the sound came a light: The rest of that vast
chamber dimmed as with a sudden mist that shadowed the

corners and clung to the walls, a vague and somber mantle cloaking us all, and light fell from the air on the quaich that Mordryth still held in his hands, where Gweniver had thrust it.

It was from that cup that both sound and light, aye, and darkness too, had origin: The bowl of the quaich was beginning to vibrate and shimmer, the sound building, the light beginning to bloom blue on the whiteness of the polished metal. As the note reached a pitch on the edge of pain, suddenly Mordryth gave a harsh cry, and threw his hands wide, thinking to fling the cup from him.

But though he loosed his hold on it perforce—we saw later the red and black scorches across his palms, where the quaich had burned the skin—the magic that was now at work in the cup was not the magic that had been before. This was not the magic on which Marguessan had relied for her evil, not the enchantment laid on this thing from of old. Nay, this now at work was no sorcery that any of us had ever seen, and we were as feared and dazed as he.

For the cup that Mordryth flung away did not fall and clatter to the floor, but floated high in the air, a span above the heads of even the tallest among us; and there came a fragrance from it, that seemed somehow to partner the light and the mist and the clear high note that transfixed us like a spear, and there came in the room a sound of thunder.

It takes longer to describe than the event itself required: As we stared and stared—none of us could move by now, not even Marguessan, not even my Morgan, we were all frozen where we stood—the cup suddenly grew, enlarging and overlapping itself as it hung floating above our heads. The black pearls round its rim—rough-shapen, not perfect rounds—now blazed blue-white in the strange eerie luminescence; and the cup, or the light, began now to pulsate and contract and spin, in a three-armed spiral such as we see graven on dolmens from Tara to Vannin.

Faster and faster the spiral whirled throbbing; the note grew plangent and unbearable in beauty; the light coming from the cup, or resting on it, I could not tell which, grew brighter still; the fragrance stronger, as of roses and burned iron together, a hot wind, surely the Forge of Gavida himself must give off such a scent as this—And then all in one blinding flash it was gone. The hall of Micuarta was as it was, and we who had not been able to stir nor hand nor foot could move once more.

And still we did not so.

It was all settled very quickly after that. Once we found ourselves free to move, Arthur's Fian guards cleared the hall of everyone save the immediate participants in what was, after all, merely a little family drama—once the other elements were set for the moment aside. But the aonach guests were most respectfully if firmly moved along; and not one of them was other than eager and grateful to take leave.

We were perhaps a score or so left in the banqueting-hall: Arthur and Gweniver and Majanah standing off to one side, Marguessan and Mordryth over against them, Malgan somewhere between. Irian was not there; indeed, I could not recall seeing Marguessan's husband at all that evening. But Morgan and I stood with Donah, each of us with one arm round the child, who was shivering a little and staring at her parents; she did not weep and carry on, I was pleased to see—but she was a princess.

Of others who remained at Arthur's command, I noted Tari Douglas—well, as Taoiseach, no question but she would be present—Comyn the Archdruid, and Alair Kinmont who was now Chief Brehon, and Therrian the new Ban-draoi Mathr'achtaran; and, unobtrusive in the shadows by the wall, shadows cast now by purely natural sconces, several of the strongest and most trusted of Arthur's personal guard of Companions.

It was the time for justice, Keltic justice according to the law of the brehons that came with us from Earth, and justice was the least and the swiftest of it: Arthur spoke, few words, cold and to the point. Marguessan and Mordryth were banished forever from Court, and to my thinking they were much to thank the King that they went from there with their lives. The Chief Brehon herself was witness to the lawful execution of the doom, I spoke for the Bardic Association, Therrian and Comyn for their orders, Tari for the Council and government. Gweniver stood unmoving, and she said no word at all.

Only Majanah, looking after Marguessan and Mordryth as they were escorted from the hall by stone-faced Fians, into their exile, voiced what we must all have surely been feeling.

"Artho," she said clearly and honestly, "you had done better to kill them."

And we knew, gods help us all, that she was right.

CHAPTER
30

As for the rest of that night's remarkable events: Well, even Morgan could not give us the truth of what had taken place there in Mi-cuarta. The cup had been a genuine relic of Olwen and Llariau, two noble and notably maritorious queens of old, which Marguessan had somehow come by; and the spell that had been on it was its own, naught owing to my matesister, merely used by her for her own hateful ends. Why it had worked to her detriment, none could say for certain, though there was no lack of theories, and much joy too that it had done so.

Again, it was Majanah who came perhaps the closest of us all to what may have been the truth, when she tossed her own thought like a ball of string into the midst of our discussions.

"I know from your sojourn in our midst, as well as mine here, that magic is different on every world," she said reflectively. "But to me it seems that here the form of the magic itself, the integrity of the cup, was what came back against the Princess Morgaes"—so she turned Marguessan's name in the tongue of Aojun.

"And that is?" asked Therrian.

"Truth is ever the best defense. She called down shame on any who had violated sworn vows. Well, neither I nor the Queen Janfarie has ever done so; hence the magic would distinguish, and could not hold."

Tari breathed an incredulous laugh. "And so the wine was wine only."

"Just so."

I stirred and shifted in my chair; we were all weary beyond speech, but some things must be addressed.

"And the rest of it? That was no simple magic worked five hundred years ago by a loving and notoriously faithful queen! You were there, you saw what it did! The cup, or whatever in all the hells it was—"

Silence reigned, for they had no answer any more than I did. We were sitting slouched around the Council chamber, those of the royal family and associates whom the thing concerned most nearly, still shaking from our ordeal, tired and angry and cranky and feared, trying to make some sense of what seemed like in the end to have no sense to it at all; or no earthly sense, at the least.

For myself, I firmly believed that we had witnessed a miracle of some sort: a portent, perhaps, a foreshadowing of some greater thing to come. But that thought too held fresh fears: If this was the omen, what then must be the magnitude of the event to come, so mighty and so perilous the sign . . .

But we were all of us too shaken by far to come at any solution that night, and after perhaps another hour of vain crosstalk Arthur abruptly rose and ordered us all off to our beds, and we obeyed with glad grace.

Once there, though, even with Morgan warm and sleepy cuddled against my side, I could not keep my mind from scrolling through the events of that night, again and again, replaying them like a viewtape, and something caught at the edges of my thought. I pushed at Morgan, and she muttered some swart swearing word back at me.

"Talyn, let me sleep—"

"Why think you Gweniver so readily accepted the cup from Majanah? She had heard Marguessan say what would befall any faithless who drank from it—"

Morgan snuggled closer. "Two things, and then I will sleep, and by gods so shall you— Gweniver knew she had been faithful, and she knew she could trust Majanah. That is all. Go to sleep."

But I lay awake a while yet, listening to Morgan's even breathing in the room's stillness. She was doubtless correct in her assessment: Gweniver had been true and faithful in the smallest particular to the bonds of her marriage with Arthur—it had been only tonight that it had in truth become a marriage—she had not violated her vows, therefore she knew she could drink safely. And even if she had not known, she had a genuine trust and respect for Majanah; and if the Yamazai queen bade her drink, then drink she would, and did . . .

I thought about that for a while, as I waited impatiently for sleep to claim me. All praise to the Goddess that Majanah was cut of the fine cloth she was; had she been another Gwenwynbar, say, who knows what disaster might have come to be? But Janjan and Gwennach were equals, in mind and soul and spirit, true queens; and because they were, and were both Arthur's chosen, it did honor and credit to all three of them, and instead of contempt and scorn and enmity there was understanding; respect also, even friendship. And I was glad it had fallen out so, for I loved all three of them.

But the more vexing question remained. Marguessan had been exiled only, not destroyed. Perhaps Arthur had not wished to condemn his own sister and nephew to death for what had been—as our Chief Brehon Alair Kinmont had taken pains to point out—an act well short of treason, however ill-advised. We had honor-prices for that sort of thing, after all . . .

Still, even exiled, Marguessan would be free on her own lands, amongst folk loyal to her and her husband and their offspring, free to make what plots and plans she would. And, oh, she would surely do so: Marguessan had never from childhood been one to leave a grudge before it had given its all to her purpose; and this particular grudge had much service left in it. She would be fueled, too, by her very public humiliation; well aware that we intended to keep close watch on her, she would also know we could not, would not, go beyond the bounds of our own laws and customs. Within the maigen of her lands and Irian's, Marguessan would be free to do as she wished; and, I doubted not, she would take full advantage of that fact.

I yawned prodigiously, and prepared to follow Morgan down into slumber at long last; then was jolted awake again by a thought that had been niggling at the edge of

my awareness all night long. And the thought was this:
What had become of Olwen's cup, that had so spectacularly confounded its abuser?

The silver quaich had duly performed its astounding
transformation, the which had still not been satisfactorily in-
terpreted by the sorry parcel of brilliant brains loitering
round the Council table until three past middlenight. But it
had not been seen or found or heard of since: We had
thought to find it lying on the floor of Mi-cuarta, after; or
perhaps magically restored to the place whence Marguessan
had filched it. But it had vanished without a trace; and,
somehow, that troubled me even more than all the rest of it.

Still, though we at Turusachan thought much on the
matter, it was soon all but forgotten by the rest of Keltia:
The thinking being, Aye, well, so the High King has banished his sister and her brood; she had never been well
loved by the populace, and they were neither glad nor
stricken to see the back of her. Doubtless, they thought,
all would blow over, next month, next year, fifty years
from now, and Arthur and Marguessan be friends. No
matter that they had never been friends in all their lives,
those two; but so the folk thought, and we considered it
best to let them think so.

But we were greatly sorry on another matter entirely:
Majanah was returning to Aojun, and we did not want her
to go.

"A sixmonth is substantial enough for a first visit,
Talghen," she said when I went to her to plead for a stay
of departure.

"Aye, well, when *we* came to *your* planet we stayed
seven years—"

"True enough, I could not get rid of you tried I never
so hard . . ." We laughed, but quickly grew solemn again.
"I will be coming back, you know! Any road, I have con-
sented to let Donah remain here with her father for a
while. It is good that she should come to know him, and
Janfarie and you and Morgauna and the other dear friends
we have here. Also Roric will be near to help her—it will
be best so. Most especially now that Artho and Janfarie
are truemates—"

I gaped. "My soul to the mountain! How do you know
that?"

Majanah laughed again. "A cavebat could have seen it coming—even though Artho and I are no longer each other's in love, nor have wish to be, still can we tell how it is with one another. He was wedded when he came to me in Mistissyn—you were there, you know how it was—but he and Janfarie were not partnered, indeed, were not so until last night. So we had each other, and she had the Lord Keils ... If they two had been truemates then I should not have taken Artho for all the life of the world; but now they are so, and for my part I have my own lord, Brone, who rules Aojun and the Aojunni while I am away. Even Lord Keils has found a new friend in the Lady Meloran; and if she is not his truemate he will find her in another, but all will go rightly on. You will see."

"Aye, I daresay I shall—but in the end?"

"In the end, Donah will be Jamadarin over Aojun in her turn; she will bring her Keltic half to that estate as well as that part of her which is Aojunese. And you too will have had a hand in the queen she shall become ... Which is why I ask you now to look after her while she is here, you and Morgauna. I know Gerrans is still from home, and that Morgauna prefers it so, but there is in Donah that which a Ban-draoi can teach to grow and flower, and I would she did."

"Surely Artos—"

A wise smile. "Artho and Janfarie will soon have cares of their own, heirs of their own— I have read it in the wind, it will surely be. A boy and a girl, not of the same birthing but of the same heart ... Any road, I know you and your lady will care for my daughter; she loves you both."

"I will make a bard of her yet," I promised; but I was deeply moved by what she had said. "Janjan—"

"Ah, you do not know the good it does me to hear you call me that! But sit now, and I will sift the stars in your hand one more time."

I obeyed, dropping to a cushion by her feet and holding out to her my open right hand, palm uppermost, for I remembered well her skill at this form of kenning. Majanah took my hand across her knee, running a fingertip over the lines and creases of my palm, smiling as she saw again a thing she had seen before, or had not seen until now.

"Your hand is still full of stars," she said, "as it was when first I read it. Deeper, finer, higher—it is all still there." She turned my hand this way and that, bending it backward to make the lines leap out plain, then nearly folding it closed. "But there is more in it now—"

"What things?" I asked humbly, after she had been silent what seemed a long time.

"I do not entirely understand, but—there is a question you have not asked, a question of long standing, and you must ask it of one who is hidden? The secret valley? Is there such a place? Well, your hand tells me you must go there, and you must ask about your mother; time it is for you to know at last. Your mother wishes it so."

I gasped, for of all things I had been expecting I never thought her to say aught like this.

"My mother is dead, Jamadarin," I said after a while. "She died when I was barely two years old."

The golden eyes were soft as summer, the smile full of love. "Well, surely she is! How else would she be telling me this, how putting it into her son's hand for me to find? Because she is no more in the body this life round does not mean she no longer cares for her dear ones, or has abandoned looking after them—but I do not have to tell you this."

"Nay," I said, after another long pause, for I did not trust my voice. "Nay, you do not. What more?"

She stared into my hand for many moments. "Someone else," she said at last. "But he sleeps and dreams—I cannot reach him, he cannot speak to me. Your mother knows him. Go to the secret valley. That is all I can say. You will be glad of it."

She returned my hand to my keeping, and we sat on for a while in companionable silence. But my mind was reeling. My *mother*! Speaking to Majanah? It seemed impossible, but I knew that my friend had read my hand aright. I would go to Glenshee, then, and I would ask that question I had been given leave, so long ago now, to ask. I would ask Seli, Queen of the Shining Folk, about my mother, and I would hear what she had to tell me. Time it was that I should know.

But summer had passed its height, warm and green and slow, the trees heavy with full leaf yet just beginning to be touched by autumn's oncoming, by the time I made ready for my journey to the valley of Glenshee.

Majanah had gone home to Aojun at Midsummer, leaving Donah here with us as she had promised; and a fine time we were all having of it. The one twingeing note in that summer's tune was that Donah and Malgan were often in each other's company. But—so far, at least—it seemed they dealt with one another as brother and younger sister, Malgan protective and instructive, Donah admiring and teasing and altogether adoring. As for the other couple on whom all eyes were fixed: Well, so far, again, there was no sign of the prophesied heir Majanah had foretold; but from all appearances, Arthur and Gweniver would not be delaying the starting of one very much longer.

It was partly for that very reason that I delayed my going: I wished to see them happy and settled before I went, though I knew perfectly well that after all their years of marriage they were familiar enough to and with each other not to need my henwife's fussing. Yet by another kind of reckoning they were but new in love; all Keltia, indeed, could see they were besotted, and the folk were as delirious with the joy of it as were the lovers themselves. We had all waited long enough for it to come.

But both of them urged me to go, in no uncertain terms; Morgan, too, insisted, though it was Arthur who was most persuasive.

"The Queen Seli gave you leave to ask," he reminded me more times than I could count, "and you delayed the query; and for that she gave you the praise. But I too think the time is come for you to know—and too," he added, faltering a little, "there is that other thing she spoke of."

He could not say the name any more than could I: But I can write it down—Merlynn. He was the sleeper and dreamer Majanah had seen in my hand's palimpsest; would he be, too, at Glenshee?

Gweniver had followed my thought, and spoke gently. "The only way to know is to go."

And so I did.

In the interests of speed I went by aircar to Methven, the market town that lies on the edge of the great plain of the Litherlands, east of the Hollow Mountains, and which was the nearest settlement of size to Glenshee. Not that any of the townsfolk knew of the existence of the hidden vale; but I thought it best to continue on the side of caution, and did not speak of my errand nor yet my destination.

Arthur had given orders, and two horses were ready waiting, a well-gaited mount and a packbeast; the stabler was incurious, seemed not to twig my assumed name, and I daresay had forgotten all about me by the time I had ridden out of the townland.

All the same, I took a circuitous route through the dales and fells, until I had satisfied myself, with a few Druid tricks here and there, that I was free from possible trackers. Only then did I allow myself to relax and revel in the passing loveliness: blue hills heavily forested, steep streams clattering from the heights of Mount Keltia away in the south. Here so far north autumn was already moving upon the land, and the weather was cool and bright and windy—as those say who live on Tara, the Hawk was out, the northeast wind that is the precursor to An-Lasca.

I was ridiculously, causelessly happy; I sang as I rode, and recited great chunks of classic chaunts to my horses. But mostly I thought of how things had worked themselves: of Majanah, and Donah, and Artos and Gwennach, and even Marguessan . . . A corner had turned, and here alone in the boundless North I could feel the changes as I had not been able to sense them back in Caerdroia.

Keltia had become itself again, in far shorter a time than we might have thought, back when first we started to try to make it so. Those great reforms and restorals that Gweniver had begun and Arthur had expanded were more firmly in place each day, each hour. High doings, to be sure: Perhaps not since the days of the great Astrogator had all the ideals of the Keltia he had intended been so clearly and so patently in force.

To me, though, an even greater thing than this was the way the folk had blossomed in the presence of those restorings. In my days as journeyman bard—well, spy, if you insist—when I had wandered round Gwynedd for Arthur and the Companions, I had seen the despair of my people as few others who worked for the Counterinsurgency had ever seen it. They merely observed it: I was out in it, lived with it, and with them, those sufferers under Edeyrn's heel. I endured it with them, bled for them as they endured it, quietly encouraged them as they struggled to change it and resist it. And so quietly had that work been done that they never noticed at all, maybe, that it had been words that had given them heart to fight back—a song or chaunt or poem sung them by a travelling bard, lodged in their souls to give them strength when they came to call upon it.

And it was right that they should not remember where the strength had come from: I was glad it should be so, gladder still that I had lived to see this. It was what we had all worked for, given our lives and hearts and minds to, given our souls to, whether we lived or died in the giving. Now it was here, and Arthur and Gweniver the ones of whom it had sprung; and soon now, very soon, that life would go on in a life that would be both Arthur's and Gweniver's joined at last, and Keltia would have found its way back to itself.

So I thought as I rode.

You will remember I had been this way but once before, and that guided by Gwyn himself. I could well have been lost entirely in that trackless wild; but somehow I knew that I was called, was but following a path laid out for me, which would bring me safe to my journey's end.

So when I rode at last over the lip of the valley in which Sychan lay, I was not at all surprised to see waiting for me a figure cloaked in gray, seated still as stone upon a stallion as gray and still as that stone itself.

"Well met, Birogue of the Mountain," I said, in the bard's voice that can carry like a far bell across a crowded room, though unraised and unstressed in the speaking.

"Three times met, and this not yet our last," she answered, and I could tell from her tone that she was smiling, though I could not see her face in the shadow of her gray hood. She turned her horse and fell in beside me as we rode down to the Dry River.

"So, then?" she said as we dismounted to lead the beasts to the hidden stable behind the water-curtain. "How is it with you and my star pupil? I like to know that those whom I have wedded go strong together in their joinings—"

I laughed, and balanced the saddles on the wall between the looseboxes. "Oh, we are well wedded, you and my lord Gwyn did your joinery to last. Morgan sends you greeting," I added as we left the stables, making the damp noisy scuttle behind the falls to the great guarded gate. "As do Artos and Gwennach; but you will know that."

Birogue smiled. "I will, and I do. But it was none of them that sent you here, I think."

"Majanah, Jamadarin of the Yamazai, bade me come; she read it in my hand, and so I am here."

We had halted before the huge silver gate I remembered, and as before I divested myself of all the steel I bore upon me. As once she had done long ago, once more Birogue laid her hand upon the gate, and once more the magic barrier swung silently wide for us, and we passed through, into Dún Aengus.

We went this time not to the majestic hall with the silver walls and golden roof and the crystal throne whence Nudd, King of the Sidhe, disposed his majesty and rule over his folk, but to a smaller chamber, no less fair, hung about with tapestries and lit with sconces.

"This is my dwelling-place here in Dún Aengus," said Birogue, shedding her gray cloak and taking mine from my shoulders. "Though I go still to Collimare—My home is here now."

I seated myself where she bade me, accepted a cup of cool ale and a soft whiteflour bannock enclosing a grilled meatcake and a cut of half-melted cheese; I was hungry, and the simple food had savor and sustenance.

Birogue watched with a wistful smile; then, when I looked my question, "It is not every Kelt would feel safe to fare and feed in the halls of the Sidhe."

I waved my goblet dismissively. "More fools they, then. Am I to insult the law of the coire ainsec, which is the same under the hill as upon the land, and, very like, beneath the wave? I think not—any road, did you wish to keep me here, other ways there are than stuffing and sating."

"Well spoken, Lord Taliesin," came a cool voice that was most definitely *not* Birogue's, and I leaped to my feet before I could see who it was had spoken, and hastily wiped face and fingers with the mealcloth I had been given.

She came in unattended: Seli the queen, wife to Nudd ap Llyr, mother to Gwyn—and to Edeyrn. I made her a deeper, longer reverence than ever I would have made to Gweniver Ard-rían, and looked her in the face as I straightened from my bow.

She was no whit changed from the time I had last beheld her, what, twenty years since, had it been? Hair like soft flame, eyes like emeralds in the rock—and her younger son was slain, dead at mortal hands . . .

She saw what I was thinking, and nodded once. "Be not shamed for that, Talyn," she said. "All is dán—aye, did you think we of the hill did not ourselves answer to dán even as do you? Truly! If it is not *quite* the same for us as it is for you, it is dán all the same, and we too are bound to its call."

"And free of it also," said Birogue softly.

"That too," agreed Seli after a pause. "But there are reasons for your coming beyond the courtesies of bards."

"Aye," I said, and drew the deepest breath of my life. "Once before, Lady, in this palace where now we stand, you promised me an answer to a question I never have dared to ask. You spoke of my mother, and you told me of the friendship you and she shared." I threw a glance over my shoulder. "And the Lady Birogue, too, claimed her friendship, here under the hill. I would know—would know of my mother, and how she came to die. My father never told me, my sibs have never spoken of it. You have said you would."

I ceased, trembling with a terrible inward shivering; my nerve-net was flittering like the skin of a borraun in thunder-rain, and my voice was that of a child fighting back tears. Which is worse, to know the truth whatsoever it might be or to so fear the knowing?

Seli made no answer, but gestured me to seat myself again, and did so herself. After a hesitation, I took my chair once more, fists clenched now, a knot forming between my shoulder-blades. Birogue moved behind and beside Seli's chair, and did not look at me.

When the silence had grown all but unbearable, and I thinking to run screaming back the way we had come, to throw myself onto the stone fangs that lay in the roaring pool below Sychan's curtain, Seli raised her eyes to me and spoke.

"Have you never wondered, Taliesin, that you were born so late after the rest of your sibs?"

I was at a strange place within myself: ravelled and quivering with my fear and doubt, but also clear and cold and unexpectant; and so her question seemed not at all off the mark.

"Well—sometimes, truly, I have wondered. There are twenty years between me and the next-nearest, Shelia and Rainild—twins they were, both dead now—a score of years between them and myself."

"There is more than years between you, Taliesin," said Birogue, and now she too was watching me, her eyes silver in the golden light. "Your sibs were bound by your father to keep it from you, but you and they come of different stock. You are all of you children of Gwyddno, that brave kind lord; but you, Taliesin, had a different mother than the rest."

If I had not been safely seated, I think I would have met the floor; as it was, my entire body felt as if I had taken a step that was not there, or missed a step that was. And yet what Birogue had said, carried, somehow, the immediate solid ring of truth. This was real, this was true, this had happened. This was mine; and now I was about to learn how Arthur had felt, so long ago . . .

"Then—" was all I managed to croak, and stared helplessly, desperately, at Seli.

She met my eyes full on, and through and past them, and I knew then why all the old chaunts and ballads warn against gazing into the eyes of the Sidhe.

"The Lady Medeni was your mother, as you have been told. But she was not the woman who gave birth to you. That lady, who was valiant and lovely and wise, was your father's ban-charach. The rest of your sibs are children of Medeni and your father; but you are of Gwyddno and your mother's begetting. Now Medeni loved you as her own child: She was a woman of great benevolence and warmth, older than your mother by many years, and she took up gladly the care of you when your mother came here to be with us."

"And just why, Lady, did my mother come here?" My voice sounded harsh as a hawk's cry in my own ears.

Birogue it was who answered, and I thought I would die of the gentleness in her tone.

"She came here, Taliesin, because she was dying, and we thought thereby to save her, for her years were but eight-and-forty."

I wrenched the words out now past a disabling muteness, as if someone had laid a spear-haft across my throat and set a foot upon it.

"How can that be? Kelts are but youths at such an age, even under Edeyrn we did not die so young—save in battle. It cannot have been so!"

And now it came, the spear's bladed point. "It was so, Talyn, for that your mother was no Kelt. She was a woman of Earth."

I felt the words falling upon me, blows struck from a very long way away. I was—well, I have no words for how I was, I a bard, wordless. And yet I could not say I was surprised: All the little things over the years that had flagged a puzzle and a mystery, things that my own brothers and sisters would not speak of, not even Tegau to whom I was closer than to all the rest together ... Of Earth. My mother was of Earth. I was half a Terran.

Birogue was speaking again. "Your father, Talyn, went on the very last of the secret voyages Kelts made back to Earth, the *immram-tuathal*. All the more daring, for that it was made in Edeyrn's despite: Kelts had been returning to Earth, on rare occasions, to be sure, since first these worlds were settled; for adventure, or curiosity, or even to pillage ideas. They seldom if ever revealed themselves to the Earthfolk, save in the very earliest days, when they were still helping stranded Kelts to come away. But your father and his comrades had a different, graver purpose: They went in hopes of getting Earth's aid against the Marbh-draoi. They failed, and so returned."

"But not without bringing away a few more souls as brave as they," said Seli. "When they came to Earth, they made contact with certain Terrans whom they had kenned from afar. Terrans whose natural gifts had run along the same track as your own—and *they* were not afraid! Nay, they were glad, and they told the visitors, to all their sorrow, how it was on Earth just then; they were themselves beset by war, had a Marbh-draoi of their own ... When your father and his company despaired of getting the help they sought, and prepared to return again to Keltia, these Terrans begged to be permitted to come also, though they were told of how it was here just then. And leave was given them: They were the very last of Earth to come to Keltia, and maybe ever will be."

"And my mother?"

"She was one of the first to ask to come—your father fell in love with her, and though he was already wedded to Medeni, and had six children by her, he brought your mother home with him. They contracted a céile-charach union, and you were born to them twenty years later."

I was beyond all thought or reason by now, sat there shaking as with fever, dully listening, letting it fall upon me; though whether I truly *heard* was another matter . . .

Birogue spoke so softly now. "She became my dear friend; in those days I came often to Tair Rhamant, that small fair place, and others of our kin too."

"If they so loved—how came it that it took twenty years before my birth?"

For the first time, Seli smiled. "Not for the same reasons it has taken Arthur and Gweniver so long, I can assure you! Nay, perhaps it was merely a matter of breeding—the strain your mother brought from Earth perhaps needed time to adapt itself to Keltic bloodlines . . . But then she sickened in earnest," and now Seli did not smile. "A sickness of Earth, maybe, naught that we could treat, not even here, where Gwyddno brought her when mortal healers failed. But we made her comfortable and happy—she was our friend—she did not suffer, save only from weakness at the last, and she died here under the hill, with Gwyddno and my son Gwyn beside her, and Birogue and Merlynn Llwyd and I myself to ease her passing."

Even Merlynn's name did not stir me where I sat huddled, and after a moment Birogue continued the tale.

"No other mortal has ever died beneath the roof of Dún Aengus, Talyn, and only one other ever shall . . . So Medeni took care of you, loved you well, owned you publicly as hers; then when you were not yet two, she also died, of a plague of Edeyrn's."

I glanced up, but Seli's face did not change.

"Then it was," Birogue went on evenly, "that your father required his other children to take a vow that they should never, on pain of dán, speak of this to you until he himself had told you first. But he died when you were short of six; and they kept their vow to him."

"And now *you* tell me—" My daze and dullness had been overcome by some feeling I have no name for: not anger, not frustration, not resentment—it was all nots, and questions bristled in me like fire-arrows, but all came down to one: *Tell me! Tell me everything! Now! Sooner! Forever! TELL!*

But there would be time for all that; now, here, I had one question, one only . . .

"If not Medeni—how was she called? What was my mother's name?"

Again Birogue smiled, a smile born of loving memory. "I cannot say it in the tongue of Earth—it is graven on the rock in the place where she wished to be laid, you shall see it if such is your wish—but your father gave her a new name when she came away with him. Like to her Terran name, but Keltic—as she chose to become for love of him. He called her Cathelin."

And when I heard Birogue pronounce my mother's name, all the strain and struggle and hardship, all the hammer-blows I had taken in the past quarter-hour and all those in my life before, came together and somehow took flight; sorrow left me, and as I felt it take wing, and peace come in its place to nest in my soul, I wept.

CHAPTER
31

When at last I raised my face from my hands, my sobbing done with, it was to see an empty chamber; Seli and Birogue had left me alone with my grief, and I was grateful for their tact.

I poured myself another cup of ale, then another, with a shaking hand, and began as the bard I was and ever would be to sort out my feelings. The revelations concerning my mother, my true mother, had shaken me to my soul; and not least for that in the moment of learning of her I had lost her. Though Kelts look on death in a manner different to most folk, the actual losing is no less difficult for us than for any other race. No one who has stood in those winds ever forgets it, the chill goes never from his bones or from his soul.

Nor should it: We should live with our losses, not strive to forget them as if they had not been; must make them part of ourselves, weave the black strand into the rest of the looming that is our lives—all our lives, for we do not think in Keltia of one only. My mother, this Cathelin I had never known, would be part of my life again, and I of hers: perhaps we would be given to know the reasons things had been as they were in this particular go-around, perhaps not. It made no differ; the living it was what mattered, then, now, ever.

When I found my way to that truth again, I stood up,

a little shaky still, splashed some water on my face from the fountain that bubbled in a corner of the chamber and went out to seek those of whom I was guest here. They were not far: Seli and Birogue were in the next chamber but one, a spacious open gallery; and they were plainly waiting on my coming, for they stood up at once.

"How is it with you, Taliesin?" asked Birogue. "Shall we leave you to yourself a while longer?"

"Nay, lady, it is well with me now." And the amazing, the incredible thing was that it was: I was suffused by a feeling of joy and light and peace after storm that I had never before known, and I was unspeakably weary, and strangest of all I was suddenly ravenously hungry.

"But I would see my mother's resting place," I added after a pause in which neither woman spoke. "And after that—"

"You would see Merlynn Llwyd," said Birogue, and I started to find myself so easily kenned, though I was not much surprised. "It is for that too that you have come, and then there is a thing we must speak of, a word you must carry back to Arthur and Gweniver. But another than Seli or I shall give it you."

My curiosity was twigged; but even that was overshadowed by what she had just spoken of Merlynn. Was it possible? The last I or any mortal Kelt had seen of Merlynn Llwyd had been on the battlefield of Nandruidion, when Edeyrn's magic had caught him up in so strange and terrible a way ...

But after I had been fed—good plain wholesome food, fare as solid and real as you would find in any cookplace in Keltia—and felt myself restored at least in body, I gave thanks for my meal and went with Birogue to the place where my mother rested. Seli did not go with us, but remained behind, and Birogue assured me we would see her again before I left the Dún.

We went together through a maze of galleries and corridors; the palace of Dún Aengus was the chiefest stronghold of the Sidhe in Keltia, the oldest established and to my thinking by far the fairest. We passed through exquisite chambers rich with tapestries of every description, all most skillfully worked; through arcades of armor where the walls were hung with helms and swords and shields and loricas, wrought of silver and findruinna and gold;

along balconies and balustrades; past feasting-halls and dancing-floors and places set aside for study or contemplation. And in all our passage I saw not one other of those here residing; not soldier nor faery-bard nor hand-maid nor lord—not even a faerie beast, no cu-sith, nor one of the great tawny hunting-cats—and did not dare to ask.

After what seemed a long time—hard it is to measure hours under the Hollow Mountains, a day can be a moment, a year a century, an hour the rest of your life—we came to a place unlike all the rest of the Dún. It was a cavern where the hand of the Sidhe artificers had been stayed, for sheer loveliness of the untouched place: It minded me at once of our dens on Gwynedd, the beauty we had lived amid at Llwynarth.

From where we stood, a pool spread out at our feet, and round to one side was a ledge overlooking the silver water. At the far end of this ledge, a flat plate of polished stone had been made of the cavern's natural rock, and upon this had been carved words in Gaeloch and in Englic and in runes, and in what I guessed to be the written script used by the Sidhe among themselves. My heart began a slow pounding, and I moved forward as if I walked in dreams.

I came to a halt before the carven stone, and put out a trembling hand to touch the incised letters. This was where my mother lay for all time; or rather, I corrected myself, where her mortal form was barrowed, for she herself was long gone from here, on her own road. But the bones that lay behind that stone seal had been bones that had borne me, that flesh now dust had been flesh that had made my own . . . I did not weep; it did not seem a thing for tears. But I smiled, and drew my fingers over the letters of her name. So far from her home—had she thought, when she went with Gwyddno for love and fate, that she would one day come to leave her body behind in such a place as this? Than which there could be no fairer in all Keltia; but still it was not her home, not hers by birth . . . *Cathelin*: My fingers moved on, to rest on the unfamiliar Earth rendering of that most familiar Keltic name. But I would not say it, would not pronounce it as surely my father had in the moment of her going out. It was not for me to say her name; but looking on the stone, touching the letters, I said the name it was my right to say, the name I had never been able to say to her in life.

"Mathra," I said to the woman who had waited so long to hear it. "Mamaith." And she sighed, and touched my hand, and went on, though she was ever with me.

Birogue had waited at the cavern entrance, again to honor my privacy; and when I rejoined her it was with a new certainty.

She smiled to see it. "You are strong now with the truth; my friend is proud of her son. She came to tell me so."

"She told me too," I said, and it was no more than truth, and also no less. "I have learned the truth of my mother; now I would learn that of my teacher."

And she conducted me once more through the halls beneath the hill.

But this time we went a different way, back to the builded regions, and came at length to what seemed, incredibly, to be a small annat or fane, set apart from other chambers; a place of power and peace. Glancing at my guide for permission, I stepped inside, making the reverence that as Druid I had been taught long since to make on holy ground.

Though my mother's grave had been imbued with much the same feeling, still had that been a grave, a resting-place for the cast-off form; sanctified, but a place of ending, where the voyaging spirit leaves the body as easily and instinctively as a snake leaves the shedded skin it has outgrown; for new and greater garb awaits both soul and serpent, and it would be against all laws of dán and nature to stay clad in the old.

But this was not the same—it was more a place of holding, of rest and abeyance, of a matter that although suspended for the moment was by no means concluded . . . At the center of the fane there was a niche in the back wall, and it was there I was drawn as in another dreaming, an ashling—and knew it was no dream.

Within the niche glittered the crystal tree of Edeyrn's magic that had taken my teacher; and within the sparkling lattices, half veiled by pellucid milky swirls that ran like frosty galaxies through the trunk of the sorcerous tree, lay Merlynn Llwyd.

By some trick of the swirls his face was but half-hidden; I stepped closer, but was halted by the light touch of Birogue's hand upon my arm. This was my beloved teacher, but he had also been her beloved mate; and was still, if what I sensed had any validity: For Merlynn was not dead as we had thought.

"Nay," said Birogue with a smile of the most piercing tenderness, "he does but slumber. Even Edeyrn could not destroy him, and did not study to try; the magic was meant to take Merlynn out of time awhile, and Edeyrn acted but in accord with dán, his and my lord's and Keltia's all in one."

I stared at the face I knew so well: Merlynn it was, and yet not so—or maybe more so, aye, perhaps that was it, a kind of refining and reducing of the essential soul that here indwelled . . .

"Not dead," I breathed wonderingly. "What, then?"

Birogue put out a hand, but did not touch the crystal of the tree. "He will sleep until he wakes. And wake he shall, Talyn, when he is needed: a year, a hundred years, a thousand years from now. And I shall be here to greet him when he does." She laughed at the look on my face. "Oh, we are not gods! Even the Shining Folk have a set span to their days, though our fate is not your own after. But I shall have days enough, I think, for that; to be with him again, and to help him help those he will wake to meet."

I was adrift in dazzled possibility. "Who will they be? What like shall they be?"

"Not even the Sidhe can answer that. They will be Kelts, right enough; more than that I know not. But he foretold this long since, you know: what would befall him, and Edeyrn, and Keltia. So far it has spun out in accordance with his foretelling."

I stepped nearer again, though like her I did not touch the surface of the crystal. So close as I was, I could feel what radiated off it: not cold, precisely; more a sort of frozen energy, a kind of charge that made me slow and sleepy, hot and angry, all at once.

"I miss him so much," I said then. "And so does Artos—May I tell him of this? So that he can know too—"

"Aye, Artos, aye," said Birogue, laughing. "I would

not keep him in sorrow any longer, I love him too dearly, and any road he will need to know the truth of it, sometime down along. Gwennach too, she is Ard-rían; and Morgan and Ygrawn, for that they three will be the three who—" She broke off suddenly, as if she had said too much.

But I was only half-listening, nodded in absent promise. I was recalling a long trudge through mountains in autumn, this man my protector and more a father to me than my real father had ever been, me on my short sturdy not-yet-six-year-old legs; and that only the beginning ... But what would the ending be! As a bard I was caught up in a web of words and glory; my fingers itched for my harp, for a song of a crystal tree and a sleeping guardian—I glanced anxiously at Birogue, struck by my own presumption. But that is how artists think in times even of pain and loss; nay, especially in such times. It is how we do our work, for ourselves and for the rest of the world.

"Aye, it is permitted," Birogue assured me. "Songs too will be needed, must be part of it; and who better to make them than a onetime student, now the Pen-bardd of Keltia himself?"

She stood there a moment longer, in a silence that was as loving and as palpable as a kiss; then she smiled again, and drew my arm through hers, and we went back to the chambers where others lived their lives.

As we walked I said no word to my companion, but reflected on what I alone of Kelts now knew, what I had been given to know this day. I had come to know two paired truths: One was that the woman who was my mother, though dead, was with me, and the other was that my teacher, thought dead, yet lived. Cathelin I should not come to know save in a life to come; but with Merlynn it was a different tale. Perhaps a many-times-great-grandchild would live in the time of his returning, would know him, even be taught by him as I had been. Perhaps even I myself, in a future life ... But my task just now was to make sure that every child born in Keltia for the next ten thousand years should know of Merlynn Llwyd. My future descendants should know too of Morgan and of me, should be able to speak to Merlynn of us, when he came again; and would hear from him in turn of Arthur and Gweniver, and the Company, and of us. All the great tales should be kept alive, and the breach of years be mended . . .

Caught up in my ashling, I did not realize that we had come again to Seli's chambers. She was waiting for us this time, seated in her high-backed chair, and this time she did not wait alone.

From the facing chair across the hearth—at least I think it was a hearth, though I could not tell you if the Sidhe even had need of such to warm their halls—Gwyn son of Nudd rose up at our entrance, and smiled upon me.

I was halfway across the room to him, glad greeting tumbling over my tongue in haste, before I recalled that he was after all Prince of the Sidhe, and I but brother to a mortal monarch. I tried to recover my dignity, made him the reverence I had made Seli, but it was no good; we were both laughing, and he met me with the embrace of two friends long parted.

But when we drew apart, I could see something in his face that I had never before seen upon the countenance of any of his race, and I was suddenly afraid.

"So, Taliesin," said Seli then, "you have seen."

I bowed, and took the seat she indicated. "Aye, and thanks to all in this Dún that it was granted me . . . There will be more questions," I added after the briefest of pauses, almost as much in query as in statement; or in warning.

But Seli only laughed. "Very like! Well, they shall all be answered in the Goddess's good time, as many and as often as you will. I am glad you had peace of the seeing. But now we must speak of something that touches more Kelts than the House of Glyndour only." Turning to Gwyn: "My son?"

Gwyn bowed deferentially to his mother before he spoke, and such was his beauty, there in the silver-walled room with the golden light upon his face, that I all but forgot to listen to his words. But when I remembered, and listened, all else was soon forgotten . . .

"You will remember, Taliesin," he said, in a voice of a deep-mouthed musicality that even Plenyth First-bard would have envied, "the night that the Cup came to Caerdroia."

"How not! But—you say 'Cup' as if— Was it not Olwen's quaich, that Marguessan used to try her tricks?"

Gwyn's eyes rested on me; or perhaps not *on* me, who can say what he saw sitting there in my chair—was it I, Talyn, or who, that the night-dark gaze rested on?

"Aye and nay," he said after a while. "That cup of Olwen's was never found, not so?"

"We searched for many days," I admitted. "Marguessan had it not when she left Turusachan, nor did Mordryth her son; and it was not to be found in the hall, nor anywhere in the palace, nor had any of the others present taken it. It was gone."

"In a way. In another way, not so."

Awestruck as I was, still was I beginning to lose patience with the riddling replies I had so far been given; I knew well that the Sidhe move to another measure than do the rest of us, but I was a creature of time, and the glass was running down.

"Speak plainly, then!" I heard myself snapping, and was appalled to hear it. But Gwyn only smiled.

"Even as a lad, you were ever impatient to get to the heart of the thing," he said. "Perran saw that straightway, back at Daars, in the lane near the city walls."

"Aye, well, my sorrow," I muttered gracelessly, for I remembered well that day whereof he spoke. "But still, lord—"

"If I seem to speak in fancies, hear me out. It is a tremendous thing I must tell you, and you have already been whelmed with strain and strangeness twice this day."

I subsided, and now all my attention was fixed on what he had to tell me; even Seli and Birogue were forgotten, so caught up was I with Gwyn.

"Well, then," he said. "The cup Marguessan used to try to trap Gweniver and the Yamazai queen—whose acquaintance we must make, I think, another time; we shall have more than a few things to speak of—was indeed the cup of Olwen White-track, that she passed on to her grandniece Llariau; you know all that tale. But what perhaps you have not known, what not even many of the Pheryllt have known, is where such vessels—and Olwen's is by no means the only such in Keltia—draw upon for the power they bear."

I stared blankly at him, for what seemed a week; and which, given the way of the Sidhe with time, may well have been. Then:

"Pair Dadeni! The One Cup—but that is here! We saw it, Artos and Morgan and I, when we came here before the King your father; you yourself held up the Cup for us to see, the other Treasures also—"

I was remembering that day, that sight: Nudd enthroned, Gwyn revealing to us one by one the Thirteen Treasures that had come from Earth with Brendan and Nia; and chief among the Thirteen were the Four. The Spear Birgha, that roars for blood; the Sword Fragarach, that now hung by Arthur's side in Turusachan; the Stone of Fál, that is the gaze of death itself; and Pair Dadeni, the great Cup, the Graal as some have called it, that can restore the dead—the newly dead—to life.

"The Cup, the Cauldron, the Graal—call it what name you will, it is the same, and it is itself. And from it every other healing thing in Keltia takes power: every crochan, every saining-pool, every healing-rann, every specific and restorative and palliative, even that wondrous tool by which you mend wounds with light. All come from the Cup in the end."

"And Olwen's quaich—"

"—has power to know love's true touch, and derives that power from the Pair itself. It is one of the lesser graals, and all those are children of the greater."

I was beginning to have a first faint inkling of what he was making ready to tell me, and I say to you, not even in the time of my dreaming before Cadarachta did I have such a feeling of dread at what I might be made to know . . .

Gwyn drew himself up. "Taliesin. The Cup is gone, the Pair. It is not in its place with the other Treasures, and we have sought for it long and hard. It is not here. It vanished the night Olwen's cup disappeared from under your sight in Mi-cuarta, as have all such vessels throughout Keltia; indeed, it appeared to you there in the hall, in token of its going. And soon now, even the healing tools and ranns and all the rest will no longer be able to perform their tasks; as you will find."

"Goddess, is there then no healing left in the land?" I cried out, aghast at the thought.

"Only its echo," said Seli. "Illnesses may still be cured, so that they are not grave ones; but no more. There is yet an overflow into your world from where the Pair now is, to make such small healings possible. But the greater ills—not so."

"Nay, this cannot be!" I was as good a theologian as any of my calling. "When Uthyr gave up his life, when he took the unhealing wound—he did it so that Keltia might be healed, that the land made waste might be whole again. It was the royal sacrifice, the given-death—that paid for all! For you see yourself how the land was healed—at Nandruidion, you were there—"

"Truly," said Birogue, and now she was as somber as the other two, and fear rose up to choke me. "That was a debt paid and purchased; this is another matter entirely."

"What then are you telling me?" I asked in a very small voice; I could bear no more of this, I was beaten and afraid. "Just let you say it straight out, let it be told me."

And it was Gwyn who did so. "It is the Princess Marguessan. She it is who has stolen the Cup, and you must seek to find it."

I opened my mouth to speak, but no word came out; it seemed that no more could be said, ever, to shock or surprise me. I had already taken two hard hits this day, as Gwyn had said earlier, and in all honesty I did not know how much more I could bear, not and stay sane. First my mother, then Merlynn, now this . . . I think I made some little small sound, and then I am quite sure I fainted; for the next memory I have is of lying on a low couch where Gwyn must have carried me, and Birogue looking down upon me, dabbing my face with cool water on a silk cloth dipped in a silver bowl.

At the memory the sight of the bowl put on me, I started violently upright, struggling against the sick dizziness. "The Cup—"

But Gwyn pressed my shoulders gently down again upon the pillows. "Even the Cup can wait on your senses returning," he said. "But as you see, Talyn, it is a grave thing."

I saw; oh gods, I Saw all! Marguessan's sleeveless antic in Mi-cuarta—merely a covering screen for this greater, more terrible thing: Pair Dadeni stolen, I could still hardly believe it ...

"How?" I asked after a while. "And if so, to what purpose?"

"Naught good, you may be sure," said Seli. "As to how, we are not certain. But it is so beyond all doubt, that Marguessan has taken it. And yet there may be some hope here."

"What hope?" I asked, for I was all but hopeless.

"The Cup protects itself, Talyn," said Birogue. "As do all the other Treasures ... It may be that it has betaken itself to a place of safety in face of Marguessan's attack; where if it cannot be used for good then at least it may not be used for harm. Marguessan may not be able to come at it just now any more than we ourselves."

Well, that was some comfort—perhaps. "More pity Artos took it not what time Nudd offered," I muttered, and Gwyn laughed.

"As to that," he said, "who knows but that Marguessan would only have gotten her hands on it all the sooner? Nay, Arthur did well, and will do better still. But this is Gweniver's task. And she shall not go alone: Women must seek the Cup, and men of art shall help in the seeking. It is not a task for a warrior alone, this one; be sure that Arthur knows and accepts that, else the quest will be all in vain."

"I will tell him, lord," I said doubtfully, for I knew already that Arthur would claim this quest for his given the taish of a chance.

"Nay, Talyn," said Birogue, softly but with iron-bite in her voice. "In this you must command him."

"He is the High King! Or had you forgotten?"

"He is our High King also," said Gwyn. "In all mortal things we are lieges of the Ard-tiarnas of Keltia even as you yourselves, bound to the Copper Crown in more ways than you can know. But this is one matter in which Arthur has no dominion. This is not for him to settle, and so you must tell him."

"He will like it not."

"Nay," he answered. "But he will do it even so. I know Arthur, he will recognize the necessity, and do what he must do. It is all part of the dán he began to work at

Cadarachta, and it was not completed at Nandruidion, for there is one thing more you must be told—"

At that word my spirit all but failed and fled me; I closed my eyes, then opened them again—I would take my very deathblow with open eyes, I ever like to know whence comes the stroke—and when I had heard that last they had to tell me, I knew that Arthur would indeed stand away from this quest; for it was geis, and geis was a thing he well comprehended.

"Aye," was all I said; and all I had time to say, for I felt again that lurch and dislocation of reality—even such reality as this!—the spinning, the roaring in my ears; and then as once before I was lying on the cold grassy ground without, on the edge of Sychan's gorge, my horses both grazing nearby.

I lay there a while unmoving, wondering why with all their magic the Shining Folk could not contrive a gentler method of sending their guests back to the road when the visit was over. Then I sat carefully up, and glared in the direction of the great hidden hall behind the waters.

"Gods but I *hate* that—" I sent a protest, aloud also, and bitterly, and heard a faint friendly echo of mirthful understanding. But I was not angry, nor even much annoyed, at the matter of my summary dismissal. There were greater and higher and deeper things to hand, and time it was I got back to Turusachan so that others besides myself could deal with them.

I caught the horses easily, mounted and rode slowly up the track to where I had entered the valley of Glenshee, for all the urgency of my errand still reluctant to leave so lovely and powerful a place. Argialla was rising in the east, and I saw unsurprised that, judging by the curve of the waning crescent, I had been within Dún Aengus one full month, perhaps longer. But now there was no more time to tarry, if indeed there had ever been, and already it might be too late.

I kneed my horse to a canter, and we dropped down over the edge of the ridge; Glenshee closed up behind us as if it had never been. And if it were ever to be again, for me or for Gwyn or for Keltia, if Keltia itself were to continue to be, all might ride on my returning timely to Arthur and to Gwen. Surely, it was ever *somewhat;* but this was a far more terrible somewhat than aught before it.

For what Gwyn had said to me at the last was naught to do with my mother, or with Merlynn; naught even to do directly with the vanishing of the Cup. Nay; what he had given me at last was the answer to a thing we had beaten at in vain these many years; you may well remember.

Long since, when Edeyrn had caused Morguenna and myself to be brought to him in Ratherne, on the eve of Nandruidion, he had told us one thing in especial among the many dreadful things with which he had taunted us. And this it was: "There is another; one who has sat at my feet to learn skills and secrets, one whom I have raised up so that all they may be thrown down. And even should I myself be destroyed in the fight to come, or all of them perish likewise, this one I have taught may live to rule Keltia in their despite, and raise an heir to follow."

The 'they' he spoke of was, of course, the kindred of Pendreic, the royal House of Dôn. And the 'one' he spoke of—well, all of us had ever thought that Edeyrn meant Gwenwynbar, whose son Malgan had been heir to Edeyrn's own heir Owein Rheged. Indeed, she had shown us a certain crude facility with things of power, as witnessed by the events at Tyntagel, and what went before. But now I knew for certain it was not so, and was racing to tell Arthur before another sun could set on the truth. We might not have many suns left to rise over Tara, and I would waste no more.

For the truth Gwyn had told me was this: Arthur's great enemy, Edeyrn's last pupil, was not his onetime now-dead wife. Nay; it was his own sister. It was Marguessan Pendreic. Daughter of Uthyr and Ygrawn, sister to Morgan, cousin to Gweniver: She it was who had worked against us all this time. "Now shall boar be set against bear": I had heard it myself, and had not guessed it. And now she had stolen the Cup of our Treasures, and we must quest to take it back again.

I rode east under the rising moons all that long, long night, back to Methven town, one thought only in my mind and soul and heart: Marguessan must be stopped. The Cup must be found and restored. And it was for Gweniver, and women of her choosing, and men of art, to do the seeking and the stopping and the finding—once the High Queen had given the word.

But before it could be given, that word must first be brought. And so I rode; and, after a while, very softly, I began to chaunt.

(Here ends *The Oak Above the Kings,* the second book in the *Tales of Arthur* sequence of THE KELTIAD. The third book is called *The Hedge of Mist.*)

Appendices

GLOSSARY

Aengus: one of the **High Dânu;** god of wind, journeys and love

aer: sung satirical verse, usually made by bards

Aes Sidhe: (pron. *eyes-shee*) the Shining Ones, a race of possibly divine or immortal beings; their king at this time is Nudd (or Neith) ap Llyr

afanc: (or **avanc**) large, savage carnivorous beast native to the planet Gwynedd (as **Avanc:** mythological water-dragon whose roaring is the sound of catastrophic floods)

aircar: small personal transport vehicle used on Keltic worlds; at the time in question, very rare in private hands

Airts: the four magical directions to which sacred circles are oriented—North, East, South and West; as **airts,** general directions

ashling: (or **aisling**) waking, wishful dream; daydream

Alterator: one of the three High Powers of the Keltic pantheon; neither male nor female, the Alterator works with the Mother Goddess and the Father God to effect the changes they decree (not to be confused with **Yr Mawreth,** the Highest God, q.v.)

amhic: "my son"; used in the vocative

anama-chara: "soul-friend"; term for those close and strong friends limited to one or two in a person's life

an-da-shalla: "The Second Sight"; Keltic precognitive gift (also **Sight** or **Seeing**)

An-Lasca: "The Whip"; in autumn, northwest wind at Caerdroia, on the planet Tara; herald of winter

annat: place of formal indoor worship, public or private, as opposed to **nemetons** (q.v.); usually attached to institutions such as convents, colleges or monasteries, but frequently found in private homes as well

annic: small white virulently poisonous snake, not native to Keltia; called **marbh-fionn**, "white death," by Kelts

annir-choille: "lass of the wood"; place-spirit that inhabits upland woods and forests, appearing in form of a young girl

Annwn: (pron. *Annoon*) equivalent in Keltic theology to the underworld, ruled over by **Arawn**, Lord of the Dead; lowest of the **Three Circles of the World** (q.v.)

an uachdar: lit., "uppermost"; in salutations (e.g., *Pendreic an uachdar!*) usually translated as "Long live _____!"

aonach: formal gathering, assembly or fair

ap: "son of"

ard-na-spéire: "the height of heaven"; hyperspace, the over-heaven

Ard-rían, Ard-rígh: "High Queen," "High King"; title of the Keltic sovereign

Ard-tiarnas: "High Dominion"; the supreme rulership over Keltia

Argialla: the innermost of the two moons of Tara

Arvor: chief planet of the Brytaned system, renowned for its vineyards

asrai: water-spirit found near cataracts, especially before a rainstorm (they vanish swiftly afterwards)

athra: "father"; a formal style

athra-cheile: "father-in-law"; lit., "mate-father" (**mathra-cheile**, "mother-in-law")

athro: "teacher," "master"

Avred (also **Abred** and **Hollfyd**): the visible, imperfect world of everyday life and appearances

Awen: (usually **Sacred** or **Holy Awen**) lit., the Muse or sacred poetic gift of inspiration; as used by bards, the personified creative spirit, represented by three lines, the center one vertical, the outer two angling in opposite directions (/|\)

bach: (also **-bach,** added as suffix to male names) denotes affection; used to all ages and ranks, can be translated as "lad" (fem., **fach** or **-fach,** "lass")

ban-charach: lit., "the loved woman"; term for a woman formally and legally associated with a man short of lawful marriage (cf. **far-charach, céile-charach**)

Ban-draoi: lit., "woman-Druid"; Keltic order of priestess-sorceresses in the service of the **Ban-dia,** the Mother Goddess

bannock: thick, soft bread or roll; biscuit or muffin

bansha: female spirit, often red-cloaked, that sings and wails before a death in many ruling Erinnach families; often seen as a wild rider in the air or over water

bards: Keltic order of poets, chaunters and loremasters; they often function as teachers, mediators, marriage brokers and spies

barguest: malevolent place-spirit appearing in form of a huge black dog (not related to the **Púca**)

beannacht: "blessing"; used as salutation of greeting and farewell

Beira: Keltic goddess; the Queen of Winter

Beltain: festival of the beginning of summer, celebrated on 1 May

Birgha: the Spear, one of the Four Chief Treasures of Keltia

bodach: term of opprobrium or commiseration, depending on context; roughly equivalent to "bastard"

borraun: wood-framed, tambourine-style drum, played by hand or with a small flat wooden drumstick

brambling: small songbird native to the planet Gwynedd; similar to Terran nuthatch or chickadee

Bratach Bán: "The White Banneret"; the Faerie Flag given by Seli to the line of Pendreic; it may be waved three times to summon the help of the Sidhe to the Keltic people

braud: "brother"

breastling: nurseling, a suckling child

brehons: Keltic lawgivers and judges

Brighnasa: the feast day of the goddess Brighid or Briginda, celebrated on 2 February

Briginda: the goddess Brighid in her aspect as Lady of Spring

brugh: fortified manor house, usually belonging to one of the gentry or nobility; in cities, a town-palace or townhouse of great elegance and size

caer: fortress, stronghold

Caer Coronach: "Castle Lamentation" or "Crown of the North"; in Keltic theology, the silver-walled castle (also known as **Argetros,** "Silver Wheel") behind the north wind, to which souls journey as the first stop after death; a place of joy, light, refreshment and peace, to which the newly dead soul is guided (and guarded en route) by those who have loved it in life

Caer Dathyl: capital city of the planet Gwynedd, in the Kymric system

Caerdroia: capital city of Keltia, on the Throneworld of Tara

cailleach na luaith: "hag of the ashes"; divination by means of embers—the spirit of the fire is invoked and visions are revealed in the coals

caltrap: three-spiked iron ball, tossed into the path of horses in battle to bring them down with their riders

cam-anfa: "crooked storm"; violent localized cyclonic disturbance of the sort known to Terrans as a tornado

cantred: political division of planets in most Keltic systems; roughly equivalent to a county or shire; province

cantrip: very small, simple spell or minor magic

caoine: "keen"; lament or dirge of mourning, usually chanted or sung

caredd, pl. **careddau:** "heart," "dear one"; used to family and friends

cariad: "heart," "beloved"; used to a lover

cathbarr: fillet or coronet, usually a band of precious metal ornamented with jewels

cat-of-a-kind: two things or persons, both alike and both objectionable

cat's-lick: perfunctory attention

céile-charach: "loved mate"; word for either partner

to a legal and formal union short of lawful marriage, or for the partnership itself

clarsa: Keltic musical instrument similar to a harpsichord

cleggan: vicious biting insect that buzzes annoyingly

clochan: dome- or yurt-like structure used by the Fianna in the field

clune: small open meadow

coelbren: magical alphabet used by Druids

coire ainsec: "the undry cauldron of guestship"; obligation, in law, to provide hospitality to any who claim it; failure to do so will result in any of a number of fines and charges

Common Tongue: at this time, not based on the Terran tongue Englic but on a form of Hastaic, the Coranian mother-language

compall: dueling-ground used by Fianna and others, especially for the **fíor-comlainn** (q.v.)

Companions: also, **Company** or **Circle;** those who are known to history as Arthur Ard-rígh's earliest and closest supporters and friends, latterly raised to knighthood

Coranians: ruling race of the Cabiri Imperium, hereditary enemies of the Kelts; they are the descendants of the Atlandean Telchines, as the Kelts are the descendants of the Atlandean Danaans

coron-solais: "crown of light"; personal aura

crabjaw: slant-tongue; false speaker who stays just this side of lying

creagh-rígh: "royal reiving"; in very ancient times, the traditional raid led by a newly made monarch to consolidate his or her rule

Cremave: magical clearing-stone of the House of Brendan; it has the infallible power to tell truth from falsehood

cribbins: humble food eaten by travellers, usually a stew of whatever is available or can be hunted

crimbeul: lit., "droop-mouth"; mustache

crimmock: maggot, noisome parasite

Criosanna: "The Woven Belts"; the rings that circle the planet Tara

crochan: magical healing-pool that can cure almost any injury, provided the spinal column has not been severed and the brain and bone marrow are undamaged

curragh: small leather-hulled or clinker-built wooden boat rowed with oars

cu-sith: faerie hounds, green-furred and golden-eyed

cwm: (pron. *coom*) hollow; a natural amphitheatre found in hilly lands

Cwn Annwn (or **Cwn Arawn**): (pron. *Coon Annoon*) in Keltic religion, the hounds that belong to Arawn Lord of the Dead; red-eared, white-coated dogs the size of a yearling calf, that hunt down and destroy guilty souls, especially those of traitors

Dakdak: race of biped furred marsupials dwelling on the planet Inalery

dán: "doom"; fate or karma

Daynighting: spring or fall equinox

deosil: righthandwise or sunwise (on a ship, the starboard side); clockwise

dermasealer: skinfuser; medical tool used to repair injuries by means of laser sutures; invented by a Fian healer, Lady Liaun Darroway

dichtal: bardic finger-language, often used as secret code

Dobhar and Iar-Dobhar: the Lands of Water and Beyond-Water; magical planes attained to by sorcerers in trance

dolmen: sacred pillar-stone

Domina: in the Ban-draoi order, title of a high priestess

drench: philtre, potion, compelling drink; commonly, a love potion

Druids: magical order of Keltic sorcerer-priests, in the service of the **Ollathair,** the Lord-father, the Goddess's mate

drystorm: rainless thunderstorm, marked by strong lightning and gusty, heavily ionized winds

dubhachas: "gloom"; melancholy characterized by causeless depression and an inexpressible longing for unnameable things

dúchas: lordship or holding; usually carries a title with it

duergar: in Kernish folklore, an evil elemental or place-spirit

dulcaun: leech, bloodsucker

dún: a stronghold of the Sidhe (also **liss** or **rath**)

dwimmer: evilly sorcerous (**dwimmercraft,** black magic)

enech-clann: brehon law system of honor-price violations

éraic: "blood-price"; payment exacted for murder or other capital crime by the kin of the victim, or, if victim was kinless, by the Crown

Ercileas: the mythological/historical personage known as Hercules

faha: courtyard or enclosed lawn-space in a castle complex or encampment

Fainne: "The Ring"; the six system viceroys and vice-reines of Keltia; instituted by Saint Brendan and abolished by early Pendreic monarchs, the Council was re-established by Arthur and Gweniver

far-charach: "loved man"; term for a man formally and legally associated with a woman short of marriage (cf. **ban-charach, céile-charach**)

Far Darrig: "The Red Man"; particularly gruesome place-spirit or elemental that appears as a tall, emaciated man covered head to foot in blood; strongly omened for disaster or other great personal evil

ferch: "daughter of"

Fianna: Keltic order of military supremacy; officer class above all other armed forces and ranks; **Fian bedding,** traditional sleeping-materials for Fians in the field, consisting of one layer each of green brushwood, dry moss and fresh rushes

fidchell: chess-style board game

fidil: four-stringed musical instrument played with a bow

findruinna: superhard, silvery metal used in swords, armor and other offensive or defensive applications

Fionnasa: feast of the god **Fionn,** celebrated on 29 September

fíor-comlainn: "truth-of-combat"; legally binding trial by personal combat

fireflaw: lightning-bolt

fith-fath: spell of shapeshifting or glamourie; magical illusion

Fomori: ancient enemies of the Kelts, inhabiting the planet Fomor and many colony worlds

fostern: relation by fosterage; foster-brother or foster-sister

Fragarach: "The Answerer"; also translated "Retaliator"; the Sword that is one of the Four Chief Treasures of Keltia

Gaeloch: language spoken throughout Keltia (in addition to the six major planetary languages and numberless dialects thereof)

Gál-greine: "Sunburst"; the white-and-gold vexillum or battle-flag of the Counterinsurgency; heraldically blazoned as *argent, or a sun in splendor* (a gold many-rayed sun on a white field)

galláin: "foreigners"; sing. **gall;** fem. **gallwyn;** generic term for all humanoid non-Kelts (and often used for non-humanoids as well); similarly, **outfrenne**

Ganaster: third planet of the Nicanor system; seat of the **High Justiciary,** a voluntary interstellar court to which systems may make petition for arbitrated settlement of grievances short of war (and sometimes of war also)

gauran: plow-beast similar to ox or bullock

Gavida: Keltic god of fire, lightning, metals and handcraft; known as the Smith of the Gods

geis, pl. **geisa:** (pron. *gesh, gesha*) any prohibition or moral injunction placed upon a person, often at birth or other significant moment; to break geis means certain ill-luck and misfortune, if not worse

glaive: lightsword; laser weapon used throughout civilized galaxy

goleor: "in great numbers, overabundance"; Englic word *galore* is derived from it

graal: shallow, two-handled cup or dish, usually (though not always) made of precious metal and decorated with gemstones and carving

grá-tintreach: "lightning-love"; love at first sight

Grian: primary of the Throneworld system of Tara

grianan: "sun-place"; solar, private chamber

grieshoch: embers, low-smoldering fire

gúna: generic name for various styles of long robe or gown

gutling: gluttonous person

Gwenhidw: (pron. *GWEN-ih-due*) sky-goddess who is consort to **Manaan; Gwenhidw's flocks,** high white puffy clouds on a strong wind

Gwynedd: chief world of the system of Kymry

hai atton: "heigh to us"; horn-note or cry that rallies an army

handfasting: rite of religious marriage (as distinguished from civil marriage); a spiritual linking of souls, which is marked by the making of the third of the **Three Cuts** (q.v.)

hanes: (pron. *hah-ness*) "secret," "tale," "reporting" (**Hanes Taliesin:** the bardic code devised by Taliesin Glyndour ap Gwyddno while yet a student of his craft)

the Hawk: cold northeasterly spring or autumn wind on the planet Tara ("The Hawk is out")

High Dânu: the eight (or, by other counts, seven, nine, twelve or fourteen) gods and goddesses of the general Keltic pantheon who are raised up above the rest, to act as intermediary Powers between mortals, the lesser deities and the Highest God (**Yr Mawreth** or **Kelu,** q.v.)

Hui Corra: flagship of Saint Brendan in first immram of Kelts

Hu Mawr: Hu the Mighty (**Hu** is pronounced *hee*); father of the gods in the Kymric pantheon

húracán: severe windstorm of tropical origin

immram, pl. **immrama:** "voyage"; the great migrations from Earth to Keltia; **immram-tuathal,** the reverse voyages of spying and information-gathering that went from Keltia back to Earth

inghearrad: intaglio carving; anything incised or engraved

jurisconsult: brehon engaged in law-court cases

keeve: beaker or barrel

Kelu: "the Crown"; the One High God above all gods, held by Kelts to be both Father God and Mother Goddess (though the Goddess and the God are also separate and different entities, worshipped apart from Kelu), or neither, or beyond such distinctions altogether; cannot be known in earthly life, though Kelu is frequently besought as *Artzan Janco,* "Shepherd of Heaven" and **Yr Mawreth,** "The Highest"

kenning: telepathic technique originally developed (and now used almost exclusively) by Druids and Bandraoi

laeth-fraoch: "hero-light"; exceptionally visible aura that surrounds a person of advanced spiritual development

lai: unit of distance measurement, equal to approximately one-half mile

laighen: sharp, leaf-bladed spearpoint

lasathair: "half-father"; stepfather

launa-vaula: "lashings and leavings"; full and plenty (said of meals)

leatherwing: bat or other similar creature

leinna: long, full-sleeved shirt usually worn under a tunic

lennaun: lover without benefit of formal arrangement

Llacharn: "Flamebright"; the sword that Arthur took from the stone on the island of Collimare, and which was broken at the battle of Ratherne

llan: retreat-place, cell or enclosure for religious anchorite

lochan: small lake or mountain tarn

lonna: light war-spear favored by the Fianna; also, hydrofoil-type vessel used by Keltic sea-navy

Lughnasa: feast of the god **Lugh,** celebrated on 1 August

maenor: hereditary dwelling-place, usually a family seat, in the countryside or city

maigen: "sanctuary"; border, fixed by law and its extent set according to rank, that surrounds a noble's lands, within which that lord is responsible for the peace and safety of all folk and their goods

mailin: purse, money-pouch; by extension, imputed wealth

Malen: Kymric name of Keltic goddess of war (usually **Malen Ruadh, Red Malen**)

mamaith: child's word for "mother"; equivalent to "mama" or "mommy"

Manaan: Keltic god of the seas and salt waters, consort to **Gwenhidw** (q.v.)

mankeeper: small lizard that changes coloration as a protective device

Marbh-draoi: "Death-druid"; universal byname for Edeyrn ap Seli ac Rhûn, usurper, assassin and Theocrat

Mari Llwyd: the Ghost Mare; in Keltic mythology, a giant phantom horse of bones, with fire in her eyes; the Mari Llwyd is an omen of great and terrible significance, and its appearances always presage disaster

mataun: mattock or other dull-bladed tool

Mathr'achtaran: "Reverend Mother"; mode of address used to chief priestess of the Ban-draoi order

m'chara: "my friend"; used in the vocative

mether: four-cornered drinking vessel, usually made of wood or pottery

methryn: foster-mother (**maeth,** foster-father)

Midir: Keltic god of meaning, plan, words and literature; one of the **High Dânu** (q.v.)

Mihangel: Keltic god of battle, known as Prince of Warriors (also **Maharrion**); legend says he will command the forces of Light at the great final battle of Cymynedd, which will decide the fate of the universe between good and evil; also aspected as **Fionn** and **Arawn** (q.v.)

mormaor: civic official, usually the chief elected governor of a town or settlement

Mór-rían: "Great Queen"; title for the Goddess in Her aspect as Lady of Battles, when in shape of a raven She hovers above the field

Mountain Mother: place-goddess of hill and mountain regions; the ranges are combs for her long green hair

nathair: generic term for any sort of snake, not necessarily the poisonous sort; Kelts hold ophidians in honor as prophetic creatures

nemeton: ceremonial stone circle or henge; **Caer-na-gael** is chief of these in Keltia, while **Ni-maen** is the royal nemeton above Caerdroia

Nevermas: a time that never comes

ollave: master-bard, usually; by extension, anyone with supreme command of any art or science

Olwen White-track: in legend and history, a queen's daughter (later queen herself) of such power and holiness that white flowers sprang up before and behind her as she walked; **Olwen's Cup,** a quaich belonging to this queen from which only faithful spouses could drink, according to a geis she laid upon it herself in love for and honor of her own mate, Rhydian (later passed on to her grandniece Llariau)

orcaun: killer whale

oréadach: cloth-of-gold

Pair Dadeni: the Cauldron of Rebirth, or Cup of Wonder, one of the Four Chief Treasures of Keltia

palug: graceful, red-furred, ferocious lynx-like feline, native to the island-continent of Môn on the planet Gwynedd

Pen-bardd: "Chiefest of Bards"; ancient title given to two bards only in all Keltic history—Plenyth ap Alun, founder of the Bardic Order, and Taliesin ap Gwyddno, its greatest exemplar

Pheryllt: class of master-Druids who serve as instructors in the order's schools and colleges (**Ro-sai,** head of the Pheryllt, a title once held by the Marbh-draoi Edeyrn)

piast: large amphibious water-beast found in deepwater lakes on the planets Erinna and Scota; the species was known to Terrans as the Loch Ness Monster (**piast-tears,** "crocodile-tears," false tears of hypocritically feigned emotion)

pibroch: battle-song, usually played on pipes

pig-i'-the-wood: children's game in which those in a "safe" place are lured out by those who are "it"

pirn: spindle, thread-winder

pishogue: small magic, cantrip

quaich: low, wide, double-handled drinking-vessel

rann: chanted verse stanza used in magic; spell of any sort

Ravens: Edeyrn's enforcers, used as terror-police; his crack troops used against the Counterinsurgency armies

rechtair: steward in royal, noble or wealthy households

riachtanas: "necessity"; involuntary urgent memory, usually prophetic in some way

rígh-domhna: members of any of the Keltic royal families, as reckoned from a common ancestor, any of whom may (theoretically, at least) be elected to the Sovereignty

riomhall: magical circle used for ritual or protective purposes

ros-catha: battle-cry; Arthur's was "Lean thusa orm!", usually translated as "Follow on!" or "Follow thou me!"

saining: rite of Keltic baptism, administered anywhere from seven days to a year and a day after the child's birth

Samhain: (pron. *Sah-win*) festival of the beginning of winter and start of the Keltic year; New Year's Day for Kelts; celebrated on 31 October (Great Samhain) and continuing until 11 November (Little Samhain)

scallaun: "shelter"; magical shield that can be used as protection against wind, rain, cold and the like

scallogue: planetoid, asteroid, any small rocky orbiting interplanetary body

schiltron: military formation much used and favored by Kelts; very compact and organized, it is extremely difficult to break

seastone: the gem aquamarine

sgian: small black-handled knife universally worn in Keltia, usually in boot-top (**table-sgian,** knife commonly used at meals, duller and longer-bladed)

shakla: chocolate-tasting beverage brewed with water from the berries of the brown ash; drunk throughout Keltia as a caffeine-supplying stimulant

shieling: mountain cavern where herds are stabled against the rough weather; also, the hidden refuges operated by the Counterinsurgency to protect its people and technology, during the days of Edeyrn's Theocracy

silkies: the **Sluagh-rón,** the seal-folk; a phocine race originally native to the Out Isles of Caledon, perhaps brought from Earth with the first **immrama**

síodarainn: (pron. *shee-dah-RAWN*) "silk-iron"; black metal alloy, extremely strong and tough, often used for starship hulls

sith-silk: very fine, very costly silk fabric

Six Nations of Keltia: the six star systems of Keltia (excluding the Throneworld system of Tara); in order of their founding, they are Erinna, Kymry, Scota, Kernow, Vannin and Brytaned (or Arvor)

sleaghán: a type of spear

slothel: lazy, stupidly dull-witted person

snowstones: hail, sleet, frozen rain

softsauder: to butter up or flatter someone; also, the flattery itself

Solas Sidhe: "The Faery Fire"; natural phenomenon similar to the will-o'-the-wisp but occurring over rocky ground; usually seen in the spring and the fall

spancel: rope or tether, usually for use on beasts

Stone of Fál: one of the Four Chief Treasures of Keltia

stour: uproar, tumult, outcry

stravaiging: idle wandering about, rampaging

stray-sod: place-magic of very ancient derivation; to step on the stray-sod means disorientation in the extreme—often the afflicted person or beast will wander for hours, even die, in plain sight of help or escape

streppoch: term of opprobrium; roughly, "bitch"

Sulla vhic Dhau: the historical/mythological personage known as Solomon, king of Israel (**vhic Dhau rígh,** "son of David the King"), renowned for his poetry and insightful justice

sulter: great heat and humidity of climate; any kind of oppressive warmth

sun-gun: moon-sized (and -based) laser cannon, used to defend planets and even whole systems

sunspecks: freckles

Sunstanding: the summer or winter solstice

taish: magical projection of a person's face or form; common slang for "ghost" or any kind of extraordinary phantom or apparition

talpa: blind, blunt-snouted digger animal native to the planet Kernow

Tanist, Tanista: designated heir of line to the Keltic throne

Taoiseach: (pron. *TEE-shaakh*) the Prime Minister of Keltia

telyn: Kymric lap-harp

tenaigin: (the "g" is hard) "forced-fire"; sacred flame used in rituals

thrawn: stubborn, unreasonably perverse

Three Circles: in Keltic theology, the three levels of existence—**Annwn,** the Underworld; **Avred,** "The Path of Changes" (also **Hollfyd** or **Abred**), the visible, everyday world of imperfections and striving; and **Gwynfyd,** "The Circle of Perfection", only to be attained to after many cycles of rebirth

Three Cuts: tiny ceremonial nicks made on one's wrist, with a consecrated sgian, during rites of saining, fostering and handfast marriage, to obtain a few drops of blood for the purposes of these three most solemn rituals

tinnól: the marriage-gift each partner gives the other the morning after the handfasting (or wedding)

tinnscra: the marriage portion given to a man or woman, or to them as a couple, by their families, clanns or (in the case of royalty or high nobility) by the reigning monarch; generally something substantial, like land or income, with reversion rights vested in each partner in case of subsequent divorce

tirr: cloaking effect, part magical, part mechanical in nature; used to conceal ships, buildings and the like; does not work on living or moving things

torc: massive neck ornament worn by Kelts of rank; heavy, open-ended circle usually of gold or silver

Torc Truith: the Great Boar of Keltic mythology; a terrifying emanation of great antiquity, held to lead souls to hell

traha: "arrogance"; more than mere arrogance, wanton pride or hubris

triad: poetic triplet used by bards, in which three similar things, events or people are linked for instructive purposes

Turusachan: "Place of Gathering"; the royal palace at Caerdroia; by extension, the entire central government of Keltia; also, the plateau area above the city of Caerdroia where the governmental buildings are located

usqueba: "water of life"; often **usqua,** whiskey, invariably unblended

Vallican: Kymric dialect, most frequently used in the westlands of Gwynedd

watchpot: greedy person; overly fond of food

widdershins: lefthandwise or countersunwise; in a counterclockwise direction

Yamazai: dominant race of the planet Aojun; usually refers to the fierce and able woman warriors of this matriarchal and matrilineal system

Yr Mawreth: "The Highest"; usual name for Keltic Supreme Being

CHARACTERS

Alannagh Ruthven, Companion, friend to Arthur

Amris Pendreic, Prince of Dôn; late Tanist of Keltia, eldest son of Darowen Ard-rían and King Gwain; brother to Leowyn and Uthyr; far-charach to Ygrawn Tregaron; father to Arthur

Arthur Pendreic, known also as **Arthur Penarvon,** Prince of the House of Dôn; son of Amris and Ygrawn, adopted son of Gorlas Penarvon; nephew to Leowyn and Uthyr; foster-brother to Taliesin Glyndour; Ardrígh of Keltia, by joint rule with Gweniver his second wife; by Majanah, Queen of Aojun, Jamadarin of the Yamazai, father to Donah

Berain nic Elheron, Companion; Fian warrior; friend to Arthur

Betwyr ap Benoic, Companion; friend to Arthur

Birogue of the Mountain, a lady of the Sidhe, mate to Merlynn Llwyd

Daronwy ferch Anwas, Companion; heir to the Lord of Endellion; friend to Arthur **(Ronwyn, Ronwynna)**

Donah, Heir of Aojun; daughter of Arthur and Majanah

Edeyrn ap Seli ac Rhûn, Archdruid; known also as **the Marbh-draoi;** usurper, traitor and Theocrat

Elen Llydaw, Companion; daughter of the Duchess of Arvor; friend to Arthur **(Elenna)**

Elphin Carannoc, Companion; ollave; friend to Arthur; chief teacher to Taliesin

Ferdia mac Kenver, Companion; friend to Arthur **(Feradach)**

Grehan Aoibhell, Companion; the Master of Thomond (heir to the Prince of Thomond); friend and warlord to Arthur

Gorlas Penarvon, Lord of Daars; first husband to Ygrawn Tregaron; adoptive father to Arthur

Gweniver Pendreic, Tanista of Keltia; only child of Leowyn Ard-rígh and Queen Seren; niece to Amris and Uthyr; cousin to Arthur, Morguenna and Marguessan; Ard-rían of Keltia by joint rule with Arthur her husband

Gwenwynbar; daughter of Gerwin, Lord of Plymon, and Tamise Rospaen; first wife to Arthur; mother of Malgan

Gwyddno Glyndour, Lord of Gwaelod; husband to Medeni ferch Elain; father to Taliesin, Tegau, _et al.;_ murdered by Edeyrn

Gwyn ap Nudd, Prince of the Sidhe; heir to Nudd ap Llyr, King of the Sidhe, and Seli his queen; half-brother to Edeyrn Marbh-draoi

Irian Locryn, Lord of Lleyn; husband to Marguessan Pendreic; father to Mordryth, Gwain and Galeron

Kei ap Rhydir, Companion; friend to Arthur

Keils Rathen, Companion; warlord and friend to Uthyr Ard-rígh and Arthur Ard-rígh; lover of Gweniver Ard-rían

Leowyn Pendreic, Ard-rígh of Keltia; second son of Darowen Ard-rían and King Gwain; husband to Seren Princess of Galloway; father to Gweniver

Majanah, Jamadarin of the Yamazai, Queen of Aojun; ban-charach to Arthur; by him, mother to Donah, Heir of Aojun

Malgan ap Owein; son of Gwenwynbar, reputed son of Owein Rheged

Marguessan Pendreic, Princess of Keltia, Duchess of Eildon; elder daughter of Uthyr Ard-rígh and Queen Ygrawn; cousin and half-sister to Arthur; cousin to Gweniver; wife to Irian Locryn; mother to Mordryth, Gwain and Galeron

Marigh Aberdaron, late Taoiseach of Keltia in Uthyr's service

Medeni ferch Elain, Lady of Gwaelod; wife to Gwyddno; mother to Tagau *et al.;* reputed mother to Taliesin

Melwas, prince of Fomor; son of Tisaran, heir to Nanteos

Merlynn Llwyd, known also as **Ailithir;** Druid; Archdruid; teacher and friend to Arthur and Taliesin

Mordryth Pendreic ap Irian; heir of Lleyn; son to Irian and the Princess Marguessan

Morguenna Pendreic, known as Morgan; Princess of Keltia, Duchess of Ys; Companion; younger daughter of Uthyr Ard-rígh and Queen Ygrawn; cousin and half-sister to Arthur; cousin to Gweniver; wife to Taliesin; by him, mother to Geraint (Gerrans)

Nanteos, King of Fomor; grandfather to Melwas, father to the Heir of Fomor, Tisaran

Nudd ap Llyr, King of the Sidhe; husband to Seli; father to Gwyn

Owein Rheged, Lord of Gwynedd by Edeyrn's grace; the Marbh-draoi's regent over Gwynedd; second husband to Gwenwynbar; reputed father to Malgan

Roric Davacho, Companion; friend to Arthur; warlord to Majanah; husband to Daronwy

Scathach Aodann, Companion; Fian general; teacher to Arthur and Taliesin

Seli, Queen of the Sidhe; wife to Nudd; mother to Gwyn

Taliesin Glyndour ap Gwyddno, narrator; Companion; youngest son of Gwyddno and his Terran ban-charach Cathelin; foster-brother to Arthur; husband to Morguenna Pendreic; by her, father to Geraint

Tarian Douglas, Companion; the Mistress of Douglas

(heir to the Prince of Scots); Taoiseach of Keltia; friend
and warlord to Arthur

Tegau Glyndour, known as Tegau Goldbreast; Companion; eldest daughter of Gwyddno and Medeni; sister to
Taliesin; wife to Eidier Lord of Sinadon

Tryffin Tregaron, Companion; son of Marc'h Duke of
Kernow; nephew to Ygrawn; cousin and friend to Arthur; latterly Duke of Kernow and husband to the
Duchess Ysild; by her, father to Loherin

Uthyr Pendreic, Ard-rígh of Keltia; youngest son of
Darowen Ard-rían and King Gwain; brother to Leowyn
and Amris; second husband to Ygrawn; father by her to
Marguessan and Morguenna; uncle to Arthur and
Gweniver

Ygrawn Tregaron, daughter of Bregon Duke of Kernow;
sister to Marc'h Duke of Kernow; ban-charach to
Amris Pendreic; wife to Gorlas Penarvon; wife and
Queen to Uthyr Pendreic; mother to Arthur (by Amris)
and Marguessan and Morguenna (by Uthyr)

Ysild Formartine, Heir of Arrochar; Companion; abducted by Marc'h of Kernow; wife and Duchess to
Tryffin

Taliesin is pronounced tal-YES-in, *not* tally-essin, ta-LEE-uh-sin, tal-uh-SEEN or any other erroneous exoticism.

Marguessan is pronounced as spelled.

Morguenna is pronounced mor-GWEN-a.

Nudd is pronounced neethe (to rhyme with seethe; and
sometimes spelled *Neith*).

Tegau is pronounced TEG-eye.

Ysild is pronounced iz-ZILD.

Ygrawn is pronounced ig-GRAWN.

And you're on your own for the rest of them . . .

THE BOOKS OF THE KELTIAD

The Tales of Brendan
*The Rock Beyond the Billow
*The Song of Amergin
*The Deer's Cry

*The Sails of the Hui Corra **(An Immram)**

*Blackmantle **(The Tale of Athyn)**

The Tales of Arthur
The Hawk's Gray Feather
The Oak Above the Kings
*The Hedge of Mist

The House of the Wolf
*The Wolf's Cub
*The King's Peace
*The Beltane Queen

The Tales of Aeron
The Silver Branch
The Copper Crown
The Throne of Scone

The Tales of Gwydion
*The Shield of Fire
*The Sword of Light
*The Cloak of Gold

*forthcoming

THE ROYAL HOUSE OF DÓN: Rulers of the Druid Interregnum (Theocracy) and the Dóniaid Restoration

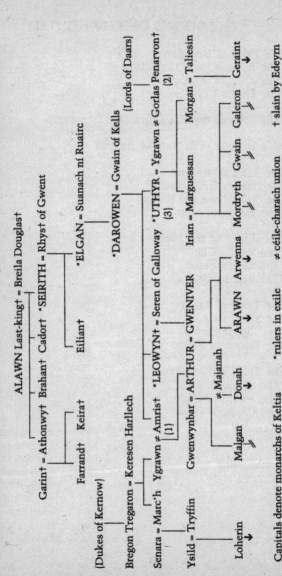

Capitals denote monarchs of Keltia   *rulers in exile   ≠ céile-charach union   † slain by Edeyrn

THE BOOKS OF THE KELTIAD by Patricia Kennealy-Morrison

In the Earth year 453 by the Common Reckoning, a small fleet of ships left Ireland, carrying emigrants seeking a new home in a new land. But the ships were not the leather-hulled boats of later legend, and though the great exodus was indeed led by a man called Brendan, he was not the Christian navigator-monk who later chroniclers would claim had discovered a New World across the western oceans.

These ships were starships; their passengers the Danaans, descendants of—and heirs to the secrets of—Atlantis, that they themselves called Atland. The new world they sought was a distant double-ringed planet, itself unknown and half-legend; and he who led them in that seeking would come to be known as St. Brendan the Astrogator.

Fleeing persecution and a world that was no longer home to their ancient magics, the Danaans, who long ages since had come to Earth in flight from a dying sun's agonies, now went back to those far stars and after two years' desperate wandering they found their promised heaven. They named it Keltia, and Brendan, though he refused to call himself its king, ruled there long and well.

In all the centuries that followed, Keltia grew and prospered. The kings and queens who were Brendan's heirs, whatever else they did, kept unbroken his great command: that, until the time was right, Keltia should not for peril of its very existence reveal itself to the Earth that its folk had fled from; nor forget, for like peril, those other children of Atland who had followed them into the stars—the Telchines, close kin and mortal foes, who became the Coranians as the Danaans had become the Kelts.

Yet Brendan himself had said that a day must come at last when Kelts and Terrans should meet again as cousins;

three thousand years later, that day had not yet come, and many there were among Brendan's people who prayed it never would.

THE SILVER BRANCH
Volume I of the Tales of Aeron

The Silver Branch is Aeron's tale—from the events long before her birth, which would shape the worlds and the burden she would inherit . . . to her first discovery of the magic that could move the very sun from its path . . . to the dangerous rites of passage that would make her sorcerer, warrior, avenger, and ultimately, queen. It is a spellbinding recounting of forbidden passion and of honor betrayed, of jealousies that will plant the seeds of future treachery, of love and loyalty tested to the very limits of the great Abyss—and of a people and a ruler so convincingly portrayed that *The Keltiad* is transformed for readers from the stuff of legend to the very essence of life.

The COPPER CROWN
Volume II of the Tales of Aeron

When lore became legend on ancient Earth and the powers of magic waned, the Kelts and their allies fled the planet for the freedom of distant star realms.

But the stars were home to dangerous foes, and millennia later, the worlds of Keltia still maintained an uneasy truce with two enemy empires—the Imperium and the Phalanx. Then, at the start of the reign of Aeron, mistress of high magic and queen of all the Kelts, an Earthship made contact with her long-fled children. And while Earth and Keltia reached out to form alliance, the star fleets of the enemy mobilized for final, devastating war. . . .

THE THRONE OF SCONE
Volume III of the Tales of Aeron

Aeron has fled to the stars on a desperate mission to find the fabled Thirteen Treasures of King Arthur, hidden from his Keltic descendants for fifteen hundred years. Her search will lead from the depths of space, where worlds are born, to the heart of an ancient enemy's stronghold and on to a trial of courage and magic that even the Queen of the Kelts may not survive!

And while Aeron pursues her destiny among the stars, all the forces of Keltia are mobilizing for a war that could set the very worlds ablaze—a war that can only be won if Aeron returns triumphant from her doom-shadowed quest. . . .

THE HAWK'S GRAY FEATHER
Volume I of the Tales of Arthur

It was a time out of legend, an early age in the history of the worlds of Keltia when a youth named Arthur dared to regain the throne for the royal House of Don from the usurper Ederyn. The greatest of druids and sworn enemy to all who defied his will, Ederyn vowed when he seized power that he would crush the House of Don—by cutting the people off from their greatest strength, the ancient arts of druids, warriors, and bards. Still, some had managed to keep the secret knowledge alive . . . preparing for a time when their skills—and the penetrating genius of one called Arthur—would be called upon to strike out against their oppressor. . . .

About the Author

Patricia Kennealy-Morrison was born in New York City and has lived there for most of her life. She is the author of The Keltiad fantasy series; her novels include *The Hawk's Gray Feather* and *The Oak Above the Kings*. The former editor of *Jazz & Pop* magazine, she was one of the first women rock critics and has written extensively in the field. In 1970, she married Jim Morrison, lead singer of The Doors, in a private religious ceremony. Her memoir, *Strange Days: My Life with and Without Jim Morrison*, was published in 1992. She is a Dame of the Ordo Supremus Militaris Templi Hierosolymitani, a High Priestess in a Celtic pagan tradition and a member of Mensa.

If you and/or a friend would like to receive the *ROC Advance*, a bimonthly newsletter featuring all the newest and hottest ROC books and authors, on a complimentary basis, please fill out this form and return it to:

ROC Books/Penguin USA
375 Hudson Street
New York, NY 10014

Your Address
Name _____
Street _____ Apt. # _____
City _____ State _____ Zip _____

Friend's Address
Name _____
Street _____ Apt. # _____
City _____ State _____ Zip _____